Bound in Black

By

Steven De Luca

Also by Steven De Luca

Bound in Scales

Copyright © 2020 by Steven De Luca

Edition 1.

All characters and events in this publication are fictitious and any resemblance to real persons, living or dead, is purely coincidental

Original cover art by Dario D'Alatri

ISBN: 9798629229827

Part One

Hope and Desperation

Chapter 1

Rumblings of Disagreement

Galdor called the moot to order rearing up on hind legs and spreading his green wings wide in the traditional closing. He stood in the middle of the moot chamber—a spacious underground cavern—five dragons to each side of him. Ten dragons made up his council, a mix of the oldest and wisest in their community.

"The moot is closed," Galdor said. "Let the wisdom and strength of the eleven, forever guide us." He folded his wings and inclined his head to the assembled members.

Dragons passed their leader, dipping their heads in respect as they departed. Dragons of all colours, light blue, fiery orange, bright yellow, green, bronze and even a silvery platinum. Different varieties of varying shapes and sizes, large and small, left the cavern of the moot until only one remained. Blaze the Black.

Galdor marvelled at Blaze's jet black scales and the flash of white, like a bolt of lightning emblazoned upon the dragon's chest. Black dragons were rare and Blaze was the only black that made his home on the Lifting Plateau. Blaze waited until the rest of the moot departed before he spoke.

"I would talk with you, moot leader. Of sensitive matters," he glanced at the last few retiring dragons, "for your ears only," waiting until they departed the large cavern.

"Could these matters not have been discussed before the moot ended?" Galdor asked. This was an unusual request as Blaze was always vocal in the moot.

"Not when you hear of what I have discovered." The concern in his voice wasn't something Galdor was used to hearing. Blaze was always confident and sure. His hushed tone and this secretive request to speak alone, sounded serious.

"Very well. What's sensitive enough that you would keep it from our moot?"

"Treachery," Blaze said. "I fear some of our brothers and sisters of the moot plot against us." He glanced furtively at the exit to the cavern as if to check they weren't being overheard. "Perhaps it may be prudent to find somewhere more private."

"Treachery?" Galdor questioned. He couldn't believe it. "Are you sure? Who would betray the moot? And why?"

"I'm as sure as I can be, but we shouldn't discuss this here. I'll tell you all I have uncovered, but I would rather do it where there is no chance of us being overheard."

Galdor was shocked. Blaze must be wrong. The moot were his most trusted advisors and he knew them all as friends. They were good dragons. Blaze was the only new member of the moot and had arrived at the Lifting Plateau eleven summers ago. Maybe the newest dragon to join the moot could see things he might have missed, his perspective being newer than most. A fresh pair of eyes would see things differently. Either that or he was utterly and completely mistaken.

"While I do not doubt your loyalty," Galdor said, "I would ponder on your words. Let me observe our brothers and sisters now that you have alerted me. I do not wish to rush into this blind. I have known these dragons a long time and trust them all." He didn't want Blaze to feel he couldn't come to him with his concerns, yet his accusations were ludicrous. "I ask you to be my eyes and ears and keep me informed of anything unusual." Hopefully that would keep him placated until all this blew over. "Between us both, we should be able to monitor the situation before we jump to any conclusions and be in a better position to take action, *should* we need to. If we need to talk in private, we can always take a flight away from the plateau and discuss our business outside these walls." He felt bad humouring Blaze but it was better than confronting the moot with false accusations of treachery.

"A wise decision, moot leader," Blaze agreed, "but do not wait too long, I fear if you do, all will be lost." The black dragon turned abruptly, head swaying from side to side as he surveyed the chamber and the surrounding tunnels, still cautious of being overheard. He took one quick glance back at Galdor and departed the cavern in a display of uncharacteristic behaviour.

Galdor couldn't think why anyone would plot against him. What would be their reason? He had led the moot successfully and other than the normal rumblings of disagreement, the dragons of the Lifting Plateau were content.

Or so he thought. Blaze's words were deeply disturbing. It might be something, but he doubted it was treachery. He would need to pay more attention to the comments and actions of his colony, see if there was anything he was missing. Surely, now he was aware of any possible dissention it would be easier to recognise. He still couldn't quite believe Blaze's ill tidings and hoped the black dragon was mistaken. If something was wrong his *perception* would have alerted him.

He was tired, caught unaware by Blaze's imagined conspiracy and reading too much into it. After a good night's sleep he would see things more clearly. He was sure he would be able to dismiss the black dragon's words and reassure him no plot existed. Still, Blaze wasn't a dragon to entertain such fantasies and it was extremely out of character for him. He was a practical and confident dragon. He wouldn't embarrass himself with information that would make him look like a fool. Was there something to his concerns?

With a heart heavier than it should have been, Galdor ambled from the moot chamber. The words of the black dragon a gnawing burden he never would have anticipated he would carry.

* * *

Weeks passed and Galdor observed his fellow dragons, searching for any traces of conspiracy or subterfuge, yet finding none. Blaze came to him regularly, catching him early in the morning or late in the evening, sharing his findings but never having the chance to elaborate before they were disturbed. The more Blaze told him, the less he believed it was true. He was beginning to think Blaze had imagined everything.

Galdor looked out from the ledge he was perched on outside his sleeping cavern. The morning sun heralded a bright new day, but the idyllic sunrise was spoiled as Blaze appeared like a dark cloud, hurrying along the outer ledge of the plateau to Galdor's cavern. It was early and most dragons were still slumbering. By the way Blaze purposefully strode towards him and the fact that he was seeking him out this early, Galdor concluded the black dragon brought with him, what he believed, were more ill tidings.

"Galdor," the black dragon hissed, "we need to speak." He turned his head, looking behind. "In private. I have uncovered something vital. A human mage is involved!"

Galdor dreaded his furtive meetings with Blaze. The black dragon's hatred for humans was well known. It wasn't the black dragon's fault, he was only trying to help, but every time they were alone, he would have more bad news. Some other small detail about the conspiring dragons or something else about the supposed plot. He would inform him of a conversation overheard, implicating one of his trusted moot members in the conspiracy. There was never any proof; everything was conjecture and speculation, nothing ever implicated any dragon directly.

Enough was enough, he needed to get to the bottom of what was going on. It was time to call the black dragon's bluff and tell him his annoying theories were fiction. Hopefully once Galdor intervened he could get Blaze to accept there was no conspiracy.

"Meet me on the southern slopes of the plateau, where the Silver River falls to the valley below," he told Blaze. Better to take the black away from the plateau and address this dragon to dragon. "And let us not depart together." He would play along with Blaze for now. The waterfall was far enough away to be private and there were many secluded caves in the rocky cliff face where they could discuss Blaze's concerns.

"Agreed, moot leader. Your caution is wise. Leaving separately is clever." Blaze turned and hurried from the cavern, hesitating at the exit to look around before spreading his wings and jumping from the ledge.

Blaze certainly believed something was wrong and Galdor wondered what could have upset the black dragon so much. His own *perception* niggled him. He was always mindful of his dragon sense and listened when it warned him something was amiss. The trouble with *perception*, Galdor mused, was it always more of a hunch, a sixth sense, and how you understood the message it conveyed, was open to interpretation. All dragons were influenced by it, some strongly, others ever so slightly. There was no rule as to how it worked, it just happened. As dragons said, *it is what it is.*

Sometime he wished his *perception* was a little more obvious. Still, when it niggled him like this, regardless of what it conveyed, he would be wise to stay alert. What made Blaze feel it was necessary to leave their home and speak in private?

He worried for his friend's sanity. Important matters were rarely discussed beyond the ears of the moot. It was strange behaviour and extremely unsettling. Galdor hoped it wasn't more about the humans again. Blaze didn't like humans. Maybe his unhealthy hate of mankind was causing him to see things that just weren't there. Blaze strongly believed dragons should take back what was theirs and destroy all the human towns and villages, driving them from the land.

Hundreds of years ago there had been no humans and all lands belonged to the dragons. Time passed and their numbers grew, their towns and villages always expanding. Humans settled on once empty lands, spreading through the wilderness, building and breeding, their numbers increased faster than any other species. They were like a plague, infesting the valleys and forests, always taking more.

It was a familiar story wherever dragons made their home.

Galdor decided the dragons of his colony should keep to themselves. Dragons had a poor reputation as far as humans were concerned. The humans didn't realise dragon kind were intelligent and sociable creatures. The moot decided, prior to Galdor's rule, to withdraw and keep their distance and maintain the peace. Galdor saw wisdom in this and followed in the talon steps of his predecessors. Although this was the majority view of his own moot, it wasn't everyone's opinion.

Blaze believed dragons shouldn't let humans populate lands that once belonged to them. Even though he was relatively new to the Lifting Plateau and had been with them for over a decade, his silver tongue often attempted to convince other dragons they should fight and take back what was lost to them.

Galdor maintained the peace he had preserved for generations and there was enough land for both humans and dragons. Their continent was huge and they could live where humans could not.

Blaze argued, dragons should take back what was once theirs. It was weak to let humans have the best land and the best feeding grounds. They should burn the cities of man and crush them with their superior strength. It was a grave mistake to ignore the human advance and sit idly by as their numbers continually expanded. Humans learned quickly as their race evolved and their grasp on their own magic grew stronger.

Galdor maintained the peace. Dragons from the tales of men behaved in this way, not dragons from the Lifting Plateau. They would be no better than tyrants if they eradicated humans. Every race should be allowed to live and there was a whole world to explore. He wouldn't throw away thousands of years of peace and disrupt the balance his ancestors sought to maintain.

He hoped the moot still saw wisdom in his words and realised his way was best for all concerned. He needed to speak with Blaze and find out what was wrong. What exactly this so called conspiracy entailed and who he thought was involved. Surely then he could convince Blaze it wasn't real and help him see he was mistaken.

Galdor ambled from the cavern, not wishing to hear what the black dragon wanted to tell him, but unable to ignore it. He would meet him as agreed, but not right away. He needed time to think on the best approach.

"Galdor," a voice called to him from below. It was Sapphire the Cerulean. Her blue scales were somewhere between the colour of a bright summer sky and the gemstones she was named after. She was a beauty to behold and her scales sparkled. He pushed himself from the ledge, dropping from the cave mouth to land next to the blue female.

"Sapphire," he greeted her, "You are up early." He didn't want to get caught up in a conversation with the blue dragon and while he was hesitant to hear the latest dark foreboding from Blaze, he didn't want to put it off, either.

"As are you," she replied, tilting her head and making her statement a question.

"I have..." he hesitated. He was sure he could trust Sapphire, she was one of the longest serving members of the council of the moot. Blaze never mentioned her in his whisperings or implicated her in any plots. Galdor exercised caution and hated himself for feeling this way with Sapphire, "...something that needs my attention."

He leaned in close, deciding to trust her in spite of his reservations and lowered his voice, "I have heard a rumour about a human mage causing trouble." Blaze had at least told him that much in his whisperings. He didn't want to tell Sapphire too much about his own suspicions, not until he was sure Blaze was wrong. He was almost sure he was, yet his responsibilities as moot leader dictated he should investigate everything thoroughly. He would be remiss in his duties if he didn't check. He would let Sapphire believe this for now. It was much better than telling her he suspected Blaze was losing his mind. He could always tell her later there was no mage, no trouble. He would deal with Blaze's issues first and if the moot needed to intervene, then he would tell them all.

"A mage? Here on the plateau?" She raised the hard bony ridge above her left eye, quizzically.

"No, not here, but if he is stirring up trouble I will deal with it and we won't need to involve the others." That should reassure her temporarily. "It will just stir up unrest and I don't want that." She knew how he felt about keeping to themselves and maintaining the peace. He didn't want to risk another debate about humans again. It would only add fuel to the fire Blaze favoured. The sooner he could show Blaze everything was fine, the better. This was all starting to get overly complicated.

"Please, Sapphire, keep this to yourself for now. I am handling it. I am sure it's nothing, but if there is anything actually going on, I need to know before I bring this to the moot."

"But what if—"

"Please, trust me and do as I ask. I'm sure there is no cause for concern, in fact I'm confident everything will be resolved shortly. I'll speak with you when I'm done and explain everything. Can I count on your discretion?" He didn't want the moot stirred up because of Blaze's unwarranted suspicions.

"Always, moot leader. Are you sure I cannot help?" Sapphire cocked her head in question again, as was her way.

"I am sure. Thank you, Sapphire. Your understanding and support is something I value, as I do our friendship." It was true, his respect for the cerulean blue was great.

"And I yours. So be it," she agreed, "But," and she looked at him, meeting his eye, "I expect you to come hunt with me and we can discuss it over our kills." Sapphire loved to hunt and she was a worthy adversary, blues were known for their competitive streak.

"I would enjoy that." He could think of nothing better right now. "It has been over long since we last flew together in the hunt. I will speak with you on my return." She stood back as he lifted into the air, propelling himself up is a tight spiral. When he was high enough, he closed his wings tightly to his flanks. Air rushed over him as he angled downward, waiting until the last second before opening his wings and gliding towards the plateau's edge.

The sensation of flying, the freedom of the open air and exhilaration of speed, soothed him. Galdor loved the wide open skies and the thrill of the flight. He sped over the ground, gliding to the edge of the plateau, crossing over the boundary where the land ended, dropping steeply away from the flat ground where he made his home. Wings stretched wide, he waited. Warm air pushed against the thick leathery membranes of his reaching wings, the pressure of the updraft filling them like giant sails and catapulting him high into the morning sky.

The first dragons to settle on the plateau named their home aptly; the Lifting Plateau. Galdor always marvelled at the natural phenomenon as he rose effortlessly, propelled upward by strong thermal currents. The change in air pressure and the accelerating uplift temporarily eased his troubled mind. He reached the apex of his lift and beat his wings, banking steeply downward, turning in lazy circles as he surveyed the flat land below. A few airborne dragons crossed the plateau and Galdor observed a red dragon, gleaming as the rising sun caught her scales and set them alight.

He circled the perimeter of the plateau, taking his time, observing the cave mouths in the rocky slopes sweeping down from the mountains above. The lofty peaks pierced the clouds, shrouding their height, high and cool, but not cold enough for snow. Opposite the mountain slopes, on the other side of the grassy plateau, the land dropped again. Far below, the warm humid jungle sprawled off to the west. The heat from the jungle and the cold from the mountains met at the edge of the plateau, forcing the warm air upward. When a dragon flew across the divide between warm and cold, the warmer air thermals pushed up along the plateau's natural rock walls creating the lift.

Galdor crossed the divide again and rose once more, like a leaf on a strong wind, effortlessly extending his wings, expending little effort. The rush of warm winds carrying him higher felt wonderful on his scales. He never tired of the sensation and today was no exception. It made him feel alive, forcing Blaze's words from his mind and giving small respite from the troubles the black dragon shared with him.

Sometimes dragons reflected the nature of their colour and Blaze the black certainly brought dark tidings with his stories of treachery and betrayal. Ultimately, Galdor knew he was avoiding the issue. As moot leader he would fail in his responsibilities if he didn't find out what exactly was going on and put a stop to it. Whatever *it* was.

He watched as a black shape far below lifted into the sky and turned towards the south. It could only be Blaze. Galdor waited as the black form grew smaller. He drifted on the thermals, spiralling in ever widening circles, not yet ready to confront his friend, but he could find no reason to put it off any longer. Reluctantly he set off in pursuit of the black dragon, casting a keen eye over the plateau, confusion and a little paranoia clouding his reasoning.

Banking steeply, Galdor followed Blaze's path, leaving the Lifting Plataea behind. The ground far below levelled out and soon he was above the Silver River. He flew along its winding course as it turned and twisted, killing time rather than taking the straight route to his destination. The water beneath him reflected brightly like the metal it was named after.

As the river neared the waterfall its current grew noisy and turbulent. The land dropped away and a spray of mist hung in the air, rainbow hues glistening as the thundering roar from the falls reached his ears. It would make the perfect place to talk, the noise from the waterfall drowning out words destined for his ears alone. This whole situation with Blaze had him on edge. He shouldn't be worried if another dragon overheard their conversation. He was sure Blaze was mistaken, his claims unfounded, and his caution unnecessary. But there was still the hint of hidden doubt. What if he was wrong? Deep down his *perception* warned him there was something else he was missing and he would be a fool to ignore it. Their covert meeting was an unusual request and although it tugged at his subconscious, he was loathed to admit he could be wrong.

Flying above the falls, Galdor enjoyed the feel of the cool mist as it coated his scales. Beads of water ran from his hide, water resistant scales repelling the moisture. Small rivulets swept out behind him as he plummeted over the edge of the waterfall and descended through the spray. He pulled up as he reached the bottom of his vertical dive, spreading his wings and gliding over the large pool at the foot of the falls, angling towards the grassy shore.

Blaze perched on a rocky ledge of the cliff top, not far from the rushing water, waiting as Galdor alighted onto the riverbank. The green dragon reared up and shook his body, twisting from side to side, droplets of silver flying from his scales. When he was finished removing the excess water he hopped up from the shore and landed on the narrow ledge beside Blaze, talons scrabbling for purchase on the mossy stone.

"Is this a better place to discuss your concerns?" Galdor asked, raising his voice to be heard over the roar of the rushing waterfall.

"I suppose it will suffice," Blaze answered, craning his neck and looking above, checking to see if Galdor had been followed.

"There are dry caves farther down the river," Galdor said, "secluded and more private," he added, hoping to reassure his companion.

"That sounds better," Blaze said, "I will follow you there." Galdor wondered at Blaze's reply. He was almost never one to follow and usually took the lead. He was definitely acting strangely and Galdor grew more concerned.

Galdor pivoted on the ledge and the loose scree crumbled as has talons gouged the rock face. He pushed backwards as he sailed out from the cliff face, propelling himself upwards. He turned and flew parallel with the river, glancing back as he heard the crack of Blaze's wings, the black dragon mimicking his manoeuvre.

The caves he mentioned to Blaze weren't that far away and he led the black dragon downstream for a short distance. Below his wings the ground changed from flat grasslands as the river entered a large canyon of red coloured rock. The river slowed and deepened, no longer silver now, but dark blue, almost black, shaded by the steep canyon walls. A few cave mouths were visible, dark holes against the contrast of red. Galdor set course towards them, looking back under his wing to make sure Blaze still followed. The black dragon, much like the river below, stood out against the red of the rocks, making him difficult to miss.

Galdor selected one of the larger caves on the canyon wall, dipped his wings, dropping slightly before tipping them back and catching the air in huge green sails. His body propelled upward, gliding over the rock until he passed the bottom lip of the cave entrance. He closed his wings, pulling them tight into his flanks and shot inside the cave mouth, his talons churning up dust as he came to a spectacular halt on the cave floor.

Blaze drifted up to the ledge and caught the outer ridge of the cave mouth with his talons, awkwardly scrabbling for purchase and attempting to close his wings and stop his forward momentum. Wings whipped the rock, cracking loudly and echoing through the cave, accompanied by claws scraping over stone. Blaze managed to fold his wings and entered the cave, coming to a halt next to Galdor. His landing was functional, but Galdor's own prowess in the air was more efficient and, the green dragon thought, much more stylish.

"Nice trick." Blaze commented. "It's a tight fit for open wings."

"And if anyone followed us or tries to approach," Galdor reassured his friend, "we'll hear them." He moved deeper into the cave, ducking his head and squeezing under a low part of the cave's ceiling. "Now, tell me of this supposed treachery," he commanded, getting straight to the matter. He still didn't believe the black dragon and hoped this was all a misunderstanding.

"A human mage has wormed his way into our moot. He promises power, gold and silver, tempting some of our brothers and sisters. He tells of a great hoard of treasures ripe for the taking, of conquering the humans and taking what is rightfully ours."

"What advantage would this mage gain from dragons overthrowing humans? It doesn't make any sense. Why would he convince us to break the peace and invite defeat for his race?"

"Why indeed. Think Galdor, he must stand to profit in some way. He tells of great wealth, perhaps he plans to profit from the unrest. I don't have the answer to why a human mage would incite war against his own kind. Who knows the minds of humans? Not dragons!"

"You have often argued that we should overthrow mankind, why are you telling me?" Wouldn't this be exactly what Blaze wanted? It didn't sound right.

"We don't need a human telling us what to do, we can do it ourselves should we desire it!" Blaze spat. "I respect your decisions, even if I don't always agree with them. You are our leader and that is how it is. We follow you because we know you have our best interests at heart."

"Thank you, Blaze. Before I act, I need proof of this conspiracy. I need to be sure before I take this to the moot." He wanted Blaze to know he would check thoroughly before making any decision. "Do you have names or any evidence to support your accusations?"

"I have better than that. I know where the mage is. I followed him and discovered where his lair is. I can take you there and we can confront him together. But we should do it now, as I think he is ready to start a rebellion and the opportunity of catching him unaware probably won't present itself again. And," Blaze purred, "we can take his hoard of gold and silver, it would only be right after the trouble he has stirred up."

"A fitting punishment," Galdor said. "Extracting vengeance on this upstart and taking his hoard is an appropriate course of action. If we let the mage continue unchecked, it would cause dissention and unrest, not what we want for the dragons of the Lifting Plateau." He would play along with Blaze and once he realised there was no mage, perhaps he would admit to himself there was no conspiracy.

"There is no time like the present, moot leader. We should fly now, stop this man before his promises and lies corrupt our kin. The decision must be yours, but show weakness now and the moot will believe his words. He is a powerful creature and I think he may have used a glamour to beguile or kin. He must be strong indeed if he has the ability to fool our brothers and sisters. He believes himself a match for the strongest of dragons."

Galdor growled. His patience over the last few months was coming to an end. This would finish today. He only needed to play along with Blaze for a little longer. He was sure now it was all in the black dragon's mind. Even if Blaze were right, he was Galdor the Green, strong and smart. No mage, fictitious or otherwise, would dare to undermine him and challenge his authority.

"You are right, Blaze. Take me to his lair and we will end this before his plan begins." Galdor's tail whipped back and forth in anger. He didn't hate humans and knew only too well it was better to keep the peace between their species. He expected the mage would not be found, and even if he was real, he would be no competition. He was filled with a desire to crush this imaginary mage and even though his gold and silver didn't exist, he still felt the attraction of precious metals. He almost wished the mage and his hoard were real. Gold and silver would be a welcome payment for the inconvenience.

He turned and perched on the ledge of the cave. "I will follow you, Blaze. Let us not waste any more time. I would see this ended today."

Blaze leapt from the cave mouth and Galdor took off after the black dragon. His wingbeats thrashed the air as the pent up frustration coursed through his body. He didn't know where the black dragon was leading him and didn't much care, his *perception* hummed like an irritating insect, no help at all.

* * *

The land below was barren as Galdor followed Blaze in pursuit of their quarry. They travelled for an hour and the farther they flew from the Lifting Plateau, the more desolate the land became. No man or beast made their home out here in the wilderness. The trees and the plants were scarce and the lands empty of life. An ideal place for a rogue mage to hide and plot— unseen by both human or dragon eyes.

The mountainous terrain they flew over was pitted with black foreboding holes, cave mouths that burrowed into the barren rock. Blaze began to descend, spiralling downward until he arrived at a large gaping cave entrance. Galdor dropped down beside his black guide, dust clouding round them both as they came to a halt.

"This is the entrance to his lair," Blaze said. "The mage hides inside a labyrinth of tunnels that is difficult to navigate. I should go first and show you the way."

Galdor pushed passed Blaze entering into the cave mouth before the black dragon. He wanted to take charge of this situation.

"This is my fight, Blaze and I will confront the mage. How difficult can it be to follow a tunnel and sniff out his lair?" He wanted to show Blaze he was prepared to listen and act, if necessary. He peered into the dark, his eyes adjusting to the gloom. A long straight passageway led off into the heart of the mountain. Galdor could see tracks on the dusty cave floor; dragon and human! Was Blaze right? Was there more to this that he believed? Hurrying down the tunnel, he inhaled great breaths and sniffed the air. His sensitive snout picked up the unmistakable tang of magic, distant but strong. It tickled his *perception*, the sharp stinging tang of human magic, unpleasant and recognisable.

Blaze followed and called out directions when the tunnel forked, leading them closer to their destination. Eventually the passageway opened out into a large underground cavern and Galdor stopped, surveying the darkness for any signs of a mage. He could smell him now, he was close, his scent strong in the confines of the tunnels. Surely Blaze was mistaken. It was possible the mage had nothing whatsoever to do with Blaze's stories and was here for his own reasons. Employing stealth, Galdor crept forward, his head low, ears alert for any sound that would give the mage's location away.

A pale light glowed from the rear of the cavern and as he watched, Galdor saw the shadow of what could only be a man flicker across the cave ceiling. This cave appeared to lead into a smaller cavern, the archway barely large enough for a dragon to pass through. This must be the inner sanctum of the mage and this was where he would hide his treasures, perform his magic and conjure his spells. Galdor was overcome with the compulsion to act. He wasted no time. The time for caution and creeping around was over. Dragons should not have to sneak around, especially a moot leader. It was time to get some long awaited answers.

He charged across the expanse of the large cavern, his head ducked low, clawed talons gouging grooves in the cave floor as he ran. He was more used to flying at speed than running, but was able to cross the cavern floor to the inner cave in the blink of a dragon's eye. Blaze followed, but he wasn't as fast. That was fine, he didn't need Blaze's help now. It was up to him to deal with the mage and find out if Blaze's accusations held any credence. Blaze could observe and learn how a moot leader handled a human who incited rebellion amongst his dragons, *if* he was guilty.

He didn't slow as he approached the smaller cavern and leapt through the gap, pulling his wings tight against his body as he passed through the narrow space in the rocks. His *perception* alerted him to a change, like a faint memory he couldn't quite recall. Was it the proximity of the mage or something more? He cleared the archway as he pounced, like a giant cat after a tiny human mouse. The mage turned, unfazed by his spectacular entrance, and smiled at Galdor, contempt plain on his small round face. He looked beyond Galdor's head as Blaze appeared at the entrance to his underground lair.

Considering Galdor's swift appearance inside his domain, and another dragon standing guard behind him, the mage did not look at all surprised.

"Greetings Galdor the Stupid. I thought you'd be here earlier. Still better late than never."

Galdor was astounded. This man should be trembling in fear. How dare he speak like this, with apparently no concern for the potential danger he was in. He made light of his situation and was flippant and rude. A man should always tread carefully when speaking with a dragon, especially a green. His anger flared and the heat of his dragon fire grew deep inside his chest, a rumble escaped his throat and small wisps of smoke curled from his nostrils.

"You look confused Galdor. Have you not yet realised you have been taken for a fool!" The thrum of human magic became obvious and Galdor could feel the electricity in the air, like the anticipation after the sound of thunder, knowing the lightning would strike at any second. He looked back towards Blaze and realised the entrance to the cave he entered was changing. The edges of the rocky archway blurred and small sparks crackled and jumped. He could see Blaze through the diminishing gap as the black dragon retreated into the main cavern, withdrawing into the darkness.

Where was he going? He had said nothing after being so vocal about the mage and how they must confront him. He was... No! It couldn't be. He could see the deception in the black dragon's eyes, read his deceit. The pain of betrayal slammed him like a blow.

"I see you have finally worked it out," the mage sneered. "Blaze has played his part well. There is no plot within the moot, unless it is ours." He side stepped and attempted to dash for the archway, which was growing smaller, too small for Galdor to pass back through.

"Your black friend led you here, tempted you with his stories and my gold. No gold or treasures for you Galdor, only confinement and death!" The Mage sprang for the exit to the cave, attempting escape before the shrinking hole in the rock reduced anymore. Human magic filled the cave and Galdor detected the entrance was controlled by the mage, who was desperate to depart before it became too small even for him to pass through.

Galdor was not about to let the man get away, emotion boiled inside him, along with the fire in his chest. The green dragon could no longer hold his rage in check and he lashed out at the mage before he could return to Blaze, who was laughing, safe on the other side of the gap. A terrible gout of flame spewed forth from wide jaws as Galdor flamed the mage, unleashing his wrath. The intense heat of the fire, fuelled by his betrayal, engulfed the doomed man as he tried to escape.

Hair ignited, clothes incinerated and flesh burned, blistering and blackening as skin slewed from bone like melting wax. A sickening stench filled Galdor's nostrils and his stomach churned as flame ravaged the human. Even though it was over quickly, it was a horrible way to end another life. The mage died instantly and as his life force faded, so too did the last remaining gap between the two caves.

Solid rock filled the empty space and the momentum of the fleeing mage carried his dead body into the cave wall, his smoking remains slumping to the floor. The smug face of Blaze was the last thing Galdor saw before it disappeared behind the newly formed rock.

Galdor roared in frustration, expelling another barrage of fire at the lifeless mage. Intense flames licked around the already charred carcass, curling up the rock and illuminating the darkness in a grotesque tableau of anger.

The mage was already dead and there was nothing more he could do other than lash out in frustration. Frantically he clawed at the wall, hoping he could break through and get to the black dragon on the other side but his efforts were futile and Blaze was beyond his reach.

The stink of burned human filled the cave and as his flames diminished, so did the light. Galdor focused himself, searching for control and peered into the darkness, his eyes growing accustomed to the ominous black.

There was nothing to see. He was alone in an empty cave with only the dead mage for company.

Realisation dawned like a blinding light in the dark.

He was trapped in this cave without any visible means of escape.

Chapter 2

Outside Looking In

Blaze watched as Galdor rushed headlong through the portal, talons leaving furrows in the soft cave floor as he charged towards his demise. He must be able to sense the human mage, the caves stank of man odour and magic. He was so caught up in the moment and desperately close to confronting the enemy, he didn't stop to consider his fatal mistake.

The black dragon followed, slowing his pace. *He* wasn't foolhardy enough to get too close to either mage or dragon. Not now things were turning interesting. Hanging back on this side of the mage's passageway to who knows where, and observing Galdor's poor lack of judgement, was a much safer option. Cultivating the seeds of doubt and watching the green dragon unknowingly blunder into his trap would be entertaining—as long as he kept his distance.

The mage appeared inside the smaller cave and turned and smiled at Galdor, ruining the green dragon's dramatic entrance. He was a smug human, full of confidence and clever words. He thought he was smart with his complex plans and convoluted theories. Blaze was sick of hearing him talk, his squeaky voice and superior attitude were more than he could stand. He was a necessary evil and his usefulness was nearing its end. He would learn that black dragons were smarter and so much more intelligent.

And devious.

The stupid mage put on a good show and followed the script Blaze set out for him. If anybody knew how to get under Galdor's scales, it was him. He had spent the last few weeks setting the scene, convincing Galdor there was unrest in the moot, that a mage was inciting a rebellion with his trusted followers. Small snippets of information dropped into the conversation at the right moment, a secret meeting late at night. He played the green dragon for a fool and Galdor swallowed down his stories without chewing.

The mage grinned at Galdor, called him stupid and berated his tardiness. The green dragon stood motionless, rage twisting his usually calm demeanour, completely dumbstruck a man would speak to him in this way. Moot leaders were used to respect. Perhaps now he would see the wisdom in his words and realise humans were a scourge to be cleansed. He didn't blame Galdor entirely, the mage had that effect on him too. The moot leader expected subservience and compliance, the mage showed him disrespect and flippancy. That was sure to anger the usually calm dragon. The stupid man might think he was safe, but he wasn't. If he believed Blaze would help him and take his side against Galdor, he was sadly mistaken. It would be educational for them both... and interesting to see how this played out.

Blaze had set two fools against each other, fed them their lines and given them each their motivation. All that was left to do now, was to sit back and watch as they confronted each other, both believing they held an advantage over the other. They would find out how wrong they were.

Galdor's anger made itself obvious as his chest rumbled, a distant thunder deep inside heralding the oncoming dragon fire. Blaze kept to the shadows outside the magical portal, his black scales a cloak of invisibility in the darkness. He had to give the mage credit, the passageway was fashioned in such a way that it looked just like a smaller cave adjoining the larger cavern. There was no indication that it was really a gateway to some other world. It appeared to be the perfect lair for a greedy mage. He performed his magic more than adequately and Galdor hadn't detected anything was amiss. His usual snout for such matters, this time, had failed him. Galdor's snout was keenly attuned to all sorts of magic, but in his rush to catch the mage unaware, he charged through the hidden portal and crossed the threshold between worlds. Little did he suspect he was now standing in a cavern, deep underground, no longer on his own world.

Blaze marvelled at the magical bridge spanning a distance he could barely imagine. It was a magic beyond his ability and the mage explained, at great length, when they conspired. He spoke to Blaze as an inferior as if his spellcasting and knowledge were too far above the black dragon's understanding. He would learn there was more to this plan than his self-proclaimed genius, even though he had done well to set this part of the trap.

Realising that Blaze hadn't followed him through, Galdor turned to see where the black dragon was, just as the archway disguising the portal started to diminish. The mage berated the green dragon asking if Galdor had worked their plan out yet and the arrogant human praised the black dragon for his part in their scheme.

Blaze drew farther back, the pain of betrayal in Galdor's eyes too much for him to bear. He didn't want it to be like this, but Galdor wouldn't listen to any of his ideas or suggestions. If the moot leader had taken him seriously and listened to his advice, he wouldn't be in this predicament. But Galdor knew best and he only had himself to blame. He was always ready with an answer or a reason why they should do things his way. A politician's answer. He listened to the others members of the moot when their ideas, stupid as they were, were voiced. What did Blaze have to do to be heard? What was necessary; what Galdor had forced him to do. Get rid of him.

With the moot leader out of the way, Blaze would be free to lead the Lifting Plateau to greatness. He would start anew, removing Galdor was just the first part of his grand scheme. When he was finished he would have the power he truly desired and a wealth of knowledge no dragon had ever possessed before. With his new found responsibilities he would be able to lead the colony in a manner befitting dragons.

He could have challenged for leadership of the moot and fought Galdor to the death. It was still one of the rules, barbaric as it was, that could be used to determine the moot leader. But he didn't want to risk a fight and even though he knew he could best the green, he didn't want Galdor to die that way. He didn't deserve a dishonourable death, misguided as he was, he only had the best interests of the Lifting Plateau at heart. This way, he would be gone and still have a chance of survival. It was possible he might like his new home, living out his life in a new land, on a new world. It sounded quite exciting. Perhaps Galdor would think so too, once he had time to adjust.

The mage couldn't resist telling Galdor there was no gold or treasure to be found as he sprang around the dragon and tried to exit the cave. The portal shrank, getting smaller and its edges were difficult to see, blurring like a heat haze, little sparks crackled and popped, jumping across the stone where it met its border.

Blaze had to admit, the little human was agile as he attempted to get back to his own side of the passageway. The original plan was to leave Galdor on the far side. The mage, with Blaze's help, would return back through the portal to the soil of his own world, leaving the green dragon trapped, but unharmed. The man dodged to one side, Galdor obstructed his path to the shrinking portal, blocking what should have been an easy retreat. The portal was still large enough for a human to pass through, but Galdor's chances at squeezing through it had gone.

Blaze laughed. The idiot mage had left it too late, spending valuable time taunting Galdor more than he was instructed. He had to show off, prove to himself he was smarter than Galdor. If he was trapped on the other side with Galdor, what was to stop him making a bargain with the green, reopening the portal and them both returning home? He should never have trusted the little human, all his planning would be ruined if...

Bright flame, white hot, blasted from Galdor's throat, driving away the darkness and causing Blaze to squint. Galdor's normal calm gave way to a madness, the intense wave of fire was proof of that. Usually dragon fire was orange, yellow or red. White was the flame of frustration, pent up rage and cleansing retribution.

Blaze didn't need to worry about the mage any longer, Galdor solved that problem for him. The mage had been close to escaping, but not close enough. It was a harsh lesson to learn... and much too late. Blaze could appreciate its outcome. The mage, understandably, wasn't nearly as impressed by the lesson.

Hair ignited as the flames engulfed him, clothes and flesh burned to black. It was strangely fitting as the mage's skin changed colour to mimic the scales of his former accomplice. Unfortunately the irony was lost on the charred human body.

Blaze leaned in close, peering into the closing portal, sensing the mage's death. No ordinary human would be able to withstand a flaming like that, but he was a mage and might have a spell of protection. Blaze needed to make sure. The portal snapped shut, a muted popping sound accompanied its disappearance. And the spell died along with its source, confirming the mage's demise.

The last thing Galdor saw before the portal died was his victorious opponent and soon to be leader of the moot. He hadn't been pleased, venting his anger by launching another gout of flame at the rapidly closing portal. But he was too late. The mage's spell ended abruptly and the flames failed to pass through the gap in the rock as it vanished from existence.

He stared at the solid rock wondering if Galdor appreciated his kindness at letting him live.

They had been friends and no matter their differences, he had liked the green dragon. He was sure he would be fine, he had always been lucky and often managed to fall on the right side of good fortune. Well, maybe not today, but at least he was alive.

Blaze grinned to himself, happy that this part of his plan had worked out better than anticipated. Both Galdor and the bothersome—but necessary—mage were gone. He had planned on using the mage for a little while longer, but that didn't matter now. At least he wouldn't have to dispose of him later. His old friend had managed to help him one last time before leaving his moot leaderless. It was a favour he would gladly repay.

Blaze casually wandered back through the caves. There was much to do, but now there was time. With Galdor out of the way, he was ready to fill the void.

Chapter 3

Fungi and Fishing

Galdor surveyed the cavern once more, prowling around its circumference examining the rock walls. It didn't matter how many times he checked, there was no way out, no exit or passageway large enough for a dragon to squeeze through. It was no different from the last dozen times he had inspected his new prison. He discovered a few narrow tunnels leading into the large chamber he was trapped in, but nothing even remotely dragon sized. He even tried digging with his claws, scraping and scratching, but the rock was solid and unyielding.

The charred smell from the dead mage had grown weaker, but he could still sense the human magic emanating from his remains. It must have been strong magic for it to still be detectable. It was a mystery to him why the magic should linger now that the mage was dead. He didn't know enough about human magic to understand why its presence remained. Human magic was different from the magic dragons called upon. The opening between this cave and the one Blaze occupied, abruptly closed when the mage's life ended. He would expect that the magic should have dissipated too.

He wasn't sure if he regretted killing the human. Taking a life—even a human life—was not something he enjoyed. Anger gave way to frustration and he couldn't help thinking the mage deserved nothing less for his actions. But he did regret being fooled by a man... and the treacherous black dragon that conspired against him. He may have exacted his revenge on the mage, but Blaze was out there— somewhere—free to wreak havoc unchecked. Galdor didn't like to think about what Blaze would do and currently he was powerless to stop him, stuck in here.

Just where was here exactly? Galdor's *perception*, his dragon sense, told him he was no longer on his own world. He knew this to be true, even if he didn't know how. He suspected the mage's powerful spell had opened a passageway between worlds. Probably the reason why the residual magic he sensed was so strong.

Not something a dragon was familiar with and as far as he knew, not a spell his magic could recreate

He also sensed he was deep underground. His *perception* was rarely wrong. He wished he had paid it more attention before leaping through the disguised passageway and acting on impulse.

The cave was cold, the air musty and undisturbed and smelled of fungus. If anything had ever visited this cave before, it had been a long time ago and hadn't bothered to stay.

There were dark mushrooms sprouting from the cave floor and Galdor snuffled in the dirt, digging a few free with his snout. They were small and he would have to eat a lot if they were to provide him any sustenance. Dragons needed meat, but if mushrooms were all that were on the menu he might as well give them a try; even though they didn't smell appetising. He gobbled a few down and instantly regretted it. The taste was revolting! Mouldy and rancid. They possessed some strange magical property he was unfamiliar with, that reacted with his own. Their potency must be extremely strong as they were tiny compared to his body size. He gagged and coughed up the mushrooms, vomiting them onto the cave floor. His head swam and his stomach roiled, cramping in agony. These would be of no help, they were poison to him.

He flopped down on to the cold floor, resting his head on outstretched front legs and assessed his predicament. No food or water. No way of escape. Nothing at all to help him. Even his magic was of little use down here in the subterranean depths. Blaze was gone, the passageway closed and there was no way home.

The conversations with Blaze, the lies he invented to create a fictitious conspiracy within the moot, all of it was a trick. He had never fully believed and should have never assumed Blaze was mistaken. How had he not seen through his subterfuge? The black dragon had spent weeks undermining his confidence, whispering in his ear about plots that didn't exist, tempting him with gold and treasure ripe for the taking. When he had seen the mage, especially after expecting no one to be there, he had reacted on instinct.

It was obvious to Galdor now. Blaze coveted his position as moot leader and wanted to rule. He had employed the mage to trap him, the only dragon that stood in his way. Galdor wondered why the mage trusted Blaze and had thrown his lot in with the black dragon. He could contemplate the reasons for ever, but he would never know for sure. It was easy to see how fully Blaze had fooled him. Cruel retrospection was as bitter as the mushrooms. The taste of the foul fungi would fade in time, unlike the memory of how he was tricked.

What lies would Blaze tell the dragons of the Lifting Plateau? How would he explain why their moot leader was missing? Would they even suspect the black dragon at all, or follow him as blindly as he had? Blaze, he realised, was a master of deception. He was skilled in weaving a compelling tale and clever with his words. Galdor was powerless to intervene now he knew the truth, knew exactly who the real conspirator was. He couldn't help feeling a little conflicted at the satisfaction the death of the mage brought. He had probably done Blaze a favour, the mage's life expectancy was likely to be shorter than planned and Galdor had only hastened his end. Blaze wouldn't need to get rid of the human now, Galdor had unintentionally solved that problem for him.

Blaze had never liked humans, always maintaining dragons should destroy them, calling them a plague against nature. Galdor should have paid more attention to the black dragon's grumblings, seen beyond the words and discovered his true colour; black like his scales, like his heart.

Now he had time to reflect, there was something strange about a black dragon with a white flash on his chest. It could just be an unusual mark, but Galdor didn't know of any other dragon that had such a unique adornment on their scales. Blaze hadn't been hatched at the plateau, but joined their colony. There was nothing odd about that, but on reflection, he didn't really know much about him other that what he had shared. Now he wondered if what Blaze shared with them about his past was real or if it was more of his lies. Was the black dragon's intention always to get rid of the moot leader and take his place?

Galdor breathed out a long sigh, the sound of exasperation echoing through the empty cavern. What did it matter now? Stuck here with no means to return home and stop Blaze, whatever his plans. The black dragon had arrived at the Plateau and Galdor accepted him at face value. A dragon was a dragon and shouldn't plot against his own. Black dragons were rare and perhaps they weren't the same as greens when it came to looking out for one another.

All dragons squabbled and had differences of opinion, sometimes they even fought, but actively conspiring with man, against one's brother, was unthinkable. Galdor hoped the moot would see Blaze for the black hearted, black scaled enemy he was, but hope was in short supply, especially here. With no obvious source of food or water he wouldn't be able to survive. Dragons were able to live for short periods of time without sustenance, but eventually he would wither and die.

Galdor closed his eyes and drifted slowly towards sleep. He could dream of escaping this place, but... Sleep!

He could sleep! Of course he could. Not the *long sleep* of old dragons, dragons who had grown tired and were near the end of their life cycle. He knew the secret of the long sleep and how to enter it and, if he was clever, he could use this knowledge to extend his life. He needed time to think through his plight. This was a magic he *could* use to help. He wouldn't have to worry about eating and if he was lucky, in a decade or so, an opportunity for escape might present itself. It wasn't much, but it was all he had. He would not give up hope even though his future looked bleak.

He would wait.

Dragons were a patient lot and greens were the most patient of them all. He wouldn't lie down and die, not as long as he still drew breath.

He rose and paced the cavern until he found an earthy part of the floor, free from rocks and stone. He scraped his selected spot raking it with his talons and loosening the compacted ground. When he was satisfied, he dropped down, pushing his bulk and shifting his weight until he made a hollow depression. If he were to sleep for any length of time, the more time he spent preparing the ground, the less uncomfortable it would be. He didn't want his magically enhanced slumber to be disturbed by a sharp rock or awkwardly placed boulder. Dragon scales were tough, one of the hardest and more resilient armours known, but if he lay down and something annoyed him, it would disturb his focus and keep him from sustaining his extended rest.

He shuffled around at bit more, making sure he was as comfortable as possible, then finally settled. His huge wings were tucked in tightly and he wrapped his tail around his body, turning his neck to complete the circle — tail to snout—like a cat curled up in front of a fire. He took a few huge breaths, slowly inhaling and exhaling, and drew on his magic.

Pushing the bitter taste of Blaze's betrayal from his mind, he focused on relaxing, clearing his mind of any distractions. He reached for his magic, not too deeply as he would have to get the amount he needed perfect. He didn't dare invoke the long sleep, as once he crossed that threshold, there would be no return. He wasn't ready to lie down and give up. He released the magic, letting it flow through his body. The warmth of the spell chased away the chill of the cavern and the glow of magic emanating from his scales, pushed back the darkness.

Galdor glowed, his green scales bathed in a soft golden light that radiated from their edges, a warm wash of hazy magical light covering him entirely. His eyelids fluttered and a few small wisps of smoke drifted from his nostrils as he succumbed to a deep resting slumber. He sank below consciousness, embracing the spell that allowed him to preserve his energy and slow down his metabolic rate. He would rest and wait, without the need of sustenance. He found the balance and could remain this way for decades, even centuries, should he need to. He wouldn't give up. He would find a way forward, a way out, he only needed to wait. Just how long that wait would be he didn't know, but for now, it was enough.

* * *

Blaze launched himself from the cave ledge and soared out over the mountainside, leaving the maze of tunnels behind. He wouldn't need to return to the fictitious lair of the mage any time soon. Galdor was trapped on another world with no means of escape. Galdor the Gone!

He flew deeper into the desolate lands, there was one more errand to perform before returning to the Lifting Plateau. He was careful when Galdor had still been here, exercising extreme caution, but now he was free from the green dragon's rule and he could relax a little. His prize was well hidden and far away from the caves where he trapped Galdor. He reasoned the green dragon wouldn't be able to detect anything that unusual such a long distance from the mage's fictitious lair. And he didn't know if the mage would sense it either and come snooping where he didn't belong.

He flew above the valley, the Silver River cut deeply through the barren rocks, dark and slow flowing. The river travelled hundreds of miles across the land and its nature changed with the terrain. Its surface was no longer the silver that gave the river its name. The flow was slow moving and shaded by the sheer rock that bordered its shores, the steep canyon walls it cut through, cast their shade across its surface. The deep dark water appeared devoid of life, but Blaze knew what lay hidden beneath its surface.

He navigated the canyon following the twists and turns of the deep water below, until it widened. Pillars of rock, tall and straight, rose out of the water, their height level with the top of the canyon. Bands of colour, shades of red and orange, ringed the giant monoliths, marking off the millennia, mimicking the cliff walls.

Blaze closed his wings and tipped his head forward, plummeting towards the river's surface, he inhaled deeply and filled his lungs. He cut the water's surface cleanly, closing his nostrils as he entered smoothly into the dark depths. The chill of the cold water cooled his scales as his body's momentum pushed him deeper below the surface.

Visibility in the murky depths wasn't a problem. Dragon eyes could see in the dark, whether it be the night sky or deep water. Blaze used his tail, swishing it casually from side to side and propelling himself with little effort. He loved to swim and had chanced upon his discovery purely by accident, or so he had believed. Now he wasn't so sure.

Blaze had swam in this river many times and loved to catch the giant eels that inhabited the deep waters. They were fast, but so was he. The effort of chasing them through the depths was worth the reward. He loved the taste of the eels and often came here to fish, rather than hunting on the plains.

He recalled the day last summer when he made his discovery, his memory vivid...

...it was hotter than normal and he'd been flying above the river, observing the waters beneath. A shoal of giant eels breached the surface, disturbing the calm waters. One of the eels was massive, almost the length of his body and as thick as a tree trunk. Blaze targeted the eel, diving down and trying to grab it in his talons. The huge creature was strong and didn't give up without a fight. It writhed, twisting and turning as it thrashed wildly until it managed to wriggle free of his grasp. Blaze chased his prey, following it as it slipped below the surface, blood flowing from where his claws had torn the eel's leathery skin. He pursued it through the murky waters, the scent of fresh blood easy for a dragon to follow.

In an attempt to evade its chasing predator, the eel swam deeper, diving down to seek sanctuary on the dark riverbed, but it was weak from its injury and loss of blood. Blaze was closing in on his prey when a purple glow, radiating out from beneath him, caught his attention. The riverbed was bathed in a strange purple light which didn't originate from the sky above, but from below.

The eel pulled away, taking advantage of the distraction that slowed its dark pursuer, but Blaze wasn't quite ready to give up the chase. Ignoring the strong attraction from the purple glow, he put all his effort into propelling himself through the murky water, his tail stirring up the silt as it thrashed, putting him back in the chase.

The eel weaved, swimming from side to side, its motion snakelike as it rippled through the water. Even though it wasn't travelling in a straight line, Blaze was hard pushed to keep up. This was the eel's domain, a creature evolution had designed perfectly for its environment. Dragons were best suited for flight and were adept on land, but Blaze had spent many hours swimming and fishing and was no stranger to the water. He lunged forward, whipping his tail up and down in an attempt to generate more movement and pulled unfurled wings, using them like giant flippers, speeding him closer to the escaping eel.

He snapped once, narrowly missing the eel, a burst of bubbles spilling from his nostrils. He closed them quickly to avoid snorting in water, knowing that he would need to surface soon. He ignored his burning lungs as they ached for air. Putting all his power into a last desperate attempt he thrust forward once more and this time jaws clamped on slippery skin, gouging teeth biting into the eel's flesh. The water turned red and the taste of warm blood exploded inside his mouth. The eel, sensing it was close to death and unable to break free of the dragon's jaws, coiled its body around Blaze's head and neck like a constricting snake, in a desperate attempt to fight back.

The black dragon bit down harder, twisting and turning, deadly jaws locked tight, rolling in the silt of the riverbed like a huge black crocodile. The writhing limbs of a dragon and a twisting eel, added to the mix of sandy soil and blood clouded water.

Lungs now bursting for air, Blaze found purchase on the muddy riverbed, pushing his powerful rear legs and launching himself—and the eel—upwards. He rose from the river's depths, tail and wings working together to speed his assent through the dragging water.

As he rose towards the surface the purple glow caught his attention once more, shining weakly through the stirred up cloud of silt. Blaze slowed, mesmerised by the light, drawn to investigate its unknown source. He wanted to find out where the light originated from and why it compelled him to search it out.

The eel reminded him there were more important matters he needed to take care of first, its body curled and tightened, crushing his throat. Blaze swam towards the natural light of the sky, finally breaking clear from the water's pull and into the air. Water ran from his black scales, his wings whipping the river's surface as he exited, climbing upward. The giant eel added extra weight, straining his tired, oxygen starved muscles. Flying with a writhing eel, twisting and turning, altered his balance and made it harder to maintain his direction and gain height. The easy option would be to open his jaws and release the eel, but Blaze wasn't prepared to do that

He drew in what air he could, widening his now opened nostrils and inhaling as much as the constricting coils around his throat would allow. His wingbeats steadied and stroke by stroke, he cleared the steep canyon wall. He flew out over the rocky cliff side, the water below him replaced with bright sand. He opened his jaws, relinquishing his hold on the eel and was rewarded as the pressure around his throat vanished. The eel detached itself from Blaze and fell, uncoiling as it sensed freedom. If it thought the clever ploy of strangling its attacker successful, it would learn its mistake when it landed on the barren ground below.

Blaze turned, banking back to claim his meal, but the eel hadn't surrendered yet. He admired its resolve never to give up as it hit the ground with a puff of dust and instantly started wriggling towards the cliff edge. It contracted and expanded its coils, pushing across the ground, probably sensing the river below, instinct driving it on to freedom. Sand and dust stuck to its sides, mixing with the blood oozing from its wounds. If it reached the water, it knew it still had a chance of surviving.

That—Blaze decided—wasn't going to happen. He filled his lungs and dropped from the sky, talons outstretched. The eel reached the cliff edge and slithered, head first, out into the empty air. Gravity took over and pulled its body downward, moving faster as more of its weight slid out over the cliff edge.

Blaze hit the edge of the cliff, talons closing around the tail of the eel, snatching it just before it began to fall clear. Blood spurted from the fresh puncture wounds, coating the black dragon's claws. He flapped his wings, dragging the eel back over the land. It hung lifeless in his grip now, spent after its final desperate exertion.

Blaze hit the ground, crushing the eel's tail as he landed, not wanting to let go. He released the dying creature and it lay still, the only movement it was capable of now was the flapping of its gills as it struggled to breathe. Blaze gripped it below the head with his front talon, crushing its throat, satisfaction flooding through him. Just as the eel had tried to strangle him, he now had that advantage over it. He squeezed, his sharp claws burying themselves into the eel's skin, the crushing strength of his grip tearing flesh. Raising the eel up, he stared into its black eyes finding no sign of intelligence. It wasn't aware of its defeat as it hung limply from his claws.

Blaze crushed its head between his jaws, enjoying the warm flesh and blood as he tore it free from its body. He devoured some of the eel, savouring its taste. It was a huge specimen and he was unable finish it all, leaving the remains of his feast for scavengers.

His thoughts returned to the purple light, deep beneath the river's surface.

He needed to bathe and clean the blood from his scales and now there was no giant eel to capture, he could focus on the strange light source. He balanced on the canyon's edge at exactly the same spot the eel had attempted its escape. Tipping his weight forward, he pushed himself out from the rock and dropped from the cliff. Head thrust forward, wings tucked to his flanks, he hit the water perfectly, slipping below the surface with minimal resistance.

He let his speed carry him down into the depths once more, gliding through the water effortlessly. The disturbed silt had settled after his underwater struggle. He neared the riverbed and was rewarded with the compelling purple light, a beacon in the darkness, calling him closer. It was difficult to see where the light source originated from as it was spread out over a large area.

He swam nearer and a few smaller eels darted from the path of the oncoming predator. Blaze had expected the shoal to have scattered after the earlier disturbance. Eels would usually seek out nooks and crannies in the rocks or go to ground on the riverbed, burying themselves in the soft silty mud. Now that he had time to observe, he wasn't the only one attracted to the compelling purple glow. There was an unusual amount of aquatic activity in the area, all just as curious.

But he wasn't another onlooker basking in the strangely lit water, he was an intelligent dragon bursting with curiosity and a compulsion to discover where the light came from... and why.

Taking care not to disturb the riverbed silt, he cruised slowly along the submerged canyon wall. The purple glow intensified and he twisted his neck, looking upwards and realised why he hadn't been able to locate the light's source. An overhanging shelf jutted outward from the rock and viewing it from straight on, it looked like part of the underwater canyon wall. From the angle of Blaze's head, he could see there was a space behind the overhang, shielding the light and causing it to deflect downward rather than out. No wonder he couldn't see where it was coming from, when he was parallel with the rock its source was completely disguised.

Determined to see what was hidden behind the rock shelf, he twisted his body, turning himself upside down and swimming with his back facing the riverbed. There was a gap between the riverbed and the bottom of the overhanging rock where the light shone out. It was such a beautiful colour, its glow intoxicating and almost magical. Blaze pushed his head and neck deeper under the gap, wriggling like the eel and forcing his bulk under the rock. He swam upward towards the light, aware that he needed to make haste, only able to hold his breath for a limited time. Dragon lungs may be large, but so was the amount of oxygen they needed to breathe. Even though he was practiced at underwater swimming, he still needed to come up for air.

He examined the hidden area behind the rock shelf, knowing he would have to call off his search soon and head back up to the surface. He needed to breath and was reaching his limit when his head broke free of the water and he emerged into an underwater cave... filled with air! He pushed farther into the entrance, claws scrabbling for purchase on the rim of the opening, until he managed to pull himself inside.

The cave would have remained hidden if it wasn't for the purple glow lighting the way. It was dark this deep down in the river's depths and the light appeared brighter than it really was, exaggerated by the surrounding blackness.

Blaze stood at the edge of the pool he'd used to enter the cave, water dripping from his black scales. He was amazed at this secret underwater cave and the fact that it held air, musty damp breathable air. The inside of the cave was decorated with stalagmites rising from the floor. Stalactites, like giant icicles, reached down from the ceiling to meet them. The roof was higher where he stood, sloping back toward the rear of the cave at an angle. Some of the thick trunks of the stalagmites were fixed to the bare rock floor while others rose from shallow pools. Drips rained down intermittently, dropping from the ceiling or from the pointed tips of the stalagmites. The echoing drips filled the silence with their soothing sound.

Any formations Blaze had previously witnessed had been white in colour, but these ones glowed with a deep purple phosphorescence. The walls of the cave were lit by the glowing structures and their colour reflected off the pools of water, casting various shades of light blue, dark blue and purple, rippling in time to the dripping water's movement.

Between the formations, smaller alcoves had been formed where pillars had grown and thickened over the millennia. Blaze knew the cave was ancient, these formations would have taken thousands of years to develop and his *perception* confirmed this. He wondered if any other living creature had ever witnessed this amazing place or if he was the first intelligent being to visit here. There was something magical about the cave and it wasn't just the spectacular view. He sensed something more, just under the surface of his conscience mind, gently compelling.

Blaze drank in the incredible scene he had stumbled upon, wondering why the unusual stalagmites and the stalactites glowed. He sensed an unknown magic, but it wasn't from the rock formation, they appeared to be natural in origin.

He moved away from the pool, slowly examining the inside of the cave, mesmerised by the moving reflections. The cave was larger than he expected and he squeezed between the rock formations, exploring the deep recesses behind the purple pillars.

The cave turned back on itself and Blaze navigated through the spaces between the stalactites, following the tunnel. The light grew dim but there was still enough to see by. The pull of magic was stronger here, and the deeper he explored, the stronger it became. The angle of the ceiling sloped towards the floor and Blaze had to crouch, making it harder for him to navigate the diminishing passageway.

The tunnel came to an abrupt end. A solid rock wall signalled to the black dragon he had arrived at his unknown destination.

And Blaze came face to face with the source of the magic that had drawn him here...

He snapped back to the present, his memory of the discovery fading. A warm purple glow illuminated the depths of the riverbed, welcoming him back to the secret underwater cave.

Chapter 4

Tired Bones

Galdor opened his eyes and sniffed the musty air. His *perception* alerted him to the distress and panic invading his senses. These were emotions not solely his own. His forced open eyelids heavy with sleep and blinked a few times until they moved freely. He had slept for a long time and something disturbed his slumber, breaking the spell and forcing him into a state of wakefulness. Even through his enhanced sleep he was alerted to any change in his environment. He didn't want anyone or anything approaching undetected and catching him unawares. Groggy and a little disorientated, he focused on waking fully.

The last 23 years had passed in the blink of the Earth Mother's eye. His internal calendar was never wrong and his *perception* unerringly accurate. Memories came flooding back, a harsh reminder of how he was trapped and who was responsible. He cleared his head, shaking lose the cobwebs of prolonged slumber. An impressive yawn split his jaws and he inhaled loudly, displaying sharp teeth to an empty cavern.

The sensation of fear tickled his nostrils and as he became more aware of his barren surroundings, he realised he wasn't alone! Something had unintentionally woken him, its fear invading his subconscious, and he could hear movement from the far end of the empty chamber where the narrow tunnels entered.

He turned his head, slow and quiet, his curiosity peaked. He had drifted in his magically enhanced slumber, his metabolism slowed down to preserve and prolong his life, careful not to embrace the long sleep. Although he knew its secret and how to use it, the long sleep was something for old dragons. His technique was similar, but he didn't put himself fully under. He was still partially aware of his surroundings when he rested, but any change in environment, a noise or even a bright light, would register and alert him, bringing him back into a wakened state.

The scuffling sound moved closer and a low pitiful bleating echoed softly around the rocky cavern. Galdor smelled blood. Warm blood, alive and pulsing through the creature's veins, tantalising his senses. Senses starved and malnourished for over 20 years. The creature was small, Galdor could see the dark shape as he focused his eyes in the dark. As his vision adjusted, the dark shape became clearer until he identified a coat of shaggy brown hair. It was a goat. Little horns protruded from the goat's head and it even had a small beard. Galdor's belly grumbled, loud as thunder in the quiet cavern. The goat froze and hunkered down, spooked by the sound.

The hungry green dragon could now see the blood he smelled, seeping from the goat's torn and twisted front leg. How it had found its way down here was a mystery, but judging from its wound, it hadn't been able to escape. For a moment, Galdor appreciated the trapped beast's plight. Like him, it was stuck underground, lost and alone, with no means of getting home. However, unlike Galdor, this unfortunate creature was going to die today. It might be scabby and flea ridden, but to him it was a feast. He hadn't eaten for far too long and even though he was able to stave off the worst of it, hunger still gnawed his empty stomach. Sleeping though the constant gnawing was at best bearable, but it wasn't pleasant.

Galdor pounced, covering the distance between himself and the goat with ease. He snapped his jaws around the defenceless beast, crushing its neck and savouring the hot blood as it splashed inside his mouth. The goat was lean and stringy and he knew it would have been tasteless and bland under any other circumstances, but today it was divine. He tore meat from bone, ripping large mouthfuls of warm flesh and savouring them. He controlled an urge to swallow it down without chewing, his stomach crying out for sustenance. With all the self-control he could muster, he slowly chewed the meat, drawing out each mouthful, relishing his first meal in over two decades. Sweet juices mixed with blood trickled from his jaws as he devoured every scrap he could. He ate everything, even consuming the skin, the part of a kill he would normally leave. That wasn't an option now, he didn't want to waste a single scrap. He couldn't afford to be fussy. When he was finished, he picked at the carcass, cleaning every tiny morsel of flesh from the bones until only a skeleton remained. He even cracked the bones open, crunching them between sharp teeth and sucking out the tasty marrow from their insides.

When he was done, hardly anything remained of the goat. Galdor was glad it had found its way down to his cavern and hadn't laid down and died in one of the narrow tunnels. He would surely have smelled it had it been stuck somewhere beyond his reach, torturing him with its scent, close enough to smell but too far out of reach.

Galdor sniffed the air and followed the scent of the goat, tracking its passage across the cavern until he discovered the tunnel it had emerged from. Pushing his snout as far as possible into the narrow tunnels, he sniffed again, hoping to smell another stray animal, lost in the darkness. He knew his surprise meal was probably a lucky accident, but he was awake now and there was no harm in checking.

The small tunnel was unyielding, there was no give or lose rock as he pushed and prodded and he thought once more about digging his way free. If the goat had entered this way—had he been able to fit—he was positive the tunnel would eventually take him above ground. He gave up exploring the tunnel, there were no more goats and absolutely no way he was going to get through there. He could scrape and dig for centuries and wouldn't be able to get any distance. And, he wouldn't have the energy without anything to sustain him.

He prowled the cavern, sniffing and scratching, hoping against everything he already knew, that he had missed a hidden tunnel, an undiscovered passage, anything that would provide a means to get him outside and above ground. He was only fooling himself, there was no way out.

Galdor returned to his hollowed out depression, settling down next to the scant remains of the goat. Just a few small bones were all that remained of his meal, a cruel reminder there was nothing here to eat. He longed for blue skies, to feel the sun's heat on outstretched wings. To fly, to swim, to eat, anything was preferable to the depressing darkness and colourless rock of the musty cave.

He closed his eyes and embraced his magic, slipping back towards his dream state. He cursed the thought of Blaze, victorious and no doubt smug that his plan to be rid of him had worked. He couldn't shake the hatred that ran deep inside, he still had trouble believing his former friend tricked him and their friendship had been a lie.

A soft scratching close to his muzzle broke his train of thought. He cracked open one eye, raising the eyelid enough to squint out. Another unexpected visitor! His lonely cavern was a hive of activity today—Galdor the Popular, receiving another visitor. He caught the slightest movement as he peered out into the blackness. Crawling over one of the goat's bones was a skinny rat. It sniffed the remains then began to lick one of the broken splinters, scavenging the marrow Galdor had missed. Galdor observed the beady eyed rodent, its soulless black eyes reminding him of the final look he shared with Blaze before the portal closed.

The green dragon relaxed his jaws, ever so slowly opening them and poking his tongue out. Inch by inch his tongue slithered quietly across the floor. The rat stopped and sat up on its hind legs, its instinct for survival alerting it to danger. Galdor's tongue lashed out, striking like a viper, too fast for the rat to dodge. Curling around the scrawny rodent, Galdor tightened his grip; from viper to constrictor. The rat squealed and wriggled, attempting to bite its captor, but Galdor had a firm hold on it and it wasn't able to use its teeth to any effect. He opened the one eye fully, eyeing the rat and wondering if the smell from the dead goat had attracted the tiny creature.

Hunger won over curiosity and he pulled his tongue into his mouth, unravelling it from the rat and launching the rodent into his gullet. At the same time, he called forth a little of his dragon's breath, covering the writhing rat in a short burst of flame. He coughed and regurgitated the rodent, snapping it smartly between his teeth before it flew out onto the cave floor. Barbequed rat was better than raw rat, only slightly, but it was better. He crunched the charred snack and swallowed it down. It might be small, but every little helped.

How low had he fallen? Galdor the Green, once moot leader of the Lifting Plateau, respected by his peers, wise and fair, reduced to eating rats! Desperate times called for desperate actions and devouring roast rat wasn't something he was proud of. But, looking at it positively, he had food in his belly and was surprisingly content. He cleared his throat and blew out a tiny flame, expelling the remaining fire called up to cook the rat.

Wisps of smoke curled upwards from his nostrils, disappearing to become part of the dark as the flame faded.

Galdor embraced sleep and glowed golden as his magic radiated out from between his scales, lighting up the dancing trails of smoke for an instant before fading and the cavern returned to darkness.

* * *

The years passed slowly and Galdor drifted along with them, with nothing to do but wait. What he was waiting for, he wasn't quite sure, but his *perception* told him, so he remained patient.

He awoke a second time from his hibernating slumber, groggy but fully aware of where he was and how many years had passed. Galdor was always able to understand the passage of time and how to mark it accurately. It was another ability that came easy to him, similar to his snout for sniffing out magic. He knew with unerring confidence that he had been in this cavern now for 47 lonely years, his latest *nap* dragging painfully for the last 24.

He stretched stiff muscles and unravelled his wings, shaking free a thick coating of dust that settled on him while he slept. He paced, first around the edges of the cavern, listening to the sound of his own breathing and nothing else. Not a single thing stirred, no goat or rat, nothing but himself. Alone.

Then he covered the rest of the large cavern, moving back and forth, traversing every inch of the floor. He was thankful the area of confinement was large enough for him to move about freely. Freely; perhaps not the best word to describe his actions, he mused.

The goat's bones lay pitted and decayed. The body of the mage still stank of magic when he got close enough for it to be obvious. The smell of the unknown human magic dredged up the bitter taste of his memories from the day he was trapped, and he deliberately kept his distance from that part of the cavern.

He would prefer to sleep and let the years pass by in a state of semi-oblivion. He found it easier to deal with being only vaguely aware of his surrounding and the length of time spent being a guest at the pleasure of Blaze and his schemes.

Even though it made things a little more bearable, he was conscious he must be careful not to rely on sleep as a means of escape. He also needed to be mindful of descending too deep into his enhanced slumber and slipping into the long sleep. Once his body reached that point, there was no hope of return. So, he would have to wake up every now and then as a preventative measure. Every 24 years or so was a good time to wake. It was short enough to keep him from sinking too deeply into his sleep, yet long enough for a substantial period of time to elapse. If he checked his circumstances regularly, hopefully something may have changed for the better.

Hunger gnawed like a rat chewing its way out from his insides and his throat was as dry as the dusty cave floor. There wasn't anything he could do at present to change the hunger or thirst, so he pushed it to the back of his mind. All he could do was return to his slumber, slow down his metabolism and hope for something to change. What that was he didn't know. He couldn't think exactly what change might help him escape his underground prison. Any possibility that offered escape, no matter how small, was worth holding on to. And, he thought, his choices were extremely limited.

A seismic event might cause a movement in the rock tunnels. An earthquake might crack the walls that surrounded him, opening a fissure to the outside world. A volcanic eruption could force huge fissures through his solid prison walls or force molten magma to the surface and create a chimney to freedom. But these weren't common occurrences and he had felt no seismic activity, no rumbling except that of his starving belly.

Still, stranger things had happened. Last time he awoke, he feasted on goat and consumed roast rat for seconds. Always, his thoughts returned to food, like a yellow dragon thinking only of his stomach. He hadn't counted on his previous opportunistic meal, even though it was small he would take his good fortune and remain positive. He was patient and would wait. Most greens were known for their patience and Galdor the Green was more patient than many. With perseverance and a little more luck, next time he emerged from his sleeping state, something might have changed.

Galdor returned to his familiar hollow and settled down into a comfortable position. The depression now a well-worn Galdor shape, fitting him perfectly. Closing his eyes, he focused on his magic and was grateful it was in plentiful supply. Dragon magic was not unlimited and recharged itself over time, and time was in plentiful supply. If only there were some way he could employ his magic to help him escape. But dragon magic, while useful for many things, couldn't offer him a way through solid rock.

He wondered at the human magic the mage employed to manipulate the portal and the vast difference between human and dragon magic. Dragons couldn't master human magic, so whatever spell the mage cast to open the passageway, Galdor, no matter how powerful his own magic, could not.

He embraced sleep and let himself be pulled under, his last waking thought was of how different man and dragon were. And, if he were man sized, would he have been able to retrace the path of the ill-fated goat and return to the outside world?

* * *

Galdor slept for another 34 years, hardly ageing as time slowly marched forward. His breathing slowed, almost to a stop and his body relaxed in its temporary condition of stasis. He awoke out of necessity, although this time he was a little later between his periods of magical slumber. He assessed the time spent in his prison. He had been trapped here for 81 years. 81 long, unchanging years.

The cavern remained unaltered since he had last awoken. No disturbances, no unexpected goats, no earthquakes or volcanic activity. Nothing had changed to alter the solid rock walls holding him captive. He didn't even need to open his tired eyes to know this. His *perception* was enough to confirm it. Was there any point to rising and wandering aimlessly in the dank darkness? What would it achieve?

The empty cavern was the same as always, no way out, no different from before. No unexpected opportunity for escape presented itself. He had remained in his life preserving slumber a full decade longer than the last time, pushing the amount of time he believed he needed between wakeful periods.

Staying in his sleeping hollow, too ambivalent to bother with moving or stretching, his awareness slowly manifesting from his drowsy state to become fully alert and awake. Sleeping was his only escape from his surroundings, dreaming of colours and light, food and water, conversations and debates. Living.

This was no life for a dragon, a dragon in his prime. He still had centuries to live his life, but not trapped in here. If he were free, he would live for at least another 300 years, even after his time endured underground. His magic had preserved him, but he was aware the longer he was imprisoned here, the more chance he would eventually have to succumb to the long sleep.

He didn't want to sleep for centuries, only to be able to awake for short periods of time, then be forced to return to his slumber indefinitely. And if the long sleep overcame him, that would be exactly what happened. He wanted out, he needed to be free. The torture of being trapped, helplessly and horribly trapped, with nothing to look forward to but more of the same, was beginning to wear him down. There was nothing he could do to change this, nothing but sleep away the years and hope for something—anything–to change.

He didn't feel like getting up and stretching, he was comfortable and didn't see the point in moving. He would only have to settle back down again, so he would just stay where he was and it would save him the time. Save time. The irony of this nearly made him laugh at himself. He had all the time he ever needed. Why would he want to save time? The constant sleep and unchanging environment were crushing his spirit, altering his mood. He needed to keep going, keep hoping and keep waiting. Stick to his resolve. Something would change, needed to change, and soon. Soon. When? In the next decade? The next century? How much longer could he stand it? How much longer could he survive without going mad?

Galdor tried to shake of the haunting misery of defeat. He wouldn't give up, couldn't give up, as long as Blaze was out there, spreading his lies, deceiving his colony. There was something wrong with the black dragon, something different Galdor couldn't quite lay a claw on. He knew it wasn't just the hatred he felt for him, a dragon who was once his friend and now his adversary. He contemplated long and hard when he was in his dreaming state and was convinced. If he ever escaped this cavern, no! *When* he escaped, he would track down the black dragon and hold him accountable for his devious actions.

Galdor's blood boiled and the heat of fire in his belly replaced his hunger. Blaze would pay. He would pay for the stolen years, for his lies and deception. Galdor would have answers, would know why Blaze had betrayed his friendship and turned against him. It couldn't just be for the position of moot leader, that wasn't even guaranteed. The dragons of the plateau would debate for years on who should replace him, they might even wait to see if he would return. Blaze would surely feed them some falsehood about where he was and why he was missing.

If he could convince the moot Galdor would never return, it would leave the vacancy of leader open. Blaze wouldn't stop until he was in charge and it was his words guiding the moot and making the decisions. Then would come the war against the humans he longed for. The suggestion he never tired of presenting. Dragon and humans were not friends, but Galdor had maintained the peace between their races. Blaze wouldn't follow his lead. Not if he were chosen as leader. Galdor was unsure why Blaze despised humans so much. Now that he had ample time to contemplate it, when he remembered his conversations with the black dragon, he had always pushed for war.

Galdor sighed, his musings were nothing but idle dreams. The dragons of the moot might have waited, but that was decades ago now. Whatever happened to his moot, was buried in the past. Whatever mischief Blaze had wrought, would already be done. The black dragon's scheming was decades gone.

It probably wasn't good for his mood to guess what had happened, he had no way of knowing and he would naturally assume the worst. The more he thought about it, the more it would influence his mood and the anger and the frustration he felt could only lead to a negative disposition.

Something he needed to avoid if he were to stay sane. He needed to focus on his survival, on staying calm and outlasting his captivity. Once he was free, then he would be able to address Blaze's wrongdoings.

Claw and Fang! Lying here wasn't helping. Galdor stood up. If he didn't move around a little, next time he was due to wake, he might not bother and that would be bad. He needed to maintain perspective. He decided he would wake every 25 years from now on. Each time he emerged from sleep, he would rise. He spent more than enough time in his comfortable hollow. Complacency was not in his nature, he was Galdor the Green and he would win free of this prison.

He extended his wings, the wide cavern accommodating his full wingspan, and flexed them. Drafts of wind blasted dust that had remained undisturbed for decades. He turned his neck, rotating his head, clearing a stiffness he hadn't been aware of. His scales were supple and it felt good to stretch and move about. Extending his neck, he opened his jaws and roared into the darkness. The quietness of the cavern was shattered and the sound echoed from the hard stone, answering his call. It was satisfying to roar his defiance into the blackness.

He examined the bones of the long departed goat, ancient and almost decayed to dust, years of erosion breaking them down to nothing. He compared them to the mage's remains, which lay across the cavern where he had fallen. He lay unchanged, crumpled against the cave wall where he had attempted to escape through the passageway between worlds. Smugly satisfied, Galdor sniffed the blackened corpse, even after all the decades that had passed, the stench of human magic remained. The mage hadn't succumbed to the decay that had eaten away at the goat's bones. What remained of his charred flesh clung to the bones and his robes were dusty, but intact. It was as if a preservation spell similar to Galdor's sleep, was holding the body together, a constant companion accompanying him, unchanged, down through the decades.

The reminder of how he was tricked still cut deeply and he turned from the body, drawing in breaths through his nostrils to clear his snout of the unnatural smell. Human magic was acrid and offensive to him, its sharp tang the opposite of the sweet fresh smell of dragon magic.

Galdor paced around the cavern, this time in an attempt to exercise his limbs. He knew if there was a way out, he would have discovered it during one of his previous hundred inspections.

He stomach cramped with pangs of hunger, another skinny goat or even a fat rat, would be a welcome luxury. He was extremely fortunate before and he didn't expect that his luck would land him another meal anytime soon. His mood was a little brighter now, having shaken off the encroaching despair, he was ready to return to his slumber, and wait. It was only a matter of time and he had all the time he needed.

Patience was his ally, hope his armour and vengeance his weapon. He returned to his hollow, familiar and worn, surprisingly reassuring in the dark cavern. He would prevail, he wasn't destined to spend the remainder of his life here and he *was* going to escape. An opportunity would present itself. He had to believe it or he would be lost.

He turned around a few times, folding in his wings and wrapped his tail tightly round his body until it touched the end of his snout. He blew a small puff of air from his nostrils, scattering dust as he sighed and embraced his magic, sinking back into his slow slumber.

Chapter 5

Troubled Waters

Blaze swam deeper. He knew exactly where to find the hidden entrance to the underwater cave. *His* cave. He had visited it many times and loved the tranquil peace and its soothing purple light. He felt lucky to have made his accidental discovery and, not for the first time, he thanked the giant eel that initially led him to find his secret place.

It wasn't just the calming effect of his hidden treasure that put him at ease; he enjoyed the natural beauty of the cave. The mystical purple light and the subdued dripping had a certain peacefulness that focused him when he needed time to think. Today he didn't need any more time to think or plot, his plan was already progressing. Today he was ready to act.

The purple light illuminated the riverbed, its soft glow guiding the black dragon home to his underwater lair. He swam through the waters and the inhabitants of the river—drawn to the mystical light—scattered from the dark foreboding stranger in their midst. He located the now familiar entrance, wider now with his constant visits, making it easier for him to squeeze through. With his passage back and forth he had worn away the silt and mud, shaping a depression below the overhanging rock.

Blaze entered the water filled tunnel, pushing upward into the cave, his lungs crying out for air. The depth of the dive, added to the time he spent swimming underwater to locate the entrance, made the trip a close call. His head emerged from the tunnel, bursting into the cave, gasping giant breaths of much needed air into his aching lungs.

He was glad it was a difficult journey for a few reasons. The Cave was safe from interlopers discovering his secret place. Having stumbled over the entrance purely by chance the odds of someone else finding it were slim. And they would have to be an excellent swimmer to get this deep and not drown.

He crawled out of the pool, shaking himself vigorously and flicking his wings. Droplets of water shot from his body in a cascade of purple rain, catching the light from the glowing pillars. The white flash on his chest took on a purple hue, gleaming strangely in the phosphorescent brightness. The unusual marking—a jagged lightning bolt on the scales of his chest—wasn't a mystery to him. It was part of who he was. It identified him as different, made him unique. He knew how different he was. He was marked for greatness and when he plan came to fruition, every dragon would know it.

As far as he knew, no other dragons displayed such an obvious distinguishing feature. Yes, they were all unique in their colours, shades and hues. Two greens of exactly the same shade would look similar, but they would still be recognisable as individuals. All dragons featured many different attributes to mark their individuality. His white flash, the blaze that had given him his name, was unusual. Usually dragons had a base colour and darker and lighter shades on their scales and hide, rather than a patch or shape of an entirely different colour.

He made his way quickly through the maze of stalagmites rising from the floor. No matter how many times he visited the cave, he couldn't help marvelling at the soothing purple light. It really was a wonderful place and he was happy that it was only his to look upon. Other dragons would spoil the tranquillity he found here. He didn't want to share it as it rightly belonged to him. He discovered it and only he was worthy of it.

And of the magical treasure hidden within its depths.

He had found the treasure, or perhaps it had found him. Had it drawn him into its secret domain and revealed the way? Led him here to make his discovery? It didn't matter. All that mattered was it was his. It belonged to him, he found it and now he would use it as he saw fit. It would change the world and grant him mastery over all the weak, misguided dragons Galdor had abandoned.

Everyone would learn that Blaze the Black was the better dragon. He was smarter, wiser and more generous than Galdor and he knew dragons were the superior race of beings. He would be infinitely more powerful than any dragon that had ever existed and he would become a legend in his own lifetime.

He hurried towards the recess at the rear of the cave, twisting and turning through the giant pillars with practiced ease, his black scales glowing a deep purple as their light shone upon him.

Slipping into the space where the recess started, he wondered if it was coincidence that it was hard to see, hidden as it was. The rock folded back and the cave wall appeared solid, the entrance to the rear tunnel disguised from casual inspection. Even after finding the cave, the treasure it protected was cleverly hidden. An optical illusion designed to keep the unworthy away. The unworthy. Not him.

Blaze contemplated how his treasure came to be here. Who could have left it unattended? Surely whoever it was would not have wanted it to be found. But luck, or something more, revealed it to him. Perhaps it was his destiny.

Whoever placed it here must have done so a long time ago and by now would either be gone, or be dead. Nobody would abandon a treasure this valuable. They would be mad just to hide it away and never utilise it to its full potential. They must be dead, it was the only reasonable explanation. Their loss was his gain and he would never make the mistake its previous owner had.

Slowing as he reached the end of the smaller tunnel, he drank in the allure of the wondrous object resting on a small rock plinth before him.

Nestled comfortably on a hollowed out part of the plinth sat a circular globe. It was large, but no too large and would snugly fit into the palm of his claw. Sometimes, when he came to gaze upon his treasure, it appeared smaller than it was now. Blaze didn't know why it changed size, but he understood it was magical and he thought that his interaction might have something to do with the change.

The globe pulsed faintly in the ambient purple light, but it wasn't the colour of the stalagmites that lit the rest of the surroundings. The surface was a little like marble and appeared solid, with a polished glossy shine. But it could also look opaque and muted with a pastel finish rather than the shine it wore today. It resembled a celestial moon and wouldn't look out of place in the midnight sky.

Blaze flicked out his tongue, tasting the magic in the air around the globe, pungent and honey sweet, heavy with the anticipation of a power beyond any magic he knew or understood. It was a fresh magic, not truly dragon magic, but he knew, *perception* clear, he would learn to master it.

He had already experienced its depth, carefully testing its boundaries and cautiously probing deeper into its mysteries. The secrets within the globe were immense and he had only scratched the surface of the forbidden knowledge it held. It should have been larger than the sun, and twice as bright, with the vast wealth of information it contained, but it wasn't.

Blaze knew he had uncovered something special. While Galdor had been lurking around, leading the moot nowhere and avoiding issues that needed addressing, he had taken every care not to delve too far into the globe and its secrets. Galdor was a fool but he was most certainly not stupid. Well, not *that* stupid. He didn't want his fated green leader to unearth his secret and foil his plans before they began, so he remained cautious of too much interaction with the globe while Galdor was around.

He waited and learned to be patient but it was hard to resist the temptation of the globe and all the wonders it offered. But he knew he must—or risk losing everything. And he wouldn't lose the globe or surrender it, he would have died before he let it fall into Galdor's petty claws. The former leader would have stored the globe away, too cautious to learn from the knowledge within. He took forever to make decisions. Galdor the Careful. And where had that landed him?

Blaze would reap the rewards of his patience now that Galdor the Gone was no longer a threat. Galdor the Gone! It amused him every time he thought of this new name. Gone and soon to be forgotten. For good. Galdor, green, gone, good! A rumble of laughter sounded deep within his chest and he snorted a small puff of smoke, content his adversary was finally out of the way.

The globe changed. Blaze instantly aware and serious. A curl of black drifted below its surface, a wisp of smoke to match his own, but this one was alive and sentient, swirling through the globe's cloudy white insides.

Blaze pushed his snout up close to the surface of the globe, sniffing deeply and inhaling the scent of magic. This was no pearl of wisdom, no fabled moonstone or orb of enlightenment. Blaze knew of them, knew of their powers and the legends surrounding these mystical artefacts. They were steeped deep in dragon culture and all dragons were taught the lore. This was something more, something greater than the most powerful pearl. It wasn't just a receptacle of knowledge or a vague predictor of some possible future.

This globe was Galdor's bane and had already shown its worth and helped him best the green dragon. It was a tool to use, a weapon Blaze would wield to free the dragons of the Lifting Plateau, returning them all to their rightful place in the world. This was a globe of destruction, a weapon of power. It was also an opportunity to improve every dragon life. No longer would dragons hide, cowering from humans and retreating into the wilderness. The time of being afraid to upset the balance was in the past.

He would teach mankind their centuries of pathetic complacency were at an end and return dragons to their rightful place.

The globe reacted to the proximity of the black dragon, the small black curl inside its misty seas, attracted to the touch of his snout, pressing against its cold smooth surface.

Blaze relaxed as the globe connected with his consciousness, he was still aware of the cave and his surroundings, but he was aware of so much more. The secrets the globe shared with him were an unknown addiction, a whispering insight his *perception* understood, enlightening him and feeding a thirst for more than he had ever known he wanted. He knew that if he fed the globe, gave it what it needed to grow more powerful, it in turn, would feed him. With this power and knowledge at his disposal, he could do whatever he wanted. Nothing, be it dragon or man, would stop him.

When he communed with the globe, he was close to understanding the foresight of its wisdom. He knew he needed to give it more in order for it to give him its secrets. He needed to break through the final barrier and embrace what was inside. He arrived at the threshold and now he was ready to step through. He understood how to do this and was prepared to make the ultimate sacrifice to gain what he desired.

His mind floated through the white swirls of ideas and ethereal wisps of knowledge stored within the globe. He could see the shapes of information circulating, feel the magic and sense the millennia of stored secrets and spells, but he couldn't quite interpret their meaning or understand their message. The knowledge teased him, just beyond his reach. He must give it more before it unlocked its secrets and enlightened him with its mystical and arcane intelligence.

He pulled away and broke contact with its surface, his snout chilled and comfortably numb, unaware of the passage of time. That was one of the strange side effects of the globe, the loss of time. Dragons were known for their accuracy when it came to counting the years. Their inherent magic could follow the passage of time unerringly, be it seconds or decades, like an internal clock. He never understood why men built devices to measure time. Dragons comprehend it instinctually. Yet more proof that they were below dragons as a species.

He grasped the globe with his front claws and sat back on his haunches, removing it from its resting place. It was the first time he had lifted it from the plinth, being content to touch and caress it before today. Anxiety hit him like a wave and a dark foreboding presence awoke. He clung to the globe, fearful that if it dropped, he would lose everything he coveted. The dread that filled him wasn't coming from the beautiful globe, as he'd first suspected. He must protect it from the presence. It didn't like him taking possession, but it would not stop him.

He curled the treasured globe in one talon, his claws wrapping protectively around it. A cage of sharp black bone locking it securely in his grasp. It sat perfectly inside his talons as if it belonged there. Nothing would stop him taking it with him. He knew it was more resilient than it looked and doubted it would break, should it be dropped, yet the urge to keep it safe from any potential danger was strong.

He left the bare plinth and traversed the stalagmite covered floor, returning to the pool and peered down into the clear water. For the first time since discovering the cave he sensed something was wrong. Apprehension stopped him entering the water. He wanted to leave and take the globe with him, but the fearful feeling of a dark presence hampered his departure.

Leviathan.

The word sounded in his head! *Perception* informed him the globe had spoken! This was new.

His heart pounded, blood pulsing as his breath quickened. A combination of fear and something else coursed through him. Excitement.

He didn't know what was happening but he was sure it was connected to removing the globe from its resting place.

It had probably been resting there for an extremely long time and his interaction had triggered this strange reaction. He sensed the globe was fine, it hadn't become malevolent towards him for disturbing its rest. If anything, he felt it was as excited as him. The cave was still the same, serene and filled with beauty. He gazed at his surroundings, took control of his breathing, and let the peaceful purple light sooth him, as he searched for calm.

He held the globe aloft, peering through his claws at the encased treasure. A vortex of tiny black whirlpools tore through the white cloudy mists inside. The globe had never been this active before. Moving it had certainly stirred it up, but had also awoke something more, another presence. It was a hostile and vengeful force and Blaze would rather not wait around to encounter what he sensed was coming.

It was time to leave.

Chapter 6

Unexpected Visitors

Galdor slept. His slumber plagued with restless dreams, filled with desolation and despair. Feelings of isolation and confinement haunted his sleep, familiar and unwanted. His incarceration spanned the last 105 years. Long eventless years. He wasn't due to wake up for another year, yet something tugged at his subconscious. The niggling pulled him slowly back towards wakefulness.

He checked his internal body clock; he had only slept for 24 years and planned another year of deep sleep before he emerged. Why was his *perception*, his dragon sense, attempting to wake him early? When he had last been awake his mood was low. Now he felt different. He was aware of another consciousness influencing his thoughts.

Darkness and hunger were his only companions, a prisoner in a world not his own; trapped in the blackness with no way out. What was changing his mood? As he became more alert, surfacing from the depths of sleep, he recalled his plight, once more reliving the difficult truth of his entrapment

The passageways and tunnels exiting the cavern were too narrow for a dragon his size, his huge green body impossibly large, preventing him the escape he longed for. A reoccurring theme as he slept and a constant reminder of his predicament. The memory of his capture stung like a fresh wound each time he surfaced to relive. He wondered if this was part of the black dragon's cruel scheme.

The magic he needed to leave, using the way he entered, was denied to him. He was a dragon and the portal he travelled through was created by a sorcerer wielding human magic. Even if he could learn the spell, which he doubted, he wouldn't be able to employ his own dragon magic to cast it. Another subtle torture inflicted upon him, enduring his imprisonment in the knowledge it was possible to return home to his own world, unaware of the spell required to do so and unable to wield the necessary magic.

He missed the heat of the sun on his green scales, the blue sky, and the pleasure of flight. He missed fresh meat and the thrill of the hunt. All of the things that were part of everyday life were beyond his reach and he longed for them.

He remembered the fateful day of his incarceration. It was a reoccurring dream, a frequent reminder he would rather forget. But his cruel subconscious wouldn't let him, punishing him for his mistake.

His eyes snapped open, his heart pounding as it would after a fast flight or steep dive, adrenaline pushing him to an awakened state. His *perception*, now wakening him fully and bringing him out of his dreams and musings, drew him from the deep slumber, not quite the long sleep. That would be the final act of surrender, eventually admitting defeat after all this time. It was something he was forced to contemplate more often.

But not yet.

Something stirred above him, he could feel it. A life. There were only two previous occasions when other living creatures ventured into his cavern of confinement. A scrawny goat and a skinny rat. He had eaten them both, savouring the warm blood and living flesh, meagre morsels offering little sustenance in his barren existence.

His cavern must be far below this world's surface, buried deep under the hard unyielding granite of mountains. He reasoned that if he was closer to the surface, he would encounter more living creatures, stumbling and lost in the darkness. He had contemplated trying to dig himself out, widening the small passageways and tunnel to the surface like a giant green mole, but that had proved impossible. Even dragon talons couldn't dig through stone. A desperate act.

Galdor sniffed the musty air, peering deep into the dark cave, hoping another mangy goat or even a skinny rat were visiting his demesne. Nothing. Everything was as it had been, day after day, week after week, decade after decade. Unchanging and boring. Incredibly boring.

He let his mind drift once more, thinking of goats, sheep, cattle and deer. One fat buck would be a feast for his grumbling stomach. He imagined flying low over the grassy plains, the scent of summer in his nostrils, the sweet smell of the herd, the warm blood of his prey, the…

A noise, distant and muffled, jerked him back into an alert state. He really needed to focus. A scraping sound, dragging and scuffling. Something *was* in the tunnels above him and it was coming this way, he was positive.

Dragon sense was seldom wrong. He had been dozing down here far too long, slipping slowly towards the eternal long sleep. He knew exactly how much time had passed, but was unable to tell if it were night or day, summer or winter, above ground. Slowly and steadily he was moving towards the inevitable last choice. Once he decided to slow his body down and embrace the long sleep, there was no return. It was what old dragons did, not a younger dragon like him. But what other choice did he have? Wither and die, his resources depleted, no food, no sun and no life worth living.

The scuffling sound was louder now, his sensitive ears picking up a distinctive pattern. He sniffed the air, the usual dank odour of stone contained a hint of something new. Something he remembered—and had grown to despise.

Human.

A turmoil of emotions writhed within. He hated humans. Once, long ago, he was happy to keep a respectful distance from them, avoiding any contact. After his incarceration in which a human mage was directly involved, regardless of the part played by Blaze, his opinions had undergone a change. Humans were deceitful and dishonest. Liars and tricksters. Conflict warred between a much needed change in his boring existence and confronting a human. It was decades since any visitors had come here and certainly nothing intelligent. He waited, listening intently as the dragging footsteps stopped and started, dragging and scuffling, painstakingly slow as they drew nearer. What would a human be doing down here in his cavern. *His* cavern, his home, it was odd that he saw it this way, when his greatest desire was to leave.

Galdor retreated to the far end of the cavern, he needed to shake of the mental cobwebs, gather his wits and find out why a human would be wandering through these caves. What would possess a surface dwelling human to venture deep under the ground? Nothing good. Of that he was sure. Did the human know of Galdor's existence? Surely his *perception* would have alerted him to any previous visits and woken him. He would observe and deliberate, it was the clever choice. It wasn't as if he lacked the patience. He had waited here long enough, been patient all this time. Now, perhaps he would be rewarded.

Let the human find him. He would be waiting. Waiting and watching. This time he would be ready, this human wouldn't catch him unaware or fool him. He had fallen foul of human magic once. Never again.

A light radiated from the far wall of the cavern, blindingly bright to his eyes after a century of darkness. Galdor squeezed his eyelids tightly shut. The light probably wasn't as bright as he imagined it to be. His eyes were sensitive after their prolonged exposure to the darkness. Dragon's eyes were powerful and could easily see in the dark. The little illumination the human provided, bathed his cavern in an entirely new light, illuminating it in a way that was different to how his eyes usually saw it. Slowly he cracked open his eyelids and followed the moving figure as he—it was a male—trudged with no particular direction, across his floor.

The human entered deeper into the darkness of his cavern. He was holding a glowing orb in an outstretched arm, causing shadows to dance over the rocky walls. Magic radiated from the human and his light emitting orb.

Human magic.

He could smell it now, pungent and unpleasant, assaulting his nostrils. It was similar to the smell that emanated from the dead mage. It was an aroma he didn't care for and the reason he was trapped here. The stench stirred up painful memories. There were also other scents stimulating his keen olfactory senses. Mushrooms and horses. There was fungi growing in the cavern and this human stank of them. Galdor hated mushrooms. They made him sick. The smell brought back the memory of when he first arrived, snuffling through the dirt of the cavern, sniffing them out and eating them in the hope they would fill the void in his empty belly. They had not. He could still remember the feeling of light-headedness and nausea.

The foul black mushrooms contained a magic not unlike human magic. Galdor soon discovered that they didn't agree with him and suspected they were poisonous to dragons. He quickly decided he would rather starve than ever eat another foul fungi. The very thought of them made his stomach churn. Not a pleasant experience after being starved for so long.

The human was searching the cavern floor, stopping every so often when he located a mushroom. He picked the perceived treasure and deposited it into a sack he carried. He would get a surprise if he tried to eat them, or maybe humans wouldn't react in the same way. The man wasn't lost, he was here collecting the mushrooms. He also smelled of horse and Galdor wished that it wasn't just the tantalising aroma he had brought with him. A horse would be delicious, a tasty treat and a decent size too. Warm fresh horse flesh was more than he could hope for, the thought of it made him salivate.

Galdor crept towards the human, crouching low to the floor, taking care to employ a stealthy approach. He knew the human couldn't see him and didn't have the eyes of a dragon, but it would be prudent to assume his ears worked well enough. If he made any noise, he would alert the human to his presence.

He focused on the small figure as he moved, stealthily closing the distance to his prey.

His prey? Was he really going to eat the man? Was he that hungry he would stoop so low as to devour a man? He probably wouldn't taste as good as the rat. He could have lived on rats if they had been plentiful. He wasn't proud, but he would take rats over a human any day. What they lacked in size, he was sure they would make up for in flavour. Humans were not appetising to him in the slightest. This one stank of human magic and black mushrooms, not a combination that appealed to his empty stomach. But in his starving state, after his years of unintentional fasting, he would try anything once.

He waited as the human crossed the cavern floor, his eyes the only thing that moved, following the man's path, the rest of his body as still as stone, patiently letting his next meal come to him.

* * *

Blaze took a deep breath and dived head first into the pool. He gripped the globe tighter and pulled his talon close to his hide. He didn't want to drop it on his swim to the surface. He felt a strong desire to protect it and bring it safely out of the river. He was a more than competent swimmer and could cut through the water just as effectively holding his prize in one talon, his powerful tail and rear legs providing the required propulsion. He could also use his wings for steering and seldom relied on his forelegs, having much practice swimming to and from the underwater cavern.

Reaching the bottom of the water filled tunnel he scrabbled beneath the overhanging rock and into the main river. The foreboding presence stronger now he was away from the shelter of the cave. He felt uneasy as there was little protection out here in the open water. The purple light that had first attracted him to the hidden entrance was momentarily blocked as his body exited the gap and entered the river's depths.

It was dark this deep down and for a moment he assumed the night sky was responsible for the lack of light. His time spent in the cave was longer than he expected and if the sun had already set, natural daylight would no longer filter down from above. He craned his neck upward in search of the surface and the darkness vanished! Weak daylight was once again visible, filtering down from far above.

Something had blocked out the sunlight. Something huge!

He was aware of a giant black form cutting through the water above, half way between the riverbed and the surface, blocking his path to freedom.

An overwhelming wave of panic set in, an unfamiliar emotion for any dragon. The turbulent wake from the passing giant crashed into him with unexpected force, buffeting him like a leaf in a storm. He clung to the globe, fearful it would fall from his grasp and be lost to the murky waters as he fought to right himself, wrapping his other foreleg over his precious cargo, scared that he would lose it for good.

Blaze understood now what the presence was, having witnessed the physical manifestation as it swept by a Leviathan. The globe had warned him, knew it would be there and told him. These creatures were massive and more than a match for a dragon. Especially a swimming dragon caught between it and the surface.

This was the dark presence he felt, a dark and vengeful guardian come to stop him taking the mystical globe.

Leviathans did not live in rivers. The river was wide and deep enough for the creature's massive size, but Leviathans were creatures of the vast oceans. At home in the depths with the whales and sea serpents, not the eels and fish of a river.

This river ran all the way to the coast, flowing through the canyon and eventually into a wide estuary spanning miles of coastland. It must have swam upriver, taking advantage of the deep water to get here. It was fitting the globe would be protected by such a creature. How could he have been so naive to believe it hadn't? Its previous owner must have enchanted the leviathan, casting a spell of protection and compulsion on the creature. The leviathan must be aware the globe had been disturbed, sensed it was moved from its secret hiding place and it was here to stop it.

What better guardian than a massive leviathan for something so valuable. Leviathans were almost immortal and lived for millennia, were extremely fierce, excellent swimmers, highly aggressive and more dangerous than dragons.

Blaze could sense it was closing in, he felt the dread as it oozed into his hide, he couldn't see it but he knew it was coming for him. He had taken the globe and now this terrifying guardian was going to make him pay.

He pivoted as fast as he was able, the water slowing his movements more than he liked. His tail flailed wildly, wings beating at the water as he manoeuvred himself back into the safety of the tunnel. He strained, twisting his neck to look out from under the overhanging rock, only to draw back as his pursuer neared, his horns scraping on the solid rock.

The leviathan swam parallel to the riverbed, its passage stirring up the mud and silt. As it cruised by the opening to the tunnel, Blaze risked a look and was confronted by a huge yellow eye staring malevolently into his own. He burst back up the tunnel, panic increased his speed, fear driving him away from the ancient predator, overwhelmed with dread.

He was a dragon and the emotions the leviathan inflicted upon him were foreign; he should never feel scared. This creature was a true predator, unfeeling and emotionless and with the magical geas imposed on it to protect the globe, it wasn't an adversary Blaze wanted to face.

He fought to stem the rising panic, still cradling the globe protectively, trying to think of his next move. He hadn't bested Galdor only to be stuck in a cave like him. No, that was not going to happen. He had come too far to let a dumb creature, an enormous, massive, dumb creature, trap him. These creatures weren't known for their intelligence, they were vicious and strong, as was their nature. And while the leviathan was bigger, they were only marginally intelligent. They were hunters and killers, but dragons were smarter. And smaller.

The inner cave led nowhere. There was only one way in and out. It was completely submerged and his initial search for an alternative entrance or exit proved that. The only way out was through the underwater passageway. His only option was to leave the way he came in. The leviathan knew he was here, he was its prey and it wasn't going to let him swim away with the globe it had been charged with protecting.

He could cower in here, waiting for it to give up, but a compulsion spell, one that had to be extremely strong to control a leviathan, wasn't going to let it forget him any time soon.

He needed a distraction. If he could sneak past the guardian and make it to the surface, it wouldn't be able to follow him once he was clear of the water. It owned the advantage down here in the river depths, but Blaze ruled the skies and he would like to see it try and fly after him.

He searched for calm, pushing his fear to the back of his mind and stared at the peaceful glowing stalagmites, drawing on their familiar presence and forcing himself to relax. As he gazed upon their soothing beauty, the dread lessened and an idea came to him. It was risky, but it was the best he could think of.

Chapter 7

Second Chances

Galdor observed the approaching human as he wandered across his cavern. He wasn't following any path, but he was obviously searching for something. He must have come from the surface, did not appear to be lost or injured and moved with a purpose... of sorts. He would never fully understand what motivated these tiny beings. All he did know was they were driven by many forces, wealth and power high on their list. Humans were unable to live in harmony with nature and destroyed everything they touched. If he made this man his next meal this world would be a better place.

The human turned his arm and the light from the glowing orb shone directly into Galdor's eyes. He shut them from the bright glare, exaggerated by years of darkness, remaining stationary. He moved his long neck, positioning his head away from where his eyes reflected the light. He opened his eyelids fractionally to reduce the chance of being seen, cautious he may have already alerted the human to his presence. If his visitor had spotted him, he hadn't reacted.

The light dulled and Galdor could see the human shielding the orb with his hand and peering into the darkness. He must have seen something. He held the orb high throwing its radiance farther and directing its light to where Galdor's head had been a moment before. Yes, the human had noticed something unusual in the dark and was searching for its source. Galdor did not think he would realise it was the eyes of a dragon he had glimpsed. If he realised there was a dragon lurking in the darkness, he was sure the small man would have reacted differently. He would have probably panicked and bolted back the way he had come. Instead this curious man turned towards him, waving his light around the vast cavern. The searching light was too fast to hide from and it shone directly in front of Galdor's snout before he could evade its revealing illumination.

This time the annoying interloper reacted, dropping the orb onto the sandy cave floor with a satisfying thud. Galdor was convinced beyond any doubt the human now realised he was not alone. He shared the cave with a dragon. Call it a wild guess, or perhaps it was his *perception,* but he believed the human expected these caves to be empty of life. The look on his ratty little face was evidence enough his *perception* was correct.

Galdor didn't move; the game was up. Light from the fallen orb reflected on his metallic scales, bathing the surrounding stone walls in a soft green glow. The human stood frozen to the spot, his hand empty and open, just like his mouth. He was close enough for Galdor to lick him. He could taste the salty sweat in the air between them. He breathed out and the air ruffled the man's hair as he stood mesmerised, almost certainly terrified.

Galdor was impressed he didn't flinch or cry out in surprise. Perhaps he was too scared. What little human wouldn't be? Stumbling across an impressive green dragon in the depths of a dark underground cavern. The noise of the man inhaling was the only sound in the silence of the cave. His eyes darted from side to side searching the darkness around Galdor. Did he expect to see other dragons? Highly unlikely. The clever little human was looking for a means of escape.

Before Galdor could take charge of the situation, the man bent down, recovering his light orb and held it aloft, shining the light along his scales. Then, instead of running as Galdor expected, he spoke.

"Greetings, magnificent dragon," he said. His voice thin and squeaky, not like a rat as Galdor expected, more like a timid little mouse. "I am Alduce and I mean you no harm. I've come in search of black mushrooms and I... er... didn't mean to... you know... disturb you."

Galdor was amazed. The man, obviously in fear of his life, actually possessed the tenacity to speak to him! This day—or night—he didn't know which, was turning out to be the most interesting time he had experienced over the last century... if you didn't count the goat or the rat.

He would play this out. The man wasn't going anywhere. Galdor held the advantage, the human was as trapped he was. Not because he couldn't leave but because Galdor wouldn't let him. He could easily stop him from leaving the way he came in. The man might be small and flighty, but a dragon was faster than a mere human. He stared into the tiny eyes, calling on his hypnotic powers to draw the man under his spell, but the man didn't appear to be affected. How could a man resist his dragonly glamour?

Human magic! It protected him and its power was strong. This was no mere human; he was a practitioner of magic. Human magic, foul tasting and as black as the mushrooms he searched for. Galdor tried another approach.

"Greetings, Alduce, collector of mushrooms," he boomed, puffing himself up. "I am Galdor the Green," he paused for dramatic effect. "It has been many years since anyone has ventured this deep into these caverns and disturbed me." His commanding reply stunned the man. His mouth dropped open a little wider than before and he resembled the ill-fated goat, just before Galdor ate it. But Galdor grudgingly gave the man credit as he pulled himself together and responded once more.

"It is my great honour to meet you, mighty Galdor. I'm terribly sorry I've disturbed you." His voice was a little steadier. Reluctantly the green dragon felt the faintest slither of admiration for the man who named himself Alduce. To remain calm in what must be a highly unusual and extremely daunting situation for him, was quite impressive. This was someone not to be underestimated. Galdor was still paying for the last time he underestimated a human and he wouldn't make the same mistake twice. His *perception* told him there was definitely something unique about this man but he couldn't quite put his talon on it.

The little man was clever, paying Galdor a compliment and apologising for disturbing him. A quick witted thinker. He was trying to flatter his way out of his predicament, but Galdor was smarter and wouldn't fall for his ruse. He didn't understand the intrusion was a welcome distraction and he wasn't disturbing him in the slightest. After all the years spent alone, even a conversation with a mere human was an unexpected delight, a break from the monotony of slumber.

Galdor would glean some enjoyment from this man, this Alduce, before he ate him. He would test his mettle and see just what he was made of.

He sniffed at the man, moving in as close as he could without his snout touching him. The man stood his ground and didn't flinch or back off. He held his resolve. Galdor made a show of his sniffing, flaring his nostrils wide and drawing in air as noisily as he could. Then, he flashed his fangs and licked them, teasing his tongue along razor sharp teeth in an attempt to intimidate Alduce. Maybe the man wasn't smart at all, perhaps he was just stupid. Did he not realise he was one quick snap from death? Galdor could swallow him whole if he wanted, crush and grind his soft warm flesh to a bloody pulp. It was time to take a more direct approach.

"You smell of magic," he growled with fierce menace. "Magic and mushrooms. I am hungry, little human. I've been trapped here a long time." This time Alduce did have the decency to look frightened.

"Trapped?" Alduce questioned, sounding more curious than he looked. He omitted to mention the dragon's hunger. This human was clever, he would have to be careful with this one.

"Yessss, trapped," he hissed. Then reminded him, "and *hungry*." He could smell the man's fear.

Galdor moved forward threateningly, as if stalking a frightened deer, positioning his body between Alduce and the tunnel he'd emerged from, cutting off any hope of escape. He understood that feeling all too well himself. Let the human experience the despair he had felt for the last hundred years, see how he reacted to that.

"Well, perhaps I could assist you, magnificent dragon," Alduce said.

Galdor was interested to see how Alduce would assist him. "I could bring you some food, if you wish."

The man understood he was hungry. Was he was hoping to use this to bargain with? As he tempted the dragon with the promise of food, Galdor wondered what this man could deliver that would satisfy his aching belly. And just how he planned to deliver a dragon sized meal, this deep underground. He started to squirm, trying to see around Galdor to the now blocked cave mouth.

"Really?" Galdor crooned. "You would leave and return with something for me to eat?" Just when he thought the man was smarter than he expected. Did he honestly believe a dragon was going to fall for such an obvious deception? Did he think so little of dragons as to believe they were such fools? "Most kind little Alduce, most kind." Galdor purred, leading him on.

Alduce stepped slowly towards the cave mouth, nodding convincingly. "Yes, that's exactly what I would do, bring you back a feast, a feast fit for a... dragon, yes."

Galdor had heard enough. It was time to give Alduce a lesson on how to treat his superiors.

He snapped, "How stupid do you think I am?" He thrust his neck past Alduce and turned his head back, staring directly into his face. He swayed his neck from side to side like an angry snake, once more attempting to mesmerize him. He didn't like it that he was immune to his beguiling voice. He may not have used this enchantment in a long time, but a dragon didn't lose his magical prowess or forget how to employ it. Was Alduce playing him for a fool? Pretending to be slow and dim-witted in an attempt to lull him into a false sense of security. Waiting to make his move and spring some human spell on him?

Alduce had nowhere to run and Galdor's head was strategically placed, blocking his only means of escape. If he moved forward, the only place he would find himself was between his jaws.

"Maybe I shall eat you. Better to take what I have in front of me now." Galdor snorted, blasting another wave of hot breath over the human, feeling satisfaction when Alduce cowered a little. He would understand the hot air could easily be replaced with dragon fire, unless he was completely stupid. And if he was, it wouldn't matter one bit. It bothered him that he was unable to ensnare Alduce with his voice or hypnotise him. He wanted to test him to see if he was aware he was protected by human magic. The way he acted it was as if he was oblivious to his immunity.

"Nor are you enthralled by my voice. Your magic prevents you from falling under my hypnotic spell." Alduce didn't respond or divulge any of his secrets, neither confirming nor denying Galdor's suspicions.

Galdor shook his head, convincing himself and reinforcing to Alduce that he wasn't going to let him go.

"No, I think if I let you leave, you would not return with food." Every time he was reminded of food, his stomach ached. He tried for so long to ignore the pangs of hunger, distance himself from the gnawing emptiness and had almost forgotten it. Almost.

He flicked out his tongue, imagining the taste of warm blood, even if it was human. He licked his dazzling white teeth, teeth that hadn't been used to tear flesh for far too long and spat venomous words at Alduce.

"You would return with more magic wielders, foul sorcerers and stinking mages. You would slaughter me after you cast your enchantments." Humans were not to be trusted. They didn't know the true nature of dragons. He shared his true name with this one. Deep down he knew he wasn't going to let him leave and it wouldn't matter.

"Very well," Alduce said, surprising him. The man displayed backbone, facing up to a dragon that was about to consume him. "Eat me if you must," he continued, "but know this mighty Galdor, I am your best chance at freedom, eat me now and you'll never know if I could have freed you."

Galdor was momentarily stunned, this impudent little human was telling him, Galdor the Green, he was his best change at freedom. Impossible!

After contemplating his escape for over one hundred years this impudent creature, this arrogant and disrespectful little man, thought after a few minutes he knew better than a dragon.

Galdor pulled back his head, shaking it slowly from side to side like an agitated viper, eyeing Alduce as he stood waiting to accept his impending demise. It was time to end this farce. Alduce had stopped being an amusement and become an annoyance. Galdor thrust forward, his roar echoing around the cavern, jaws opening wide, ready to grind this irritating insect from existence.

Alduce just stood there, his eyes shut tight and never even flinched. Galdor pulled short his killing strike, facing the man. Surely this human wouldn't be able to help him gain his freedom. It must be a ploy. Being stuck here all this time was causing Galdor to question his decisions. He was concerned he was experiencing the onset of madness. For a moment he contemplated eating this human. There was something about Alduce, something unusual, he sensed it. His *perception* niggled him too. Could he really help? He would never know if he killed him. There was time to explore all eventualities. Time was something he had in abundance.

He tilted his head, closely scrutinising the terrified man. There *was* something about him. He couldn't quite work out what it was, but it was there, just out of reach. Was this human his saviour? There was nothing to lose and everything to gain. Blind anger subsided and Galdor, once known for his good reasoning, decided to give this man a chance. He still wasn't sure why, but dragon *perception* was seldom wrong. He wouldn't give in to the maddening boredom and become just another irrational beast. Deep down he didn't want to eat a human. Humans looked at dragons and all they saw was a terrifying creature, bent on rampage and destruction. None had ever taken the time to learn about what a dragon really was. Perhaps if he could give the man before him a chance, he would see beyond the fire breathing monster and discover the real dragon beneath the scales.

Alduce opened his eyes, surprise written over his ratty little face. He must be wondering why he wasn't dead. It was time to try a different approach. A different tact that would show the human how dragons behaved, how civilized and intelligent he was.

"You think you can free me?" Galdor asked, hoping his words sounded friendly.

"I don't see why not," Alduce said, "I am a sorcerer. I have magic at my disposal." Galdor wanted to believe, needed to believe. He was desperate and would give this human a chance to prove his claim. And If he betrayed his trust, like the mage before him, he would end his life.

"Before I decide on the best approach to your... our predicament, you better tell me how you came to be stuck deep underground." He couldn't fault Alduce for trying. He offered the man a chance and he certainly rose to the challenge.

"And, just so you know, mighty Galdor," Alduce continued, "I would have returned with food for you. I intended no deception. I am a man of my word before anything else. Use your beastly magic, you will know I speak the truth!" Galdor looked into the man's eyes and read the man's heart, as much as he could with the interference of his magic. Alduce might be bluffing, but Galdor believed, if given the opportunity, he *may* have returned with food, even if the man doubted it himself. This man was an enigma and Galdor liked a good puzzle. After so long alone it was good to finally have something to stimulate his mind.

It was time to be magnanimous with this strange human sorcerer.

"Very well, little sorcerer with the big heart, Galdor will tell you his tale. We will see what you can do to assist and if after that, you deceive me, you will return to being my next meal. Agreed?" He set the terms of his proposal, leaving no room for ambiguity.

Alduce didn't answer right away. He took his time contemplating the offer. "Agreed, however, when I succeed, I shall ask a boon of you and you will grant it. These are my terms, if they are unacceptable, eat me now and be done with it."

Galdor growled. This was his proposal and he set the terms. He felt a grudging admiration for Alduce for proposing his counter offer. He wanted a boon but it may prove to be more than he bargained for. He would play this out and let Alduce believe he had struck a better deal. He let him wait for his answer, then thrust his snout close to the man's face without touching him. He stared menacingly into Alduce's eyes, playing the part of a man eating dragon. After all, this was how humans expected dragons to behave. He didn't like it, but needed to show his resolve. It was unclear how powerful this sorcerer was and he was hard to read, his *perception* was not as sharp with this human.

"Agreed," Galdor finally said. "But do not test my patience, I warn you. I have become a touch less tolerant since being trapped in this underground prison." He was beginning to have fun with this little man.

Alduce expelled his breath and appeared to relax. Galdor sensed he wasn't as confident as his outward appearance suggested.

"Good. Tell me then, Galdor the Green," Alduce said, "how you came to be trapped in these caverns. I am intrigued to learn your story. I admit, I'm puzzled as to how such a large creature as yourself was confined here. Especially when the actual tunnels I used to get here are so narrow. I had to squeeze through at places and I'm small compared to you."

Alduce was inquisitive and Galdor understood he would have to relent and tell him how he had come to be trapped here. It was difficult for him to relive the pain of his story and admit to the human how he had been fooled. How he was stupid enough to fall for a ruse he should have detected. It was shameful and embarrassing, but he would tell his tale and give Alduce the knowledge he wanted. There was no reason, other than the painful memories, he shouldn't share his story. It may even help the sorcerer find him a way out. It was human magic that trapped him. It stood to reason that human magic might be the answer to his problems.

"Very well, human, listen well and do not interrupt me, green dragons do not appreciate interruptions. There will be ample time for any questions you may have after I finish."

Galdor settled himself on the sandy cave floor, folding his wings comfortably and resting his head on outstretched front legs. He took a huge breath, swallowing his pride and by the light of the orb, he began telling his sorrowful story.

He told Alduce all about Blaze, about the lies and deception. The betrayal of a dragon he believed was a friend. Of how he had fallen foul of the human sorcerer Blaze conspired and plotted with. But he told Alduce more. He shared his past life with the man, something he never would have thought he would ever do. Perhaps, he didn't know for sure, he wanted at least one human to truly understand most dragons were not the fire breathing monsters humans thought they were. He explained about his home and his culture. How dragons lived and how they understood nature and lived in harmony with it. Of how his colony had drawn away from humans and their society, rather than fight with them. He told it all and when he started, he could hold nothing back. His passion for his colony and his role as moot leader invigorated his spirit, and his tale flooded out.

Alduce interrupted from time to time and Galdor, even though he disliked the intrusions, realised it was in the man's nature. The questions he asked were relevant and he didn't mind too much. Alduce wasn't as uneducated as he first thought and Galdor understood why he asked. Galdor knew he wasn't a great story teller, yellow dragons had the gift of telling tales and enthralling their audience, but at least he was a good one.

Alduce listened attentively and was genuinely interested in Galdor's plight. When he finished, the man looked saddened. Perhaps he did have some yellow blood in him after all. His story had touched the small man. While he would never understand what it was to be a dragon, to fly unhampered as the sun warmed your scales, Alduce would know the wrong Galdor suffered. Even a human could appreciate being held in a dark prison with no hope of freedom and the cruel mental torture it imposed. The withering of a free spirit, the confinement of a life that thrived on freedom. He was sure dragons and humans could at least agree on that.

There was more to share, something else he needed to make the man aware of that would help him understand fully. "Come, Alduce," Galdor said. "Come and meet the mage who trapped me here." The mage was part of the reason he was imprisoned here. It was his spell that tricked him from his own world and lured him here. He turned and walked into the darkness, towards where the mage's body lay. He still hated him, even though he was dead. The thought of his trap and the spell the foul sorcerer cast upon him, brought forth an agitation that was hard to control. He tried to hold it in check, but his tail swished from side to side, betraying his anger.

He craned his neck back in Alduce's direction. "And bring your light with you, there is something I believe you should examine." Perhaps the sorcerer who was alive, might be able to figure out the spell of his dead counterpart.

Alduce heeding his words, stood and dusted himself off, gathering up his orb and scuttled behind. He really was a bit like a two-legged rat. Nimble too, carefully avoiding his flicking tail as he hurried to catch up. Galdor led him to the edge of the cavern and stood before the body of the dead mage.

"Meet the nameless mage," Galdor said, a hint of humour in his voice. "He lies where he fell, no gold or treasures did he have. Even though he was in league with Blaze, I do not think my black hearted adversary ever intended for him to survive, but instead to be trapped on this side of the portal with an angry dragon. Circumstances dictated he die with me, but had he survived and made it back through the archway to my own world, I suspect his life expectancy would have been short. He served his purpose and would have no further use to Blaze, of that I am sure. I do not know what lies he was fed or what promises were made to him. He surely must have believed it was worth the risk, meddling with our kind. He was no match for the black dragon's treachery." He sniffed the ancient corpse. It still reeked of human magic. The blackened body somehow preserved after all this time, dry withered skin stretched and ancient.

Alduce came to stand beside him and held the orb out, examining the mage's remains. "He looks like he's grinning," he said.

Galdor noticed it for the first time, Alduce's observations were correct. The mummified head, with its tightly stretched skin, did indeed look like it was smiling in a deathly grimace.

"Although I doubt his thoughts were pleasant while you seared his living body to charcoal." Alduce added. His words, while accurate, were upsetting. He despised this mage as much as he despised Blaze. They were both responsible for trapping him.

"He deserved his fate," Galdor snapped, the memory of the betrayal an old wound newly opened. He glowered at the corpse and then at Alduce. "I fought for my freedom when I realised their game. He wouldn't be this way had he not intended me harm!" It was true, the mage only had himself to blame. The satisfaction of ending his life was little consolation.

"I'm sorry Galdor, truly I am," Alduce squeaked. Galdor sensed the words were spoken from the heart.

"This man made a choice to oppose you, I am only here by chance and do not intend you any harm. I gave you my word that I would do everything I could to help you." He pointed to the charred remains of the mage. "You will have to excuse my comments, it's my way of dealing with a difficult situation. I don't wish to end up like the mage," then he quietly added, "or in your belly."

The man's words held truth. He hadn't come here with the intention of harming Galdor, he didn't even know he was stuck underground. He stumbled over Galdor's cavern by accident and found himself just as trapped. He faced the little man, his face pale and tense. Galdor was projecting his rage and hate onto this human. He was still angry at events one hundred years in the past, remaining fresh in his mind. Sleeping away the years didn't diminish the pain and hurt. It was there every time he awoke. Alduce had been unfortunate enough to be a target for his displeasure. He stared at the man and started to chuckle, the sound reverberating around the cavern and breaking the tension.

Puzzlement showed on Alduce's face, he appeared relieved but also confused. Galdor understood how he must feel. An angry dragon growling and threatening him one minute, chuckling the next.

"Forgive me, Alduce," Galdor said. "I am not use to dealing with men." His predetermined opinion that all humans were evil was a result of his long incarceration. "Seeing the mage after telling you my story has opened old wounds. I was angry at being deceived, reliving the events are unpleasant for me. You show a spirit that is worthy of a dragon and I have been rude to the only intelligent guest I have had in over a century." He didn't know why he felt he must explain himself to the man, but somehow it felt right.

"A century! You've been trapped in this darkness all this time?" Alduce blurted out. "One hundred years of imprisonment without seeing the sun. Galdor, that's terrible."

Terrible didn't even come close but he held his feelings in check, understanding Alduce was truly sympathetic to his plight. He was right about this man, he was different from the others he had known.

"I too would be angry and bitter if our positions were reversed. There is no need for forgiveness, I was flippant because I was scared. I didn't stop to think. I didn't know. How have you survived so long? What do you... eat?" He was a curious man, this Alduce, always asking questions. His inquisitive nature would surely get him into more trouble than he bargained for. He was asking a starving, food deprived dragon, what he ate. Galdor ignored the hunger pangs that plagued his empty stomach.

He decided he wouldn't eat Alduce. If he were to spend the rest of his existence in this miserable cave, he wouldn't unjustly punish this man.

Alduce was not responsible for his predicament. Green dragons were better than that. An idea occurred to him.

"I can see we have both formed pre-conceived ideas regarding one another. I believe I have misjudged you too, Alduce. Despite my predicament, I was once a good judge of character and my stay here has undermined that. What say we start anew? A fresh beginning is what is needed here." He reared up and spread his wings in the traditional dragon greeting, treating Alduce as a peer and showing him respect.

"Greetings Alduce, I am Galdor the Green and I am pleased to make your acquaintance. I have been trapped in this underground cavern for over one hundred years and I am not my usual self. I'm sure you can appreciate why, after hearing my tale. I would be eternally grateful if you could help me with my plight, however, should you wish to leave, I will not stand in your way, nor will I eat you or burn you to death, like the unfortunate stinking mago," he snorted. There, he said it. Alduce was free to leave. Surprisingly, the little human stood, listening intently, waiting for Galdor to finish. Even the skinny rat hadn't looked as dumbstruck.

"I am able to sleep for long periods of time," Galdor explained, filling the silence, "decades or longer, it's something dragons can do." A vague explanation would do as Alduce did not need to know dragon secrets. "I can preserve my strength that way without the need for food, which I admit, is incredibly scarce down here. I've managed to scavenge a few meals over the years, but only when something wanders into my prison." It wasn't worth elaborating that he had eaten a flea ridden goat or a skinny rat and this time the inquisitive sorcerer never questioned him about it. They had found a common ground. He wouldn't tell Alduce what he had eaten and Alduce was omitting to mention food. It appeared the man was a quick study and had more sense that he had given him credit for.

Alduce didn't move, staring at Galdor. "Stinking mage?"

"Yes, he stinks, but not of charred flesh. He stinks of a strong magic. I can smell it from his corpse even after all these years, an acrid taste, bitter and foul."

Alduce stepped close to the ancient corpse inhaling deeply. It was a wonder the small snout holes in his face could smell anything. Galdor gave another rumbling chuckle as Alduce sniffed.

"Can humans smell magic? Tell me you can, tell me he stinks of it."

"No, Galdor, I smell nothing. The mage is totally free from any odour I can detect, be it magic or decay. However." He crouched, stretching out his hand, "I can *feel* it." He turned to face Galdor, amazement plain on his face. "And you are correct, it's strong!" He was captivated with his discovery. Galdor always suspected the magic performed by the mage was powerful. The mage's body was over a century old, yet his remains lay partially intact. Compared to the bones of the goat, which were nothing but dust, it was logical to ascertain the residual strength of the human spell had kept the body preserved. If the surprised reaction of Alduce was anything to go by, he was sure his assumption was accurate.

Alduce reached out apprehensively, slowly extending his arm and touching the corpse, running his tiny hand along its length. Galdor leaned in close, something was happening here, his dragon senses tingled. If Alduce discovered why the mage still radiated magic, he didn't want to miss it. He didn't dare hope, but any clue the human might discover could prove vital to his release.

Alduce jumped back as if bitten, nearly swatting Galdor's snout. He pulled back instinctively and then felt foolish. The change in circumstances was making him jittery. Nervous anticipation at finding the elusive answers he sought for so long, filled his empty belly with nausea. That and being so close to the human magic, thrumming through the cavern. The magic appeared to be responding to Alduce.

"Sorry, Galdor, I didn't mean to make you jump." Alduce grinned. He actually grinned at him. As if a small human could scare a dragon.

"I was taken unawares by the power I feel emanating from the dead mage, "Alduce continued, thankfully ignoring his embarrassment. "After one hundred years any residual magic he may have held on to should long have dissipated." Alduce shook his hand, wafting it from side to side, keeping it away from his snout this time.

"My hand is tingling from the magic I feel, as if the body is charged, like the air before a thunder storm." He rubbed his hands together. "Interesting. Very interesting," he murmured distantly.

Galdor moved back in, studying him. He was like a different person. The pitiful man who attempted to bargain for his life was gone. Alduce was showing his true colours now he knew he was in no danger from his host. The man was thrilled at the prospect of learning something new, a scholar on the verge of an important discovery. It was obvious to Galdor there was another side to this inquisitive human. His excitement at the prospect of uncovering the mystery before them gave back Galdor something he had lost.

Hope.

"If he died over one hundred years ago, why is his body still whole? He should be naught but dust and bone," Alduce mused running his hands back over the mage's body, more confident now. He slowed as he reached the neck, rummaging in the folds of his tattered robe.

A sliver glint flashed as Alduce removed something from the mage, pulling it over the remains of his head. A finely wrought chain dangled from his hand and something small twirled at its end. Alduce tugged, freeing the chain from the tangles of the tattered robe. As he removed his discovery from the body, dead one hundred years, time caught up with the intact corpse.

The body of the mage crumbled, disintegrating to dust until all that remained were ancient looking bones, pitted and stained as if they had been there for centuries. Whatever Alduce held in his hand, had kept the mage from decaying naturally.

"Strong magic," Galdor said into Alduce's ear, attempting to get his attention. "That is what I have been smelling. That is the answer to why he remained whole. You have removed what preserved his remains and he perished before our eyes."

Alduce held the chain at arm's length, a small pendant dangled down. It caught the light from the orb and Galdor was surprised to see it was fashioned in the image of a tiny dragon, superbly crafted. The metal looked clean, no tarnish or soot tainted the surface. It had withstood a dragon's flame and it hadn't blackened or melted. Strong magic. Human magic. Galdor marvelled at its beauty, the detail of the dragon was perfect. Whoever had created such a treasure and imbued it with magic was skilled in more ways than one.

"I've never seen anything like this. The metal is light and hasn't discoloured, even though the mage was engulfed in flames. There's no sign of any stain or corrosion. It must be substantially strong too, as it didn't melt."

It was strange that the man echoed what he had been thinking. If they had both arrived at the same conclusion, surely it must be true.

Alduce gave the mage's remains one last look then asked, "Sniff the mage now Galdor, can you still smell magic from his bones?" He stepped back from the remains, making space.

Galdor sniffed at the mage's remains, he drew in a huge breath, unable now to smell any scent of magic. He poked at the skull with his snout, nudging it to make sure. Nothing.

"I can smell no magic. It smells as it should, dead. Very old and very dead, that is all," he told Alduce.

"And what if you smell the pendant?" Alduce asked. Galdor leaned in, eyeing the silver image of the dragon hanging from the chain in the sorcerer's fist and repeated his sniffing. "Strong magic, stinks like all human magic, yes, potent and powerful." The mage may have been powerful, but *his* magic had died with him. The source of the power was the little dragon pendant. Memories flooded back. When he had been trapped, the smell of magic, this same smell, assaulted his sensitive nostrils. Galdor didn't make the connection until he sniffed the pendant, but his *perception* wasn't wrong. This was important, he knew this had something to do with the portal.

"Do you know what it is Alduce? I believe this might be how the portal from your world to mine was controlled. It stands to reason, powerful magic would be required for a spell of that magnitude. I remember when I flamed the mage," he stopped, looking from the pendant into the eyes of the man, regretfully reminding Alduce how he had killed the mage. He didn't know why, but he almost felt bad for the little man. "That is when the portal started to shrink," he finished.

"You may just have something there, Galdor. I suspect the pendant is some kind of focal charm that can store magic. It certainly feels powerful, extremely powerful. If the mage was using this to assist in a bridge between our two worlds, when his life was ended, his hold on the magic would have ended and his control over it too, causing the spell to end." It made sense. How had he not seen this before?

Now it was explained to him it all fell into place. There was more to Alduce than met the eye. He *knew* there was something different about this man, something special. Listening to him theorise on how the magic worked, what the mage had done and how it might be linked to the pendant, Galdor believed Alduce to be a sorcerer of incredible power and knowledge. His *perception* echoed his gut feeling. He just didn't know it himself yet. That was something the man needed to discover for himself, such was the way of the arcane. It wasn't a dragon's place to tell a human his magical potential. Perhaps he could convince Alduce he was endowed with the power to perform great magic. Galdor could see no harm in nudging him gently in the correct direction and lending a little encouragement.

"Alduce," he purred, "do you think it would be possible, since you now possess this magical charm, that you could use it to re-open the way home for me?" He put his own magic into his words, unsure his silver tongue would beguile Alduce, but there was no harm in trying. It wasn't necessary, Alduce was already one step ahead of him.

"Galdor, why don't we see?" He studied the spinning pendant as he spoke. "As my master is fond of telling me, you never know until you try!"

Chapter 8

Escape

Blaze set the globe down, careful to keep it away from the edge of the pool, then moved to the rear of the cave to where the thinnest columns stood. Bracing his legs, talons set wide, he gripped the rock, took a deep breath then roared. His voice echoed around the cave and he swung his tail in time to the roar, putting every piece of anger and frustration he felt into his effort.

His tail smashed into the targeted column and the force of the blow reverberated through his body. The tail of a dragon was strong and Blaze's tail was filled with muscle, honed daily through flight and all his swimming. He was rewarded with a sharp cracking sound and he drew his tail back for second strike. This time when it collided with the weakened pillar, it shattered, sending huge chunks of glowing stone scattering across the cave floor.

He waved his tail from side to side, flexing the muscles and shaking off the pain from the blow. It would be tender and bruised for a few weeks, but if his gamble worked, it would be worth it.

He collected the chucks of glowing rock, purple light bathing his black scales as he gathered up as many as he could cradle in his front claws. Making his way back to the pool he tipped the rocks into the tunnel, watching them fall through the water. They lit up the bottom of the passageway, adding to the light that shone out into the main river. He went back for a second load, scooping up the remaining fragments and adding them to the glowing pile at the bottom of the tunnel.

Leaving the globe unattended—it wasn't hidden but it would be safe—he jumped back into the tunnel, taking a huge lungful of air before hitting the water. He pushed down to the bottom, grabbing chunks of glowing stalagmite and throwing them under the overhanging rock, out into the river.

He moved backwards and forwards along the gap, using the space between the overhang as a shield against the leviathan. He could still sense its malevolent presence and he fought off the impending dread, sure now it was a magical enhancement of the spell ensnaring it.

When all the pieces of the shattered pillar were distributed, he swam back up the tunnel for what he hoped was the final time. The farther away he moved from the leviathan, the more the feeling of dread lessened. He pulled himself out of the pool, gasping in air and slowed his breathing, forcing himself to relax. He regretted destroying the pillar and marring the beauty of his secret lair, but it was necessary for his survival.

He wanted to leave, but he waited a few minutes more, hoping the extra time would help his plan. His breathing returned to normal and he scooped up the globe, eyeing the swirling mists inside and sensing their agitation. He would have time to examine it more fully on dry land and unlock its hidden secrets, but first he needed to escape its vengeful guardian.

Securing the globe in one talon and pulling it tightly against his chest, he dropped back into the tunnel, drawing in a mighty lungful of air before closing his nostrils. He swam to the bottom and carefully peered out under the rock, surveying the river. His plan had worked! The glowing chunks of rock lit up the riverbed, attracting shoals of fish. And the giant eels.

They swarmed around the glowing rocks, drawn by the ethereal purple light, filling the river with a horde of seething activity. There was no sign of the leviathan, although its presence could still be felt. Blaze made his move, aware his time was limited to how long he could hold his breath. He squeezed through the gap, wriggling out into the open water and swam, unprotected, directly into the midst of the writhing mass. The river's inhabitants didn't scatter as they usually did, mesmerised by the brighter than normal glow. Then the river darkened, exaggerating the glow of the rocks as the patrolling leviathan attacked, sweeping down from above and blotting out the skylight.

Blaze shot out from the centre of the shoal, smaller and more agile than the huge bulk of the leviathan, his tail thrashing violently, bruises forgotten. The unstoppable leviathan crashed into the midst of the living distraction like an avalanche, huge elongated jaws crushing everything in its path. An explosion of mud and silt clouded the water, churning up the riverbed, the strong scent of fresh blood identifiable even through his tightly closed nostrils.

Pieces of giant eel and severed fish littered the river and Blaze used the confusion to swim for the surface. The leviathan turned, faster than Blaze would have believed possible, its huge mass pushing out waves of water and creating a vortex of swirling riptides. Blaze rode the turbulent undercurrents as they propelled him upwards, gripping the globe as he turned and twisted, attempting to control his ascent. He was sure if he dropped it, the leviathan would chase it and not him, but that wasn't an option. He would escape with his prize... or the leviathan would catch him.

He didn't deserve to die and he didn't want to let all his careful planning and hard work go to waste. He wasn't going to let a monster that relied on brute strength and sheer ignorance, beat him. He was superior to the leviathan. He had a destiny to fulfil and nothing, no matter how fast or fearful, would stand in his way.

The huge leviathan bore down on him, closing the distance. Blaze had one last move to make, but he needed to time it to perfection. He waited as the creature closed in, swimming for his life it was difficult to hold back and wait for the perfect opportunity. Panic-stricken at being devoured, adrenalin surged through his distressed body and kept him from freezing in terror.

The leviathan lunged, jaws open, ready to crush the black dragon between rows of sharp teeth. Blaze twisted and let go what he clasped in his other talon. A piece of glowing rock, exposed from the protection of the tightly curled claw, lit up the water as it dropped toward the bottom of the river. The leviathan's jaws snapped shut in the place where Blaze had been, its aim distracted by the falling piece of glowing stalagmite, as it twisted to follow its bright new prey.

Blaze had managed to grab it when he swam out into the midst of the swarming mass of fish, scooping it up in his free claw and shielding it tightly, tucking it into his chest.

It was time to leave, he had no more tricks to play. The leviathan chased after the glowing rock, pursuing it down and Blaze altered his angle of escape in the opposite direction, riding the upward current created by the diving creature's huge tail. His lungs burned and his own tail throbbed, but he was still alive to feel the pain and he could taste victory.

Welcoming daylight shone down from above as he neared the surface and a final surge of energy propelled him out of the river and into the beautiful air. He beat his wings for all he was worth, gaining height as the water sprayed from his body, catching the sunlight—the wonderful golden sunlight—and tiny rainbows shone through the misty spray, heralding his triumphant return from underwater.

He glanced down through the sparkling surface of the river, sunlight reflecting and distorting what lay beneath.

The river darkened.

The water beneath him changed from a flat even surface to a bulging, rising curve. Inside the dome of swelling water, the huge bulk of his pursuer was clearly visible. As it rose, Blaze could pick out each and every detail of its body, the swelling water magnifying the already gargantuan creature.

Its huge scales a gleaming pattern of grey-green, beautiful as they caught the sunlight. Hard dorsal spikes ran from the back of its neck, decorating the spine and ending at the thick powerful tail, which propelled it upwards.

The leviathan exploded through the river's surface, launching into the air beneath the black dragon.

Blaze beat the air, forcing the last of his energy into exhausted wings. This creature never gave up! He climbed, too slowly for his liking, as the leviathan's speed carried it out of the water towards him. It was too close! He couldn't gain the height he needed before it caught him. Twisting, he pivoted his entire body sideways, rather than upwards. The leviathan, its momentum carrying it straight up, was unable to correct its trajectory to match. Jaws snapped, three times in quick succession, clacking in the empty air the black dragon had vacated.

Realising its prey had managed to evade it, the leviathan attempted to twist its bulk mid-air and follow, the geas compelling it, driving it relentlessly on. It massive body writhed, its tail whipping frantically as it attempted to control its pathway through the air.

Blaze cleared the river, crossing over the canyons cliffs, leaving the water behind, never more grateful to see solid rock beneath his wings. Every muscle in his body throbbed—he could easily collapse and sleep for a year—relying on every drop of energy that remained to keep himself airborne. The leviathan roared in anger, the deafening sound echoing along the canyon walls.

The black dragon climbed higher, wings aching from exertion, tension and fear coursing through his entire body, the terrible dread forcing him on. He twisted his neck and watched as the leviathan reached its zenith, hanging momentarily, before dropping back towards the river. It struck the canyon's edge, pectoral fins flapping like undersized wings, bouncing from the rock and deflecting back at an angle. It plummeted back towards the waiting river, colliding with one of the many pillars rising from the water. Rock exploded as the leviathan's weight ploughed into the pillar, its collision destroying, in seconds, what a millennia of erosion had sculpted. Colourful chunks of red rock rained down into the water like a meteor storm, thrashing its dark surface to boiling froth, closely followed by the descending leviathan.

The creature smacked into the river's surface with an almighty crack, a sound like peeling thunder assaulted Blaze's ears, still ringing from its deafening roar. A geyser of water shot upwards, a mighty wave drenched the surrounding canyon walls, soaking the parched rock to a deeper red. The river swallowed the leviathan, a swirling vortex of frothing water filling the giant hole where its body punched into the river. A tidal wave surged out, rushing waves lashed the canyon walls as they thundered outward, churning the usually placid surface to white foam.

Blaze landed on the wet cliff edge, careful to avoid the crumbling rock damaged by the impact of the leviathan. The leviathan's body sunk below the surface, unmoving as the river claimed it. The wash from the massive wave dissipated, undulating waves rippling like a spring tide, stretching in both directions along the river, eventually diminishing.

That, Blaze thought, must have hurt. The huge leviathan's body impacted the river, striking with the flat of its belly after a painful collision with the solid pillar. It must have been like hitting a second solid wall of rock; he didn't think anything could have survived that. High up on the canyon walls, the watermark remained, the only sign of the creature's passing. The pillar it had collided with was completely gone, creating an obvious gap in the familiar view.

The river's surface swirled and a small whirlpool formed, bubbles bursting as they rose from the depths. Wisps of black smoke hovered above the disturbance, escaping from the bubbles and gradually thickening. Blaze felt a warmth in his claw, reminding him of the globe still clutched tightly to his chest. Heat grew and he placed the globe on the rock, careful to keep it away from the canyon's edge. If it fell back into the river, he didn't want to go back down there to retrieve it. He'd had enough of swimming for one day.

The cloud of smoke rose, winding its way up the canyon, the earie stillness making it all the more unusual. It wove like a serpent, as if searching for something, then changed direction and headed straight towards the black dragon. The globe flared, bright even under the sunlight, attracting the smoky thread as it twisted though the air.

Blaze stepped back as the globe called the smoke to it, drawing it closer. He knew he was witnessing something magical as the smoky threads circled around the globe, covering the surface in a dark swirling cloud. He could sense the globe had drawn the threads from deep below the water's surface. It pulsed, shining through the dark mist, its insides writhing like a maelstrom. The smoke exploded outward, then rushed back towards the smooth surface, passing through the outer shell and joining with the turbulent essence inside.

Blaze tentatively reached out a talon, lightly resting it on the surface of the globe. A rush of elation overwhelmed his weariness as the globe settled and the swirling inside calmed. His tiredness vanished and he felt amazing. No longer was he exhausted, it was as if his near death brush with the leviathan never happened.

He had felt weak and powerless against the leviathan, ashamed a dragon would be scared and flee for his life. But now he was victorious, evading a stronger adversary and snatching the globe from its protection. He was in no doubt now that the leviathan had been compelled to guard it and was alerted when he removed the globe from its ancient resting.

The globe was his now, no longer hidden away and guarded. He had rescued it from the clutches of the leviathan. It had failed. He had won and that was what counted.

The globe returned to its dormant state, calm and peaceful. Blaze, unsure that whatever had just happened was over, closed his talons over the surface. It was now cool to the touch and he experienced strong feelings of gratitude and acceptance.

Water splashed below and sharp dorsal ridges broke through the river's surface moving slowly at first then gathering speed. Blaze stared, amazed the leviathan had survived. Its huge tail swept from side to side under the water, propelling it downriver towards the great ocean.

It raised its head above the water and called out, a mournful sound, so different from the roar of rage. Blaze understood. It had lost. Lost against a better opponent, but it also lost something more, something the globe had taken.

He watched as it sank back into the river and vanished, defeated. It might have survived the fall, but he knew it wouldn't live for much longer. The globe had taken something vital from it, its essence of life. It was going home to die. The leviathan's loss was his gain. The victor claimed his reward.

Blaze picked up the globe—his prize—and headed for the Lifting Plateau.

Chapter 9

Out of the Darkness

Galdor didn't know anything about Alduce's master; he sounded like a wise mentor indeed. It was possible he might be another human who might surprise him. Could this sorcerer really have the ability to help him escape? His *perception* tickled his senses, but it wasn't able to provide an answer.

He needed to focus and drag himself beyond the complacency of continued sleep. This was the most eventful day he had experienced in his long incarceration. Was this the day he had been waiting for? He was bursting with anticipation, this unlikely disturbance to his slumber had delivered someone to him who was willing to try and help him escape. When Alduce had first arrived, he had felt nothing but suspicion and mistrust. His *perception* had shown him this human was different, changing his hatred to hope. He could barely contain his excitement as he focused intently on the human.

Alduce fixed his gaze on the spinning pendant, intense concentration written over his rodent like features. Galdor's scales tingled, human magic thick in the confines of the cave. He could sense a change in his surroundings, an expectant feeling, the air charged with anticipation. The unpleasant taste of human magic filled his nostrils, potent and strong. He hoped Alduce knew what he was doing. Magic this powerful, unleashed in a confined space, could be dangerous. Still, it was a risk he wanted to take, anything was better than being stuck here for eternity.

Lightning crackled along the cavern roof, small blue sparks building to larger arcs, spitting and jumping as they swarmed across the rock overhead. Bolts flew from the cave roof, drawn to the dragon pendant, absorbed into the unusual metal, filling it with power.

Galdor exhaled, his breath whistled as he puffed in surprise, Alduce glancing at him as he held onto the chain, a corona of light enveloping the man. The lightning poured into the small dragon, filling it with more and more power. Alduce stood, bravely gripping the chain as the power intensified. Just when Galdor thought the pendant was about to explode the power blasted from it. Eight trails of lightning leapt from the metal dragon, bursting free from containment, rushing towards the far wall where the portal had been. The lightning streaked over the rock like a spider's web, spreading out in a circle, a spinning whirlpool of magical light. Eight points in the wall glowed as the lightning spread, lighting up the cavern, the blue sparks blurring into a continuous circle, faster and faster as it spun around the points fixed into the rock.

Galdor examined the whirling pool of light, it grew brighter, opening from the centre. Was it possible the eight points on the wall had been deliberately set there by the mage to create the original portal? It was a mystery, yet Alduce had managed to imitate the spell and create a passageway. This time, it was the way home, the path to freedom rather than imprisonment.

Galdor blinked, clearing the moisture of tears from his eyes. A great euphoria filled him as he watched the small man wield the hated human magic. Confusing emotions mixed with excitement and anticipation. This was the day he had waited so patiently for, his long ordeal almost over.

The newly created passageway expanded outwards until it reached the edge of the whirling lightning, rippling like waves on water. It slowed and calmed and the blurring cleared, the surface steady. A vision of beauty. To think he had contemplated eating Alduce! The taste of the sorcerer's unbelievable success was a thousand times better than his flesh ever would have been.

Galdor was in awe, "Alduce, you have done it!" This little man was indeed a sorcerer worthy of his talent. "You have restored the archway. You are truly a sorcerer of great knowledge and power. You have opened the way home for me after more than one hundred years." He couldn't express his gratitude enough, and any further words failed him, all he could do was stare at the gateway in wonder.

"Galdor," Alduce said, his voice low, "I am but an apprentice and you pay me a great compliment for accidentally stumbling across the answer you so desperately desired." His modest reply only reinforced Galdor's opinion that this man was special. Of that he was positive, his perception strong about it. Alduce would be like no other human sorcerer and was destined for great things. Galdor would truly have liked to spend more time with the man and get to know him better, but the urgency of returning to his own home was too intense.

"Well then," he told Alduce, "Apprentice you may be now, I can only believe when you become a master, you will be the most powerful human who ever practiced magic!" The man had tamed the magic from an artefact he had never seen, opening a gateway to another world. This wasn't something a mere apprentice should be able to accomplish. There was no time to waste, no time to discuss this with Alduce. He needed to act.

"I would dearly love to stay and discuss the how and the why, Alduce, my rescuer, but I fear to waste another second stuck in this dank prison. I must return and see how the years and that black hearted dragon have changed the home I once knew."

Galdor tested the portal, sliding his neck through the shimmering ring of light, nervous it would work as he hoped and still not fully believing it was real. He pulled it back through and looked Alduce in the eye, no longer was there any trace of fear, rather a sense of great wonder and respect. Something they both shared.

"You asked me a boon when we made our deal, sorcerer." Galdor said. "Name it now and I will grant it." Whatever Alduce wished for, if it was within Galdor's power, he would give it freely.

Alduce nodded, bobbling his tiny head with little conviction. "My boon, mighty Galdor, was not to meet my end in this cave," he grinned. "And remaining on the outside of your belly is reward enough for me."

Galdor couldn't help the laughter that rumbled deep from within. When he first met Alduce, he had hated the man, another despised human, filled with poison and lies. He would never have believed after a century of confinement that a human sorcerer would make him happy enough to laugh. Let alone free him.

"I desire no more," Alduce continued, surprising the dragon, "to see you gain your freedom is more than enough payment. It's not every day I'm given the opportunity to meet a dragon." Galdor knew the words were true and spoken from the heart. This man had a spirit worthy of reward. Any man who could rise above his prejudices and save a dragon for no reason other than helping—when he thought he was going to die—was more than human. And Galdor would proudly call him a friend.

"You are a humble man, Alduce, I doubt there are many among your race that would turn down such an offer. It gives me hope for the human race." He pulled his leg back, tucking it under his chest and bent low, bowing to the man before him and showing him the respect of an equal. An equal with the spirit of a dragon.

"I will remember this and the lesson you have taught me here today, that dragon kind and human beings can become friends."

Galdor drew himself up on his hind legs and spread his wings, the light from the portal highlighting his green scales. The man would receive a boon, he deserved to be rewarded with more than just praise.

Galdor called on his own magic and a gold light emanated from his body, bathing him in a shimmering haze. He was ready to transform, be born anew, leave his prison and start fresh. Releasing the magic, he glowed brighter and separated his skin and scales from his body. There was no pain as his outer layer shed, sliding free, as it dropped to the cave floor. New scales radiated from below the old, gleaming with all the colours of the spectrum, shimmering and pulsing like waves as they surrounded his form. The pulsing slowed and the new scales glowed brightly before settling to their natural green.

He felt reborn. The shedding was rare and not all dragons were able to renew their skin and scales. Galdor had only done this once before and it was a private, secret act. Alduce would never know how privileged he was to witness a shedding, but he did look suitably impressed.

"I leave you my hide of skin and scales," Galdor proudly announced. "A sorcerer such as yourself will find many uses for it, I am sure." He stepped free of his former skin and leapt through the portal like a mighty green salmon in a waterfall of swirling light.

He stood on the other side, his home world, free at last. Looking back through the shimmering portal, Alduce stood, fixed to the spot, stunned and amazed. Perhaps he understood the shedding and just how lucky he was. He had been gifted a boon from a dragon, survived where others less talented would have met their demise. And he now owned a powerful magical pendant. Much better, Galdor mused, than ending up in a dragon's belly.

He pushed his head back through the hole in the cave wall, talons firmly planted on his home ground.

"Galdor the Green owes you much more than the hide he has shed and the magical necklace you hold," he said. "Remember this Alduce, for I shall not forget. If you ever chance to visit this world, seek me out." He quickly pulled his head back through the portal and spoke from his own side.

"Quick, now, close the archway behind me," he called out. He didn't want anything to happen to the man, not after everything he accomplished. The unknown magic was still a concern and it wouldn't sit well with him if Alduce was hurt or injured as a result of holding the portal open.

The circle of the gateway started to diminish, drawing in on itself, closing. It grew smaller and smaller and the light began to fade. Alduce must have released his hold on the magic. He would be safe.

"Thank you," Galdor said to the small hole of the closing portal. He hoped the little man could hear him.

The portal closed, winking out of existence and the cave wall on Galdor's world returned to being solid rock.

Part Two

Manipulation and Subterfuge

Excerpt from the private journals of Alduce.

The Earth Mother and dragon magic.

The Earth Mother is believed to be the first ever dragon to have existed. She is regarded as something close to a deity—but not worshipped as a goddess—yet held in reverence. She is credited as being part of the natural order and the creator of all things. Dragons believe the origins of magic were gifted by the Earth Mother giving her magic to the land, the birthing of all dragons and the bringing of life. Similar to Mother Nature?

    She is referred to and often thanked, but still remains a mystery outside true dragon perception. She is accepted and known without the need of explanation and just is, in typical dragon logic.

    There are many stories that tell where she originated from and how she came to exist, depending on which colony elder tells the tale. The common belief is that long before humans walked the lands, dragons inhabited the worlds and every dragon is a distant descendant of the Earth Mother. Her magic was great, allowing her to span the galaxies, seeding the worlds she visited with her eggs, then moving on. This might be why dragon eggs are attributed to be naturally resistant to almost everything and do not need attention to incubate or hatch. And also why so much dragon lore and history follows a similar path, though the details and circumstances can differ from world to world.

    Some worlds are no longer home to dragons as they have died out and become extinct, fading into myth. However, if there is magic in that place, no matter how strong or weak, it is because dragons once flew the skies.

    Dragon magic is much older than the magic employed by sorcerers, mages, magicians or any other human practitioner of the mystical arts. On worlds where magic fades, another power fills the void: science waits to be *discovered and fill the vacuum. Technology and scientific discovery replace the unknown with the known and where once mystery and belief were strong, explanation and reasoning now prevail. This raises the long pondered question. Has the lack of belief in magic caused it to fade once science is discovered? Would the academic scholar of science, on a world that has lost magic, be the magician or sorcerer of that world's past age?*

The lifespan of dragons long exceeds that of humans, but they are less prolific. It is the fate of most worlds that are the home of dragons, that eventually, these wonderful creatures are forced into extinction by humans. Humans on any world will eventually rise to the top of the evolutionary pile, becoming the dominant species. As humans thrive, be it magically or technologically, dragons suffer. It is an age old pattern that ultimately eliminates the dragon species, even though they are stronger both physically and magically.

It should be noted, that there are many types of magic, the two most common being dragon and human, neither of which is interchangeable.

I have concluded that other worlds that are devoid of any magic at all, while they may be inhabited by man, have never known dragons in their history.

Some worlds believe dragons to be mythical, creatures of legend never having truly existed, only stories and tales of fantasy, inventions of the imagination. The sad fact is, even though there may be no scientific evidence to prove their existence, dragons were once inhabitants of these worlds.

Chapter 10

Dragon of Stone

Galdor hurried through the labyrinth of caves, eager to be above ground. He followed the passageways he had traversed over one hundred years ago, remembering the route he had taken. It may have been a long time ago, but his memory was as sharp as his teeth. The pathway he followed was a reminder of his stupidity, a bitter memory of how he had been tricked. Now he was leaving his captivity it was easier to bear.

He weaved through the caverns and archways, desperate to see the sky once more, but something slowed him. He stopped, his *perception* tingling; he was sure he had seen another dragon inside the cave mouth he just passed. Cautiously he turned round and peered into the recess he'd hurried by.

It was another dragon. It stood there in the darkness, staring away from him, completely stationary, as if it was intently studying something. Strange that it failed to notice his presence. Surely its own *perception* would have alerted it to the fact another dragon was close.

"Hello?" Galdor spoke, more a question than a greeting. The other dragon never moved and there was no indication the stranger even heard his words. The smaller spikes on his neck stood up like the hackles of an angry wolf. Was this another trick? A trap set by Blaze? He would not be fooled again, not after a century of torture. He wouldn't fall foul of the black dragon's deceptions a second time. He couldn't stand to suffer imprisonment ever again.

"I am Galdor the Green, once moot leader of the Lifting Plateau. Identify yourself." After one hundred years, his voice hadn't lost its tone of authority, yet there was no response. Nothing! It was as if the unusually still dragon never heard him. There was something amiss, this wasn't right. He prepared his fire, drawing deep from within, ready for confrontation and prepared to defend himself. He was appalled that he should think of attacking first, but he wouldn't risk his freedom—or his sanity—again.

The dragon didn't move and Galdor crept closer, on full alert and waiting for a trap to spring or an attack to come. Nothing happened. He approached the mysterious dragon, vigilant for any trickery, then realised why it was still and unmoving.

It was because the dragon before him wasn't alive. It was made entirely of stone! He hadn't noticed any statues when he came here to confront his would be adversary all those years ago. It was possible he missed seeing the statue when he had last been here. It was fair to say he hadn't been his usual observant self that day, extremely distracted and only focused on one thing: the mage. Blaze managed to knock him off balance, distracting his normally keen eye with his whispering and suspicions. He couldn't blame himself for not noticing if this stone dragon was part of the shadows or not, on that fateful day.

The statue looked vaguely familiar and it had a distant sense of... something, he wasn't sure what. It was spectacularly realistic, perfectly rendered in every detail and entirely lifelike.

Galdor examined the workmanship, the attention to detail was magnificent. Who would create such a work of art where no one would ever see it? Dragons weren't known for carving statues. It was a mystery that he...

"Baelross the Blue?" This was no statue! Realisation hit him like a blow; his legs felt weak and it wasn't from his years of incarceration and starvation. This was once a real dragon, no longer made of flesh and blood. Skin and scales! No wonder the stone image appeared so authentic.

Who would do this to a dragon? Why would anyone want to? Had the mage cast a conjuration on Baelross? He didn't believe it was the mage. The mage was in the other cave, waiting for him. And he never mentioned anything about turning a dragon to stone. If he was able to perform such a powerful spell, Galdor was sure that would have been easier than luring him into the portal.

Blaze! This must his doing. He was the only other dragon—as far as he knew—that had been here before. It could only be the black dragon's evil work. What had he done? What could he have told Baelross to lure him here? And more importantly, if he was responsible for this atrocity, how had he changed a living dragon to stone? If Blaze possessed this ability prior to trapping him, it didn't make any sense he wouldn't use it. The more he thought about it, he was positive this unfortunate stone dragon hadn't been here on his previous visit.

He needed to find out what had happened in his prolonged absence. If this was any indication, he suspected it was nothing good.

"I'm sorry Baelross," Galdor said to the stone dragon. "I promise you will be avenged."

From deep inside the stone, Galdor could sense a tiny spark of magic. Was it possible that somewhere, locked within the solid rock, something of the blue dragon still existed? Was he crying out for help? He probed gently, reaching out with his mind and searched for signs of life, but all he could sense was cold dead stone, the wisp of magic gone. It was maybe just as well. The horror of being turned to stone and still being aware would be unbearable. He hoped Baelross wasn't trapped inside, still conscious and suffering some cruel eternal torment.

Galdor would rather be dead if it were him.

Unbidden, tears came and he blinked them from his eyes, saddened that the first kindred spirit he should encounter on his return home, had suffered a fate worse than his own. Dragons should never turn against their kin. To do so would be to stoop to the level of humans warring amongst themselves like animals. He checked himself. He was judging all humans with his preconceived prejudice. They weren't all like that. He owed his freedom—and his life—to a human. Alduce had proved to him that all men weren't bad, just as Blaze had shown him all dragons were not good.

He need to get out of these caves, they held nothing but despair and he'd had his fill.

Leaving the stone dragon to the darkness, unaware of how long the former blue dragon stood his silent vigil, he rushed to escape the confines of the bleak caverns. He had spent enough time below ground to last him two lifetimes.

The air grew sweeter as he made his way to the surface. It had been far too long since he breathed in fresh air.

Emerging from the cave mouth he had entered one hundred years previous, he looked up into an afternoon sky. More tears came, but this time it wasn't from sadness. The outside world was beautiful, filled with colour and light. The sun was passed its zenith but it would still be a long time before it set. He blinked a few times, clearing the tears, the bright daylight harsh upon eyes that had only seen darkness for too many years. The blue of the sky, welcome and intense. The green of his new scales vibrant and full of life. So many colours and so many emotions, so many years lost.

Galdor would not shed any more tears. He choked the overwhelming emotion back. He wouldn't waste time on the past. He pushed up from the ground, his mighty wings lifting, pulling his huge body skyward. He gave silent thanks to the Earth Mother, she who seeded worlds and gave her magic to all dragons, grateful his wings still worked. He was tired and weak and hadn't wanted to contemplate what he would do if his wings hadn't carried him into the air.

The breeze wafted over his hide, fresh and clean after his confinement. The afternoon sun warmed his scales, replenishing his magic and his spirit. The pleasure of simple flight was wonderful as he beat his wings. His stomach growled, reminding him of his ravenous state. After all of this day's unusual events his mind truly had been distracted, allowing him to forget the ever present need to eat.

When he awoke to Alduce's presence, his gnawing hunger was the first thing he felt. Now, after a century of fasting, he was able to do something about it. Goats and rats were off the menu. In the confines of his cave he would have been thankful for anything. He had even contemplated eating a human! He had reached his nadir and now, like his flight, the only way was up. He needed to feed, to hunt, to live.

First he would fill his empty belly. He would gorge himself until his burning hunger was sated. Then he would find a lake to bathe in, wash away the stink of dust and cleanse himself in crystal clear waters. The simple pleasures of life that he had been denied for so long, would be a luxury. Once that was taken care of, he would go in search of Blaze.

There was a debt to be paid and it was time to collect.

Chapter 11
New Horizons

It was dark when Blaze finally arrived back at the Lifting Plateau. Most dragons would be settled down in their own private caves for the evening. If any of the plateau's residents should chance to look up, it would be less noticeable to spot his black scales against the night sky.

He decided after his encounter with the leviathan, bringing the globe home with him might not be the smartest idea at present. He circled high above the ground deliberately sweeping the land below, observing what would soon be *his* colony.

He longed to study his prize and learn the secrets it held, but was afraid the other dragons would sense it. It was his and he didn't want anyone to know he had it. The globe was special and gave off a magical aura that might attract some of the more inquisitive dragons. It was his and he wasn't prepared to share it. If Galdor were here he would have kept it for the moot, like a pearl of wisdom or a moonstone, hiding it away and denying it from others. Blaze knew he would have justified his actions saying it was for the good of their community. But he knew better. Galdor would deprive dragons like him the opportunity to learn and become powerful, keeping its secrets for himself. The green dragon would have felt threatened if others were smarter and stronger than he was. Only the moot leader was allowed to consult with a pearl of wisdom and the globe would have been treated the same, and that was unfair. Blaze didn't need to worry about that now. He had proved to himself he could outsmart Galdor. He was the one who would take over the moot and lead the dragons to a better way of life. Their former moot leader wouldn't be there to hold them back anymore.

Why shouldn't all dragons learn the forbidden secrets? Why were they only accessible to some and not to all? It was because weak leaders like Galdor feared competition. They were complacent in their laziness. Happy to idly sit back and watch as dragons were slowly driven from their rightful lands by humans. This world was theirs and if Galdor didn't want to defend it, the humans would multiply and spread. The time for retreating had ended, those days were passed. Now was the time for stopping the rot for good, before it set in.

Galdor was gone. The dragons of the Lifting Plateau would show their true colours now they were free of the green dragon's rule. Human lives might be precious to Galdor but there were others who felt as he did. Others who would see the brilliance of his vision and could be convinced to follow his lead and know his path was the only way forward. A new dawn for dragons was on the horizon and Blaze the Black would be their saviour.

He swept up over the edge of the plateau, the strong updrafts lifting him higher into the night sky. This was his home and he wouldn't leave because the human population spread to their lands. His lands. The unique wind patterns of the plateau were exhilarating and he would miss them if they moved.

Galdor was content to avoid conflict and the humans seemed to think they could take what belonged to others and there would be no consequences. They would learn that Blaze was a stronger leader and his dragons were to be feared. No more would they slowly retreat, avoiding human contact, now was the time to stand and fight. But before this happened, he needed to implement the next part of his plan.

He didn't want to leave his globe unattended in his cave when he was away from the plateau. That would be too risky. Someone might sniff it out and steal it.

He had rescued it from its underwater stronghold and now Galdor was out of the way, he needed to study it, learn its secrets, and use it to its full potential. It wasn't convenient to return it to the underwater cave each time, even though it was a safer place, beyond the reach of most. That place was too far away and he wanted to be closer to the globe.

He had made a detour on his way home and returned to the caves where he had lured Galdor. They were far enough away to be remote and were difficult to reach if you didn't fly. The globe would be safe there for now. Using his magic, he warded the cave entrance against interlopers. If anyone entered, his protection spell would alert him. He had communed with the globe and it showed him how to do this, teaching him the secret and weaving a connecting spell between them both. The bond he formed would alert him should the globe be disturbed.

It was intoxicating, discovering a new magic. The depths of the globe's secrets, wrapped inside its swirling inner mists, were infinite. A vast store of knowledge, there to be learned for a small price. For him to learn those secrets and gain access to the spells, it needed to be fed. It had gorged itself on the leviathan's life force. The creature had been huge and the globe had taken its spirit, using up its life force in order to grow stronger. It lay dormant in the underwater cavern until Blaze removed it, stirring its gargantuan protector. It was as if he had awoken it from its rest. While it rested on the plinth in the cave of the purple stalagmites, it had been quietly content.

Now it was eager to be more than a swirling mystery. It hungered to grow and Blaze hungered with it.

The more it evolved, the more it revealed. All Blaze needed to do was provide it with what it desired and it would reciprocate.

He understood what it needed and it would work with him, rather than take his own life force because it knew they were alike. It had a *perception*, a sentient sense, all of its own and it understood him. It wasn't a charm or a vessel, it was alive.

He glided down onto the plateau, his black scales cloaking him in darkness as he descended, landing gracefully. Being a black dragon had its advantages and night flying was his speciality. It was quiet and he hoped to retire to his cave and avoid any contact with others. Now he was away from the globe, tiredness crept back over him. His battered tail throbbed and his wings ached.

When he had escaped the leviathan he was spent, his strength gone. When the globe had consumed the life force, drawing it from the leviathan's body, it infused him with energy. The globe had known, recognised he was weakened and it provided him with the sustenance he needed.

And it felt good. No, it felt wonderful!

With the strength of the defeated guardian coursing through him, lifting the weariness from his aching body, it refreshed him physically, chasing away the stress of the conflict and his near death encounter.

He was ashamed at being afraid when the leviathan's dread force hit him. He knew it was natural for leviathans to project a feeling of fear at their enemies and understood this was the nature of such creatures. The dread had been amplified by the spell that consumed it and drove it on, but it still annoyed him, he was a mighty dragon and shouldn't be afraid. Terror had filled him, taking over his usually calm demeanour and dragons should never have to feel like that. Dragons were the ones that should instil terror in their enemies. Now he possessed the globe, he would never give in to any weakness again, *he* would be the bringer of dread and any who stood against him would learn real terror.

"Blaze," a voice called from behind. That was the last thing he needed, someone catching him returning. He had taken care fooling Galdor into not leaving together and, as far as he was aware, the others wouldn't have seen them together before they left. Dragons came and went on the plateau, were answerable only to themselves, but Galdor was a different story. He had been their moot leader and was embroiled in everyone's business. If they associated Galdor's mysterious disappearance with him, suspecting he knew anything that he wasn't sharing, it might upset his plan to take over the moot.

The voice called out a second time. "Blaze?" It wasn't going to be ignored. He turned and saw its owner, a blue dragon, appearing almost as black as he was in the absence of the sun's light, bright yellow eyes peering into his own.

"Baelross," Blaze answered, catching himself from snapping at the blue. "I was just retiring for the evening. I've had a long day," he sighed, adding a weariness to his words. "Fishing for eels."

"Was Galdor with you?" Baelross asked.

"Galdor? He doesn't swim as well as I do," he snorted, making light of his quip and avoiding the question.

"Have you seen him? I've been looking for him and he isn't on the plateau. He asked me to meet with him, sounded serious but he wouldn't elaborate. He told me he was investigating something and he needed my help."

"I spoke with him this morning," Blaze stalled. Had Galdor told Baelross about the mage? Had he shared their fictitious secret with the blue or any others? If the dragons knew about the supposed plot, they would be suspicious when Galdor didn't return. If the moot leader had shared Blaze's involvement, they would look to him for answers and that was going to make his plan to take Galdor's place, less likely. "Have you tried the moot chamber? He often goes there to think."

"He isn't on the plateau. My *perception* is never wrong." Blaze couldn't argue with that. Baelross was known for the accuracy of his dragon sense. The *perception* wasn't a sense to be ignored and while most dragons didn't let it control the paths they travelled, they were aware it was a sense they should take heed of when it provided insight. He would have to be careful. If the blue dragon shared his concern with the others, months of careful planning would be ruined. He needed the dragons to support him if his plans were to succeed. "I'm sure he'll be back soon." He leaned in close to Baelross, furtively glancing over his shoulder and dropping his voice. "He told me not to say anything."

The blue dragon's eyes widened, "I knew it," he said, unconsciously lowering his own voice. "Something *is* wrong, something bad has befallen him. We should alert the rest of the moot." That wasn't good and Blaze didn't want this blue causing problems that could be avoided.

"Galdor doesn't want that," Blaze said. He needed to convince Baelross not to go blabbing to the others and stirring them up. The last thing he wanted was for them turning their search for their missing leader into some sort of crusade. They would be out scouring the lands, snooping were they didn't belong and might find his globe

"I know where he is," he said to Baelross. On another world, too far for you to help him. "I gave him my word. I wouldn't break his trust, but..." Baelross hung on his words. He was as gullible as Galdor. Galdor the Gullible! He controlled his laughter before the blue's *perception* alerted him something was amiss. It wasn't a lie, he did know where Galdor was. It was surprisingly simple to fool others when they trusted you.

"But?" Baelross insisted. All Blaze wanted to do was sleep. This annoying blue was keeping him from a well-deserved rest. It had been an extremely full day and he was tired.

"He told me to meet him tomorrow. He has asked me to help him as well. Help him with... " Again he made a show of checking to see there wasn't anyone about. "I think you should come too. I know he trusts you, he told me he valued your discretion. But it's probably best if you keep it to yourself, for now. I don't want him mad at me, especially when he was explicit with his instructions. You *must* keep this between us, it is vital If Galdor finds out you've stirred up everyone unnecessarily, especially before he's ready, you'll have to take the blame. Agreed?" There! That ought to force the inquisitive blue into a corner. Hopefully he would keep quiet.

"I'm not sure—" Baelross started.

"Baelross!" Blaze retorted sharply. "You need to listen to me. Galdor is the wisest dragon I know. He is also moot leader. Do not go against his wishes, please." It stuck in his throat to beg compliance from the annoying blue, but he needed to get him to stay quiet and stoking a blue's ego was a sure way to succeed. "Look, I'm sure he will share everything with you, but you must understand, a black dragon *never* breaks his word." The blue dragon slumped his shoulders and Blaze knew he would keep their secret.

"Meet me tomorrow, south of the plateau, just after dawn. We will fly out to meet Galdor together and I'm sure he will explain everything to you. I'll vouch for you, he listens to my council. But be warned, Baelross the Blue," Blaze addressed him by his formal title, sounding serious. "This is bigger than black or blue. I am trusting you not to let me down and remain loyal to Galdor." He leaned in close, whispering, "And all the dragons of the Lifting Plateau."

Baelross nodded, "Blue dragons are loyal, your trust is well-placed, Blaze. You can count on my discretion."

"Thank you. Remember, just after dawn." Blaze headed for his cave. "I must sleep now, it has been a tiring day." Adding the truth to his lies gave them more credibility. He imagined the yellow eyes burning into his hide as Baelross—Baelross the Bungler—watched him leave.

Blaze would be asleep in a few minutes, but he doubted the blue dragon would get much rest tonight.

* * *

Blaze woke from a deep restful sleep, his exhaustion from the previous day's exploits gone. His night's rest chased away the tiredness and he was ready to move forward with the next phase of his plan. Renewed strength and energy coursed through his body. It felt good to be alive.

He considered his close call with the leviathan yesterday and he shouldn't have felt this good. His tail wasn't as tender as it had been, in fact, when he flexed his muscles there was only an uncomfortable twinge, the bruising all but healed.

Dragons were resilient creatures and their magical nature protected them from serious injury and assisted in a speedy recovery, should they be harmed. He had smashed his tail into solid rock and expected it would take a little longer than one night's sleep for the throbbing pain to lessen. The pain was a small sacrifice to pay for escaping with the globe... and his life. The globe had shared its inner strength with him and fed off the spirit of the leviathan, draining its life force and absorbing its essence. Blaze tasted that power when he communed with the globe, feeling it replenish his tired and aching body. It gifted him a small piece of the leviathan's spirit and it had done more than replenish him.

The globe was small in size compared to a dragon and tiny when measured against the vast bulk of the leviathan. It was a mystery how such a small thing could contain so much. Blaze suspected it already held more secrets than he could imagine and it was nowhere near full. There was a deep well of knowledge, magic, and undiscovered power, and it was all there for the taking, if he could unlock it.

He reached out with his mind and could sense its presence in the caves, the bond between them intact and undisturbed. He found it comforting, knowing it remained safely where he had hidden it, waiting patiently on his return.

He stretched, flexing his wings. There was much to do today and he needed to take care of Baelross before he disrupted his plans. He hadn't counted on the blue meddling with his schedule, but if he didn't act today, he was sure Baelross would start talking. The blue dragon wouldn't be able to hold his tongue for long, it was an annoying trait of blues. If—no when—Baelross started blowing empty smoke about Galdor's disappearance, every dragon on the plateau would look to him for answers about Galdor's disappearance. Once Baelross informed them Galdor was missing and his conversation—with the last dragon to see him—things would become awkward. It was a complication he could do without.

He exited his cave into the cold of predawn, perching on his ledge. The light from the east changing the black of night to deep blue. He was hungry, but breakfast would have to wait. Leaping into the dark sky and pushing air downward as he beat his wings, he climbed, turning and pointing himself towards the thin slither of light that divided sky from ground. Leaving the plateau he flew east, dropping over the edge as he cleared its boundaries and rode the currents as they propelled him higher into the early morning sky.

Winds pushed the underneath of his wing membranes, filling the huge black sails and lifting him vertically, the power of their pressure rippling his tough dragon skin. The sensation was exhilarating and he spun through the air currents tilting his wings and twisting with the invisible air. He reached the apex of the lift and banked south, setting his wings and gliding away from the plateau, casually turning full circle and observing the ground below, before correcting his course southwards again. No other dragons were up this early, which was fortunate as it allowed him to leave unnoticed.

The secrecy and the covert actions he maintained were vital for his success and he was good at remaining unseen. A dragon's sight was remarkable, even at night—or in the early morning dusk before sunrise. Being a black dragon helped a little as his scales were difficult to see when the sky was dark; his dull colouring less metallic than most, absorbing light rather than reflecting it.

Baelross was waiting south of the plateau and as Blaze approached, he smelled blood. The blue dragon was devouring something, the scent of it making his stomach grumble, reminding him he hadn't eaten. There was another hunger inside him, but it wouldn't be silenced with food, this new hunger he shared with the globe.

Blaze dropped down beside Baelross and waited patiently while the blue dragon finished stripping the animal carcass. It was poor manners to disturb a dragon when feeding and although Blaze wanted to hurry, he allowed Baelross the courtesy of finishing his food. Let him enjoy his meal, even though he didn't know it would be his last.

Baelross flicked out a forked tongue cleaning the blood from his snout. His tongue was a lighter blue than his scales and the red blood painted it purple as he worked the bloody smears from his scales.

"Are you ready?" Blaze asked. "And you made sure you left the plateau without being followed?"

"I was hungry!" Baelross answered, pure dragon logic that needed no explanation. "I am ready now. Nobody knows I've left. I made sure. Galdor can trust my discretion. Blue dragons are more circumspect than most."

It was true, Baelross was painstakingly meticulous on a good day; if he said he was unseen leaving, Blaze didn't doubt it. He didn't dislike the blue and didn't *want* to do him harm. Dragons shouldn't fight with their own, but it was unavoidable; the blue asked too many awkward questions and he only had himself to blame. Blue dragons were naturally snouty, poking their muzzles where they didn't belong. Baelross was no exception, sticking his snout in Blaze's business when he could have been an ally. But he was also loyal. Loyal to Galdor. Even when he learned the green moot leader would never be coming back, he would support the old ways, rather than the rightful path Blaze would show them. Blaze may be black but he felt green with envy at the way other dragons mindlessly worshiped Galdor.

"Excellent. Galdor will be pleased you have been cautious," Blaze complimented. He needed the blue compliant for now. "Our leader values intelligence." Flattering him would make this easier to accomplish. "Come, follow me and I'll take you to him. He can explain to you himself what he has discovered." It was better to entice Baelross into following and laying the responsibility of an explanation with Galdor. Many dragons of the plateau were besotted with Galdor and would follow him blindly, never questioning his decisions.

There were those who, while they would miss their old leader, would embrace the change in leadership. Blaze was hopeful they were as likeminded as him, would follow his lead, and were open to his ideas. He had already had conversations with a few hopeful candidates and was confident they could be easily swayed to his way of thinking. He must move slowly, one small wingbeat at a time, winning their trust and allegiance. And ultimately their obedience.

He respected the blue dragon's loyalty, but the cause he believed in was a poor one and he had chosen the wrong dragon to follow. He would have liked to have Baelross as a trusted supporter, but knew he wouldn't be swayed to follow him, he was too set in his ways.

"Where are we going, Blaze?"

"We are going to show you something amazing." It was true, what Blaze planned was so much more than amazing, it was spiritual. Baelross could interpret the *we* as Galdor and himself, but it was his partnership with the globe Blaze referred to. Let the blue dragon believe what he would. It wasn't his fault he didn't understand.

"Follow me!" Blaze leapt into the air, powerful wing beats lifting him effortlessly. Baelross would have to follow if he wanted an explanation. The blue dragon hadn't come all this way, secretly met with him and taken care not to be seen leaving the plateau, only to return back now without any answers. He was too inquisitive, too snouty, to resist.

Blaze had given him enough to lure him away and keep quiet, promising more. He was good at gaining the confidence of others, it was easy for him to persuade them, enticing them with the promise of something more. He wished he had been able to convince Galdor rather than exile him, but the green dragon's will was stronger than most.

Blaze risked a fleeting glance behind and saw Baelross taking off and following, the morning sun catching his blue scales as he rose into the air. He pushed onward, the presence of the globe drawing him back towards the cave where it waited, its anticipation strong.

They flew across the barren lands, Blaze leading the way. He deliberately stayed ahead of Baelross, luring the blue with the promise of finding Galdor and the secrets he would reveal. He didn't like flying and talking, shouting at each other when flying side by side. It was awkward and uncouth, he was more refined than that. He was a better flier than Baelross, so the blue catching up and asking more questions wasn't an option as long as he kept pushing on.

The sun climbed higher and the morning brightened. Out here in the barren lands it was hot, and today was shaping up to be another intense one, as far as the weather was concerned. Blaze was prepared to take the next step in his interaction with the globe. The blue dragon was going to help him discover what the globe could do, he just didn't know it... yet.

The ground below changed from open desert to rocky hills, the bright sand changing to grey rock as they neared their destination. As they approached the caves where Blaze had stored the globe, the connection strengthened. His treasured prize was aware he approached and was anticipating his arrival. He stole a look at his aerial companion, conscious that if he could feel the magic emanating from the globe, Baelross would too. The blue dragon didn't show any sign he sensed anything unusual and Blaze glowed inside, content it was only him who could feel its touch.

If the blue dragon was unaware of the magic the globe possessed, there was less chance of someone else discovering it. He might even be safe bringing it back to the Lifting Plateau, but he needed to be sure. Baelross was going to help him test his theory.

He tilted his left wing and raised the right, beginning his descent, air spilling from underneath the membrane. Wind rushed over his scales, warm and dry as he dropped to towards the sun heated rocks, the shimmering heat haze blurring the ground as it rushed up to meet him.

He landed outside the warren of caves and waited for Baelross to join him. The Blue dragon dropped from the air, wings thrown back and talons outstretched as they scraped the rocky ground halting his forward motion.

"We are here," Blaze announced, "but before we proceed, I would ask you something." Baelross folded his wings as he joined the black dragon in front of the fated cave mouth that had led Galdor to his demise. Baelross tilted his head in anticipation of Blaze's question.

"Do you feel anything different? Sense anything unusual? I think Galdor will want to know." He waited, letting his questions hang in the air between them.

Baelross took his time before he spoke, swaying his head from side to side, tasting the air with his tongue and sniffing, nostrils snorting loudly as he drew in great breaths.

"I smell the dankness that is usual with unoccupied caves, nothing more. My *perception* senses... something, but it is faint and distant, almost as if it is disguised, hiding just out of reach."

Blaze was delighted. He could feel the globe, strong and obvious. If Baelross barely sensed it and didn't know what it was, it was reasonably safe to assume others wouldn't either. It must be because the globe was rightfully his. It was connected to him alone and only he was destined to learn its secrets and share in its power.

"That is good. I'm sure Galdor will be pleased with your answers," he purred.

Baelross looked confused. The poor blue didn't have any idea what awaited him. While this was all new to Blaze, at least he knew what the globe was capable of. He had seen how it reacted to the leviathan's threat, feeding off the huge serpentine creature. It had been dumb, acting only from pure instinct and the compulsion cast upon it.

Baelross was smarter that any leviathan; he was a dragon. While he could never be as smart as Blaze, he was intelligent and knowledgeable. Surely the globe would thrive on the life force of a dragon and gain more nourishment than it had from the stupid leviathan. And if that were true, which he highly suspected, then what it shared with him would be more intoxicating than before.

There was only one way to find out. He wondered if Baelross would feel anything when the globe consumed him. He didn't want the blue to suffer, it wasn't really his fault he was misguided, that was a responsibility he would lay squarely upon Galdor. This wasn't the time for sentiment, this was the time to test his theory. He needed to make sure the blue dragon remained quiet and this way he could silence the blue, stop his meddling ways and he could also discover more about the globe.

"Blaze, what am I supposed to sense. What is it?"

"Come, Baelross, I'll take you to Galdor and he will be able answer all your questions." He spun on the rocky ground, talons scraping loudly as he dived into the dark cave entrance. This time he led the way and the inquisitive blue obediently followed. It was funny how his nature differed for Galdor's. The green dragon had pushed forward, taking the lead, foolishly rushing to his fate. Baelross needed to be shown the way, content to follow, but the endgame would be the same. Blaze would be the victor.

He led the blue deep into the honeycomb of caves until they reached the cavern where the globe waited. He had set it on the floor as there was no plinth or rock to sit it on. As he approached, it reacted to his presence, filling him with a feeling of welcome anticipation. Baelross came to stand next to him, his eyes drawn to the wonder of the mysterious globe, alive and alluring.

"What is it? It's too big to be a pearl of wisdom. Is this what Galdor wanted me to see? Where is he?" Questions, questions, always questions. Baelross could be annoying with his incessant questioning, almost as bad as a yellow. He like to think of himself as inquisitive. It was an excuse to stick his snout where it didn't belong. It was more like a compulsive snoutiness, he couldn't help his nature, but no matter, it would soon be over and he would be cured of his affliction.

"I'm not sure where Galdor is. He said he would meet us here. Perhaps he is late." Baelross was mesmerised, hardly listening to what he was saying.

The globe held his attention, glowing faintly as the inner mists, like white threads of cloud, swirled hypnotically below its surface. Blaze knew what it wanted and what he must do.

"Why don't you examine it," he hissed, temptation oozing from his words. Baelross crept forward, crouching until his belly was touching the floor and his snout was level with the globe. His eyes were wide, reflecting the swirling mist at the end of his snout, vivid in the darkness.

He remained transfixed then drew back as if jolted with pain, opening his mouth to roar, but no sound escaped. Blaze could feel the globe reaching out and enveloping its prey. Baelross froze and a wisp of white slowly snaked from his open jaws. It moved like a trail of smoke on a light breeze, curling and twisting as it bridged the gap between the dragon and the globe.

The cave warmed, heat radiated out from the still form of Baelross, and Blaze tasted his essence, the life force of the blue dragon, as it filled the surrounding air. It was like the warm blood of a fresh kill, the intoxicating aroma of fresh meat, hot summer winds and cold winter frosts. It filled his mind and washed through his senses, euphoric and exhilarating.

Baelross didn't find his contact with the globe as pleasant. He tried to move away, standing up. He shook, his body quivering, spasms of pain wracked though him but he couldn't move, his claws firmly planted on the floor. His scales shimmered, multi-coloured waves rippling down his flanks, torturous rainbows infused with pain, paralyzing him. His yellow eyes implored Blaze to help, but it was too late for the blue and he knew it, his *perception*, always extremely accurate, must have warned him he was beyond saving.

The misty white streak of life essence thickened, pouring from his mouth, drawn deep from within. A turbulent stream of coiling threads, ripping his life force from his protesting body.

The leviathan's essence had been black, but the essence that was drawn from Baelross was pure white. Blaze wondered if this was an indication of the spirit of the creature. Black essence from the dark psyche of the leviathan, white from the soul of a dragon?

It was horrifying. And beautiful. Blaze basked in the cave's atmosphere, drinking in the essence the globe fed him as it stole the life of the blue dragon. The euphoria lifted him up, sharing his mind with the globe and its swirling mists, each single thread individual yet part of something greater. Knowledge and secrets, power and strength, life and death. Eternal life for him, death to any who stood against him.

Just as the leviathan's essence was extracted and absorbed, so it was with Baelross. The leviathan had survived long enough to swim away and Blaze's *perception* had confirmed it was going back to the ocean to die. He didn't want Baelross to end up like that and he couldn't leave him to fly off and die. He would return to the Lifting Plataea, if he was able, and tell the others what he had seen. He couldn't allow that to happen. They would blame him for killing the blue dragon and suspect he had done the same with Galdor. He had spared Galdor out of kindness, but they would see it differently.

He knew the globe understood and it provided a solution. They needn't let poor Baelross die, there was another way.

The blue dragon was stuck to the cave floor, unable to break the connection as the globe drained his essence, as still as the rock itself. *As still as the rock itself!* That was it. The flow of the thick white threads, ethereal and smoke-like, slowed, nearing the end of the extraction.

He focussed on the globe, exerting his will before it took everything from Baelross. The thread of essence broke with a snap, one end drawn back into the throat of the dragon, the other whipping into the globe and covering its surface. It swirled and coalesced and the globe glowed brightly, shining through the opaque cloud that coated it.

Baelross drew in a huge breath, his eyes locked to Blaze's, panic-stricken. He was still alive, an empty vessel clinging to the tiny scrap of life force that kept him upright. A gift from the black dragon, even if he was too vacant to appreciate the gesture.

It started with his tail.

Crackling filled the cave as the dragon's body began to change. Blue turned to grey, the colour fading from his scales. Their appearance changed too. Living flesh and blood transformed to something new. The metamorphosis crept along his tail, crackling and snapping like wet wood burning, changing the dragon as it ran along its length. Where once a living dragon had stood, now one of stone took its place.

As Blaze wanted, the globe spared the life of Baelross. He couldn't let the blue dragon leave here and return, telling what he knew. He didn't want to kill him either. He had influenced the globe and it interpreted his intent. It hadn't been a command, he doubted if he were able to issue instructions to something as powerful. Well not yet. But it did mean there was the potential for the globe to do his bidding. He quickly banished that line of thought, aware of how the globe might perceive that as a threat.

The cloudy essence surrounding the globe swirled and writhed, then thrust out from it surface, like a stone dropped into a pond, circles of white rippling out from the centre. The cave brightened, a soft white light tinged with the exact blue of Baelross, radiating from the globe's centre.

The stone dragon—now Baelross the Basalt—was illuminated, preserved in rock, not dead but certainly not living. A compromise he hoped the blue dragon would understand.

The globe sucked in the essence, pulling the bright life force inside and Blaze, through his connection with it, experienced a surge of pleasure and the welcome reward of power that came with it.

The Baelross problem was solved. He wouldn't be discovered down here, and even if he was, no one would know what happened to him. A dragon of stone tells no tales.

He inspected the former blue dragon, marvelling at the detail wrought in stone. Every scale was exactly how it should be, but turned into solid rock, no longer alive. There was enough magic left inside the stone dragon to preserve it indefinitely, no longer would he need to breath, eat or sleep, the perfect solution for keeping an inquisitive blue from prying.

Gently, he drummed his talons on the stone flanks, the hollow sound echoing into the darkness.

"Better than the fate of the leviathan, Baelross," he told the stone statue. "I know you would thank me, if you could." He wondered if somewhere, inside the stone dragon, Baelross could sense him. Was he there, unable to speak, unable to hear? Stone deaf and completely dumb. At least he would be quiet from now on, no more annoying questions.

Blaze decided he would leave the globe where it was for now. Baelross could stand watch, vigilant in his duties as a new guardian for his treasure. The previous owner of that task had failed and Blaze had found a fitting successor for the job. He would never leave his post and would obey with blind obedience. A lesson for any who opposed him or his vision.

"Farewell, guardian of granite," he said as he departed the cave. The connection with the globe was still there, subtle but strong. If anyone came into the caverns or approached the globe, he would know.

And after what happened to Baelross, he no longer worried for its safety.

Chapter 12
Flame and Fury

Blaze tore through the sky, the anger in his belly raged, a cauldron of hate burning hotter than molten lava. His dragon flame seared through his growling insides screaming for release. He tipped his neck forward and plunged down through the clouds, a black envoy of death intent on delivering his message.

The globe had given him the ability to hold onto his flame longer than usual and intensify the heat when it was released. Normally if he breathed fire it needed to be expelled soon after it was summoned. Holding it at bay for any length of time was not only extremely uncomfortable, but could result in severe damage to his insides.

A dragon's stomach, throat, and mouth were designed to handle short bursts of intense flame, but prolonged exposure to this magically induced fire was never a good idea. Blaze could call on his flame and expel it, but it wasn't inexhaustible and needed time to replenish. Holding the inner fire allowed him to increase his volume and its temperature. The longer the thick liquid flame was regurgitated, the longer he could hold the stream when he spewed it forth, resulting in more fire, more heat, and ultimately, more devastation.

It was easy to do now, the globe shared the knowledge and revealed the secret to him. It was obvious now he knew how and he wondered why he had never worked it out on his own. Now it was learned, revealed by the globe, it was simple.

Emerging from the cloud cover of an overcast sky, Blaze loomed down on the vast city of humans, ready to implement the next stage of his plan. He drew on the knowledge rewarded from the globe, a gift for feeding it with the life force of Baelross. He called his magic and his scales shimmered, rippling from their beautiful black to the dull green of more common dragons. The transformation ran from snout to tail, each scale flickering through a spectrum of colours, like sunlight through rain, a rainbow of magic changing his appearance and disguising him in ordinary green. He didn't want to be recognisable should word of what happened here reach the Lifting Plateau. Everyone would know who the attacker was if the dragon witnessed was black.

His emergence from the cloud cover was acknowledged with the sound of panicked residents screaming as he dropped down over the buildings of their precious city. His hate for these puny humans burned within, ready to be vented, a justifiable necessity.

Opening jaws, his pent up anger gave way to the roiling magma of fire as it spewed forth, engulfing the proud rooftops and tall steeples beneath his wings. Their manmade opulence was no match for the wrath of dragons. Roofs may provide men with shelter from the rain and wind, but there were none strong enough to protect them from Blaze the Black, bringer of justice.

Dragon flame washed over the ridged surfaces, elemental fire curling over thin slate and baked clay alike. A sea of rage swallowing everything in a tidal wave of voracious orange. The grey slate scorched to black and bore the brunt of his fire, the thin stone tiles impervious to the flame. They deflected the fire from the pitched roofs, deflecting it down the sides of the buildings, setting alight anything flammable. Small clumps of sticky fire—the thick acidic fluid from his gullet—sat and melted holes through the slate, viscous and intensely hot, it bubbled and burned through the resilient slates. Less resistant clay tiles, crackled and smashed as the heat destroyed them, dragon fire searing them to brittle ash.

A wake of black smouldering clouds followed Blaze, fingers of smoke trailing in his wake as he swooped low over the rooftops, turning and twisting in the turbulent air as he sped across the city.

He beat his wings, rising higher and banked round, his left wing dipping like a rudder through water as it clove through the billowing smoke. He came in lower for a second pass, adding to the inferno that swept through the city, spitting more fire into the carnage and adding extra flames to the already burning buildings.

Glass shattered, exploding in the intense heat, wood cracked and splintered as it lost its integrity to the consuming conflagration. The roar of the flames joined with his own voice as he unleashed wave upon wave of delightful fire, a dissonance of destruction.

Backwards and forwards he flew, a deadly monster of legend, burning channel after channel of destruction through the human city. Smoke stung his eyes but he continued his razing of the buildings until his flame was exhausted. It was empowering to hold the fire, expanding his destructive scope. The exhilaration of this new found strength coursed through him, granting him freedom to finally teach humans the lesson they had long escaped.

He soared one last time above the city, surveying his work. His deliberate tactic to only destroy a swathe of buildings throughout the city's centre had worked perfectly. Multiple runs across the same area had resulted in a charred strip of incinerated dwellings. The surrounding fallout wasn't enough to set the whole city ablaze, even though that would be a sight worth seeing. Perhaps he would do that somewhere else when the seeds of his plan were sown. For now, he needed survivors to spread the word and let their neighbouring towns and cities know what had come to pass here.

If he killed everyone in the city, there would be no humans left to appreciate their plight. And nobody alive to blame the rampaging green dragon that attacked without provocation. The humans didn't know they were a constant source of provocation to him, but they would come to realise it. They would rue the error of their land stealing ways. This would be the first lesson in the re-education of mankind. They would learn that dragons were to be feared and respected.

Small figures scurried below, frantically throwing tiny amounts of water at the beautiful flames. If it wasn't for their sheer numbers and inexhaustible determination, he was sure the whole city would burn to the ground. Torn between wanting to see it all burn, and the knowledge that if his plan were to succeed, he would have to check his enthusiasm and settle for contentment with today's actions. It would have been nice to watch the fire consume everything, but he had still enjoyed himself. It was gratifying to be the one to finally deliver the flames.

He dropped down through the smoke towards a group of bucket wielding men, arrows from some brave souls bouncing harmlessly from his disguised green scales. Let them try to injure him with their tiny arrows, they would do no harm. He was a dragon and was superior to their primitive metal and wood. They had spirit, he conceded, and that was exactly what he needed, fighting vengeful spirit. Let them think they could fight back, it was just what he wanted.

Tipping his wings back he angled himself for a dive, plummeting down and thrusting out his talons at the last second, smoke billowing wildly through the disturbed air. He filled his claws with wriggling men and carried them from the ground screaming and wailing, into the hazy air above the fire.

His scales protected him from the heat of the flames but the feeble men he snatched up were not so lucky. He remained in sight of the onlookers below, circling higher above the raging inferno. Their round faces stared up at their comrades, shouting and howling, waving their arms like stupid little wings too thin to fly. It was incredible how such tiny creatures could make so much annoying noise. The ones he gripped in his claws were quiet and he didn't know if he'd crushed them to death or if they were unable to make any noise, paralyzed by fear. It wasn't everyday a dragon came into their midst and rained down fire and devastation.

Once he was directly above the flaming buildings, he opened his claws and dropped the men into the hungry flames. The audience below were quiet now, no doubt enjoying the finale to his performance.

Surprisingly some of the falling humans were still alive and they wriggled and writhed as they plummeted towards the flames. They whumped into the flames creating an extremely satisfying sound, throwing up clouds of swirling embers. Deep orange sparks drifted upwards through the smoke like fiery blossoms, painting patterns of beauty across the smoky grey.

Blaze loved fire, the way it danced, the colours, and the heat. It was perfect in every way. He was named for the flash of white on his chest, a blaze of light upon his dark scales. The dragons of the Lifting Plateau knew the old Blaze, but today the humans witnessed a new dragon, a rampaging phoenix. This dragon was forged in the flames of the devastation he wrought, reborn of fire and soon everyone would know his true nature.

He veered north, leaving the burning city in the hands of the humans fighting to control the raging inferno. The humans knew the dragon colony made its home at the Lifting Plateau and would observe his departure and know he returned to his kin. He maintained his northerly path, keeping below the cloud cover so the city's survivors could see which direction he flew. They would assume he was returning to the Lifting Plateau and they would lay the blame of today's attack with his colony. One guilty dragon would be good enough to condemn them all for his violent and unprovoked actions, be it a green or a black... but preferably green.

He rose into the clouds, obscuring himself from the city's watchful survivors and turned south, flying back over the city. The noxious smoke penetrated the cloud base, turning dull clouds darker, hiding him from sight. Even from this high above, nothing could disguise the vast bright stripe of fire carved through the heart of the city below. The dark clouds glowed with the light from the flames, like an unnatural sunset.

He was dirty and stained from the smoke and he smelled like a charred forest. He should bathe before he returned home. He didn't want the other dragons to smell the smoke on his scales. It may be remembered and raise questions. But, since he was already in need of a bath, it made sense not to waste the opportunity and visit a few more towns and villages, spreading a little more unrest with the human population.

It was practical reasoning and he was pleased to have an excuse to test brewing up more dragon fire from an empty stomach. His resources were depleted, but using the new method the globe taught him, he was confident he could call up enough to sack a few small towns and villages. He almost looked black again with all the soot that covered his body. Replenishing his colour changing magic, he altered the smoke blackened green scales he wore.

He drew on his own natural dragon magic and willed the illusion of a new colour to disguise his scales. He had always been proficient in using his natural magic and it came to him instinctually. He was better than most and didn't need to employ the wisdom of the globe when using familiar magic. However, his own magic came to him quicker than it once had and was easier to use. He suspected it was enhanced now he understood some of the workings of the globe.

He chose a brighter colour this time, something that would stand out and be more visible in the dull afternoon.

A shimmering yellow washed over the length of his body, the apt yellow of bright fire. The clouds around him glowed brightly with the ethereal light of magic, replacing the soot darkened green dragon with a clean scaled yellow.

Following the instructions learned from the globe, he focused on manufacturing more fire deep inside his chest. It was a little slower to come so soon after the torrent unleashed on the city, but it was still there. It should have taken a lot longer than it did and he could feel it replenishing inside. He wouldn't need as much this time, just enough for a few smaller fires.

The next few burnings were about quantity rather than quality. The quality of his new fire brewing was no longer in any doubt, as the burning city behind him could probably attest to. Although he doubted they appreciated his success as much as he did. The more small towns and villages he could add to his run today, would hopefully speed up this part of his plan.

His stomach churned in expectation and he began the process of filling it with the liquid fire once more. Dropping down through the clouds, he didn't care if anyone below noticed him now. All they would see was a yellow dragon flying south, another dragon of a different colour in the usually empty skies above human settlements. It would lend to the illusion that different dragons were abroad. One rogue dragon would be looked on as rare occurrence, but multiple dragons spreading unrest would incite the humans to panic. And once their panic subsided, it would turn to anger. An anger he believed would inevitably goad this violent species to war. And when they brought *their* war to the peaceful dragons of the plateau, they would have no choice but to retaliate.

Blaze peered down at the cluster of ugly structures far below, marring the once unspoiled landscape. It was time to cleanse a few of them from the world, and this far south, he was spoiled for choice.

The new batch of liquid fire was ready to use and he was eager to see how it measured up to the last brewing. Swooping down from the late afternoon sky, he followed the contours of the land, flight undulating as he approached a small town. He blasted the outskirts of the building as he sped by, turning his head and decorating the structures with flames as he passed.

On the outskirts of the town, there were fields filled with cows. He flew overhead, dropped low and skimming over the ground, snatched up two fat beasts before they even noticed he was there. The rest of the heard scattered, panicked by the appearance of the huge predator. He rose from the ground, twisting his neck and ripping the head from each cow in turn, silencing their feeble lowing. He spat the heads from his mouth and was about to drop the cows when inspiration struck. He flew on to the next village, the human dwellings all too frequent now and not that far apart, as the dragon flies.

The scurrying humans ran before the oncoming dragon, terrified and screaming. Blaze released both headless cows and watched as they sailed through the air, his speed adding to their momentum. One cow hit the corner of a large building, tearing it into two halves, one part crashing through the wood of the structure, the other spinning into a group of people, the impact knocking dumb struck humans everywhere.

The second headless cow bounced once and smashed into another dwelling, bursting straight through the wall. That ought to give them something to think about. Not only did a rampaging yellow dragon steal their livestock, after decapitating it, it threw the beasts away. This could only be seen as a deliberate act of violence; he hadn't even eaten the beasts! He hoped his disrespect would further his cause and help antagonise the human population.

He flew on, leaving destruction in his wake. He still had half a belly of fire left and emptied it all on a huge structure standing alone. He had no idea what it was for, but it blazed like a beacon, a signal to all humans that fire breathing dragons had returned to their lives and they were no longer safe.

Content with today's havoc, he was ready to return home. Burning and destroying was dirty work and he needed to scrub the stench of fire—and human despair—from his scales.

This was just the beginning and he was extremely happy with his results so far. His enhanced dragon fire worked better than he hoped. The usefulness of the globe and the secrets it held, would help him fill the void of Galdor's leadership. The moot needed new leadership and that was next on his agenda. It needed to be handled with more tact than inciting the humans. This called for some delicate manipulation, a dash of concern for missing friends, and the confidence of stepping in and offering stability for the colony.

Reluctantly, of course. If he played them just right, they would beg him to take over, appointing Blaze the Black as moot leader would be their idea. And once he was in charge, he would sway them all to his ideals, show them his vision, and protect them from the humans who waged war on them.

He would lead them to victory over their enemies and onto the true path to freedom. A land without man, where all dragons would be equal and reign supreme, with Blaze the most supreme of them all.

His work wasn't quite finished this evening. He must bathe and wash the grime of hard labour from his scales. Then, visit the globe and see if it was ready to share more secrets. Deep down he knew it was hungry for another spirit, another life force to feed on. The more he gave, the more he would get. It wasn't an easy decision to make, choosing who would be next, but he understood what had to be done.

With great power, great sacrifices were required. It was an unfortunate reality he would have to learn to live with. He was sure his sacrifices, and those of the others, would be worth it.

Chapter 13
Hidden Agenda

Blaze waited in his own private chamber and tried to remain patient. At long last the dragons of the Lifting Plateau had decided to call an emergency meeting of the moot members. They argued constantly about what to do, and finally settled on a gathering that was to be more of a meeting than an actual moot.

With Galdor gone there was no moot leader to officially call the moot to order. No dragon wanted to go against their age old tradition. If there was no moot leader, no moot could be called. If no moot was called, they couldn't take official action.

At last, after going round in circles for days, the remaining council had decided on gathering unofficially for a meeting. He didn't want to be the one to suggest it, as it wouldn't help his plans if everyone thought it was his idea, so he had resigned himself to wait. And wait.

Sometimes his need for self-restraint was a great burden; he longed for the day, which wouldn't be far off now, when he ruled and everyone waited on his word. Subtlety was required when manipulating one's inferiors. So he waited, and eventually, the remaining moot members managed to come up with this brilliant idea all on their own.

Quite honestly, he believed that if Galdor hadn't led them by the snout, nothing would ever be done. He understood the protocol and respected tradition—when it was a tradition he agreed with. Because Galdor wasn't here to officiate, it had taken them almost a week of discussions and debates to decide to convene. Meetings about having a meeting! The dragons of the Lifting Plateau, when it came to tradition, were stuck in their ways.

Only Galdor was able to call the moot to order and they held off, in hope their leader would miraculously return. Blaze knew this wasn't going to happen, but sharing that knowledge with the others would put him in an awkward positon, making him look guilty. Galdor was gone and it was for the best, they would come to understand a dragon's rightful place in this world, even if they never fully knew what had befallen their former leader. Any guilt he associated with removing Galdor from their world was justifiable. The dragons of the Lifting Plateau were not destined to stagnate and become extinct at the hands of the humans.

So Blaze waited until it was obvious to them all that Galdor wouldn't be returning any time soon and they would have to decide what to do on their own.

In the moot leader's mysterious absence, the dragons were apprehensive about taking any action themselves, procrastinating continually about what was the best way to address Galdor's disappearance. Life under Galdor's rule had encouraged this weak and indecisive attitude. It wasn't until poor Baelross followed in Galdor's clawprints, they were eventually forced into doing something. It was doubly beneficial the blue was gone. The globe had prospered from the life force taken from Baelross, and his timely disappearance helped push his peers into action. Now his waiting game was at an end and the moot that wasn't really a moot, was due to commence.

Blaze didn't want to arrive early and this is why he had waited a little longer, making sure all the remaining members hurried along to the moot chamber, eager to have their say. Let them squabble like hatchlings, directionless and unsure. They would realise they needed someone to take control and make the difficult decisions. Someone who knew exactly what to do in times of crisis, someone strong enough to lead them to their rightful glory. He was ready to become that someone, Blaze the Black, moot leader of the Lifting Plateau, the benevolent emperor of dragons. He would create a new history and would become the saviour of all dragon kind.

He departed his cave and casually made his way to the moot chamber, observed by the other dragons of the plateau. He stood a little taller as they watched him. They would remember this day, and how regal he looked before he was elected moot leader, when they told of his legend to their hatchlings. Dragons like a good tale and the story of Blaze and how he liberated the dragons of the Lifting Plateau would be an historic one.

The moot chamber was flanked by two red females, Scarlet and Vermillion, who stood guard when the moot was in progress. They'd taken up their usual post for today's gathering and Blaze approved of their loyalty to Galdor. The imposing pair were not only capable of keeping order and ensuring any moot was conducted without unnecessary interruption, but they were traditionalists and acted in the best interests of the colony. He was sure once he was their leader, they would be worthy soldiers in his army. If he could convince them Galdor wasn't coming home, he would be able to sway them to his way of thinking. It was a shame their scales weren't black but he needed to start somewhere and he saw potential in them both. Reds were notorious for their fiery temperament and he could exploit this to his advantage.

He nodded to both females as he entered the chamber and they tipped their sleek long heads as he passed, acknowledging his arrival. They had been waiting on the final member to arrive and as he joined the assembled dragons, they closed ranks, standing side by side, shutting off entry to anyone else.

The chamber was filled with the other eight remaining representatives, every dragon vying to be heard above the others. Galdor would have laid an egg at the commotion and scolded them all for their distinctly un-dragonlike behaviour. It was just as well the former moot leader wasn't here and Blaze was pleased he'd spared his old friend the embarrassment of seeing his beloved dragons act this way.

They remaining members of the moot council were so involved in their bickering that they failed to notice the ninth dragon enter. Blaze observed them, looking to see who of the eight, were his biggest rivals and who could be persuaded to follow him.

He knew them all and made it a priority to study them during his years at the plateau. Know your friends, but know your enemies better.

Ember the Orange was engaged in a heated conversation with the ancient green, Mossbeard. Blaze was confident the orange female would jump at the chance to follow him against the humans. She was outspoken and passionate and would see wisdom in his words. Her bright orange scales were the colour of flame and it was well known orange dragons were experts when it came to producing fire. She wouldn't be anywhere near as good as he was, not now he'd learned that secret from the globe—and he wouldn't be sharing that with her—but she would make a good ally.

On the other talon, Mossbeard would never be convinced. Greens stuck together, scales as thick as their heads, and he was one of Galdor's strongest supporters. He was ancient and any talk of conflict would be something he opposed. He didn't have the stomach for change, even if it was for the better. No, Mossbeard was too old and set in his ways, and he was passed his prime. He might be fine for keeping records and remembering dates, but Blaze needed dragons who could contribute to his cause. The ancient green's beard was as long as his stories and just as dull. Blaze would rewrite their history and a dusty old *mould* beard would be obsolete in his new order.

A thought occurred to him. He may have a use for the crusty old green after all. If he could ever convince Mossbeard to venture outside, he would introduce him to the wonders of the globe. A feeling of warm contentment rippled through his body and he could sense the globe, even over the distance between them, liked his idea. It was hungry and needed fed. It would be interesting to see if an older dragon, with more years under his wing than Blaze cared to count, would contribute more life force. But that, for now, was an experiment for another day.

Azyrian the Bronze spoke with the platinum female, White-silver, their necks close together and it was clear there was more to their friendship. Neither, Blaze believed, would be sympathetic to his cause. Metals were aloof and thought themselves better than colours and this pair were no exception. These two could only see as far as their own desires and wouldn't pose any real challenge to his authority. If they stood in his way, he would divide and conquer. Together they were a formidable pair, apart they would be easier to deal with.

Fern and Chestnut listened while Sapphire told them about her last conversation with Galdor, the day he vanished.

"He told me there was a human mage, stirring up trouble," Sapphire revealed to them.

"A human mage?" Fern asked. "Surely a mage would be no match for Galdor?" She turned to Chestnut as if to seek her approval. He was confident Sapphire and Chestnut would follow whoever led. Fern the Green was an emerald coloured female, smaller than the average sized dragon with nothing exceptional about her, and would also follow whoever led the moot.

The brown female however, wasn't known by her colour as dragons usually were, choosing to be different and was only ever referred to as Chestnut. Her reddish-brown scales had unusual tinges of black around their edges and Blaze wondered if she were to produce a clutch to him, if any of their potential offspring would hatch and keep their black birth colour.

"A mage you say?" Blaze joined their conversation, this was a topic he could work with. "I don't think a mage could best Galdor? He's too clever to be beaten by a human!" Everyone on the council knew how he felt toward humans and if he took Galdor's side, they would have no cause to suspect him. "Isn't he?" He left the question hanging, the way he positioned it sowing doubt with the other dragons.

Yesper the Yellow, a bright scaled practical dragon, chipped in. "What if the human mage has done something to him?"

Perfect; the unknowing yellow added more doubt into the mix. Yesper thought himself smarter than he actually was and he was everyone's friend, a typical yellow. The hours of listening to Yesper's endless prattling, while in turn, giving the gullible yellow cause to dislike humans, had been worth it. They had spent many an afternoon debating his theories on why it was dangerous allowing humans to progress unchecked. Something must have stuck in the empty space between the flighty yellow's horns.

"I would kill any human mage who harmed our moot leader," Blaze stated, making sure his voice echoed around the cave.

"How do you know Galdor has been harmed?" Mossbeard said, now interested in their conversation.

"And what of Baelross the Blue? Does anyone know what happened to him?" Blaze changed the subject, avoiding the question. "Are we being secretly targeted? And who will be next? Is this human mage picking us off one by one, Sapphire?" He deflected their attention to the cerulean blue female and all heads turned to hear her answer.

"I only spoke with Galdor," she said, "and he left early. It was before he vanished. That's all I know."

"And you never went with him? Why did you let him go off alone?" Blaze dropped in a few more questions, turning the focus of the assembled group towards her.

"He asked me not to say anything, I was—" Sapphire attempted to explain.

"And you didn't think that strange?" Azyrian the Bronze asked. "Our leader going off on his own without any support? Keeping secrets isn't like Galdor."

"And you never thought to share this information when Galdor didn't return?" White-silver accused Sapphire. Blaze couldn't have planned it any better. With a few perfectly placed questions the dragons turned on Sapphire. They harangued her with accusations, blaming her for Galdor's disappearance. They even doubted her when she said she knew nothing of Baelross. It was time to step in and take advantage of their confusion before the squabbling and hissing gave way to flames. He needed to unite them to fight against the humans and get them to realise they needed a replacement for Galdor. Once he restored order and gave them direction, they would see they were better off without him.

"I propose," Blaze interrupted, taking charge of the mayhem, "that we look for Galdor and Baelross rather than blaming Sapphire for something that is not of her doing." Surprisingly, they all shut up and listened. He was the only one making any sense, a voice of reason in the midst of his incited chaos. It gave him credibility in their eyes. He was the best choice for leadership. They just had to come to that conclusion themselves.

"Thank you, Blaze," Sapphire said. She came to stand next to him, firmly placing herself as his follower, but not yet aware of it.

"It is clear to me that Sapphire doesn't know any more than she has already told us. Yes, perhaps she should have shared her information earlier, but she was following Galdor's express command. I do not doubt her loyalty to the council of the moot." Her dark blue eyes were pools of gratitude, thankful for his support. "I'm sure that every dragon here would have done the same." The moot chamber was quiet, the other dragons, either ashamed of their misplaced accusations, or waiting to hear what Blaze would say next.

"We can't fall to pieces because Galdor is lost." He deliberately used the word *lost* and thankfully he wasn't challenged.

"Sapphire is one of the longest serving dragons on the moot. I propose she stand in as temporary leader until we can decide what to do. We need somebody to lead us through these uncertain times."

"But she should have told us earlier about the mage," White-silver said. Sapphire and the platinum female often differed in their opinions. And White-silver wouldn't want to see the blue in charge. "No offence to Sapphire, we need someone who will act when they have important information."

The blue dragon hissed at the slight, intended or not. "I do not wish it anyway." She turned her head away from White-silver, giving the aloof platinum a taste of her own flame.

"If we don't choose soon and cannot decide on what to do, I fear the plateau will fall and along with it, our colony." Blaze hoped the dragons didn't question his logic on how or why he feared this, only that it provoked a hasty response. If they didn't have time to contemplate, after a wasted week of doing nothing, they would be more likely to choose a new leader today. There was a comfortable complacency in knowing someone else was responsible for making important decisions. If all they could do was bicker with each other, then that *someone* would have to be him. It was time to stoke the fire and make another suggestion that wouldn't be unanimously received.

"Mossbeard, you were a wise and trusted advisor to Galdor, he always listened when you had something to say." The dusty old green thought himself the logical choice for moot leader. "Who would you suggest to lead the moot in Galdor's absence?" The mossy old fool hadn't been expecting that.

"I, er, think, let me see. Fern the Green, yes. She would be an acceptable choice." Mossbeard said. He hadn't sounded certain as he clearly expected Blaze to suggest him for the position. While Fern was a good choice, his hesitation undermined it.

"Acceptable!" Ember called out, "we need better than *acceptable.* A moot leader needs to be competent and confident." Blaze had seen Ember and Mossbeard arguing when he came in, the hot tempered orange female wasn't going to side with the old green. Ember's outburst succeeded in discrediting Mossbeard and made him and his suggestion look stupid. No moot would want an indecisive leader who wasn't able to make a strong choice.

"We should vote," Yesper suggested, "that is how a moot leader is properly chosen!" Most of the assembled dragons nodded in agreement.

Blaze would have liked a little more time to influence this suggested vote, but with Yesper's enthusiastic call for action, the dragons were behind the idea. There were nine dragons to choose from and Blaze concluded that after their bickering, Sapphire, Fern and Mossbeard were unlikely to be anyone's first choice.

White-silver and Azyrian wouldn't be popular choices either, except with each other, so that left Ember, Chestnut, Yesper and himself. He would try one last gambit to reduce the odds.

"Do you have someone in mind you would nominate Yesper?" Blaze asked. The yellow was unpredictable and Blaze hoped that he wouldn't suggest himself. Even if he did, he was sure the others wouldn't go for it. It was seen as poor etiquette to put yourself forward for the position.

"I'm not sure," Yesper replied, the wind pulled from beneath his wings. "It is a serious business and needs careful contemplation." Maybe the yellow thought he was a worthy candidate and wanted to stall giving an answer, in hope of being chosen himself.

"More delays," Ember said, surprising him, "while nothing is resolved!" She usually sided with Yesper, but the animated conversation Blaze witnessed with Mossbeard earlier must have upset her. "The only dragon here who has remained positive and has suggested anything sensible is Blaze." Ember tipped her head to him. "He doesn't want to sit on his tail, waiting while others debate. I propose Blaze the Black to lead the moot until Galdor's return."

Blaze was amazed at Ember's unplanned outburst. She wasn't the most patient dragon on the plateau and it was obvious she was tired of waiting for something to happen.

"I second Ember's proposal!" Sapphire said, raising her tail straight up behind her, tip pointing over her head towards Blaze.

Ember's tail repeated the gesture, giving him two votes, quickly followed by an arrow-headed yellow tail whipping up to be included in the count. Of course Yesper would side with the orange female, even after she had snapped at him for being indecisive. He was always eager to show he was interested in what she said, letting his desire for her influence his actions. His decision in siding with her on the vote would hopefully win him her good favour. Typical behaviour for a yellow. Their scales were too bright and their minds weren't bright enough. Another reason he disliked yellows.

He needed another two dragons to lift their tails for him and cast their vote, then he would have a majority.

Chestnut slowly raised her tail, tipping it forward between her horns. "I too, will vote for Blaze," her yellow eyes searching the remaining dragons to see what they would do. Of all the dragons in the moot, she was the most careful. If she decided to show her support, it could only instil confidence in the undecided.

Mossbeard followed Chestnut's lead, lifting his green tail and adding to the growing tally. Blaze knew the old green respected Sapphire's opinion. And just as Mossbeard's respect for Chestnut influenced his decision, Fern added her tail to the count and followed his example. Blaze wasn't surprised, where Mossbeard led, Fern usually followed. All his careful planning, his choice comments in the right ear at the right time, fell neatly into place. He was delighted his scheming resulted in him taking over moot leadership, but it had been far from easy. The time and effort he'd spent with each dragon had paid off today, months and months of careful planning finally coming to fruition.

All eyes turned to White-silver and Azyrian, eager to see what they would decide. It was already over, Blaze only needed five votes and he had received six. He was ecstatic! With only one round of voting he'd secured a majority share and would be the new *temporary* moot leader.

The last two dragons didn't even have to vote now and they knew it, but it would be interesting to see how they would react.

Azyrian the Bronze raised his tail, a little slow and a little late, but he showed support and respect when he could easily have abstained. White-silver did not. She sat with her tail firmly pressed to the ground in defiance, her cold blue eyes smouldering with contempt.

Blaze wasn't sure if she was angry because she desired the moot leader's position herself, or would rather it be the bronze who sat beside her. Regardless of what her reasons were, she was someone he would need to watch.

"I am flattered," he said, sounding humble. It was probably best not to acknowledge the platinum female's lack of support. She had shown her true colours to him today and revealed information she would have been wiser to conceal, playing along with the others. He would be ready for her, should she threaten his plans, and for now, she wouldn't upset the thrill of his victory.

He was bursting with delight but didn't want to outwardly show it. It was time for a little humility. "I'm honoured to be chosen and will be as worthy a successor for Galdor as I can." He paused before continuing. "And I will lead the moot and uphold our traditions, safeguarding the colony until Galdor returns to his rightful place." If he could establish he was a reluctant stand in, he was more likely to gain their support and trust. They didn't know Galdor wasn't coming back and his acknowledgement to relinquish his position, would show he wasn't hungry for the power of leadership. He would need to progress slowly with the next phase of his plan, implementing his changes gradually.

"I thank Ember for her words of confidence. We have waited long enough and should make plans on how to proceed. My first official act as moot leader," he deliberately omitted to include *temporary*, "is to ask you all to consider my proposal on how to find Galdor and Baelross." Offering up a suggestion on how to move forward and begin searching for their missing companions was a good start. The positive appearance of being in control and actually doing something proactive would give the dragons more reason to trust him. Asking the moot to consider his proposal allowed them feel empowered, giving them the impression they weren't taking his orders.

"We are a moot of nine," he continued, highlighting the two missing dragons. "For now," he added, implying they were going to find Galdor and Baelross. Let them think his positive attitude would solve the mysterious disappearances. "It is too late for today, so tomorrow I propose we pair up and have four groups for searching. One group north, one south, one east and the other west. I ask you all to think on the best tactic to take, how to efficiently cover as much ground as you can. We are dragons and flying is in our blood. We are dragons of the moot, the wisest and most experienced dragons on the plateau. If we can't work together and find our lost brothers, then no dragon can!" Heads nodded in agreement and even White-silver didn't look as opposed to his idea or his inspirational words.

"We are nine and if we pair up, there will be one odd dragon. Let me think on our best deployment of knowledge and resources. I believe if we take advantage of our combined skills and pair up strategically, we will get the best results." Maybe not the results they expected. His desired results were different from theirs.

"I will contemplate who the partners will be, and also I have an important task for the solo dragon that isn't one of the eight searchers. Go now and think about what we have achieved here today, even without Galdor's guidance, we have proved we can work together and I'm certain he would be proud of us all." As he spoke, he'd managed to position himself in the centre of the chamber, carefully manoeuvring without being obvious. He had one last act to perform to his willing audience, before ending the moot.

Rearing up slightly, Blaze stretched his hind legs to make himself taller, spreading his wings over the moot.

It felt good to stand tall and make the moot leader's traditional gesture.

"The moot is now closed. Let the wisdom of the nine help guide us through this difficult time." He folded his wings and settled down to watch as they filtered from the chamber, each one nodding deeply and showing him respect.

White-silver was last to leave and while she nodded to him as she passed, it was a shallow effort and barely acceptable for a dragon of his standing. That, he noted, was something he would need to address in the near future, and he had a good idea how he was going to do it.

Chapter 14
Hunting and Hiding

Galdor could smell wild antelope before they came into view. Dragons, especially greens, were known for their acute sense of smell. After prolonged years in the dark confines of the cave and the sensory deprivation experienced, his sense of smell developed from keen to excellent. His hearing was greatly improved too and even though his time spent underground was a torturous ordeal, these side effects were something positive.

The herd were upwind of the approaching predator and scattered, frantically kicking up clouds of dust. He wasn't surprised they were able to smell him as he was more than aware of his own pungent aroma. The sweet scent of the grassy savanna and the warm blooded antelope helped him forget the dank cavern of his imprisonment, but his nostrils still reeked with the ingrained stench. It was a foul stink of dank airless captivity; a smell he longed to be free of.

The antelope's hooves drummed as they fled from the oncoming green dragon. To Galdor's eyes, deprived of colour for so long, they were the most beautiful animals he'd seen. Stripes of red-brown, black and white covered their bodies, their natural hues spectacularly vivid in the warm, bright light of day.

His liberation from the cavern wasn't only freedom of the body. His mind had been liberated from the oppressive darkness that was slowly crushing his will to live. The monotony of never knowing night from day was gone. Freedom after incarceration made you look at life in a different way.

After shedding his skin and gifting it to Alduce, he now believed that he was reborn twofold. His initial symbolic rebirth with the casting off of his old scales, ridding himself of the last century's torment, starting afresh with a dazzling new hide that gleamed in the sunlight.

His second rebirth was living his life once more, as every dragon should be free to do. The thrill of the hunt coursing through his tired body reinforced his weakened spirit, too long bound in cruel captivity.

The charging antelope darted and weaved, like wind over waves, changing direction in an attempt to outmanoeuvre the pursuing dragon. Galdor basked in the chase, flying low and flitting one way then pivoting the other, following a turbulent river of reddish-brown backs across the undulating grasslands.

He swooped down and thrust out talons, choosing the fattest antelope, plucking it expertly from the ground and grasping it tightly in one claw. A long time had passed since he'd last hunted and he was pleased his abilities hadn't faded. The herd was big and there were plenty of animals for the taking, but prolonged exposure to starvation made him chose the largest, fattest, and hopefully, tastiest beast.

Of course it would be tasty, antelope were so much better eating than scraggly goats or tiny rats. His prize could be the stringiest and blandest antelope ever to exist and it would still be the tastiest one he'd ever caught. It wriggled wildly, hopelessly thrashing in an attempt to free itself from his deadly grip. Its efforts were in vain, this beast was going nowhere except into his stomach.

On a whim, he turned sharply and snatched another antelope in his empty claw, crushing talons tearing flesh and filling his nostrils with the scent of warm blood. Exquisite blood, its intoxicating aroma tantalising his senses, its fragrance almost driving away the smell of the cave.

Today was a day for making exceptions. He never normally made a double kill. Under the circumstances he indulged himself. Was it greed? Indeed it was. None the less, he deserved it. Most warranted and welcome.

The herd trampled the grass beneath their hooves as they widened the gap between themselves and the now slowing green. He could catch them easily if he wanted; they were quick to run and quicker to forget. By the time he devoured his first two kills, they would be far enough away to think themselves safe, forgetting about the fate of their unfortunate herd mates. It was in their nature and the Earth Mother had made them prolific and plentiful. Galdor could easily catch up to the herd and snag another helping... or three.

    He dipped one wing and pivoted mid-air, plummeting to the ground. One of the antelope was still wriggling, its instinct for survival strong, never stopping it from giving up. Galdor had never given up, like the pitiful antelope, he had clung to instinctual self-preservation for over a century, never losing hope that one day he would be free. It was easy to reflect, now he was flying in open skies, on how determined he was at regaining his freedom. Realistically it had been a hard battle and without Alduce's intervention he wasn't sure it was one he would have won.

    Galdor considered himself as practical as the next dragon. He was free now and that was all that mattered. However, he was prone to overthinking things. He couldn't help contemplating how his sanity would have fared if the wandering sorcerer hadn't stumbled into his cavern.

    Bones crunched as he hit the ground, jolting his mind back to the present, it was a mistake to dwell on what *might* have been. The struggling antelope stopped moving, its fight for survival done. Galdor's stomach growled and his jaws salivated in anticipation of his first proper meal since his liberation. He tore into the fatter of his two kills, out of practice talons ripping huge chunks of warm flesh effortlessly from the beast. Dragon's claws were always sharp and he made easy work stripping flesh from the bone.

    The satisfying taste of freedom was not a disappointment. Taste buds long deprived of any food at all, worked to make up for lost time. Decades of dreams fantasising about this moment, paled in comparison to the real thing. Incredible taste exploded in his mouth, tantalisingly good as he chewed and tore, eager to gorge himself and swallow mouthful after divine mouthful.

He buried his snout in the carcass submerging his nostrils in the scent of the kill, wondering if he would be too heavy to fly if he ate too much antelope. With the burning hunger that had gnawed his stomach for all those years, he might just find out. Systematically, he cleaned every scrap of meat from the first antelope, leaving only bones, hooves and horns. Blood and gore splattered his new green scales and he curled his tongue along his snout, cleaning the worst of it away, before staring on the second beast.

This time he wasn't as desperate, his initial longing to eat sated a little. He tore open the antelope enjoying this one just as much as the first, taking his time and savouring every mouthful. Succulent juices mixed with blood, oozed from its flesh and Galdor was careful not to lose one drop, catching any stray drips with his serpentine tongue. The flavour was strong and the taste one hundred times better than any goat... or rat.

Now he could chose his meals and eat at any time he wished, a simple luxury denied for so long. He finished his second antelope, leaving its bones beside the first, rising into the air. A welcome feeling of strength returned to his wings, his first meal giving him sustenance after so many years of starvation. His full strength would take a while to replenish and sunlight, open skies, fresh meat, and freedom, would all help towards his recovery. It wasn't just the physical act of eating his body benefited from, but the ability to eat when he pleased. He was aware the long imprisonment weakened his body, but now his mind soared, free from any restraint.

He followed the herd, sniffing out their location easily with his enhanced sense of smell. He picked off another two antelope, then took a fifth for good measure, enjoying each one as much as the first. He could probably eat five more, he mused, and still not be too heavy to fly.

He took to the air, rising on wings that felt and acted more like they should. The simple pleasure of being able to stretch them out properly and fly without any constraint was a joy.

He was ready to accomplish the next task on his list, searching the terrain below as he flew. He appreciated the act of flying anew, once more revelling in the pleasure of soaring through the sky, beating wings made strong with the recent sustenance of food. His wings had been a long time closed. As tiring as it was, the aches brought on by today's exertion, reminded him he was free. While he was able to flex them in the confines of the cavern, true flight was the only way to exercise wings in the way they were intended.

Sky blue reflected brightly from the surface of a lake, catching his eye and he turned south towards it.

Water.

After years of dusty skin and a dry throat, dreams of ice cold mountain lakes were now close enough to be a reality.

The lake wasn't one he was overly familiar with, he didn't remember what its name was—if he had known it before—and he didn't care. It was nestled in a small valley surrounded by tall trees, deep green foliage highlighted against the blue. He could drink and bathe and all he wanted to do was to submerge himself in the waters of this wonderful oasis and wash away every last trace of the cave.

He angled himself towards the centre of the lake and peered down into the clear blue depths, making sure it was deep enough. Folding wings tightly to his sides and tipping his weight forward, he dropped from the sky like an arrow, snout pushed out in front, tail straight behind, hitting the water at an angle and cutting below the surface with hardly a splash. Cold clean water engulfed his body, invigorating his skin and scales, washing clean the memory of the cave.

Galdor flicked his tail and propelled himself through the deep water, pointing back towards to the daylight of the surface. He used his wings like giant fins, pushing himself through the water like a huge fish, angling upward. He burst forth from beneath the lake's surface, water streaming from his scales and twisted, dropping back into the water with an almighty splash. Waves exploded out from his body, disturbing the lake's surface, then rushed back into the void he created, as he sank beneath them.

The cold waters cleansed his hide, washing away the blood from his feast, purifying his spirit and hydrating his life force from the drought of incarceration. He felt alive again, rejuvenated by the simplest of meals and an abundance of water. Simple pleasures once taken for granted were now bountiful gifts from the Earth Mother herself.

He swam through the lake, fish darting from his path as he entered the shallows, wading out of the lake and splashing up the stony beach. Opening his wings and shaking them in a half-hearted attempt to expel any excess lake water, the point of his tail following him like the fin of a fish as it broke the lake's surface. He lifted it free, flicking it from side to side and cast rippling arcs of water out over the lake.

He dipped his neck and lowered his head to the water, drawing in huge mouthfuls, tipped his head back, enjoying the sensation as the clear liquid ran down his throat. Cold fresh water quenched his thirst, washing away the parched years of dryness, refreshingly divine in its purity. He bent for more, greedily drinking until his stomach bloated to excess.

Perception alerted him! He sensed a presence and he knew someone or something approached. He was in no fit state to confront Blaze and didn't have any idea of what was near, so he decided to do the only thing he could at present; hide!

He scrabbled off the beach and sought the cover of the surrounding forest, pushing through the trunks and taking refuge beneath the canopy of mottled green, a natural camouflage that blended with his scales. Dragons weren't known for hiding and under any other circumstances Galdor would have stood and waited for whoever approached. He knew only too well he was still in a weakened state, even though the euphoria of his new found liberty surged through him.

Being trapped and stuck in a cave without any means of escape could do strange things to your disposition, and while he detested himself for cowering cautiously out of sight, he felt it best to remain undiscovered... for now. Perhaps it was his *perception* guiding his decision or maybe he had been alone too long and was frightened of any confrontation.

His hatred for Blaze had eaten away at him, and like the unsated hunger, it had grown inside, always there, an unscratchable itch that needed clawing. Prudence was his ally and patience a lesson well learned. He would bide his time and regain his strength before considering his next move. Something felt wrong and he would be a fool to rush headlong into the unknown. His last reckless venture was proof enough of his previous stupidity.

Whatever else Blaze was, he wasn't an adversary to be taken lightly. The devious dragon had shown his intentions were like the colour of his scales: black. Black of scales and black of heart. After his prolonged absence from the Lifting Plateau, Galdor couldn't imagine what lies Blaze had told, but there was one thing he was sure of; Blaze must have spent considerable time plotting to be rid of him and that took patience and planning. Galdor didn't think that Blaze just wanted to send him away, the black dragon had gone to considerable lengths to trick and trap him. Who would fill the void left by Galdor's disappearance? Who would step in and take charge of the moot? Who was hungry to make war on the humans? He knew the answers to his questions only too well.

With nothing to do but sleep and think for all the years spent in his cave, Galdor's conscious mind had ample time to contemplate Blaze's actions. Retrospectively, it was easy to believe he should have seen the signs, he should been able to see what Blaze was up to, but the black dragon had fooled him. If he was able to fool one dragon, there was no telling what lies had been fed to the colony. He would need to employ caution before he made the mistake of any further impetuous behaviour.

Perring up through the gaps in the leaves he scanned the sky, watching and waiting. He was an expert at waiting and patience was another skill he had learned to develop and become an expert in.

Two black shapes blotted out the sky as they passed overhead: dragons! Two *black* dragons. He was sure it wasn't just their silhouettes against the bright blue sky—his eyes weren't deceiving him. He blinked rapidly and shook his head a little, then stared back up at the dark dragons, wanting to make sure his prolonged exposure to the darkness wasn't effecting his sight. He knew he was right the first time and the shock of seeing two blacks that clearly weren't Blaze, rattled him. He would recognise his nemesis anywhere and neither black dragon overhead exhibited his tell tale mark.

Blaze was unusual and blacks were rare. He was sure that neither of the dragons passing overhead were his adversary. One hundred years was a long enough period for the duplicitous black dragon to father a clutch and beget decedents. Could these two blacks be his progeny? It was entirely possible. He assumed any offspring of the black dragon thriving here, would naturally be his enemy.

He was extremely glad of the cover provided by the trees, sheltering him from being spotted. He may have been gone for a long time and be out of practice with a lot of things, but his *perception* was as sharp as it had always been.

He followed the progress of the two black dragons as they passed between the gaps in the foliage, watching them shrink, the farther away they flew.

Galdor knew he was south west of the Lifting Plateau and these dragons were flying north east. It was a logical assumption they were heading towards his former home. He contemplated following them back; he was eager to find out what had befallen the plateau in his absence. That could prove risky and he wasn't prepared to jeopardise his hard won freedom.

He needed to recuperate, build his strength and regain his depleted magic. He would find somewhere to shelter and observe the land. He would observe the skies and watch out for any coloured dragons. Maybe he would find his former friends and be able to question them about the events of the last one hundred years. If he could learn just what was going on, it would give him some insight into how to proceed.

When he had slept, his dreams were filled with returning home to his own world, returning to the plateau and reclaiming his life. These hopes sustained him through his ordeal. Now he was free, things weren't as simple. Something was wrong and even though the world around him looked the same, his *perception* warned him otherwise.

He thought of poor Baelross and wondered how a dragon could be turned to stone. And why would someone want to do that? If this was Blaze's doing, how had the black dragon learned this magic? It was one thing to possess the ability, but entirely another to willingly commit another living creature to this torment. To transform a dragon into a statue, leaving the flicker of his life spirit deep inside, was completely evil. He hoped the blue's sentience was too far buried for him to be aware of his predicament. He couldn't imagine if it would be worse or better than the imprisonment he had suffered.

He didn't want to consider how dark the black dragon's soul had become and what other horrors he was capable of. His homecoming wasn't the glorious return he had imagined.

He emerged from the shelter of the trees, carefully scanning the skies for any signs of life. When he was sure the way was clear, he hopped up from the ground and flew above the forest canopy, keeping close to the treetops in case he needed to use them for shelter again.

He would find somewhere to hide, somewhere where food was within easy reach and there was adequate cover to obscure him from the prying eyes of what he now considered were his enemies—until he learned otherwise.

His *perception* informed him his paranoia wasn't unjustified. He would rest and get stronger. Once he was back to his former self, once he was healthy and whole, then he would be ready to confront his darkest fear: the black dragon named Blaze.

Chapter 15

Divisions

"I've spent most of the night working on a search plan," Blaze addressed the moot of nine. "Mossbeard and White-silver, you will be the searchers to the south. I think you will make an excellent team. With the pragmatism of a green and the power of a platinum, I'm confident your wisdom and strength will be the perfect pairing." He had designs for them both and wanted them together for the next part of his plan. And a little well placed flattery wouldn't do any harm in putting them at ease.

"White-silver, your eyesight is legendary amongst the dragons of the plateau. I'm sure you will spot our missing dragons, any unusual activities or trespassing humans, should there be any in the lands to the south. Mossbeard, your knowledge of our records will help you to decide what areas are more likely to produce results. Please start your search beyond the Silver River, working across the lands and head south. Do not go into the lands inhabited by men, I don't want to lose any more dragons to their dark human magic." Making it appear like humans were responsible, would keep their focus away from him.

The green and platinum paired off and surprisingly didn't argue. He knew they would probably have preferred different partners and that's why he put them together. Divide and conquer.

"We will do our best," Mossbeard said. White-silver tipped her snout, barely acknowledging his leadership. She would know respect before this day was over.

"Ember and Yesper, I would like you to range to the north." The yellow male would be delighted at the pairing with the orange female. He was easily manipulated and was quickly becoming one of Blaze's loyal supporters. He would chase Ember's tail all day, finding an excuse to be with her and any reason to prove himself a worthy mate. He would view the choice of putting them together as wise and be grateful to Blaze for pairing them, following his lead without question.

"I know you have extensive knowledge of the northlands, Ember. Range as far as the snowfields, paying particular interest to the sheltered canyons and valleys. Anything could be hidden there. It is a difficult task and one I entrust to you both." Yesper couldn't get to Ember's side quick enough and Blaze stifled a snort of humour. The orange would have her wings full all day and no doubt set a fast pace to quell Yesper's continuous chattering. If he was paired with Ember, Blaze wouldn't have to listen to the yellow's incessant babble. Yesper didn't have the stamina of the larger orange and would push himself to keep up. That would keep those two occupied and out of the way.

"Fern and Chestnut, I would ask you to range east and search the woodlands, jungles, and greenwoods. You are both colours of the forest and have the blood of forest dragons in you. You are the best suited to this region."

Chestnut had been quick to support him at the vote and he admired her black tinged scales. He was sure he would be able to convince her of his vision for the Lifting Plateau and gain her loyalty. After that was accomplished, he was certain she would see him as a potential mate. Who wouldn't want the most powerful dragon, who was now leader of the moot, as their mate?

Fern was a follower, not a leader and would take her lead from the brown. And once Mossbeard was out of the way, the green female would bend to his will.

"Sapphire and Azyrian, you have the west." White-silver glowered at the cerulean blue female with undisguised hated. The bronze male was never far from the platinum female's side and like all metals, they stuck together in their own special groups, thinking themselves superior. Driving a blue wedge between bronze and platinum would keep her attentions diverted, making it easier for him to catch her unprepared.

On the surface all eight dragons appeared to be content enough with the search mate he'd selected for them. Blaze knew his tactical deployment would cause unrest with the majority of them, especially the dragons he wouldn't be able to win over from Galdor's former rule. If he could whittle out the troublemakers and the miscreants, he could replace them with his own supporters.

Imagine a ruling body of loyal dragons, unafraid of upsetting the humans, eager to take back their lands and cleanse the human plague for good. He could feel the touch of the globe, many miles distant, as the thrill of openly destroying the cities of man filled him with a righteous satisfaction.

Eight dragons looked to him in the silence and he snapped his attention back to the present. "Fly out and search, dragons of the Lifting Plateau. By fang and by claw, find our lost brothers and bring them home, where they belong. Range as far as you must in daylight and return when night falls. I know most of you can see just as well in the dark, however, we stand a better chance of seeing anything unusual or out of the ordinary in the light of day. I will stay here and speak with the colony, surely there are some among us who saw or spoke to Galdor or Baelross before they went missing." No one challenged his decision—as it should be with a moot leader—accepting his instructions without question.

The bickering squabbles of yesterday were forgotten. Blaze the Black had united the moot, giving them a purpose. Someone needed to take charge and he was their best choice by far, even if they didn't realise it yet. It was something he'd always believed and now, after much planning, he was well on his way to enlightening the moot and educating the colony. Once the dragons were in line with his ideals, when they were able to see his insightful vision of what the future would be, he would be able to change the world for ever.

The globe pulled at his consciousness, reminding him of the part it played and the secrets it held. He would be rewarded with the hidden knowledge it possessed, its power and its wisdom. All he needed to do was feed its own hunger in return.

"Fly high and fly free, brothers and sisters. I know Galdor would be proud of you all." They stood visibly taller at the mention of their former leader. That love and respect would be his. When he was done he would have their devotion and their minds. "It will be a long day, so when you return I want you to rest. Your wellbeing and that of the colony are my greatest concern. If there is nothing of importance to report when you arrive home, get some well-earned rest. We'll gather in the moot chamber, tomorrow at sunrise, to discuss what our next actions will be."

That would allow him the opportunity to carry out the next phase of his plan and no one would be any the wiser until tomorrow. Events were unfolding at a faster pace now Galdor was gone, his months of endless scheming were reaping the rewards he desired.

The four searching pairs rose into the morning sky, each setting off in their designated direction. As Mossbeard and White-silver veered off to the south he connected with the globe. His thoughts soothed its turmoil, promising it the wait was almost over. He urged it to be at peace and remain quiet, so as not to attract the attention of the southern searchers. At least not yet.

He watched until all four groups disappeared into the blue, tiny specs of dark against the bright sky. From this far away, no colours were distinguishable even to his superior dragon eyes. Black silhouettes shrank into the distance. The colony should have more black dragons, a flight of dark destroyers filling the skies and striking fear into the ground dwelling humans. The day would come when they looked upwards and saw their oncoming demise.

He would speak with the dragons of the colony, fulfilling his part of today's brilliant plan. When the searching dragons retuned, the gossips would say their new moot leader had spoken with them, earnestly inquiring about the disappearance of their missing dragons. He would be inquisitive and interested, making a show of being concerned. The Lifting Plateau would come to realise that Blaze the Black cared for them more than Galdor. They would be content under his rule and come to see the wisdom of his vision, understand it was what they unknowingly lacked under his predecessor's rule. Blaze would be a legend and he would return dragonkind to their rightful status.

He hurried to carry out his chore, knowing the quicker he spoke and played the part of dutiful leader, the quicker he could sneak away and continue with more important matters. If he was lucky, there might be some time left to fly south and burn a few more towns and villages. A little inciting encouragement would help move things along nicely. And it was fun. He was sure he could squeeze in a few fiery visits before he returned to the cave where the globe rested. As much as he enjoyed the destruction, it was part of the master plan, just as long as he was back at the cave before Mossbeard and White-silver flew overhead on their return to the Plateau.

He wanted to spend some time alone in the globe's presence before he introduced the annoying platinum and the irritating green to its wonders.

Chapter 16
Changes

Blaze left the burning city behind, the orange flames lit the evening sky like a second sunset. Thick clouds of smoke rose from the ruined quarter of the human made buildings, darkening the horizon. The human constructions took a long time to build, their workers systematically covering the land with their dwellings, spreading ever farther. How easy it was to set them alight, burning the timber and searing the stone, tearing down what they made in a fraction of that time.

Humans would learn taking dragon land was no longer tolerated. They would know war and destruction. Annihilation would be the cost of their arrogance; a price long overdue.

Blaze shimmered, the illusion of green scales faded, returning him back to his glorious black. He was thankful to the globe for sharing the secret of illusion. He only needed to remain disguised for a little longer, making sure any word of who was responsible for yet another violent attack, would not be traced back to him.

The pull of the globe filled his mind, basking in the enjoyment of his actions. It called him home, encouraging him to return to its secret resting place. It anticipated what was to come and the promise of more life force was a thrill to them both. He longed to take the globe back to the Lifting Plateau, but it was still too soon. He needed to wait until he established his dominance over the whole colony. He would win their hearts and strengthen his hold over their minds. He would show them he was a worthy successor and make them forget their previous leader and his failings. His dragons would no longer be weakened by Galdor's memory.

Landing at the familiar cave mouth, he hurried inside the dark entrance, eyes adjusting to the gloomy interior. When the time was right, the globe would sit in his moot chamber, resting in a place worthy of its greatness, instead of a dusty cave floor. For now it was safe here, sitting beside the stone remains of Baelross. The inquisitive blue made a fine guardian, standing over the globe and protecting it in Blaze's absence.

"Thank you, Baelross the Basalt, stone protector and granite guardian," he said to the former blue dragon, whacking the solid rock of the saxified dragon affectionately with the flat of his tail. The globe lay in a sandy hollow between two stone talons, its white radiance brightening as Blaze approached. Swirling patterns rolled over its curved surface, responding to Blaze's presence, pastel blues highlighting the underside of the stony dragon above it. The song of its promised secrets a welcome distraction from the chattering squabble of the dragons he had spoken with earlier. Each one, clamouring to inform him of their thoughts regarding the disappearance of Galdor and Baelross. Not one of them knew the truth, ignorant and suspecting nothing, trusting him implicitly.

He reached out and closed his talon about the globe, sharp claws clicking on the smooth surface, hard and unyielding. The power inside flooded up through his front leg and into his whole body, washing over him like a massive wave, suffusing his spirit with invigorating energy. It welcomed him back and hungered for his next offering. It sensed his plan to deliver more life force, more living, breathing life. More energy, magic, spirit, and power. It coveted them, demanded it be fed. In return it offered knowledge and secrets beyond that of a dragon's understanding; secrets it was ready to divulge to its benefactor. It was the power he desired—and needed—that would help change his dreams to reality. The sacrifice was worth the reward.

Perception alerted him that others approached, far enough away to be sensed and slowly getting closer. His time communing with the globe passed by so quickly. It only felt like a few minutes, but as he unfurled his talon and broke contact, he realised more than an hour had elapsed. It was disappointing he couldn't spend more time here, but once all his plans came to fruition, he could spend as long as he wanted unlocking the globe's secrets.

He tore himself away and followed the tunnels back outside, remembering the day when Galdor passed through the portal to become trapped on another world forever. The human mage had been devious in his scheme to trap Galdor, and as much as it pained him to form a temporary alliance with something he despised, it was a necessary burden he was forced to endure. The mage wasn't as smart as he believed himself to be, otherwise he would have escaped the portal, as he planned. No doubt, like all of his kind, he would have gone on to betray his deal with Blaze, had he escaped. Blaze never would have let that happen, he would never trust a human and was wise enough to know when the mage's services were no longer required. The mage's timely demise was his good fortune.

The afternoon sun had long since dropped below the horizon, the last traces of light faded from the sky. He could feel the presence of dragons, still beyond sight, but nearer now. Two dragons coming from the south, tired after a day's fruitless searching. Blaze hoped they were disheartened and exhausted after a long day's tedious searching without any results. If they were tired and worn down, they would be less likely to see through his deception until it was too late.

Reaching inside himself, Blaze began the summoning of his dragon flame. A deep warmth filled his chest, accompanied by pleasant grumbling. His flame came easy, a well-practiced action of late, only taking a few minutes to brew enough to dispel an impressive fiery blast.

He walked outside onto a flat piece of ground and expelled flame, directing it over a stand of small trees and bushes, igniting them instantly. The light from the fire chased back the oncoming darkness of night, creating a signal beacon for any who saw it. Blaze added a second gout of flame over the already burning shrubbery, making sure the fire was intense and obvious. There was no way Mossbeard and White-silver would be able to miss his raging signal fire.

The heat of the flames warmed his scales as the light from the fire emphasised his silhouette, making it easy for the dragons above to see his orange tinged form. Black dragons were almost invisible in the dark and he didn't want to appear suddenly and startle his potential targets into doing something unpredictable.

Mossbeard would be defeated without much effort. He was old and slow and passed his prime. Even if he showed some hidden courage and actually put up a fight, he wouldn't stand a chance. White-silver was a different matter. She was a metal and they were known for their toughness. She was also aggressive and confrontational and she didn't care for Blaze or his ideas. She was disrespectful and arrogant, like most metals. He believed he could best her, if it came to fighting one on one, but if Mossbeard had the opportunity to side with her, his chances would be much reduced. He could always call on his new power, gifted to him from the globe, but it was untried so far. He would prefer to test it before he relied on it in a fight. The details of his aspirations were in the careful preparation, calculations rather than risks. He didn't want to leave anything to chance, especially not after all the effort of his hard work and endless planning. Not when he was this close.

A trumpeting challenge rang out from above and the voice of the platinum female split the night. "Identify!" she roared.

"Blaze the Black, moot leader of the Lifting Plateau," he responded. "Join me on the ground." Turbulence from the wingbeats above fanned the fire, blowing flames and glowing embers in every direction as the two airborne dragons alighted beside him.

"Mossbeard. White-silver. I'm glad I've found you. What news?"

"Nothing," Mossbeard said. "Hours of endless searching. My eyes are as tired as my wings." He sagged, deflated in failure.

"There is unrest in the south," White-silver added. "The humans are agitated. We kept out of sight, as you instructed, but my strong eyesight allowed me to see farther than Mossbeard. Something has upset them. They stir like angry hornets. The city we saw from afar was on fire."

She had disobeyed him. It was just like the platinum to not follow his orders. He knew she was trouble. How dare she go against his explicit wishes! He deliberately told them to keep away from the human cities. Of course the humans were angry. With his constant unprovoked attacks, the hornet's nest was ready to swarm. He swallowed down the anger that fought to rise and maintained a calm exterior. "Well it appears you've discovered something, Mossbeard. If the humans are angry, then there is a reason. Could it not be connected to our missing brothers?"

"Humans are humans," White-silver sneered. "What they do doesn't concern us."

"They steal our land!" Blaze spat, letting his mask slip. "It concerns me, so it should concern you all." He immediately regretted his reaction as Mossbeard took a step back and stared at him. The platinum upstart got right under his scales with her aloof manner. She would learn respect and he was ready to teach her. She showed no reaction to his words, as if she didn't even care.

"I have found Baelross," He announced. That should give them pause. "While everyone was out searching, I spoke to some dragons at the plateau. A young female red said she was friends with Baelross and he often visited these caves."

Both the platinum and green looked beyond Blaze to the cave mouth set in the hillside.

"Where was he? Mossbeard asked.

"Is he harmed? Has he told you what happened? Where did you find him?" White-silver asked.

"And does he know anything about Galdor's whereabouts? Can he help us locate him?" Mossbeard questioned.

"It is probably best if you ask him yourselves," Blaze said. "He's... different now, changed from how he was before."

"Different? How? What has changed?" White-silver asked. She stood alert, the spines on her neck quivered, sharp silver quills twitching with excitement, or perhaps it was agitation. It was difficult to speculate—even though she let her emotions betray her—the display could mean either. Her outward display conveyed weakness, much like his own outburst. Alerting those around you to your true feelings gave an advantage to any who were able to read them. It was a lesson he would remember and learn from White-silver's mistake, curbing any further emotional outbursts in the presence of others.

He would need to be careful of her, he could see she was wary. She would find out just how different Baelross was and see how arrogant and disrespectful dragons were treated under his rule.

"I'll take you to him and you can see for yourselves." He turned towards the caves, confident they would follow, their curiosity getting the better of them. He turned to add, "And please, be quiet. I don't want poor Baelross unnecessarily inconvenienced," spotting a shared look of concerned confusion between them.

He would take them to look upon *poor* Baelross and they would see what awaited any dragon that opposed his will. Baelross wasn't the first to get in his way and he wouldn't be the last. As the old saying went; *if you wanted dragons to hatch, their shells must be broken*. He didn't want to punish them, but if they wouldn't follow his lead and support his cause, they were no use to his colony. The weak and the rebellious would be whittled out until only the strong remained. Loyal dragons who supported his vision would be awarded the honour of helping him take back what was rightfully theirs.

He entered the dark cave, eyes adjusting to the gloom as he made his way to where the stone remains of Baelross stood. The globe sang out, its voice filled with anticipation and hunger as it connected with his eager mind. He didn't want Mossbeard or White-silver to share in its beauty, it was meant for him alone. He risked a glimpse behind, checking to see if they were aware of the globe's presence, but they stumbled through the darkness, blissfully unaware of what awaited them.

The sensation grew as he neared Baelross, filling him with an unknown expectation something wonderful was about to happen. When the globe absorbed the life force from Baelross, the energy and the power it shared, resulted in a feeling of intense euphoria. A euphoria he longed to feel again.

The blue dragon loomed out of the darkness and to his amazement, Baelross was alive!

Blaze jarred to a stop, the spikes on his neck quivered, battle ready, his talons scraping to a halt on the cave floor. How could this be?

On closer scrutiny, he saw Baelross hadn't reverted back to skin and scales. He was still made of stone, unmoving and silent. The globe pulsed, radiating out a wash of blue colour, bathing the stone scales. The illusion it created was completely lifelike, giving Baelross the appearance of a living blue dragon. He looked just as he was before he was turned to stone and if Blaze didn't know any better, he would have believed Baelross was normal.

His senses began to tingle and Blaze felt the globe's consciousness stir from sleepy anticipation to wakefully alert. The cave filled with a raw energy, tantalising his scales as it coursed over his body, the membranes of his wings vibrated, skin taught and sensitive as the feeling pulsed to a crescendo of intensity.

"Baelross?" Mossbeard's voice echoed from behind. "Thank the Earth Mother we've found you." The green pushed forward while White-silver stood where she was, her suspicious nature preventing her from following blindly.

Light exploded from the globe, violent and white, blasting away the shadows and illuminating the cave like a bright sun. The illusion dropped and Baelross was transformed from vibrant blue to granite grey, returning to lifeless stone.

"What—" Mossbeard managed to say before the globe's light silenced him forever. Blaze half closed his eyelids, squinting in the intense light, clouds of white mist swirling through his usually black pupils, mimicking the surface of the globe. The panic Mossbeard experienced flooded his senses, his thoughts one with the old green. Where Mossbeard felt fear and uncertainty, Blaze only felt pleasure and power. He was aware of everything the green experienced, but was immune to the panic, lost in self-indulgent satisfaction and the gratification of Mossbeard's demise.

White-silver sprang into action, leaping forward to assist the green. They may not have been the best of friends, yet she reacted on instinct, hoping to protect him from the unexpected attack.

Dragons should never harm other dragons. Blaze was aware of White-silver's instinctual obligation, strong in the platinum female. Lately his own views had changed. Sacrifice, however tragic, would strengthen the colony. He was the only one to see this and he must remain steadfast, detaching himself from emotion if his plans were to succeed.

Blaze called on the power of the globe, tapping into its knowledge, unaware of how he was doing it, a new instinct taking over, banishing any doubt he wasn't in perfect control.

A net of golden threads spread over White-silver, stopping the platinum dragon and freezing her in mid-air. The threads wrapped around her form, running over her body like golden ivy, twisting and writhing, sentient and aware, cocooning her in a glowing prison of gold.

The usually gloomy cave was alive with life and light. Platinum scales shone with gold, a metallic kaleidoscope of unrivalled beauty, painting its colours over the cave's dull interior, the dragon inside held fast, restrained and unable to assist Mossbeard. Cold blue hatred reflected in her eyes, as bright as the blinding light shining from her scales.

Perception sure White-silver would remain disabled, Blaze turned his focus back to the green. Mossbeard was of no use to his new order, the stuffy old green too set in his ways. He was oblivious to the stagnation of their species, blindly following Galdor's rule without question. Even now he tried to resist, too stupid to realise he was beaten. There was no place in the colony for dragons that couldn't see the truth. No place for unbelievers who resisted his will. And definitely no place for greens who thought they knew better than a black.

The globe understood his thoughts and agreed with his assessment. Mossbeard would be able to serve them another way. He would be able to give one final sacrifice for the colony. His gift would help strengthen their cause.

White strands of ethereal light whipped out from the globe, lashing themselves over the green's scales and binding his wings tightly to his flanks. Tentacles of wispy light, insubstantial as smoke, yet strong as steel, constrained the struggling dragon, growing as they increased in speed, faster and faster as they gained momentum, blurring into a spinning mass.

Blaze could feel every fibre of light, connected through his link with the globe. As the swirling threads enveloped Mossbeard and tightened their hold, he tasted the life force, coppery and thick like the warm blood of a fresh kill. The faster the threads spun, the stronger they bound, squeezing the green dragon and contracting him, crushing his physical form and drawing out his spirit. The power of the globe stronger now, like his own. There would be no stone remains this time. No shell left as it was with Baelross. This time everything would be consumed.

The swirling light changed, slowing as the intense white started to take on the green of Mossbeard's scales. Faint at first, streaks of misty green, pastel and indistinct, thickened until it resembled a marble cloud streaked with heavy green veins, vibrant against the white. The silhouette of Mossbeard was visible through the mass of changing threads, a dark bulk at the centre of their swirling dance. Blaze could feel him hanging on, struggling to maintain his grip on life, but failing.

The globe ripped at the life force, greedily tugging at Mossbeard's will, pulling it from the dying dragon's grasp. Blaze focused on strengthening the pull, lending his will to the globe, eager to help. Together they were invincible. A tearing ripped through the cloud, devoid of sound as it separated Mossbeard from his life force. The bond was broken and the green dragon's spirit beaten.

The mist turned green and all traces of white vanished as the threads slowed to a stop and reversed direction. They picked up speed as they tugged at the life force, pulling it from Mossbeard, unravelling it and absorbing it into the swirling mists, expanding until they were bloated and full. Blaze could feel the energy and power, infused with the magic of the globe, ripe for harvesting. The temptation to take all the life force for himself only held in check by the globe's own hunger.

The whirling threads twisted and separated as the spinning increased and as they coalesced back into long winding strands, Mossbeard's form grew clearer. Fine threads drifted from his body, like vapour rising from hot stone, wisps of smoke leaching out from between his scales and joining with the thicker threads. His physical form began to diminish as the last of the threads left his body, stealing the final vestiges of life as they departed.

The green dragon grew insubstantial. Tough scales, strong talons, hard bone, all began to fade. As his body grew more translucent, it also reduced in size, shrinking as its transparency intensified.

Blaze was ready.

Mossbeard vanished from sight, reduced into nothing, completely gone as if he never existed. The mass of threads filled with everything the green dragon was, his energy, his power, his very being, exploded outward in a blinding flash. The globe drew them in, pulling everything back inside itself, a torrent of smoky green threads rushing over its surface, joining with the swirling white within.

For the briefest moment, two points of red light winked inside the depths of the globe, dark and malevolent against the misty white exterior.

The onrush of euphoria slammed inside Blaze's mind. The intense pleasure, unlike before, more substantial and complete. He basked in the glow of the fiery energy as it filled his being. The magic and power no longer part of Mossbeard, pure and untarnished by his spirit, now it was free from his being; ready to be received into a new vessel, adding vitality, vigour and life, as it found a new home within the black dragon.

The life force from the leviathan had been old and primeval, scant intelligence filled with raw strength. It hadn't been fully absorbed. It had managed to swim back to the open sea before it gave up and faded into death.

The life force from Baelross was better, more substantial, filled with not just physical strength, it contained energy, intelligence and magic. A magic that was part of every dragon, a vital piece of their existence, the inner spirit and the true life source. Blaze understood the life force taken from the blue dragon wasn't everything he possessed. There was still a tiny part of his existence locked deep inside the stone. He didn't contain enough magic to break free, the globe had made sure he would remain inert. Somewhere in the stone body, the last remaining fragment of the blue dragon's spirit clung to life, resisting the finality of death.

That was the difference between Baelross and Mossbeard. The green dragon was utterly and completely gone. His physical form reduced to nothing, every single piece of his life force absorbed into the globe.

Blaze now understood why the stone body of the blue dragon remained, why he hadn't vanished, while the green was expunged from existence.

The green tinged brightness faded as the globe—and Blaze—feasted on the life-source, each absorbing an equal share.

The rush passed and as Blaze returned to normal, he was aware of the platinum female, her silvery glow, entangled with golden threads, now the only source of light.

A new power, fuelled with natural dragon magic, flooded through him, increasing his ability to manipulate the source within. A reservoir overflowing with a magic of endless possibilities, new and unknown. He marvelled at the platinum dragon suspended in the golden web. She was like a fly, waiting on the bidding of a far smarter spider, frozen in time, unable to struggle, held captive without hope of freedom.

He twisted his neck and flexed his wings, small sparks of light jumping from his black scales, crackling with energy, searching for release and hungry to be used.

White-silver's eyes were wide in terror and he could only imagine the helplessness she felt at witnessing Mossbeard's sacrifice, knowing she was powerless to stop it. She wasn't so aloof now. The platinum must understand there was nowhere for her to go and her fate was sealed. There was no way to go back to how things had been, not now she knew what Blaze was capable of. She was a problem that knew his secret and was privy to the existence of the globe. She couldn't be allowed to leave and inform the moot.

Blaze admired her spirit, defiant and assured. She was a talon in his hide and succeeded in getting under his scales with her attitude and disrespect. If only she was black. Perhaps then she would have been more inclined to follow him instead of her proud belief metals were superior. Pride would be her downfall, she...

The globe showed him the answer before he knew the question. It surfaced in his mind and suggested a fitting path for the platinum female. It was easy to understand the instructions it provided, learning from the knowledge it shared. He was eager to enlighten White-silver with this new found knowledge.

Stepping closer, he raised his head, bringing his eyes level with hers. Muscles twitched in her neck and her nostrils flared, panic showing in those cold blue eyes. Eyes, which up until now, had only shown scorn. Contempt for his lack of colour, prejudice for his beautiful black scales. He knew some other dragons thought him inferior because he remained black after hatching. That somehow he was different, strange, weaker than a colour, inferior to a metal. Did she think that now?

He wished he could show her what it was like to be black, how he struggled to be accepted. What it felt like not to be a privileged platinum. And then it came to him.

The globe's suggestion was brilliant, a perfect solution to his platinum problem, but he would add his own piece to the knowledge it provided and make it even better.

He whispered to White-silver, "Are you comfortable in there? Do you really want to know what happened to Baelross? He stuck his snout where it didn't belong. He interfered with my plans so I turned him to stone. Just one of my many new talents." He rubbed his neck gently along the web of golden threads, never quite making contact with her scales, the net keeping him from touching her. She was powerless to resist his show of affection, false as it was. He teased, aware the gesture of courtship would repulse her. He knew if he attempted such an intimate display without her consent, she would have resisted. Resisted vehemently, most likely replying with flame or fang.

"And what of Galdor? Where is our glorious leader? He isn't anywhere your search would find him. Your loyalty to him is pointless, a waste of your time and talents. Are you ready for what comes next? Do you know what fate awaits you?"

Her eyes fixed to his, a spark of defiance still there, buried beneath the fear. "I have a different role for you to play, something better than the stone of Baelross or the destruction of Mossbeard. A more industrious task. One I think you will excel at. A role more befitting of your cold demeanour. Should we try something new? Would you like to be cured of your pride?"

Blaze stepped back and opened his wings, spreading them as wide as the cave would allow. He curled them around White-silver's suspended form in a parody of the symbolic gesture performed at the moot. Gold light shone through the membranes as he encompassed her in his dark embrace. He completed the circle looking like a huge black stork shading the water's glare with its wings, while it fished.

Magic coursed through his core, abundant after feasting on Mossbeard's life force. Usually his magic was limited and took time to replenish after use. Now it was plentiful and he was filled to overflowing. There was no effort involved in calling it forth, it was eager to be used. He could feel the globe urging him to use the magic, eager to experience what was about to happen. Now the globe was the one anticipating something new, aware he was going to do something it had never experience before.

He drew on the magic, filling his wings with its essence. The membranes shimmered, bones standing out as the golden glow containing White-silver intensified. The space between his wings and the platinum dragon, filled with magic, sparkling motes of gold lifting from the net and glittering in the distorted air. A heat haze like bright sun on an ocean surface, formed in the magic void, shimmering with golden flecks. Blaze poured the essence into the seething air, flooding it with his own magic, harnessing the power from the globe and the life force taken from Mossbeard.

The powerful cocktail was a new power, a mixture of potential unknown, but Blaze knew how to use it. He increased the flow, forcing it into the void. It was easy, the essence came willingly. It felt as if he were using a stomach full of dragon flame to burn a tiny insect; overkill to the extreme—and he didn't care. The power was intoxicating and he let it flood through him, relishing the sensation. It bent to his will, hungry to do his bidding, the air charged and expectant like the anticipation of a thunderstorm. His whole body tingled, alive with magic. With power such as this he would rule everything! Nothing could stand against him.

The swirling motes brightened, throwing wide an intense golden light from under the giant black mushroom that was Blaze. The cave walls glittered and glowed as the pulsing golden aurora brightened and then began to fade. The cave grew darker as the light diminished, the extreme opposite of the vanished brightness. Black void filled the space under Blaze's wings. No longer were the dragons visible as darkness, blacker than the darkest night, filled the cave.

The sound of rushing wind shattered the silence and an unnatural force of power swept about them, a turbulent torrent of dark magic.

White-silver bucked and kicked inside the constraints of the net, all of its colour now gone. The golden strands that made up the web replaced with the dark void of black essence. It swirled over her scales flickering through the platinum in a coruscating stream.

Blaze stepped back, thin strands of magic flowed from his body, rising like steam from beneath his wings as it mixed with the magical essence. The dark void leached into the cocooning bubble of threads that held the platinum female, mixing with the net, flooding it with an intense blackness that made the rest of the cave appear lighter, even though it wasn't.

Snakes of dark thread ran around the edges of White-silver's scales, tiny rivers of black void filling the channels, platinum highlighted with black. The animated darkness pushed into the spaces between the scales forcing its way under the dragon's armour, violating her defences. It continued to flow, filling her with the essence until it was gone.

White-silver stopped struggling, hanging limply in the air, her scales oscillating from bright platinum to dark black. The pulsing quickened, alternating between both colours, faster and faster, a blur of silvery-grey, pearlescent and metallic as it rippled through every scale.

And then it stopped.

White-Silver dropped to the floor with a thud, the magical net no longer holding her captive. Her entire body now as black as Blaze's. The globe returned to normal and Blaze sensed its presence, quiet and content.

The black dragon that was once White-silver stirred, rising on unsteady legs to stand before Blaze. She stretched her wings and folded them to her flanks then tucked one leg under her chest, bowing her head low in subservience to her new master.

"You will be the first of many," Blaze purred. She retained the sleek grace of her former platinum body, more beautiful now than she had ever been. A black warrior that would fight unquestioningly for his cause, his creature to command, now and forever, until death.

The newly changed black dragon lifted her head, blue eyes replaced with fiery red. Dragons were magnificent creatures to behold, their eyes naturally mesmerising. The red jewels staring back at him were filled with a burning flame of intense adoration. Blaze knew in that moment she would follow wherever he led.

"You shall no longer be known by the name White-silver," he told her, looking into her smouldering eyes. "She is no more. Forget what you once were and embrace your rebirth." There was no resistance, no answering back, she was his. Totally.

"From now on you are Darkflame and you will be my weapon."

As much as he was pleased with his creation, he couldn't let her accompany him back to the Lifting Plateau. At least not yet. There were more seeds of doubt to sow and more schemes to put into action. For now Darkflame would remain hidden. She would do his bidding in secret and prepare the way for what was to come.

"I have an important task for you. You will fly south, far south into human lands. I want you to burn their fields, destroy their crops, steal their cattle, terrorise villages, and wreak havoc on their towns. Do you understand?"

Darkflame growled in response.

"Can you speak?" She growled again, unable to form any words. Blaze's *perception* gave him the notion it was a side effect of whatever occurred during the dark transformation. The magic he used was new to him even though the globe helped facilitate the spell, it was his doing, his idea. If she couldn't speak it meant she couldn't answer back or question his orders. He would take that as an added advantage to her transformation. One he could live with.

"As long as you understand your task. Let the humans hear you roar and learn to fear us once again. It is the only voice you need. Come." He walked her outside into the night. It was full dark now. When he spent time with the globe, it passed quicker than he perceived. Hours had passed although it didn't feel like it. He would have to be more aware of this in future. It wouldn't do to lose time.

Darkflame shadowed him in the dark and for the first time, he realise just how difficult it was to see a black dragon at night. He was used to his own black scales and never gave it a moment's thought, but looking at Darkflame, it reminded him. Her body may blend with the darkness of the night, her eyes were a different matter. They were burning fires, red and intense, standing out it the darkness with a brightness of their own.

"Return here after seven days. Forage and rest when you need. You must not fail me. Do not get captured or slain. Humans have their own vile magic, make sure you avoid those who possess it.

She growled again. Blaze liked the sound of her reply, deep and powerful, full of threating menace for the unfortunates she would encounter.

"There is one last spell to cast before you go," Blaze told her. "I don't want our black colour associated with your attacks. We need to remain uninvolved." Reaching for his own magic—he didn't need the help of the globe for this spell now—he willed the illusion of colour over Darkflame's body.

She pulsed as the colours of the spectrum altered her appearance, changing her from purple, dark then light blue, green, yellow, orange, and finally red, then back to purple.

"A temporary necessity," he said, "your beautiful black scales will return in seven days. You will take on a new colour each night. Every day you continue on your mission, the humans will know a different dragon, creating the illusion of many attackers. They will see many dragons and not just one rogue. They will be convinced our species must be stopped, that we have finished with our complacent ways and risen up. They will be forced to take action against us before it is too late for them. Then we can truly begin in earnest. No more sneaking about, no more plotting and scheming. We will be within our rights to retaliate and defend ourselves, fight back. Mankind will learn the error of their arrogant ways."

Darkflame's eyes burned with passion as she listened to his words. They were still red, untouched by the illusion of colour.

"Go now, Darkflame. Fly south and bring death and destruction to our enemies, show them your fire and flame."

She rose, great black wings rhythmically beating the night sky. Blaze watched as she turned south and vanished into the distance.

He returned to the cave for one last look at the globe, checking everything was as it should be. The globe rested between the stone talons of Baelross, a faint white glow emanating from within. There was no sign of recent events or that Mossbeard or White-silver had ever set claw inside the cave.

Mossbeard was completely gone, every scrap of life force taken until his body was reduced to nothing. He sniffed at the stone dragon, his nostrils snuffling along the cold granite scales. Baelross was stronger than the old green and the platinum. Blues were known for their strength of will. There was still the slightest spark of life inside the stone body, holding fast to what remained of his spirit. This was why he left stone remains rather than being fully taken.

Blaze ran his tail along the stone, using it to feel his way along the hard surface, probing with his magic. Whatever Baelross had done, he had resisted. Blaze touched the globe and pushed his presence at the stone, attempting to penetrate its defences. Baelross and his remaining life force were too deep to touch. It was as if he could almost grasp it, only to realise his flittering spirit was just out of reach.

The globe's presence had returned to a dormant state and it was no help at all.

It was in a state of resting, sated for now, no interest in the blue dragon's stony remains.

Baelross was no threat and could stand in this cave for centuries. Perhaps when he was more familiar with the harvesting of the life force, he could finish with the blue dragon completely. It niggled him that something of Baelross still remained inside the stone dragon, resisting his will.

"We're not done yet, my basalt friend," he said. "I know not if you can hear my words or feel my touch." He slapped his tail against the flank of stone with a satisfying whack. "We have business to finish, you and I. However, it can wait. Don't go off anywhere until we're done." He grumbled, laughing to himself.

Taking a final look at the globe, peaceful and serene in its resting place, he departed the cave. It was late and he needed to return to the plateau and get a good night's rest. Tomorrow would be an eventful day. More dragons would be missing and the moot would suffer more losses.

Mossbeard and White-silver wouldn't return from the south. The same south that was home to the humans who despised dragons. Would the remaining moot members conclude, perhaps humans were involved with the disappearance of their kin? Would it be too much to ask they made that leap themselves? With a few well-placed words and hints, it was entirely possible. His plans were slowly falling into place. With Darkflame taking on one of his time consuming tasks, enjoyable as it was, it should help speed things along. It never hurt to have an extra pair of wings.

Soon he wouldn't need to rely on the cover of darkness and the secret skulking around. He rose into the night, a black dragon in a black sky, circled the caves once and turned north towards the Lifting Plateau.

Chapter 17

Predictable Enemies

Darkflame's missions continued, increasing as the weeks passed. She returned from her original venture, successful in spreading destruction and stirring up the humans, wherever she struck. Blaze instructed her not to fully destroy the towns and cities she attacked, leaving enough survivors to spread the word of rampaging dragons and their unprovoked assaults.

His campaign of destruction and terror against the humans escalated as more black recruits were converted to his cause. His instructions to them the same as those issued to Darkflame. He let them range farther south, moving into more populated areas, escalating the attacks, always under the glamour of coloured scales.

The humans began to fight back and some of his new soldiers were lost in the conflict. Human magic and projectile weapons were a particularly effective combination for knocking dragons from the sky. He had warned them not to get too close for this very reason. Humans were weaker than dragons, but they possessed their own magic and weapons. They were considerably more plentiful, and would fight back when provoked.

The newly converted blacks they managed to kill were a loss, but if they had been too stupid and too weak to survive their appointed tasks, it was probably best they were weeded out early. The strong would prevail while the weak were culled from the colony. When he came to start his new order only the strongest dragons would be worthy.

The eight remaining dragons of the moot were all gone. Ember, the orange female, hadn't understood his vision and she met with the same fate as Mossbeard, her magic and her life force consumed until she was erased from existence. The annoying Yesper was also sacrificed to the globe in the same way. Blaze thought the yellow dragon would have been a fine recruit and would follow him unquestioningly. He had even let Yesper watch as he absorbed Ember, demonstrating his power. The yellow was always eager to please, but after seeing Ember's fate the fickle yellow developed a spine. His cruel words of ignorance would not be tolerated and his life and magic were stripped from him.

The more he thought about it, Blaze decided he didn't like yellow dragons. Not only were they too bright in colour, it seemed every yellow he had ever met was annoying in one way or another. It must have something to do with their inferior pigment, he reasoned. They probably wouldn't make good black converts and were best disposed of. Every dragon had their place and for the ones that didn't fit with his plan, their contribution was a small sacrifice for the greater good. Taking another dragon's life was not something he wanted to do, but taking their life force—and the feeling he experienced when he did—helped make it easier.

After introducing his new black dragons to the colony, some individuals overreacted. He used the magic of the globe to smooth the transition, employing just enough glamour over the colony to prevent anyone questioning too deeply where these new black dragons came from and why. If any were too outspoken, they would be converted themselves, or suffer the same fate as Mossbeard.

Opinions were like scales, all dragons had them, but only the right ones were black. How could they not see that his way was best? They were too long under the guidance of Galdor the Soft. His tolerant ways of letting the humans take everything wasn't something his colony should be disadvantaged with. It was time to fight back and show humans who the dominant species were. No longer would dragons retreat and cower in the shadows. His scales may be black, but the human race would have no difficulty in seeing him or his vision.

Fern surprised him when she hissed in his face and told him she was leaving. Blaze thought that after Mossbeard's disappearance she wouldn't be able to think for herself or survive on her own. He regretted not taking her there and then, in front of what remained of their poor excuse for a moot. He should have absorbed her into the globe and shown them all he wouldn't stand for their rebellious ways or their unwillingness to see reason.

There were some things he couldn't change and Fern's timely escape, before his power was fully established, was one of them. He would trust his instincts next time and make sure he acted before any future incidents arose. The smarter dragons would see his decisions for what they were; protection of the colony. Individuals who thought they knew better than their newly appointed leader, would soon learn his way was best.

Azyrian's support of Fern's decision was surprising. The aloof metal didn't appear to care much for green dragons or indeed other dragons who didn't share his metallic scales. Why he would have left with Fern was a mystery. Unfortunately Blaze couldn't know the minds of these misguided dragons. Azyrian would have made a competent soldier in his black army. If Darkflame was any indication, metals, it seemed, were the most successful of his converts. They took easily to the transformation and followed his instructions unerringly. They showed no signs of compassion towards humans and were masters of destruction. Perhaps it was their typically aloof attitude. He didn't care. They were loyal to the cause and as long as they performed their duties and did as they were told, that was all he required of them. He would do the thinking and planning, his followers would do as they were bid.

The mutiny that followed after Fern and Azyrian's departure reduced the colony's numbers. A lot of the original defectors had been captured and brought to justice. They now served in his black army, faithful now their scales were the colour of his own. The others who were still out there would be found. His loyal black dragons were relentless in their patrols, sweeping up any strays they discovered and keeping the colony safe.

He knew the rebels were hiding somewhere and they had managed to elude him... so far. Their time would come, they would be brought home to the Lifting Plateau, the true home of all the dragons of Alvanor.

At least Sapphire and Chestnut were still here. They were no longer part of the moot, Blaze had assigned them a new and more important duty, one that would prove vital to the future of all the dragons in Alvanor. They stayed within the deep cavern beneath the plateau, protected and kept safe by their black chaperones. They were not prisoners and he was sure they knew he only wanted what was best for them, and ultimately the colony.

He long suspected that Chestnut's offspring could possess the potential to be true black dragons. Her dark reddish-brown scales were tinged with black. They weren't just a darker shade of their base colour at the edges, like the scales of some females. They were actually edged with pure black. Beautiful black. If there was a possibility of her young hatching and retaining their dark scales, he could breed a race of *true* black dragons just like him.

Sapphire was another possible candidate, her dark blue scales not too far off the perfect hue of black. She was certainly a better colour than the bright reds or yellows, or the more common greens.

When they came into season and were ready to mate, he would win their affections and clutch with them both. If their progeny were to result in black offspring, then it stood to reason he would need to be their sire. He was willing to make that sacrifice for the colony rather than settling with a life mate.

Blaze was unsure if his black converts, be they male or female, would produce black dragonets. Their original colours may have some influence on how their eggs hatched. The magic used to transform them was still a mystery to him and he didn't know if it was just their skin and scales that were changed. Did the process of turning a coloured dragon black, render them infertile? As of yet the newly turned dragons were uninterested in pairing. He would have to experiment, when the time was right, and select the strongest of his new order. But there would be plenty of time for that *after* the humans were eradicated. After he won the war he could devote his resources to breeding natural black dragons and strengthening their species. Chestnut and Sapphire would be given the honour of birthing his new order.

Darkflame entered the cavern of the moot and Blaze's dreams of an all-black colony, were put on hold. His first black convert didn't speak, she only growled, but her meaning was clear to him.

"They are coming?"

She growled an affirmative response.

"Good, they have reacted exactly how I expected." Blaze watched as the globe glowed brightly from its new resting place, as if reacting to Darkflame's presence. Swirling mists of white disturbed the globe's calm surface and two dull points of glowing red light pierced its cloudy interior.

It was better to have the globe near to him and after his power was established, he'd brought it home and housed it in the moot chamber. The former moot members had no need for the chamber any longer and he had no desire to establish a new moot. His word was all that mattered now, his authority and his decisions would guide them all, the moot obsolete, no longer serving any purpose. He would lead and the dragons of the Lifting Plateau would follow. If they didn't obey his commands or his rules, they were of no use to him. They would be absorbed to feed the globe and lend strength to his own power, contributing to the colony in their own way and helping his cause.

"Let us view the enemy," Blaze told Darkflame. "Show me where they are." He no longer needed to conceal the globe, no one would dare steal it away from him now. It deserved a place of honour, resting by his side in his new chamber, instead of secreted away with the stony blue dragon. Baelross could rest alone in the empty caves for all eternity, no longer was he needed to stand watch and guard Blaze's secret.

It was only right that he take the former moot chamber as his own. Only his most loyal blacks were allowed entry into his inner sanctum and they knew better than to enter when he wasn't home. They were given explicit instructions to guard the chamber and make sure no one entered in his absence. The globe was bonded with him and him alone, but it was better to trust no one. He was sure no other dragon would be able to take it from him, but it was better to be safe and remain cautious.

He took one last look at the globe as it's glow diminished, the two tiny points of red light faded back into its swirling mists. He was loathed to leave it wanting to spend more time exploring its depths and unlocking its secrets. But it would have to wait until he surveyed his enemy. It was always better to commune with the globe when they absorbed a life force together. It opened itself up to his mind and was freer with its knowledge, more inclined to share, when he fed it. Perhaps later he could find a dragon that displeased him and who wasn't an asset to the colony and he could drain its magic and enjoy the euphoria it brought.

Darkflame exited the cave without being instructed. Her *perception* to his needs and wishes was highly tuned; he liked that she was able to anticipate his wants. He had grown use to interpreting her growls and deciphering her grunts. It was pleasant enough when she was around and she never questioned him or prattled on. Perhaps she would be able to clutch black dragonets if he fathered them.

The morning was dull and cloudy as she rose from the flat top of the plateau. Blaze watched as she sailed silently into the updraft, her sleek black form lifting vertically into the air. She stretched her wings, splaying them wide to catch the thermals that rose from below.

Every dragon that lived on the plateau learned from an early age to ride the currents. It was a rite of passage for fledgling flyers, stepping off the sleep ledges into oblivion and catching the updraft circulating their home.

He jumped from the plateau's edge and caught the thermals, following Darkflame. Galdor had once shared with him his passion for the plateau and the strong thermals that created the unusual, yet natural phenomenon.

The former green leader was wrong about many things, but Blaze agreed with him about the beauty and wonder of the Lifting Plateau. Why would Galdor not fight for their home? If he were still in charge he would eventually let the humans drive them from what was rightfully theirs. Galdor's love for the plateau couldn't be as strong as his own, otherwise he would have agreed with Blaze's beliefs.

No matter. Galdor was gone, Blaze was in charge now. No humans would take their home or lands again.

The thermals pushed him into the sky, his wings spread wide to catch the uprush of hot air currents rising from below. With minimal effort he dipped his right wingtip and raised his left, turning slowly in pursuit of Darkflame.

She led them south until they reached the lowland plains, far beyond the river and the underwater cave where he discovered the globe and escaped the clutches of the leviathan.

After a few hours flight the enemy came into sight.

An army of humans were assembled on the plains, their colourful makeshift shelters scattered across the grasslands, littering the ground for miles. The once empty plains were now occupied by thousands upon thousands of angry humans, come to make war on the dragon race. Their presence was a necessary sufferance and Blaze knew he would only have to tolerate them for a little longer.

His careful months of planning and his continuous assaults upon their towns and cities had paid off. The results of his campaign of terror and destruction forcing the humans to take action. Actions much like his own. He wanted a means to an end and it was almost within his grasp. The constant attacks his black converts visited on the human settlements had eventually forced them to retaliate. Ironically, they, unlike Galdor, understood that if they weren't prepared to fight for their homes, they would be wiped out. Faced with fight or flight, they chose fight. It was time for dragons to do the same.

He overtook Darkflame and signalled her to follow, leading her higher into the sky. Once they were directly above the human army, they were high enough to be well beyond the range of their weapons and magic.

Blaze could see a long snake of tiny people kicking up a dusty cloud as they arrived from the south. The humans, it would appear, had mustered as many willing people as they were able to and their numbers still grew. It was obvious, just as he intended, their choices were limited. Stay in their homes and be burned or fight back. Their predictability was what he counted on. Nothing encouraged an aggressive species like more violence.

He grudgingly appreciated their compliance with his plan even though they were reacting like cornered rats. It didn't take much for them to fight against each other, unlike dragons. So when they were provoked, as was his plan, they would focus their violent nature on his innocent dragons.

His colony were unaware of his campaign, the black dragons he sent out on missions of destruction, remained a secret.

When the shocking news broke that an army of humans was massing on the plains, only two days march from the Lifting Plateau, they would have no choice but to defend their colony. The dragons of the Lifting Plateau would not tolerate this unprovoked human invasion. He would rally them to defend their home. He would reason it was better to attack rather than let their army get too close. There were powerful magicians and sorcerers in their army, no doubt the same ones responsible for the disappearance of Galdor and all the others.

Blaze spiralled at high altitude, surveying the human army and their reaction to the dragons above. They scurried like ants, tiny in size, but large in number.

This would be no easy battle, he knew their magic wielders were powerful. It would be wrong of him to underestimate their potential, especially as he knew one of their kind had been able to open a passageway between worlds. If the mage who assisted in Galdor's downfall possessed magic of such strength, others would have access to it too. Magic like that was not to be taken lightly. He would remain wary. It would be stupid and careless of him to underestimate his enemy and throw away everything he had worked for, especially when he was so close.

As if to prove his point, bolts of blue energy rose from below. The magical attacks fell short of their targets and dissipated before they could inflict any harm. A warning intended as a message–a message telling him they were prepared to fight–fell short. It would be no fun if they made it easy.

Blaze would give them their fight and revel in their slaughter. With the might of the colony behind him, his black soldiers, and the power of the globe, he would lead them to a victory that would be legendary.

He flew around the army and turned north, Darkflame following. Even at this height he could see thousands of expectant faces turn to follow their progress.

They wouldn't have long to wait. The dragons of the Lifting Plateau would bring fire and death to the plains and would bathe in the blood of humans.

He flamed the air, spitting out a long burst of dragon fire. The bright flames offered a defiant challenge to all gathered below, a reminder they would soon taste his wrathful fire.

He circled the human host one last time, Darkflame at his flank, then flew for home.

Chapter 18

A Call to War

Blaze stood on the plateau and gazed out over the assembled dragons. A seething mass of heads and necks swayed as the restless colony waited. Once he had been the only black dragon, now there were just as many black heads as there were coloured.

His guards were instructed to gather every single dragon in readiness for his announcement. An undercurrent of anticipation hung over the plateau as they waited for their leader to reveal why they were gathered. Returning from his survey of the human army he decided it was time to share the next stage of his plan with them.

On his immediate return he visited the globe, spending what little free time was his, in preparation for this moment.

He flapped his wings, lifting himself onto a huge boulder and elevated himself above the expectant throng of dragons. A silence fell over the colony as he raised himself up on hind legs, spreading his wings wide in a dramatic gesture, attracting their attention.

"Dragons of the Lifting Plateau," he announced, his voice booming out over the assembled crowd and breaking the eerie silence. The knowledge the globe supplied, taught him how to lace his voice with magic, adding volume and authority to his words. There was also an undercurrent of persuasion but just a slight touch, keeping it at an undetectable level as some dragons might sense the glamour. It was important now, more than ever, that any decisions they came to, should not appear to be influenced.

"I know times have been difficult." There was a buzz of voices from the coloured dragons. He carried on, ignoring their grumblings. "Our fallen leader, Galdor the Green, is no longer hero to guide us. However, the

Earth Mother and her magic have provided us with new support. Some have sacrificed themselves for the greater good of the colony and taken the black." That should give them something new to ponder. Let them believe the Earth Mother's magic was responsible for the mysterious arrival of his black converts.

A slight murmur of discontent surfaced from the assembled dragons. Up until now the explanation of unknown black dragons joining the colony, had never been openly discussed. He was aware of some discontent and knew the colours grudgingly accepted his new recruits, afraid to openly question the new order, unaware of where the black dragons originated. He used the power of the globe to cast a glamour of compliance to keep them subdued and accept the newcomers. But he could only use so much before the more magically attuned, picked up on his spell.

With the colony depleted and the new blacks possessing a greater natural strength, they had no choice but to accept them into their midst. The number of black dragons slowly grew, as they were indoctrinated into the colony and Blaze's acceptance and trust in them ensured they remained unchallenged. It was too late for them to change their minds now. The black scales of his converts were here to stay, soldiers loyal to his cause. The colony should be grateful they had new leadership that cared enough to create and recruit new allies against their faceless enemy.

Faceless until today.

"Many of our friends have vanished," he continued, gently using the globe's trick of persuasion, "and there is no explanation as to where they are or what has become of them." No explanation he was willing to share. Let them believe he was just as much in the dark as they were. He waited, stretching out the moment allowing the silence to descend once more, holding their attention. "Until now," he added after his dramatic pause.

Their murmuring grew to angrier grumbling, the colony eager to find the answers. Answers that had eluded them for too long.

"I now know what evil fate has befallen our brothers and sisters. I know who is responsible for these unwarranted attacks. Attacks on our very way of life. I know who has caused us great emotional pain and suffering." He waited once more, the voices of the assembled dragons rising, their anger and frustration fuelled by his theatrics and enhanced by his magical glamour. They were impatient to find out who their enemy was. They wanted answers and were ready to retaliate.

"Humans!" Blaze called out above the angry rumblings. "It is the humans who plot our downfall. They are responsible for our missing kin. Even now they assemble on the southern plains, gathering their strength. Their armies swell as more and more flock to join their ranks. They are confident we are weak and will not fight back." Their anger grew and their voices rose.

"Mages protect their numbers," Blaze continued, "and are readying to lead them into battle. They have emerged from the shadows and are preparing to bring war to our home. No longer are they hiding their cruel intent from us with their secretive skulking. They are openly gathering for an assault on the plateau!"

The colony of dragons snarled and growled, whipped into a frenzy by his words. Some argued with those closest and Blaze listened to what was said. They still didn't truly believe him and some, even now, after all his careful planning, were hesitant to take him at his word and trust he knew best. Galdor's soft ways had poisoned their natural spirit and made them weak. They were far too accepting of humans, just as their former green leader had been. This was his opportunity to restore the balance. He would change their minds and rectify their shortcomings, show them just how a dragon of the Lifting Plateau should behave. The time for clipped wings was gone.

He reared up and stretched his neck to the south and all eyes followed his gaze. "Look to the skies!" he cried out. A small group of dragons approached from the south, small specks at first, growing larger as they neared the plateau. The colony watched and waited as they came closer.

"I have sent forth a scouting party and have asked my most trusted advisors to determine the threat."

Blaze had instructed Darkflame to accompany some coloured dragons and fly south. He needed to let them witness the human horde for themselves. If he was to sway them to his way of thinking, he needed coloured dragons to help prove it.

Five dragons came to land on the plateau, dropping down next to the rock Blaze strategically perched upon. He glanced down at his returning subjects from his position of authority and introduced them to the assembled colony.

"You all know Sapphire the Cerulean and Chestnut." They were former moot members and their word would carry a lot of weight. He had allowed them their freedom to carry out his bidding. Even if they ventured out alone—without his trusted escort—he was sure they would have been compelled to return and share their fateful news.

"They were accompanied by our green brother, Sharp-tail," he continued. His tactful inclusion of coloured dragons in the scouting party would lend it credibility. "And they were protected by Darkflame and Charcoal." Two of his most trusted converts.

The five newly arrived dragons, a blue, a brown, a green and two blacks, all made their way towards Blaze.

"What information have you gathered? What have your eyes witnessed? The colony are eager for answers and wish to learn the truth." Let them hear the words from someone other than himself. It would strengthen his argument and solidify what he had maintained all along.

"Thousands upon thousands of humans are massed on the southern plains," Sapphire answered, stirring more anger. Her confirmation only made the colony more agitated, the noise of angry dragons drowning out her voice.

"Please, brothers and sisters," Blaze called out above the cacophony of outrage, "let Sapphire speak, listen to her message. She has travelled far to bring her grim tidings to us." His commanding voice, enhanced by his magic, sounded above them. It was gratifying when they quieted enough to let her continue.

"I have never seen so many humans gathered together and they are too close to the plateau for my liking." Her statement could not have been any better. She had seen the results of his covert attacks and recognised the impending danger.

"They reek of human magic," Sharp-tail added, raising his voice to be heard above the noise. "They are prepared for war. There can be no other explanation." His words adding to the fury already stirred by Sapphire's.

Darkflame and Charcoal moved to take flanking position on either side of Blaze's makeshift podium as if to protect their leader, sensing the colony's agitation.

"Strong magic. I can sense their spells as they prepare for attack. Powerful protection wards can only mean one thing. They are gathering for battle against us." Sapphire stated, reinforcing his earlier accusations. She was less rebellious now she believed his words to be true. He had told her humans were behind all their troubles. Now she saw for it herself, she delivered the message he wanted them all to believe. Perhaps now she would become his ally rather than rebel against his every word. He hoped her strong will and argumentative nature, would be placated. She would see him as their saviour and acknowledge him as her rightful leader.

An angry army of humans preparing to attack would sway many dragons to the correct decision. His decision. He had always been right and now they would see it. They must stand and fight for what was theirs. They must fight to regain all that had been stolen from them. Take back what rightfully belonged to dragons and ultimately rid the land of the human threat once and for all. What he needed to do now was convince them all that it wasn't just his idea. He drew on the power the globe provided and launched his final gambit, adding just a touch more persuasive magic to his words.

"Do you think they gather for war against our kind?" Blaze asked, knowing their answer could only be the one he wanted everyone to hear. He wanted them to speak the words in front of the assembled colony.

"They are protected by mages who ward their numbers," Sharp-tail said. "What other reason would they have for marching on the plateau?"

The colony rumbled its agreement at the green dragon's words. Of course they were gathered for war, any dragon could see that. After his constant attacks on their homes, they had one choice left to them. They were massed and ready to fight for their very survival. A fight they were fated to lose.

"There is wisdom in what you say," Blaze said, pushing a little more of the globe's magic into his voice. It would be less detectable now the assembled host were agitated and it would do no harm to stoke the fires and kindle their mounting anger.

"I am finished waiting for more of our number to disappear. I am done sitting back and letting humans take our kin and our lands!" Blaze shouted out. His words were met with a wave of growling voices.

"Are you not tired of waiting for more of your kin to suffer at the hands of this human horde?" Blaze called out. The colony rose its voice as one in a roar of defiance.

He roared back, "Are you ready defend what is ours and to fight for the lost spirits of all who have fallen?"

The colony's answer was deafening.

"Then let us wait no longer," Blaze shouted out above their voices. "By flame and fang, with talon and claw, let us stop these impudent upstarts and end our suffering!"

The black dragons that were now part of the colony raised their own voices with those of their coloured kin. Some even blew flame into the air.

The divide between his own dark scaled soldiers and the rest of the colony was closing. They would all be allies in the battle against humans.

"What must we do to stop this impending doom?" Blaze called out.

"Fight back!" roared Sharp-tail.

"Attack them now!" Chestnut screamed, caught up in the adrenalin fuelled frenzy.

"Attack! Kill! Fight!" The angry horde took up the chant, spurred on by their peers and the subtle glamour Blaze used to incite them.

"Let us take the fight to them. Let us attack before they realise what's happening, while we have the advantage," Blaze shouted. "Ignite your fires, dragons of the Lifting Plateau. Let your vengeance burn the scourge of humanity from our lands. Rise now on wings of righteous retribution and follow me to victory!"

He stretched his neck forward, tipping his head towards the sky and spewed forth a gout of flame. A beacon of hope for all who watched. A sign of his intent. He was answered in kind as the dragons of the Lifting Plateau returned the gesture. Their bright flames burning with the heat of their hatred. A just hatred, even though it was magically inspired. His careful planning and clever manipulation, along with the strength and knowledge shared by the globe, was finally coming to fruition.

"Rise up and fly south," he screamed. "Fly with your brothers and sisters, black and coloured, visit the wrath of dragons on mankind! Fly high and fight for your freedom!"

Blaze leapt from the huge boulder pounding the air with powerful black wings. The air below him was filled with thunder as the assembled host followed him skyward. The sound of over a hundred pairs of angry dragon wings cracked and snapped as the colony rose.

It was a sight to behold and pride swelled in Blaze as he led them to battle. At last he would command their allegiance. They would see him for the glorious leader he was destined to become. He would teach them the ways of true dragons. They would rain down fiery destruction on the assembled masses of the human attack force and utterly destroy them.

There would be casualties and he knew the human magic would claim some dragon lives. Even though he would be denied using their life force for his own intent, it was a sacrifice he was willing to make. The human army would be broken and then he would be free to take back their stolen lands. His army of dragons would emerge from their conflict stronger than before, forged in battle. Those that didn't survive and fell to the human weapons and their magic would be too weak to be part of his new order. Only the strong would be worthy.

Blaze gained height and sailed out over the plateau's edge on wings of black. The updraft caught his outstretched membranes and propelled him upward, the exhilaration of flight and the oncoming battle filling him with joy.

He craned his neck backwards and watched as the sky darkened, a mass of angry, battle hungry, vengeful dragons trailed in his wake. Fire rumbled in his belly and he knew there would be flame enough to share with his enemies. The globe had given him the gift of prolonged flame. His only wish was the following horde were able to match him.

Chapter 19

Now Battle Come Down

The human army scurried into action as the dragon host approached. They scrabbled around frantically like panicked antelope, running in every direction. The stink of fear emanated from below and Blaze was pleased his dragons struck terror into their tiny hearts. If he was a small human looking up at an opposing force of dragons, preparing for attack, he would have been terrified too. His airborne host were magnificent.

Blaze felt magical barriers of protection spring hastily into life. Human magic was easy for him to detect now, after his interaction with the globe. He strongly suspected he wouldn't be able to absorb this type of magic. Dragon and human magic were nothing alike. The globe had shown him how to use dragon magic and life force, but human magic was something entirely different.

He was able to identify it when it was present and could see a hazy aura of blue surrounding the army, strong and vibrant in some places, weak and translucent in others. He would use this new ability to his advantage, an advantage he would never have had if the globe hadn't enlightened him.

The places where the barrier was thinnest were the points he would direct his attacks, his army would still need to be careful, as he knew only too well some human mages possessed power far beyond their size.

He would rely on strength of numbers and when the others attacked, he would focus his globe enhanced flame on the weakest points of the magical shield. As his dragons flamed, they would weaken the magic that held it in place and his enhanced assault should allow him to break through and destroy the mages who held it together. Hopefully.

This was all new to him, never having attempted anything like this before. His attacks on the defenceless towns and villages were unexpected. The humans didn't have time to prepare any magical defences. This time it wouldn't be as simple as appearing out of nowhere, flaming and destroying, then leaving. This was war; a confrontation with an enemy who had prepared. An enemy who were ready to fight back.

Nervous anticipation seeped into his resolve. What if he couldn't best the human magic? Was he leading his dragons to be slaughtered at the hands of vengeful humans? The globe reached out from its resting place in the chamber of the moot, soothing his worries. He was Blaze the Black, strong and fearless. The globe would guide him, fill him with a power no human magic could stand against. He was ready to conquer the enemies of dragonkind. Together they would crush anything that dared stand before their might.

He shook his head, clearing his mind and dispelled the doubt, hovering in mid-air as the host passed him by. "Onward!" He roared, encouraging his followers. A wave of heat blasted over his scales as they flew by, the fire they held already scorching the air like a hot desert wind. Blaze was glad their ire was still stoked after his rousing speech, aware they must strike at the heart of the human army before their anger cooled.

"Ready your flame," he called out as they sped through the air towards the enemy. "Burn through their defences. Scorch and sear! Claw and fang! Flame and fury!"

Darkflame, never too far from his side, led them forward. Her sleek black form aglow with the flame burning from within. She was a sight to behold, her beautiful black scales all the more perfect as she glowed from the inside, stoking her flame. She peeled off from the front of the flight, tipping into a dive and headed straight towards the centre of the assembled human force. It was a manoeuvre he would have been proud to perform himself, fearless and bold.

For a second the momentum of the following dragons slowed and the host hung in the air. Blaze thought they were going to let her attack on her own and the sight of the lone black dragon filled him with a sorrow he couldn't explain. Then, as one, the host dropped from the sky, plummeting after the brave Darkflame, joining the attack.

Screams of rage sounded as the dragons plummeted from the sky, their battle cry like an eruption from a thunderous volcano. Their voices howled in anger, giving way to the ignition of flame as they unleashed their fire and directed it against the humans.

A ragged flurry of projectiles rose from the human host. Giant dragon sized arrows flew from their catapults and ballista. The air was charged with electricity, bolts of red and blue shot from the staffs of mages, magicians and sorcerers, towards the descending wave of dragons.

Darkflame led the charge, dodging the magical attacks with ease. A huge arrow sped towards her neck and she skilfully twisted mid-dive, rolling her body and letting the arrow miss its intended target. The arrow travelled on unimpeded and plunged into the chest of a small green following her, exploding as the magically enhanced metal tip ripped through green scales, impacting with the dragon's inner flame.

The sky was ablaze with fire as his army opened their jaws as one, spewing forth their fiery anger, directing it at the sorcerous shield protecting the humans. A roar of rage accompanied by the searing voice of rushing flame, resounded through the air, like violent waves of fire crashing onto a rocky shore. Red and orange flame washed over the protective bubble of magic, rolling harmlessly across the barrier's surface. The barrier glowed blue then purple as the fire weakened its spell.

Elation fuelled Blaze as he dropped towards the glowing shield, identifying the deepest purple as the most vulnerable part of the protective spell. It was obvious now to his globe enhanced senses, after the barrage of dragon fire revealed it.

Following his host, he swooped down towards the barrier and unleashed his own fire. His advantage over the other dragons were twofold. He possessed the ability to see the weaker sections of the barrier, the difference in colour easy for him to detect. He was also able to hold his flame longer—allowing for more sustained bursts—and it burned hotter. Aiming his flame at the weakest part of the barrier, he spewed forth the fire within. Intense flame assaulted the magical surface mixing the red of his flame with the blue of the barrier. Purple waves rolled and tumbled over its surface, scorching and weakening as they battled with the opposing force.

The sting of human magic repelled him as small lightning bolts of red tore into his unprotected belly. Blaze pulled up, pounding the air and gained altitude, adrenaline surging through his body, the sounds of battle adding to the excitement of the attack. He could sustain a few hits from the human mages without injury, but it would only take one well-placed attack to ruin all his hard earned planning.

He swung round and watched his fearless host make their second run at the barrier and followed in their wake. Some dragons fell as they were hit by magical attacks, others from the huge arrows flung from the contraptions below.

But they still came.

The bodies of the slain fell from the sky, bouncing and sliding over the barrier until they crashed to the ground beyond its influence. Pride swelled his heart, a strange mixture of sadness for his fallen kin and an overwhelming joy that they would follow him to their death. Screaming above the roar of the battle he attacked again falling on the barrier with renewed vengeance.

He focused his power, channelling everything he had drawn from the globe and pushing it down through his body and into his talons. Energy and magic sparked and crackled, writhing over shiny black claws honed with razor sharp dragon magic, destructive power in need of release.

Opening huge black wings, Blaze thrust muscular rear legs forwards, black talons reaching in front of his body like a huge black eagle descending on its prey. Red bolts of magic bounced from the underside of his open wings, the humans concentrating their magic on his attack. Pain lanced through his thick hide, penetrating the strong scales and burning with foul human sorcery.

Similar attacks flashed from below, disabling weaker dragons. Blaze watched as they fell, their hearts strong but their bodies no match for the magic that disabled them. He would need to show them the way, he would give them cause to witness his strength and his bravery. There were times when a leader must lead, show his followers he was not beyond risking everything for his ideals. He was stronger than them all, the globe providing the power and the knowledge he needed to succeed.

Talons stretched out, his claws splayed wide searching empty air until they met with the surface of the barrier.

Blaze screamed in defiance as his unstoppable force met with the immovable shield. A screeching howl assaulted his ears as the two powers came together. Wings outstretched and held rigid for balance, he fought to keep control of his actions, skating and slithering over the barrier's surface, human magic clashing with his own and sending jolts of wild stabbing pain through every fibre of his body. His talons glowed with a silver blue energy as he dug them deeper, gouging them into the shield's surface, sliding and skidding as the opposing magic fought to repel him.

He pushed harder, forcing aching talons down, pushing deeper and deeper into the unyielding barrier, searching for a way through. His wings ached, his claws screamed in agony and his legs burned with intense pain. His scales felt as if they would be ripped from his hide as the human magic battled to overcome his desperate attack. Neither side yielded. Dragon and human magic deadlocked. He focused his will and the globe's presence lent him the strength he desired.

And the barrier weakened... then gave.

Talons tore through the magical shield and the pent up power found release, flowing freely, no longer held at bay by the human defence. The furrows his talons gouged, pierced the surface, penetrating the barrier and opening a tear. His magic ripped into the shield filling the tear as it expanded. A deafening boom was accompanied by a burning red flame as it ate into the shimmering blue barrier, destroying the last hope of every human gathered beneath it.

The dragons of the Lifting Plateau regrouped, this time dropping from the sky with the knowledge their path to the human army was now free from obstruction.

The first wave of winged attackers spewed gouts of flame into the human army, searing life and scorching resistance. Flame raged into the ranks of men engulfing everything in its path, black smoke choking the humans lucky enough to survive.

The next wave of dragons followed, tearing through the scattering army with an intense hatred born from lies and deception. Most dragons had spent their flame on the initial attack, weakening the magical barrier. Now that it was destroyed they would rely on the other weapons the Earth Mother had given them.

Fang and claw, talon and tooth. The strength and power that were a dragon's natural gifts were no match for a human. Dragons were powerful creatures, augmented with strong limbs, tough scales, powerful jaws and dangerous tails. Even without their magic and their flame, not many enemies could hope to stand against a dragon and survive.

There were still small groups of human magic wielders, but now there was no longer any defences for them to hide behind. Dragons had free reign to skim above the human army, raking death and destruction through the surviving ranks of men.

Blaze marvelled at the human spirit. These pitiful beings were facing extinction, they had been harried for months and their homes relentlessly attacked. Their plight was near to its end, but yet they never gave up, they stood and fought. Was it a praiseworthy attribute? A commendable action? Or was it just stupidity?

If today was any measure of the credibility in fighting to the death, then it mattered not to dragons and even less to Blaze. This was the beginning of the end for the humans of this land and, if they were stupid enough to face his army, then they deserved to be wiped out completely. His retribution for all the wrongs these horrible men had wrought on his kind, and their lands, was completely justified.

He was restoring the natural balance of his land and he needn't stop there. In time his strength would grow to span continents and the humans of this world would fear all dragons, as they once had before they learned their corrupt, unclean magic.

Even though his whole body ached and he longed to draw on more power and energy of the globe, he would wait. If he relied on it too much, it almost felt as if it was in command of him rather then he of it.

Blaze landed next to a small group of surviving soldiers, their tiny weapons no match for a dragon. Lunging forward he snapped the first man in half, blood spraying from crushing jaws. Nets and lances flew at his hide, pikes stabbed at his flanks as he waded into their midst.

A sorcerer conjuring a spell, cowered behind his comrades. Blaze pivoted, whipping his tail into the group, the black scythe a deadly weapon, cleaving human flesh and bone as it tore through his enemies.

He stomped on the survivors, crushing and rending, claws tearing furrows in the blood soaked ground, a grim reaper sowing the soil with death.

All around him similar scenes of destruction were carried out by his host. The stench of charred human flesh mixed with the sulphurous smell of expelled dragon fire, filled his nostrils. The aroma of victory.

Through the billowing smoke and hungry flames, the bodies of the dead littered the ground, human and dragon alike. There were considerably more dead men than there were dragons. The loss of dragon life regrettable, yet acceptable and necessary. There had been a time when Blaze valued all dragon life. Witnessing the death of one of their own was a sad time for all dragons, but now, the more death he saw the easier it became.

He stood in the midst of the battle listening to the moans of the wounded and dying and contemplated when it was he had lost his compassion. He had tricked Galdor because he wouldn't do what was right and wouldn't fight back. Their former leader refused to confront the humans and acted weakly, choosing the easy way out and avoiding conflict. Galdor had no stomach for war. He was stronger than Galdor ever was. He understood the harsh realisation of war was unpleasant, but unavoidable if they wished to survive.

Blaze shook his head to dispel his doubt, hardening himself to the atrocities of war and pushing away his nagging conscience. It wasn't the time to stand around thinking, now was the time to seize this opportunity and fight for what he desired. These humans deserved his justice and all the unpleasantries it brought. There could be no freedom from their scourge until they were vanquished.

His mind touched the globe and renewed his resolve, promising its power and secrets, helping him focus. He knew it held more secrets than it shared with him and he was hungry to learn them all. He must carry on his path and see his vision to its end, only then would he truly master the globe and control its power absolutely.

A pitiful keening caught his attention and he knew it originated from one of his own. He sprang towards the sound, peering through the hazy smoke searching for its owner.

His sharp eyes picked out the crumpled form of a dragon through the smoke, its green scales marred with the black scars of magical attacks. A thick iron tipped spear punctured the green's wing, the projectile tangled and twisted awkwardly through the vital membrane. Dragon skin was tough and could withstand most things but the combination of cold iron, fused with human magic, had won through the unfortunate green's defences. The barbed point dug into the dragon's neck, pinning him helplessly as he flailed wildly, attempting to dislodge the spear and shake lose the thin wire netting the humans used to hold him in place.

Blaze could feel the human magic from the net and spear and knew the little green was rendered helpless. Even if he hadn't been wounded, he would have struggled to escape the potent combination.

Soldiers danced around the fallen dragon, rushing in and stabbing at the exposed flanks with long lances, the pain of each strike as they connected with his scales causing him to keen as the magic sapped at his strength.

The slow dance of death enraged Blaze, he was angry at the humans but angrier still at the green dragon who had allowed himself to be caught and humiliated. Lunging forward he sprang to the green's defence, appearing from the cover of the shrouding smoke, black and deadly.

The soldiers with their backs to him were unaware of the new threat as they focused on tackling the green dragon. The ones facing him retreated as his savage jaws tore into their comrades. Warm blood sprayed and severed limbs flew as Blaze tore into the attackers, talons ripped and jaws crushed, reducing bodies to shredded lumps of flesh. The black dragon was a terrifying sight, claws dripping with gore, his snout drenched in human blood.

"Help me," the green dragon whined, eyes rolling in pain.

Blaze whipped his tail forwards and coiled the python-like appendage around the spear, winding it securely around the wooden haft. He clenched his jaws tightly as the human magic jolted where his tail made contact with the weapon. Even for a dragon with his strength, the foreign magic was strong, stronger than he anticipated. His breath hissed as he inhaled through clamped teeth, bracing himself against the shock and steeling himself against the burning pain. Placing his front leg over the green's damaged wing to steady himself, he smoothly pulled the shaft free, ripping the remainder of the wing to shreds. Membrane tore beyond any chance of repair.

The green dragon howled and slumped forward into the blood soaked ground. Blaze pulled the restraining net free and threw it aside. It sizzled where dragon blood touched its fine wires.

He realised his didn't know this green's name or even recognise who he was. He was neither a trouble maker nor someone who stood out.

"Thank you, Blaze," the green wheezed, "you've saved me." It was plain that although Blaze had managed to save him from the humans, the green wasn't long for this world.

Blaze bent his neck and brought his head down, level with the green's, staring into his pale yellow eyes. "You have made the ultimate sacrifice for your leader and the colony," he crooned soothingly. He felt no pity for this feeble dragon, knowing he wouldn't be missed. He was just another casualty of war.

"You are broken and near death, yet you have one more important service to perform," he whispered. Confusion reflected in the dragon's eyes as Blaze leaned close and fed upon his life force, pulling his energy from the fading body. He no longer needed the globe's help as he slowly drew what remained of the green's spirit, savouring the all too brief moment and wishing there was more.

A gentle boost of power fed his tired limbs, filling him with a second wind and rekindling the heart of his dragon fire. He wished there was more to take as the last signs of life dwindled from the sad yellow eyes staring back at him. It was a mercy, the dying dragon was closer to death than he knew, and his passing, and the small amount of life force he surrendered, would help Blaze win this war. The usual rush of euphoria followed and Blaze enjoyed the sensation. The body of the dead dragon lay at his talons, broken and maimed. His green scales dirty with the mud and blood of his final resting place.

Anger replaced the short lived rush the green dragon's life force provided. A confusing mix of emotions, caused by his death, raged for control. Blaze wanted to blame the humans; if it wasn't for them, this wouldn't be happening. Could he have saved the green? Would he have lived? No! The globe reached out from the safety of the Lifting Plateau and drove the self-doubt from his mind.

Blaze reared up and spread his wings wide, roaring in defiance. He was stronger than sentiment. He was a leader and he needed to act like one. The colony depended on his guidance to survive.

He leapt into the air, smoke billowing in his wake as his wings propelled him above the battlefield. All around, dragons fought the human army and were winning. His fallen were outnumbered by the living as they clawed and bit their way to victory. Some dragons still had some flame left to call on and Blaze could feel his own, once more burning deep within his chest, spurred on by the life force from the dead green.

He swooped low, picking out pockets of human resistance and used his dragon fire to sear them from existence. He felt superior to his kin as he sensed their surprise at his sustained flame. Only a dragon of unsurpassed power could hold and use the flame for such a prolonged period. They didn't know his secret, all they needed was this demonstration of strength. They would follow him now without question. The dragons of the Lifting Plateau had been victorious in battle. Blaze the Black had proved himself as their rightful leader. Forged now in battle, his suspicions about the plotting humans witnessed by all, they were his to command.

Now he could take the fight to the human cities and put an end to the threat once and for all. Now it would be easy to convince his host the human race must not be allowed to continue. Their defeat here guaranteed the majority of their fighters were already taken care of.

Blaze surveyed the battlefield, allowing his presence to spur on his fighters, the taste of human blood unleashing their inner hatred. Today was a valuable lesson—the discovery of the true nature of every living, breathing dragon.

He wished Galdor were here to see what a colony of dragons, united under one vision, could accomplish.

Part Three

Fang and Flame

Chapter 20

New Skies

Sunburst flew across the blue sky of Galdor's world and Nightstar followed. The sorcerer, Alduce, submerged within the black dragon's mind, still marvelled at the fearsome beauty of the magnificent yellow dragon who was his constant companion.

Sunlight shone off Sunburst's yellow scales, reminding Nightstar of his words the first time they met. His friend still burned across the sky like a celestial fire, although one of the scales upon his chest did not reflect the sun like the others. That scale was a little less vibrant and had once been coloured black. The scale donated from his own body—a living part of the black dragon—in a desperate attempt to save Sunburst's life.

It worked in a way that Nightstar still didn't completely understand, sealing in his own blood and magically repairing the fatal damage wrought by the Extractor. It didn't matter to Nightstar how it worked. It just did and that was enough. Alduce, however, dedicated far too much time contemplating why.

He was a scholar and couldn't just accept it for what it was. He wasn't as bad as he had once been. Some of what he called Nightstar's *dragon logic* had rubbed off on him. It irritated the scholar and he said it went against his nature. Deep down in his subconscious, Nightstar could almost feel it himself. He was aware of the niggling thirst for answers, but that was all the Alduce part of their unusual bond. He was aware of it and accepted this too. It was what it was.

He had saved Sunburst's life, helped heal the dying yellow dragon and brought him back from the brink of death. It was magic, probably more dragon than human, and it accomplished more than intended. It also succeeded in repairing what was broken between them, forging their friendship anew—bound in more than just blood and scales. The bond created that day resulted in the most unconventional connection between the yellow and black dragon, tying them together and impossibly mixing the blood of both human and dragon.

Nightstar would not exist if it hadn't been for the blood Sunburst had grudgingly given to save his life, when once he had hated his human side. Alduce the sorcerer would most likely have gone mad, unable to withstand the transformation from human to dragon. Two warring minds fighting for control of a dragon made flesh by alchemy, sorcery, and scientific experimentation. The sorcerer believed the accidental catalyst of Sunburst's blood helped his transition, stabilising his sanity and allowing two sentient minds to inhabit the bodies of both his human and dragon form.

The sorcerer within the dragon thrived on facts and logic. His experiment to transform from man to dragon was his greatest success and he understood the physical transition and how his metamorphosis worked. What was still a mystery to him was the mind that had been born from the life force, the sentient spirit, of the unhatched dragon foetus. How it merged with the flesh and allowed two living entities to share one physical form, was a bigger mystery to him than he cared to admit. *This* was something he had accepted and followed Nightstar's lead, accepting it for what it was, grateful for the gift it gave him.

Nightstar had moved forward, taking Alduce with him, putting the how's and why's of exactly how it all worked behind them both. It was complex enough and wasn't worth dwelling on, he was a dragon, Alduce was a human, it was easier to accept than explain. They lived and shared, individuals and the same, each present within the other, but somehow separate too.

The sorcerer inside him still pondered how it all was possible. He was Alduce the scholar and Nightstar understood his human need. Being a dragon and an individual spirit in his own right, afforded him the luxury of dragon logic. It is what it is.

He glanced at his own chest, a star of silver gleamed upon the black scales and if he looked carefully, one of those scales wasn't as dark as the rest. Losing himself to the moment and the memory, a physical reminder of who he was. The mark upon his man's body was even more obvious in human form. A small yellowish part of his lower chest in the shape of a dragon's scale, slightly raised and more than a bit tougher than rest of his human skin.

When he faced forward again, Sunburst wasn't directly in front of him anymore. The yellow dragon's habit of changing course mid-flight, no doubt distracted by something on the ground if his spiralling descent was any indication, was part of what made him who he was. It was in the yellow's impulsive nature and so much the opposite of who Nightstar was, but he understood his friend entirely.

Tipping his neck forward, he plummeted after his companion, building speed until he was moving faster. As he streaked past the casually gliding Sunburst, he turned sideways and opened his wings wide, throwing out a buffeting wave of air that blasted the unsuspecting yellow. Sunburst flapped frantically, pushed from his path by the turbulence. Righting himself, he set his wings to his sides, diving after the speeding black dragon. Nightstar could feel the difference in the air as the yellow dragon tucked himself behind, slipstreaming in his wake. The yellow might not be as fast a flier, but he made up for any shortcomings with his smaller size and airborne agility.

Quick to react to Nightstar's playful challenge of racing to land, Sunburst managed to latch on to his speedier descent. He tucked himself neatly behind and below his tail, using his substantial bulk to break the air in front. He used Nightstar as a shield, punching through the air and allowing himself to keep up. Nightstar twisted and turned and Sunburst mimicked his aerial prowess, sticking with him, unshakeable. He was competitive, but no match for the mighty Nightstar when it came to this type of flying.

He could feel the yellow dragon accelerating out from underneath him, the air moving differently across his scales, each one sensitive to the change in air flow, alerting him to Sunburst's position. He wasn't going to let his friend beat him to the ground, he would never hear the end of it should Sunburst win. He would not let him forget and constantly...

Thump!

Nightstar spiralled as Sunburst bumped his hard bony head into the softer scales where his tail joined his body. The yellow roared in pleasure as he shot away from Nightstar's wavering body as he tried to regain his downward momentum. Celestial fire his tail! Sunburst streaked ahead, a yellow comet burning towards the fast approaching ground. Nightstar used the only manoeuvre left to him, sensing the race was almost over and second place wasn't an option. Pushing himself downward with all the power he could muster, huge black wings sent him into a plunging snoutdive. Air rushed over him, sleek black scales drawing on dragon magic and charging the flow, forcing it to move faster than natural across his body.

Sunburst was close to landing, but Nightstar had one last advantage over the yellow, he was faster than him when it came to stopping. Waiting until the last possible second Nightstar drew alongside Sunburst as the shocked yellow spread open his wings for landing. He pushed out his own wings, sending strengthening magic through membrane and bone, forcing them wide like huge sails. A thunderous crack boomed out as they caught the air, deafening them both.

Dust blasted up from the ground obscuring whose claws hit the earth first as the two dragons touched down.

Sunburst folded his wings, turning to peer through the settling dust cloud at Nightstar.

"Ah, there you are. What took you?" He cocked his yellow head to the side, raising the bony plates above his eyes in a comical parody of questioning human eyebrows.

"While you were looking behind, you failed to see my claws touching the ground before yours," Nightstar replied.

"I think not, my dust was drifting upwards to meet you, when you were still opening your wings! Surely you were tasting it from way back there."

"Ha! Sunburst, admit defeat when you are bested, we both know you were second, even after banging your hard head into me mid-flight. A somewhat desperate and failed attempt to slow my descent and be first." Nightstar wore a deadly grin, exposing his teeth, a trait of his human side that he didn't feel the need to disguise in front of his friend. Another dragon might have found one of their own mimicking human facial expressions strange, but Sunburst knew better.

"I will concede to the grinning fool beside me, this once. You've said it yourself, I am generous to a fault and yellows are known for their magnanimous disposition."

"And for their cheating and modesty," Nightstar grumbled under his breath. Sunburst, if he heard, chose to ignore it, faultlessly displaying his altruism to prove the point, Nightstar suspected. "Why did you decide to land? Did you see something of interest?"

"More a feeling. We've been flying over these lands now for two days and we haven't seen another dragon. Are you sure Alduce opened a gateway to Galdor's world? Is it possible we're visiting a world where no dragons exist?"

Nightstar touched the sorcerer's mind and knew Alduce hadn't made a mistake. "We are flying in Galdor's skies. We have come to the correct place. You are right though, my *perception* is alerting me to something too."

Nightstar had learned to trust his dragon sense, an ability that was known to all others dragons as *perception*. Alduce recorded this phenomenon in his *Atlas of Dragons*, his human explanation was as accurate as any, naming it a sixth sense, naturally inherent in all dragons. It wasn't like the other senses, more of an intuition, an inexplicable awareness of the unknown, uncannily accurate and never to be dismissed. It was stronger in some than in others and Sunburst's *perception* was keener than most.

The levels of how effective this was ranged from extremely perceptive to having a hunch or gut feeling. Regardless of the scale, *perception*, when it buzzed like an annoying insect, was definitely worth paying attention to. The human part of Alduce dealt in facts and the lack of scientific evidence was difficult for the man within the dragon's mind.

"I can feel my *perception* too. It is still difficult for me, as Nightstar, to fully embrace it. A result of my human side I expect," he admitted. "Although it is getting easier."

"Come Nightstar, we have discussed this. You are a dragon, nothing less. You have proved this to me many times over. Yes, there's a difference as to how you came to be, but you are a dragon, nothing less. Let Nightstar guide you when you wear the scales and let Alduce remain a passenger. You know I respect the sorcerer, I know his soul after all and we share more than a passing acquaintance." He snorted, making light of his comment. Nightstar knew it was a topic Sunburst took seriously. The sharing of knowledge and blood between Alduce and the yellow dragon had been an ordeal they both endured.

"If we both feel there is a strangeness to this land," Sunburst continued, "we should take heed and listen to our instincts."

"Wise words, as ever, my friend. It is difficult not being the scholar all the time. In matters of skin and scales, I am your willing pupil." Sunburst was many things but when it came to living and learning about the way of the dragon, there was no better mentor, no better guide and certainly no truer a friend.

Many of the yellow dragon's peers, the dragons of the White Mountains, didn't show him the respect Nightstar believed he deserved. He saw a different side to the yellow dragon, a side he liked to keep hidden from all but Nightstar. Sunburst played the fool well and if this was how other dragons saw him, then it was them who were foolish.

After his hero's return, rescuing the dragons of the eastern continent from captivity and certain death, Sunburst's social standing improved. The dragons of the White Mountains never found out all the secrets of their adventures and the events were shrouded in mystery, which was just as well. Sunburst's telling of the tale changed a little with each rendition, deliberately disguising the facts and exaggerating the story. Even Winterfang, the moot leader didn't know everything. The sharp-witted frost drake wasn't fooled, but he chose to let their version of the facts stand, believing it best for the colony.

Winterfang admitted to Nightstar he knew only too well how smart Sunburst was, urging the black to listen when his friend spoke. It wasn't all incessant chatter as others believed and the yellow dragon's wisdom was valued by the moot leader.

Nightstar valued his friend's wisdom too, not only had the yellow saved his own life, but he knew the black dragon's deepest secret, guarding it as only a friend would. And he accepted him for what he was. A black dragon *and* human sorcerer.

Their journey had been a complicated one, filled with many obstacles. Nightstar was continually thankful they had been able to rise above their difficulties and overcome the hatred and prejudice between human and dragon. Yet another reason he appreciated the wisdom of his yellow companion and all the more reason to listen now when he sensed something was amiss.

"You are right," he told Sunburst, "something isn't quite right here. This is Galdor's world, of that we are both positive." Sunburst nodded and Nightstar knew he understood the *we* he referred to was both his dragon self and Alduce the sorcerer. Separate entities, yet one as well. "Do you think the dragons of these skies live differently from your own? Is that perhaps what we are both sensing?"

"I don't believe it is," Sunburst answered. "It is something else, something... unusual. Yes, the dragons here will be different, but they will still be dragons." It was the simple dragon logic Sunburst found so easy to accept. "They will follow their own ways and customs but we are all descended from the Earth Mother." He blew a little snort of flame from his nostrils. He always did this when he mentioned what Alduce saw as the dragon deity. Then he looked sideways at Nightstar, "Well, most of us are. What I mean is the dragons here, as with any place we inhabited, will follow the cycle. We will be plentiful and we will prosper, masters of the lands for millennia. As the human population expands, as they learn and develop intelligence, discover magic, then the balance always changes. Our kind will dwindle and humans will advance. It takes a long time, but it is the way of things. On all worlds."

"But how can you know that?" Nightstar said. "How can you be sure?"

"When night comes and darkness covers the land, we know the sun will return, bringing with it new light. We know this to be true and accept it. It is the same. I just know it. Call it instinct, *perception*, or even your so called dragon spirit. It is the same with dragons and humans. Eventually dragons die out, become creatures of myth, just as it is on your home world. I believe that once our dragon magic no longer thrives, human magic declines and eventually becomes myth too."

"Insightful," Nightstar mused, "almost scholarly." The Alduce part of his mind made a mental note to quiz Sunburst more about this when they returned home. The yellow dragon was not in the habit of speaking about the Earth Mother and often changed the subject when he was questioned.

"Call it what you will, it is a knowledge dragons are born with. I can't pretend to know what has exactly happened here in Galdor's world, but I would have expected to have encountered at least one single dragon by now." Sunburst observed. "These skies are sadly lacking any life and there are no signs of habitation, dragon or otherwise."

"Many decades have passed since I encountered Galdor and helped him return home. It wasn't that long ago in terms of a dragon's lifespan, though. I know he was concerned about Blaze and what havoc the black dragon may have wrought in his absence. I fear whatever it was, it wasn't good."

"Now that," Sunburst hissed, "is a dragon that sounds like he would be nothing but trouble."

When Nightstar first shared Galdor's story with Sunburst, his friend developed an instant dislike to Blaze and everything he had done. He didn't blame him as he felt exactly the same. What really grated on his own nerves was that he and Blaze shared the same colour. Both black and both so very different. He worked hard to gain the reputation he'd earned with the other dragons he'd met. Being the same colour as Blaze and knowing his evil reputation, Nightstar was sensitive to the fact that all black dragons would be seen as evil, especially on this world. He would set the record straight on that score and prove to Galdor that dragons shouldn't be judged by their colour alone.

"Our first priority should be to find Galdor, while exercising discretion," Nightstar said.

"While I don't like skulking, I think you are right. You know Galdor better than I. Where do you think he would be?"

"It was a long time ago and he never told me much about his world. He spoke of a place known as the Lifting Plateau. A plateau is an elevated flatland..."

"I know what a plateau is, scholar! We yellows aren't inherently stupid."

"You just act it then?" Nightstar said, still bearing his teeth in his dragon styled grin. "I'm thinking out loud. Elevated land needs to have height. Higher ground tends to be hilly or mountainous."

Both dragons turned their heads towards the north where the distant grey haze of mountains met the horizon.

"North is a good direction," Sunburst said, "and I prefer north to east." He left the rest unsaid and Nightstar understood.

"Not as warm as the south and more likely to be where we will find dragons. Alduce's studies indicate that humans are more prone to the southlands. North it is." It was sometimes beneficial to draw on the experience of the scholar. Nightstar also needed to remember to let the dragon make the decisions, trusting in himself and relying on his instinct. The sorcerer had learned to accept the dragon's behaviour. When in dragon form, Nightstar was in charge and any actions taken by dragons were best made by dragons—and by the man, for humans.

"We should use the land as cover," Sunburst suggested. "While I don't think it dragonly, we should be cautious."

Sunburst still surprised him. Dragonly? Had the yellow made that word up just to emphasise his point? Alduce could use *humanly*, so there was no reason why Sunburst couldn't use dragonly. It worked if you were a dragon. And cautious? Nightstar wasn't sure Sunburst even knew what being cautious entailed. The yellow dragon was prone to rushing in, headlong—maybe necklong in his case—throwing caution to the wind. If he was acting cautiously, then it was with good reason.

"Agreed," Nightstar said. Then after a pause asked, "Sunburst?" The yellow turned to face his friend, detecting something in the way Nightstar spoke his name like a question. "Do you think spending time with us, or rather Alduce, in human form, is influencing your decisions?"

"What? No, of course not, although... " He tilted his head and drew his gums back, exposing his teeth in a hideous attempt at a human smile. "...I do have some of your tainted blood coursing through my veins."

"Tainted? That blood saved your life!"

Sunburst couldn't hold his strange dragon smile any longer and let it go, snorting loudly, nostrils puffing out curling wisps of smoke. His version of laughing.

"Remind me to update the atlas when we get back. I need to add another annoying trait I've discovered in yellows." Nightstar took on a scholarly tone, as if narrating from a book. "*While the yellow dragon is generous to a fault, their magnanimous disposition is marred by an underlying tendency towards ingratitude and unnecessary cruelty.*"

"And another thing human scholars should be aware of," Sunburst mimicked Nightstar's tone, "*is the yellow dragon's superior intellect and clever humour, never to be bested by the minds of inferior beings.*"

"North?" Nightstar asked, ignoring Sunburst's impression.

"North," Sunburst replied as he leapt into the air, "and see if you can keep up this time!" He twisted his head back attempting his human grin again.

Nightstar rolled his eyes, a typically human reaction the black dragon managed to carry off better than his yellow counterpart. Maybe it was due to the fact his human half rested inside. Or perhaps he was better at manipulating facial expression as he knew what it was like to have a human face.

Alduce made a mental note to record this when he returned to his human form. Nightstar beat his wings, taking off after Sunburst, recalling the shared memory of Alduce's former master, Caltus. *Always a scholar first*, the old man was fond of reminding him.

He would leave human studies to Alduce, for now, Nightstar was more concerned with *dragonly* matters: finding Galdor.

Chapter 21

Topaz

The northern mountains filled the distant horizon, bleak grey peaks shrouded beneath misty clouds. Sunburst's bright yellow scales stood out in stark contrast against the ominous backdrop. Nightstar scanned the ground below, looking for signs of dragon habitation.

They had discovered the location of the Lifting Plateau two days earlier, its impressive size and height obvious, even from a far distance. As Sunburst advised, caution was the smart option. Both his own and Sunburst's perception gave warning that all was not as expected with the dragons there. Nightstar couldn't decide exactly what was wrong, but something was most definitely amiss. The whole area felt peculiar and there was a sense of dark foreboding and corruption surrounding the plateau, tainting the natural beauty of the place. He couldn't quite place what it was, but he was learning to trust his dragon sense, even though he didn't fully understand it.

Sunburst's advice on *perception* was a little hazy and Nightstar was sure his explanation on how it actually worked was a mystery to him too and he just didn't want to admit it. The dragon part of his being tried hard to embrace it and accept it for what it was, while his human side always strived to find a deeper meaning, looking for hidden answers. Answer, quite frankly, Nightstar didn't really care for. A dragon must act as dragons do, so he followed Sunburst's example and trusted to his anomalous sixth sense.

They observed the comings and goings from the plateau from a distance, taking care to remain unseen. While they remained safely hidden and avoided any direct contact, they learned little.

One thing was clear, the creatures that lived there were not dragons in the usual sense. Their coming and goings reminded Nightstar more of a bee hive than a dragon colony. Sunburst didn't like it one bit and was adamant they shouldn't approach. He urged they scout the surrounding lands looking for clues, or perhaps a single dragon they could question without the risk of exposing themselves to the unknown.

If Sunburst wasn't keen to stick his snout into another dragon's business—a trait most yellows were guilty of—Nightstar would trust his friend's instincts. He knew deep down Sunburst was right as he felt it too.

After two full days and many hours flight, keeping low and doing their best to remain out of sight, they arrived at the foothills to the sprawling mountain range. With a good distance between themselves and the Lifting Plateau, things felt more natural here. He understood Galdor's passion for his home world as it was a place of unsurpassed beauty.

Sunburst flicked his tail, attracting his attention and used the flat arrowed end to point like a human finger towards the ground underwing. Nightstar was quick enough to catch a fleeting glimpse of a large blue shape, unmistakably a dragon, flitting through the tree covered hillside. The blue scales were easy to spot against the earthy browns and greens.

Nightstar tipped his head to Sunburst acknowledging he saw the dragon too and followed him down as he dropped into a spiralling descent. There was no race this time and he was happy to follow, keeping close to Sunburst's tail and matching his speed.

The blue dragon continued on its path, apparently unaware of the strangers above. Sunburst took his time and set a course to intercept the blue, deliberately angling his path to come alongside the dragon and avoid any sudden appearance.

Dragons don't frighten or startle easily—at least not that they'd admit too—and it would be better if two strange dragons didn't suddenly appear and their behaviour be mistaken as threatening or confrontational.

Nightstar recalled his first encounter with Sunburst and the surprise he experienced. His situation was completely different and it was his first time encountering another dragon. Sunburst had been observing him before he noticed he had company and although he would never admit it to his friend, he almost jumped right out of his scales. The yellow hadn't been aware of his secret then, and the sorcerer within the black armour hadn't known how to react. He was excited, terrified, surprised and amazed, and was astonished he was able to find the words and speak to a real dragon.

The blue eventually caught sight of its escort and Sunburst nodded a friendly greeting. The blue nodded back and turned its head to see Nightstar following. The change in its attitude immediate, panic obvious, its dark green eyes widening before it doubled its efforts to try and outfly them.

"Wait!" Sunburst yelled across the sky. "We only want to speak with you."

The startled blue pounded its wings, wild and frantic as it stretched out a long serpentine neck in a desperate attempt to pull away. Sunburst paced the blue dragon, keeping up with it without hampering its flight. His behaviour wasn't aggressive and before too long, the blue realised it couldn't shake off the better flier. Sunburst was excellent at dodging and weaving and was able to keep up—and best any dragon—over a twisty, obstacle filled, terrain.

"We just want to talk," he shouted. "We're looking for Galdor. Galdor the Green."

At the mention of Galdor's name, the blue slowed. "You are with a black! Do you side with Blaze? Are you under his compulsion?" The blue twisted its head back, still fearful of Nightstar and only a little less wary of Sunburst. "You speak like you possess your own free will and are no slave of the black that accompanies you. Land and we will talk, but the black must keep his distance. Know I will fight you to the death rather than succumb to slavery!" Without further discussion, the blue dragon dropped towards the ground and landed neatly at the edge of the thicket, positioning itself behind the outer trees, using them as protection against the two unknown dragons.

"Land in the open. You may approach, but the black cannot. If you try and attack me, trick or possess me, you will taste my fire! I'll disappear into the trees and burn everything behind me, you included." A low growling emanated from the blue's stomach as it prepared to call forth its flame.

Nightstar landed in the open, keeping his distance. He folded his wings, making a show of settling, in an attempt to put the agitated blue at ease, his demeanour as relaxed as he could make it. He didn't look like he was ready to give chase and hoped he didn't appear threatening. He was larger than the blue and it was a difficult task, as dragons were, by all outwardly appearances, fearsome looking creatures.

"This calls for a touch of yellow charm," Sunburst said landing beside him. "She's clearly not enamoured by your colour." He could always rely on the witty yellow stating the obvious, finding humour at his expense.

She. Nightstar realised that Sunburst was right, the blue dragon was a female. It still took him longer than a natural born to identify a dragon's gender, although it was becoming easier. He wasn't close enough to distinguish. Alduce surmised the longer he spent in dragon form, the quicker his natural abilities would develop. It was Nightstar's hope, that one day, he would react on instinct, without the human part of his thoughts getting in the way. "I will stay back, as she bids. Try not to agitate her any more than you usually do, please. She's one step from flaming. See what information you can find out."

"My words are as radiant as my yellow scales! Remember?" The yellow dragon quoted Nightstar's own words back to him, ignoring his quip. They were the words he'd spoken to the yellow dragon on the day they first met. Sunburst was right, he was a gifted speaker and words rolled from his golden tongue. While dragons were immune to their own beguiling speech—unlike most humans—Sunburst was endowed with what Caltus liked to call the *gift of the gab*. His old master said it was easier to call it that rather than saying the long winded version he sometimes like to employ; some people have a natural oratory persuasiveness, empowering them to convince the listener in favour of their point of view. Caltus liked to simplify things and on this, Nightstar agreed. And it wasn't just people who possessed this gift, yellow dragons—Sunburst in particular—had a certain way with words.

Although Nightstar only knew Caltus through the memories of Alduce, he believed his old mentor would have enjoyed debating and arguing his point with Sunburst. The two were more alike than he would choose to admit, he certainly wouldn't be telling Sunburst he resembled the human; at least, not anytime soon.

The yellow dragon made his way across the gap toward the blue female, taking his time. She had gained a little of her composure and stood out from the trees now, awaiting his approach.

"That's close enough," she said, the rumble of fire evident in her voice. "Tell me what you know of Galdor?"

"I am known as Sunburst the Yellow, my scales are the colour of the sun. When I take flight I burn across the sky like a celestial fire," he introduced himself. "I have heard the story of how a human helped Galdor escape imprisonment and freed him from the caves that held him captive for over one hundred years."

The blue dragon cocked her head, saying nothing, her green eyes staring at Sunburst, but continually flicking towards Nightstar, making sure she knew exactly where he was. Sunburst filled the silence with his usual mellifluousness. "The teller of the tale, my friend, spoke highly of Galdor and we have travelled farther than you can know to seek council with him."

"You know of Galdor's plight. It is a secret not all dragons are aware of. How have you come by this knowledge?"

"My friend, Nightstar the Black, is a very close... friend of Alduce the sorcerer. A human of some renown and a great friend to dragons. The man who saved Galdor and gave him back his freedom." The expression on the blue's face was as close to puzzlement as a dragon could get. "My black companion is a dragon of outstanding loyalty and has risked his life and saved my hide, and that of his kin, many times over. I am curious as to why his presence troubles you."

"He is black! Like the father of lies. Black of scales, black of heart." Little sparks of flame ignited on her saliva as she spat out her reply. "He wears the mark of Blaze upon his chest. Do not seek to beguile me with your liars tongue, it won't work! I am strong of will and won't be tricked."

"I assure you it is his own mark. The Night Star. It is a symbol of light, illuminating the darkness, silvery and bright. He is neither companion nor supporter of Blaze. His scales may be black but his heart is as golden as my scales. If you knew of his deeds, the great suffering he has endured, the sacrifices he has made, you would not judge him by the colour of his scales. You do him grave injustice. I am proud to call him brother." Nightstar was touched by the passion in Sunburst's words.

"Words, Sunburst the Yellow, can be bent by any fool for their own purpose. I have heard it from the very mouth of Blaze himself. His corruption of lies, his reign of terror, and his destruction of our ways—it all began with clever words." She stole another glance at Nightstar. "Why should this black be any different from the others? Why should I listen to your defence of them? Perhaps you are under their spell, compelled to trap me and turn me into one of the enemy."

"I know not of what you speak. We are from far distant lands and are unfamiliar with what has transpired here. Would you agree to a parley? I believe that once you speak with my friend, you will realise I speak the truth."

"What could a mindless drone say that would convince me otherwise?" Her voice was filled with venom.

"The mindless drone can hear what you say," Nightstar called from where he waited. "I assure you I am nothing like Blaze and I'm disappointed you see me that way."

"It's true," Sunburst said. "He is definitely not like any other dragon you've met before, I assure you. He isn't without his faults though. Questions everything. Always looking for answers to why—"

"Sunburst! You're not helping," Nightstar stated. His ability to stick to the topic and not get distracted could often be annoying and Nightstar understood why others dismissed him so readily. The blue, however noted the exchange and thanks to Sunburst's comment, visibly relaxed.

Sunburst turned and winked one eye at Nightstar; the blue never saw the exchange. He realised his friend was using his own eccentric ways to put the nervous blue dragon at ease. Thoughts from Alduce surfaced, tinged with a wry humour, *never underestimate a yellow dragon. Especially this one!* His human counterpart knew Sunburst's personality well, as the yellow spent a lot of his time interacting with the man. He shouldn't be so surprised and was pleased his friend had overcome his inborn prejudices—just as they both had. After all they'd been through, their respect for one another had grown, despite what they both were; man and dragon.

"Nightstar and I are not your enemies and I can assure you that we aren't under any compulsion. We have travelled here from another world and are strangers. We know this is Galdor's home world and he returned here after he was freed from his prison. What we don't know is what has befallen him or this land. Perhaps it is something you will share with us?" Sunburst asked. "We would gladly offer you our help and hear your tale. We passed the Lifting Plateau and could feel... a strangeness there. We avoided any contact with its inhabitants, our *perception* warned us something was amiss. Do you truly believe we are lying? Does your *perception* not tell you otherwise?"

The blue listened to Sunburst as he smoothly guided her to a conclusion she couldn't ignore: *perception.* A dragon's sixth sense was seldom wrong.

"We have shared our names with you, sister blue. We would like to call you friend, but do not know your name. Would you at least do us the courtesy of telling us who we speak with? You are the first dragon of this world we have encountered. Well, the first we've felt comfortable approaching."

The blue rose up on hind legs and extended her neck. "I am named Topaz the Peaceful. My blue is of winter's cold ice, pure as crystal. I once made my home on the Lifting Plateau, sadly not anymore."

"You are well named, friend Topaz. You are indeed a shade of ice blue I have never encountered before, and I've seen my share of cold winters. Peaceful, you say? I can see it in your demeanour."

The sarcasm wasn't lost on Nightstar and he wondered again if Sunburst wasn't spending far too much time with Alduce.

"I've often been told that," Topaz responded in kind. "Avert!" She turned her head and vented the fire she held in her gullet. Nightstar knew brewing dragon fire was an uncomfortable experience, especially when you held on to it. Even the severest human indigestion couldn't compare to the searing sensation of roiling flames, burning from within.

Topaz releasing her fire was a promising start to her believing they told the truth. "I have questions that need honest answers, Sunburst the Yellow. If we are to share information, I must be sure I can trust you. Both of you." She stared across the gap towards Nightstar. She may have released her hold on her fiery defence, but her manner was still guarded.

"Questions. Ha! You'll get along fine with Nightstar. As I was saying, he questions everything. He's known for his irritating curiosity. I have to constantly keep him right, explaining the finer—"

"If you truly know of Galdor's rescue," Topaz interrupted, "you will know what it was the human who helped him was searching for?"

"Mushrooms," Nightstar called out. "Alduce was searching for the black mushrooms that are native to the caves. The apprentice sorcerer was on an errand for his master and the last thing he expected to find was a huge green dragon. They didn't get along at first, and Galdor even threatened to eat him. The brave human helped the imprisoned dragon and even though he feared for his life, they both managed to put aside their differences and work together, which resulted in Galdor's release. I hope we can follow Galdor's example and put aside our differences, Topaz the Peaceful."

"How do you know this? No black dragon of Blaze's army would have this information!"

"As Sunburst explained, we are new to this land. I am no emissary of Blaze, in fact, I'm a good friend of Alduce. He has rescued more dragons than just Galdor the Green."

"It is true," Sunburst agreed, "he played a vital part in rescuing the dragons of Eusavus on my home world of Salverta. Nightstar did too."

"Blaze would have his colony believe that all humans are the enemy. Galdor has a different view of men. Even before he was tricked by Blaze, he was tolerant of their ways, leaving them be. Upon his return, those of us who survived the Black Cataclysm, welcomed our rightful leader home. Your black friend doesn't appear to be one of Blaze's drones and speaks with his own voice, but you are both strangers here," Topaz said. "We independent dragons no longer have a home, hiding out here in the wilds, avoiding Blaze's patrols. He hunts us down, stealing our minds, transforming us into something far bleaker than death."

Nightstar could detect the sadness in her words. Dragons were a long lived species and the finality of death was something that brought them great sadness. If Topaz believed the dragons who followed Blaze had been transformed into mindless drones, and this was worse than death, he wasn't surprised at her sorrow.

"We are sorry to hear of your plight, Topaz. A conflict between the dragons of your world saddens my heart. Please tell me if Galdor is alive. I need to know."

"I have said too much already. For our small colony to endure, we rely on avoiding the evils of Blaze and his followers. Strangers ignorant of our troubles, be you well intentioned or not, are a risk to our survival."

"We mean you no harm," Sunburst said.

"We would help you," Nightstar said.

"I do not think you can," Topaz said. "We endure, we hide, and we live in secret, fearful of discovery and the terrible fate that it brings. We are beyond any help you can offer."

"Are you truly of Galdor's colony? You don't sound like it!" Sunburst said. "I've heard the tale of the green dragon trapped in a cave. When Galdor was at his lowest, even when he believed his life was over and he had all but given up hope, Alduce came along and changed everything. How can you give up hope? There must be something we can do? Take us to Galdor—if you even know where he is—let us speak with him. Let the green dragon speak for himself."

Topaz glowered at Sunburst and her tongue danced like a viper as she hissed her displeasure. "Do not presume to know what we have been through. Our brothers and sisters were taken by a black plague that twisted their minds and stained their hearts. A vile torture, the cruellest of torments no dragon should suffer."

"I have seen my share of evil too, Topaz. I have faced death and known the blackest despair. I have journeyed to the beyond and been brought back to life. I have watched friends die before my eyes and been powerless to do anything. Trust me when I say I know your pain." He looked back towards Nightstar, the passion of his words shone in his wet eyes. "Let us help you."

Nightstar nodded his agreement to the blue female, "At the very least, let us try," he said.

Topaz shook her head. "It isn't my decision. I must consult with the others. If you really want to help, I will carry your message to Galdor and let him decide. Be warned, he will not tolerate any deception. He is skilled in detecting lies and sniffing out untruths."

Sunburst shared a look with Nightstar that said more than words could; Galdor was alive.

"I know a little about his ability to sniff out a lie," Nightstar said. Topaz fixed her stare on him, her piercing gaze demanding an answer. "Alduce told me," he added. "He said Galdor knew when truth or lies were spoken, said he was famed for his ability to do so. Allow us the chance to meet with him and his *perception* will show him we speak the truth."

Sunburst raised one bony ridge above his eye, similar to a quizzical human eyebrow. It was a human expression the dragon had adopted. Nightstar could feel Alduce's amazement at the yellow dragon's actions, impersonating the sorcerer's questioning look perfectly. The black dragon was positive the time Sunburst spent with Alduce was resulting in him adopting some of the sorcerer's behaviours. He wasn't sure whether to be amused or distressed.

"Very well," Topaz said, missing Sunburst's human gesticulation. "Wait here. Stay out of sight and don't get into any trouble while I'm gone." She glowered once more at Sunburst as if emphasising it for him alone.

She emerged from the safety of the distant treeline pacing around Nightstar and keeping her distance, her dark green eyes examining him with an uncomfortable intensity. The black dragon stood still and endured the scrutiny.

"There is something different about you Nightstar the Black, it is clear to me now. Understand, black dragons are the cause of our misery. I meant no offence earlier. I wish to survive and did not want to be consumed by the cursed plague Blaze has brought to my kin."

"Thank you, Topaz. I would be cautious too, after what you have told us. Your words are gratefully appreciated."

"We'll see," she grumbled, leaping into the air and stirring up the dust.

Sunburst came and stood beside him and they watched the blue female as she took to the air, keeping low as she flew over the forest. Her bright blue not unlike the colour of the sky. Nightstar wondered if it helped her remain undetected, lending her a natural camouflage when in flight.

"Topaz the peaceful? I wouldn't want to meet Topaz the Antagonistic," the yellow said. "I can see what she meant about being like the colour of winter's cold ice." He gave an involuntary shiver. "That didn't go too badly. Although I don't think she likes you much."

Nightstar didn't respond, unsure of what *too badly* might entail here on this world. He watched as Topaz grew distant, difficult to see against the backdrop of the sky as she grew smaller.

"Let's have a poke around while she's away," Sunburst suggested. "Oh, and Nightstar?" The black dragon pulled his gaze from the vanishing blue and looked to the yellow dragon at his side.

Attempting another hideous parody of a human grin, Sunburst continued, "I think you should do as she says and try not to get into any trouble!"

Chapter 22

Leviathan's Gullet

"She's back!" Sunburst called out, "Topaz the Peaceful. Let's hope she's in a better mood." Nightstar scanned the sky, looking in the directing the yellow dragon was facing. The single blue speck that was Topaz grew in size as she neared. She returned alone.

The blue female tipped her wings to them in acknowledgement, circling a few times above their heads before beginning her descent. She was checking the surrounding area, Nightstar realised, looking for hidden enemies, cautious of an ambush and not fully trusting their story.

"Be careful not to upset her, Sunburst," Nightstar cautioned, "she's still wary. See how she searches the outlying trees and undergrowth. She's checking for hidden enemies. We need to build trust with this female."

"I see. Females like me, Nightstar," Sunburst stated without boast. "She wouldn't have returned if she didn't want to know more about us. She is naturally curious, almost like a yellow. I'm sure I can convince her we are no threat. Yellows and blues are not as distantly related as your atlas might think." These last words were aimed at Alduce. Conversations with Sunburst were often a three way thing.

It was as well Nightstar was able to interpret which words were meant for him and which were directed at the sorcerer. Because he was both Alduce and the dragon, he understood perfectly. The scholar within made a mental note, another example of a dragon's ability to adapt to an unusual situation. The yellow dragon was always a quick study. Sunburst only spoke to both of them when they were alone. When they were in company he never forgot their secret and was careful with his words.

"Not all *dragons* are as trusting you, Sunburst," the black dragon said, focusing on being the dragon and not the man. "Your natural curiosity has often led to... situations... that were best avoided. Fly lightly around this one, she's still nervous."

"Nervous of *you* perhaps. Where is your sense of adventure, your dragon spirit? Don't you want to find Galdor? I will convince her we are friends. Trust me."

"I do, Sunburst." The yellow dragon was many things, but firstly he was a trusted friend. Nightstar had earned his trust and proved his friendship. It was a hard road they had travelled, their friendship forged in adversity. Both sacrificed much for the other and Nightstar trusted Sunburst with his secret, and more. "I trust you with my life. As I trust you will now speak carefully to Topaz. Try not to get under her scales."

"And not all dragons are as trusting as you either, Nightstar." He raised the ridges above his eyes again in the now familiar parody of a human expression. Sunburst quite often took his words and turned them back on him. Nightstar found this talent both endearing and annoying. It was difficult to tell whether he was being sincere or making a joke at his expense. The expression on his yellow face showed nothing of the smug look he wore when he joked.

"I thank you for the complement, Sunburst." He really was getting a lot better at reading a dragon's expression.

When Alduce first manifested into Nightstar, he was a human learning the dragon way. A man inside a dragon skin. Nightstar had come a long way since then. "See if you can earn her trust. Use your charm and put her at ease," Nightstar said before Topaz neared.

She dropped into the clear ground in front of the trees she'd previously used as shelter. She kept her distance, using Sunburst as a barrier between herself and the black dragon, but was closer than before, which was surely a good sign.

"Welcome back, Topaz the Peaceful, blue as winter's ice, pure as crystal," Sunburst greeted her. He gave a short bow of his head, showing respect. "What news from Galdor the Green?"

"Galdor is well. I have talked with him at length about you both. He is curious as to why two strangers seek him out. He remembers the past. How could he not after all he endured? Alduce paid him great service and he has never forgotten the human who helped him. It is on the strength of his name alone that he has agreed to see you both."

"That is good to hear," Sunburst said. "He will not be—"

"Be warned," Topaz snapped. "Galdor is not stupid. He will not be tricked. Should your intentions be anything other than friendly you will suffer not only his wrath, but the wrath of all free dragons! By claw, fang and flame! If you attempt any treachery you will not survive against us."

"We intend no tricks, no treachery or duplicity, I assure you. We have arrived in your land, and it appears, into the middle of an unknown conflict of which we are ignorant. We will help if we can." He looked to Nightstar. "My black scaled friend here is extremely intelligent and has a way of looking at problems through different eyes. And not without some success. I am sure when Galdor meets with him, he will see his worth as both friend and ally."

"Do not presume to know what Galdor thinks," Topaz said. "If it were up to me, I would have left you here and never returned."

"I'm sure Sunburst didn't mean anything presumptuous," Nightstar said. "We are both excited to meet the legendary Galdor. We are honoured he will see us, especially as there is unrest here. It is clear to us you are concerned for his safety." It wasn't due to Sunburst's usual lack of tact that this female was difficult. The yellow dragon was making every effort not to upset her. "I know once we have spoken with him he will understand more about us, myself in particular. I give you my word and my oath that my intentions are not harmful and I am not part of any conflict or ruse." An oath between dragons was a solemn promise and was never given lightly.

"You are a strange one, Nightstar," Topaz said. Nightstar didn't risk looking at Sunburst. The yellow dragon wouldn't intentionally let slip just how strange he was. However, with Sunburst there was always a chance he would say something flippant or make a comment that may attract unwanted attention.

"Your oath and your word I will accept," Topaz said. "My trust you must earn. We have a ways to go and I am sure you are both eager to begin the last part of your journey. I will lead. Sunburst will follow. Nightstar will stay behind Sunburst at all times." Her commanding tone brooked no argument from either black or yellow. "Do not fall behind and do not crowd me. We will be flying low and keeping to cover where we can. If I drop to the ground, be ready to follow. Keep your eyes open and if you see any signs of pursuit, call out.

"I am taking you to a secret location. It is our safe haven and is unknown to Blaze and his followers. Once you have visited, you will not be granted leave unless we know we can trust you. Do you still wish to follow where I lead?"

"We do," Sunburst replied, inclining his head to Nightstar.

"Sunburst speaks for us both," Nightstar said. "We are ready, Topaz. Please take us to Galdor."

"Try to keep up," she called out as she sprang into the air.

"Try to keep up!" Sunburst started, "We... " Nightstar shook his head at Sunburst in a distinctly un-dragonlike way.

"We will surely try our best to keep up with you, Topaz," the yellow dragon said, biting back his words and swallowing what he was about to say. Nightstar silently thanked his friend for holding his tongue. Topaz did not need a lecture about how much better a flier Sunburst thought he was, even though he could most likely fly the wings off the blue female. He was sure the yellow would no doubt look for a later opportunity to prove this to her.

Sunburst like to lead and he was surprised at the restraint his friend displayed. Perhaps the time Sunburst had spent in the company of his human counterpart, wasn't just teaching him bad habits.

He followed the yellow dragon into the air as he, in turn, shadowed their blue guide, not flying too close and maintaining an acceptable distance. He was glad Sunburst recognised the importance of her request and was happy enough to go along with her instructions for now.

Originally their trip through the Flaire portal was intended to be a journey to a new world and an opportunity to seek out Galdor. It was now turning into something more serious. The feeling they both experienced when they neared the Lifting Plateau was not pleasant. If he was to describe how it made him feel as a human, he would say it made his skin crawl. Something was wrong with this world and it was only reinforced by the way Topaz reacted, adding to his suspicions.

Alduce bore a great affinity for all dragons. His experiences as Nightstar only strengthened his love for the species. He was more than a man who took the shape of a dragon. He was the spirit of Nightstar and the essence of a real dragon, even though he wasn't hatched from the shell. The blood of dragons ran through his veins, transforming him into a separate entity. He was both his own individual creature and a man.

It was difficult for the sorcerer to explain, especially as he was a scholar and took great pride in his ability to seek out the answers. Nightstar, with the help of Sunburst, was able to accept the dichotomous relationship, embracing his dragon logic without overthinking it.

If Galdor and his companions were in need of help, he would do everything in his power to assist them. Sunburst would probably have something to say on the matter, he always did. However, they shared more than blood and he would support Nightstar's decision to assist in whatever way they could and follow where he led.

Until they knew all the facts they were in the dark. He hoped after speaking with Galdor, the green dragon would be able to explain exactly what was going on. Maybe then, Nightstar, with the help of Alduce and Sunburst, could offer these dragons some help.

First he would need to convince Galdor and gain his trust. If the green dragon was as cautious as Topaz, it would prove a difficult task. Facing Galdor and gaining his trust was something he had previous experience with. When Alduce last helped the green dragon, there was a certain amount of luck involved. Alduce didn't rely on luck anymore and the apprentice he'd once been was long gone.

He was now Nightstar the Black as well as a master sorcerer. He possessed the knowledge of all his magical studies, both human and dragon. He was able to cast spells using a mixture of both human and dragon magic, unconventionally blending and mixing them to surpass the sum of their whole. It was a magic unknown and unexplored and it shouldn't exist, but it did. And he commanded it. Like any unknown magic, it could be dangerous and required discipline. It was a power beyond that of anything previously seen by the known worlds or chronicled in any writings.

If he was unable to convince Galdor his intentions were good, well, there were other means at his disposal.

* * *

Topaz led them north following the natural contours of the land. Her flight undulated, using the hills and valleys to every advantage in an effort to remain unobserved. She chose an indirect route to their secret destination, zig-zagging over the terrain, rarely flying in a straight line. She avoided leading them through open skies where possible and when it was necessary, she made haste, hurrying for the nearest shelter.

The land became more remote and as far as Nightstar was aware, there were no discernible traces of dragons to be found.

After a short while another dragon appeared, materialising out of a dense forest to their far left. The dragon paced them perfectly, remaining ahead of Topaz. She was a small emerald green. Nightstar was pleased he was able to make the distinction, his *perception* identifying her as female. She used the camouflage of the trees, the green of her scales blending in with the foliage, until she chose to make herself visible.

Topaz tipped her wings to their escort, signalling her presence, before they were able to call out a warning to her. She wasn't showing any outward signs of panic and it was obvious the distant addition to their group was expected.

From his vantage point at the rear of the group, Nightstar noted Sunburst's head, swivelling between the two indigenous dragons, observing the exchange. He faced back towards Nightstar and flared the ends of his wings, rapidly flapping them up and down a few times, the dragon equivalent of a shrug.

They continued on and another dragon appeared from above, a streak of orange-brown passing diagonally in front of Topaz and taking up a flanking position on the right, directly opposite the green female. Nightstar could tell their second chaperone was a male.

A whiff of charcoal and sulphur hung in the air. Both the orange-brown male and the green female were ready to flame, should they need to protect against the strangers in their midst. These dragons were far less trusting than the dragons of the White Mountains; the home of Sunburst. When Nightstar travelled to the world of Salverta and visited the continent of Aurentania—the land where the White Mountains were situated—his welcome had been a warm one. After proving himself in the eyes of the dragons living there, it was now his adopted home.

His experiences with these new dragons were completely different to the friendliness he had come to expect. The scholar buried deep within stored the information for his human side. Usually, Nightstar would leave thoughts that were typically human, to Alduce. As a dragon, he was concerned the species here (wherever *here* was, the Alduce side of him thought) appeared to be split into two opposing factions.

Nightstar realised, after the brief touch with his counterpart's subconscious, he didn't even know the name of Galdor's world. Alduce was eager to know what this world was called. When the sorcerer had something he wanted to know, his thoughts were more intense, reaching through the veil that was Nightstar's consciousness.

The dragon side of his being was separate from the man. Neither one fully understood how it worked, two parts of the one whole, together yet apart. Nightstar was content with how it was and accepted it; dragon logic was a lot less complicated than human. He was the dragon, Alduce was the human. He was aware of everything the man was, both manifestations different physically, yet there were two minds sharing the same body. It was what it was. Alduce still searched for a definitive answer as he just wasn't ready to stop looking for an explanation. Alduce was always a scholar at heart, it was what made him who he was.

Topaz began a slow descent, setting her wings into a fixed glide, dropping into a dark chasm cleaved into the ground beneath them. The chasm looked deep and even with the advantage of viewing it directly from above, Nightstar wasn't able to see how far down into the ground it stretched.

Sunburst stuck to Topaz as she entered the mouth of the chasm, matching her steep dive into the ominous gap. He was too close to the blue female, barely a snout's length from the tip of her tail. Nightstar hoped he remembered her warning about crowding her. The yellow would be resentful of her comment telling them to *try* and keep up with her. There was one thing he was sure of and it was that no other dragon he knew, not even he himself, could best Sunburst through terrain like this. He was the master of short fast flight, quick to turn with the ability to weave his way through tight, impossible spaces. Perhaps it was his size, perfect for ultimate manoeuvrability, the optimum power to weight ratio that proved best for aerial prowess. Furthermore, he was a yellow and most yellows possessed a serious competitive streak.

The Earth Mother, Sunburst often reminded him, gifted him with the ability to outfly any dragon and the determination to prove it to any who doubted. Nightstar himself couldn't catch the nimble yellow over an obstacle strewn flight path. Anywhere Topaz led them, his friend could surely follow. He just hoped it wasn't too much to expect Sunburst to exercise a little humility and not rub the blue female's snout in the dirt. He understood their situation and Nightstar trusted him not to upset her, even though he found it difficult not to show off. As if in answer to Nightstar's thoughts, Sunburst reigned back and let the blue pull in front a little.

Nightstar tucked his wings close to his body and entered the chasm, his eyes adjusting to its dim interior. He quickly came to understand why Sunburst had backed off his pace. The slow curving path leading down into the depths twisted sharply before him, causing him to throw out his wings to slow his speed. Thankfully the deceptive width of the chasm mouth wasn't a true indication of its inner size. He was able to open his wings fully, allowing him to slow down, then he quickly twisted in mid-air and came to rest in a huge subterranean alcove beside Topaz and Sunburst.

He peered over the edge of the rock, mighty talons gripping the stone a little harder than necessary, adrenalin surging thorough his body. A bottomless drop fell steeply into the darkness of the chasm. With his neck extended out over the precipice, Nightstar's head was buffeted by a strong current of turbulent air. No wonder turning tightly in the space before the alcove had been difficult. The turbulent updrafts surging through the chasm added to the difficulty of navigating its hidden entrance, added to that, the walls were covered with dangerous looking rocks, sharp and ragged, like the teeth filled maw of some gargantuan monster, hungry for dragon.

"Nicely done," Sunburst commented. "I wasn't sure your considerable bulk would manage such a disciplined manoeuvre."

"Isn't it strange," Nightstar retorted, his heart hammering in his chest, "the more I practice, the better I get."

If any dragon flying inside the chasm misjudged the sharp turn into the alcove, it would result in a collision with the jagged rock and a fatal tumble into the dark depths. Once you were made aware of what you needed to do to navigate it safely, it would certainly be easier, but still difficult due to the unpredictable air currents.

He wondered why Topaz hadn't given them prior warning. Did she still regard them as the enemy? Was it some kind of test to prove their worthiness? Would she have cared if they plummeted to their death? It was sad to think that she cared so little for other dragons and it was further indication things were far from well.

"Practice makes perfect," Sunburst said, lightly mimicking Alduce.

"The Leviathan's Gullet," Topaz said as Nightstar drew back from the edge. "A natural defence against uninvited guests."

A rush of wind swept through the chasm and the two dragons that had joined them for the final leg of their flight, appeared in the space opposite the alcove. They both twisted with practiced ease, turning smartly in mid-air and landing at either end of the ledge.

"Report," Topaz said to the green female.

"All clear. You weren't followed. All is as it should be," she answered.

"No sign of bla... " the orange-brown male looked at Nightstar, "the enemy," he amended, his gaze fixed on the newcomers.

They both still held their flame in check, the sulphuric stink of unreleased dragon fire heavy in the alcove.

"Nice place," Sunburst said. "Easily defended and well concealed. I can see why you would want to keep its location secret."

"You haven't seen the best of it," the orange-brown male said.

"Ryvind!" Topaz said. "Hold your tongue."

"We have allowed our guests to enter into our home, even if you disagree with Galdor's decision," Ryvind retorted. "We agreed to listen to them and hear their story. Would it hurt you to show a little courtesy?"

"Will courtesy prevent my scales from becoming black? Will it save me from the mindless torture our brothers and sisters have fallen to? I'm alive and have free will. Flame your courteous behaviour!"

"Well said, Ryvind," a deep voice echoed from deep within the alcove. "What will we become if we do not remember who we are? Understand, Topaz only has the best interests of our colony at heart. Do not judge her too harshly."

A huge green dragon emerged from the shadows behind them—Galdor the Green—flanked on either side by two equally impressive dragons, one bronze, the other a deep dark red. They appeared from the darkness to stand in the alcove mouth, blocking the passageway behind them. If there was any trouble, Nightstar and Sunburst would be at a serious disadvantage, surrounded on all sides with only one means of escape, back into the Leviathan's Gullet.

Chapter 23

Introductions

Galdor was an imposing sight, standing taller than any of the dragons on the rocky ledge. Alduce remembered him from the cavern—his first encounter with the huge green. He had looked enormous to the human and even in his dragon form, Nightstar was impressed by his size... and a little intimidated. His green scales shone as they had when he shed his scales, all those years ago, vibrant and bright. Galdor wasn't just a dragon, he was a king amongst his kind, regally majestic and spectacularly resplendent.

For all his magnificence, Galdor was no pompous monarch. He was ready to face any potential threat to his secluded colony and deal with it without hesitation. He stood ready for action, tense and alert to any danger, his followers standing alongside him. Nightstar was aware that one word from Galdor would put an end to their tentative acceptance, should he command it. But there was also a curiosity about the large green dragon, a look in his bright eyes that invited friendship, should you be worthy.

"It is my pleasure to finally meet you, Galdor the Green," Sunburst said, filling the uncomfortable silence, which until now, Nightstar hadn't been aware of. Once more he found himself transfixed by Galdor's appearance, unaware he was staring and glad Sunburst showed the good sense to speak.

Sunburst bowed low, tucking one of his forelegs beneath his bright yellow chest and paid his respects to the towering green.

He rose and said, "I am known as Sunburst the Yellow, my scales are the colour of the sun. When I take flight I—"

"Burn across the sky like a celestial fire," Galdor finished. "So I have heard."

"I see my reputation proceeds me," Sunburst said, only sounding slightly deflated at Galdor's interruption.

"Topaz has told me all about you," Galdor replied. "Or as much as she knows."

"All good, I hope," Sunburst said, winking at the blue female. Topaz chose to ignore him.

"We will see," Galdor said.

Nightstar let Sunburst speak. His friendly demeanour and good natured way were perfect for putting everyone at ease and the yellow did have his own way with words.

"I have heard the legendary tale of your encounter with Alduce the sorcerer," Sunburst continued, "and we bring you his respectful regards."

"Interesting, Sunburst the Yellow, very interesting indeed. My *legendry encounter* with Alduce is one I shall never forget. I am intrigued to learn how it is, on a world that isn't my own, you learned of this."

"A tale worthy of the telling. We have journeyed far and travelled in a most unconventional way, to stand here before you."

"I look forward to that tale, Sunburst, and you will have every opportunety to regale us with your bard's tongue." The yellow dragon dipped his head in acknowledgment and Nightstar was glad, this time Sunburst understood Galdor's meaning and knew when to hold his *bard's tongue*. He knew from his own experience Galdor desired more than clever words.

"I see you speak the truth, little yellow and can sense no evil in you. Before I listen to all you have to say, and I do believe that to be much, I would know more of your black companion. The colour of his scales gives me great concern."

Sunburst raised himself up, stretching his hind legs. "This is Nightstar the Black. The star upon his chest, silvery and bright, chases the shadows of doubt and illuminates the darkness." Trust Sunburst to add his own embellishments to his introduction. "I understand your concerns, mighty Galdor, however, know I speak the truth when I tell you Nightstar is my brother. We are bound by blood and I trust him with my life." He nodded to Nightstar. "He is also friend to Alduce the sorcerer and owes the man a debt greater than your own." Galdor cocked his head and stared at him.

Alduce had created Nightstar and he would always be thankful for to the sorcerer for giving him life. He wasn't sure he owed a debt to the man, especially as Alduce was part of him. It was time to step in and prevent Sunburst, well intentioned as he was, from complicating matters.

"Thank you Sunburst, your heartfelt words, as always, mean much to me." He copied the yellow's gesture and performed a respectful bow to Galdor. "I am saddened to hear my black scales are an omen of evil in your land. After the brief explanation Topaz gave and her reaction to my presence, I can understand why you would be distrustful of me." He straightened, meeting Galdor's yellow eyes. "Please believe me when I say I mean you no harm. I am no threat to you or you kin. Look into my eyes, Galdor, see if I lie. I know you can tell." The last few words left his mouth before he realised these were the same ones spoken by Alduce, when Galdor had confronted the man many years ago.

"I can see you are not like the other blacks we have had the misfortune to encounter. You shall answer my questions to my satisfaction and I will decide what is best for our colony. You are an enigma to me Nightstar. There is something strange about you."

"He gets that a lot," Sunburst said, then hurried to add, "I myself said that upon our first encounter and my moot leader, Winterfang thought so too. Where we come from, blacks are rare."

"We have much to discuss. Do not fear, you will be treated fairly. I need to protect what little we have left. The colony comes first, before any individuals. The decisions of a former moot leader are difficult and are never made lightly. I asked Topaz to bring you here against much protest.

You have only been allowed to come this far as you claim to know Alduce. The dragons that still reside at the Lifting Plateau do not know the sorcerer's name. If you are aware of his existence and his connection with my past, then I would learn of it. I'll admit, my curiosity is piqued." Galdor surveyed the alcove, crowded now with his five dragons, himself, Nightstar and Sunburst.

"Before we go any further, there are traditions that must be followed. As my rust coloured friend rightly pointed out, courtesies to be adhered to. Where would dragons be if we abandoned our civilised behaviour? You already know Topaz the Peaceful. Do not be fooled by her name. She will protect her kin and fight to the death, should it be required. I wish you could have met her in quieter times and known her as we did, before our dark troubles." Topaz inclined her head to her leader and then, to Nightstar's surprise, bowed to them both.

"I would have liked that very much," Sunburst said, dipping his own head towards the blue female.

"Thank you for guiding us here safely, Topaz," Nightstar said, "I understand the difficulty you have with trusting us and hope we will become friends." Topaz remained silent.

"The green and the orange-brown who accompanied Topaz are Fern of the forest and Ryvind the Rust," Galdor introduced them, acknowledging both.

Fern bowed her head, neither friendly nor aggressive. She was similar to Galdor in shape and colour, only much smaller. Ryvind sidled his way along the alcove pushing closer until he was in front of them both, bowing deeply. "Welcome," he greeted them, "I am keen to hear your story."

"As are we all, Ryvind," Galdor said, "and I am sure, once I have decided what we must do with our guests, you will."

"I like him," Sunburst whispered to Nightstar.

"We all like Ryvind," Galdor said, his voice showing emotion for the first time and rumbling in a happy laugh. "Ryvind the Rust, easy to trust. His *perception* is stronger than most and it is seldom wrong."

Galdor opened his wings, curling them round the two remaining dragons that flanked him, "These are my self-appointed guards, Azyrian the Bronze and Garnet."

Garnet dipped her head ever so slightly, her scales a rich shade of red, like the precious stone she was named after. Azyrian's scales gleamed like polished metal, his demeanour proud and serious. His stance was one of readiness, alert and prepared for action. He bowed, showing respect to the two visitors, his piercing gaze fixed on them, never wavering.

"Pleased to meet you both," Nightstar said. Sunburst stared at Garnet, drinking in her wine coloured scales, mesmerised by the red female.

"It would appear your yellow companion is taken by the beauty of the red," Galdor commented.

"Sunburst is often taken by many things," Nightstar said, bumping his head into the yellow's side in an effort stop him staring. "He's sometimes easily distracted. Garnet, please excuse Sunburst, you bear a striking resemblance to his mate, Blood Rose."

"She is a red female of extreme beauty too!" Sunburst blurted out. "The similarity is uncanny. Forgive me, Garnet, I mean no disrespect in staring."

"You pay me a great complement, Sunburst," Garnet purred, "Blood Rose must be a sight to behold." Her yellow eyes glinted with mischief as she added, "I suspect she has her talons full with such an adventurous yellow mate."

The yellow of Sunburst's snout showed a tinge of red. Nightstar wasn't sure if it was the reflection from Garnet's scales or a touch of embarrassment, although suspected it was the latter by Sunburst's expression.

"He is the sire of five dragonets with her, hatched under a great aurora," Nightstar proudly told the assembled dragons, rescuing his friend from any further embarrassment.

"Five is a good number," Garnet said.

"An aurora! A fortuitous omen," Ryvind exclaimed.

"Your good fortune lifts our spirits, Sunburst," Galdor said. "It is long since we heard such uplifting news and longer since we experienced it for ourselves."

Even Topaz looked impressed and Nightstar was glad his yellow friend had accompanied him through the Flaire gateway. Sunburst was indeed well named, lighting the lives of others he touched like a welcome ray of summer sun. He didn't want to think of what might have happened if he travelled here by himself. A lone black confronted by strangers, would not have fared well, he suspected. Bringing his yellow companion afforded him the opportunity to speak with these new dragons and gain their trust. They accepted Sunburst because he was yellow, even though he was a stranger. He doubted he would have come this far himself. It was good to have a companion, his friend, accompany him. He understood he was always learning when it came to dragon behaviour—perhaps the scholar in Alduce wasn't as far removed as he thought. Having Sunburst alongside, keeping him true, was an advantage when it came to *dragonly* ways.

"I would speak with our guests alone," Galdor announced with an air of command.

"But Galdor, we must not leave you unprotected," Azyrian protested. Fern pressed closer to Galdor's side, pushing into the small space of the crowded alcove and forcing him farther away from Nightstar.

"While I am ever grateful for your loyalty and protection," Galdor addressed his guards, "I believe I am in no immediate danger from our guests. I will take them to the cavern of the cataract where I can question them in private. Azyrian. Garnet. You may stand watch outside if you must. Ensure we are not disturbed."

All five dragons stared at Galdor, as if they couldn't believe what he was asking.

"I give you my oath," Nightstar said, "We wish only to be your friends and offer our help with your plight, if we are able."

"And only if you want it," Sunburst added. "I cannot deny Nightstar's scales are black, but that is not a reason to hold it against *him*. He may be unusual to you and I grant you, sometimes he's unusual to me too—in a good way. Give him a chance, I know you'll all be the better for knowing him." He winked at Nightstar. "I understand your previous experiences with black dragons have been bad. I give you my word, as long as he breathes, Nightstar will never be an enemy to your colony."

"Strong words and sworn oaths," Galdor said. "You give a convincing spoooh, Sunburst the Yellow. Let us retire to the cavern of the cataract, there are questions I would ask before I decide what to do with you both. Topaz, Ryvind and Fern, thank you for escorting our guests this far. Please excuse us." Galdor turned and made his way back down the dark recess.

"Nightstar. Sunburst. With me please." It was neither a command nor an instruction, yet there was an expectation they would follow him. He trundled his impressive bulk back along the narrow passageway, twisting and turning through the rock that took them behind the alcove.

Nightstar looked at Sunburst and the yellow flicked the ends of his wings in a shrug, then nodded. "We've survived the Leviathan's Gullet," the yellow said, "Now we must proceed into the belly of the beast."

Nightstar followed Galdor's swinging tail, Sunburst joining in behind, Garnet and Azyrian bringing up the rear. Green, black, yellow, red and gold dragons formed an unusual procession through the twisting cavern, the other green, blue and the rusty orange stayed behind, dismissed by their leader.

Galdor didn't appear too concerned at the reduction in numbers and Nightstar decided this was a good sign. After sharing the news about Sunburst's mate and clutch, Galdor's mood was a lot more accepting. Ryvind's opinion of them must have counted for a lot too and it was obvious Galdor valued what the rust coloured dragon's *perception* told him. Topaz, however, wasn't so trusting. She advised Galdor against their coming here and it would be hard to convince her otherwise, her mind already made up about the unknown pair, especially when one of them was a black.

The darkness of the passageway began to lighten. Nightstar followed Galdor out of the darkness, still marvelling at the ability of the dragon's eye, adjusting from the dimly illuminated cave to the brightness they now faced. He came to a halt so abruptly it caused Sunburst to bump into him from behind.

"Why are you stopping Nightstar?" The yellow dragon complained, "I've bashed my snout on the hard ridges of your tail!"

Nightstar was aware of the yellow dragon colliding into his stationary form, but he dismissed it completely, the vista before him taking priority.

They emerged from the tunnel into a grotto of wonder. Barren rock and dark cave replaced with an oasis of green and blue, bathed in bright sunlight. The hidden valley was sheltered from the sky above with an overhang of rock, partially shading the ground below, yet still letting in some sunlight. A magnificent waterfall cascaded down from the far end of the near subterranean valley, splitting the grotto into two completely different halves. The spray from the waterfall hung in the air, misty vapour shimmering with the colours of the rainbow. The spectrum of light reflected across the sparkling blue waters below, which in turn, reflected a rippling patchwork of watery colours up onto the rocky ceiling.

From his position under the vast rocky celling, Nightstar couldn't see the sky above. Where the rocky outcrop ended, sunlight shone down from out of sight, providing heat and light. From this angle, Nightstar couldn't see the blue sky outside, except in the reflection of the water that divided the grotto. The river calmed as it flowed away from the waterfall, widening into a huge clear lake, dominating almost half of the vast grotto. It flowed on through the valley's centre cutting a deep path as it wound its way to the other end, where it disappeared into the dark mouth of an overhanging cave, journeying ever onwards.

Lush green foliage covered the sunny side of the grotto floor, small trees and shrubs thriving in the sheltered valley, sustained by the water and light from above. The whole valley was protected by the natural shelter of the surrounding rock walls, keeping the worst of the elements at bay. Beneath the rocky ceiling a desert of smooth rock curved deep into the mountainside. The patterns of the strata within the rock banded with a millennia of pastel oranges and reds. Layer upon layer made up the rock wall, line upon line of times long passed, preserved in thick bands of varying colour. It was the opposite from the other side of the river, bare of any plant life and shadowed from the sky above, but just as impressive.

Dragons of all colours basked on the rocky expanse and every pair of eyes were fixed on the black dragon; the stranger who entered into the safety of their secret domain.

It was only after standing and staring at the amazing landscape—and the watching dragons—he realised the noise from the waterfall drowned out Sunburst's impatient words.

"Move over," Sunburst said, "I want to see it too! Look at that Nightstar," he bumped his head into the black dragon's flanks, "a hidden land. Perfect shelter for dragons. A superb secret hiding place and beautiful too. Look at all the dragons. They don't look too happy to see you, do they? Has that waterfall rendered you deaf?" He squeezed his way passed Nightstar's bulk, pushing in front of him for a better view. He faced Galdor. "No wonder you wanted to keep this place secret."

"It is extremely well hidden," Galdor said. "Almost impossible to detect, even when flying directly overhead. Because of the overhang curve of the mountain above and the rocky walls, it looks like there is no gap. An illusion that makes entry from above incredibly risky, even when you know it's there, it's difficult to see and even harder to navigate. Entry from the Leviathan's Gullet is much safer by comparison."

"Are there fish in the lake?" Sunburst asked.

"There are some," Galdor said, "Small and agile, not worth chasing for their size."

"The small ones can be tasty," Sunburst said. "And I've yet to meet a fish I couldn't catch."

"The lake is cold, unlike the oceans warmed by the sun. The river flows through the mountain glaciers, carrying the ice and snow melt. Too cold for my tastes."

"We passed by the Lifting Plateau," Nightstar said, "I can understand why you would miss it. This hidden valley, while not your home, is a fine place to stay until your return."

"It is my hope that one day we can," Galdor said. "I miss it, we all do. It is sad that no free dragons inhabit our ancestral home anymore." He huffed out a blast of exasperated air, reinforcing his distain. "I find it ironic I have come to reside in this grotto after escaping the prison of my underground cavern. While it isn't completely subterranean—and is a much better place altogether—it seems I am destined to live beneath the surface of the land. How the mighty have fallen, eh!"

He slowly turned to face Nightstar. "Once I sat atop the world, moot leader of the Lifting Plateau. I returned after my banishment to find it was no longer my home anymore, my world changed. He whom I once called friend took these things from me and corrupted everything. Still," Galdor continued, "let us not speak of this at present, this is not what we need to discuss."

"We are saddened by what has befallen your lands, Galdor," Nightstar said, "and we will help if we can. Does your land have a name? I would know what you call this place and the name of your home world."

"It is plain you have travelled far," said Galdor. "I too have made such a journey, though not from choice. This land is known to the dragons that reside here as Alvanor."

"Land of the silver clouds?" Nightstar asked.

"You speak the old tongue, Nightstar. You are truly an enigma. I believe you have travelled through a portal to my world and I am keen to know how you accomplished this. How is it you understand our ancient words when you are not from this world?

Nightstar wasn't sure if it was the star of silver, formed from the Flaire artefact emblazoned upon his chest, helped decipher the name of Galdor's land. Even after his metamorphosis, in the form of his dragon scales, the Flaire's properties allowed it to translate unknown languages to the wearer. There was also a good possibility Alduce might have read it in one of his many books, the sorcerer was extremely studious and his power of recall was impressive.

"I honestly don't know, Galdor," he said, telling the green the truth. "The meaning came to me after you spoke, I understood what it meant." Sunburst caught his eye, aware that his answer was missing some of the facts. He was pleased his friend remained silent, even though it was obvious he wanted to comment. Nightstar had made a promise to himself (and also to Sunburst) never to intentionally tell a lie to another dragon again. He would not lie to Galdor now, but he needed to be careful what truths he revealed. His *perception*, his dragon's sixth sense, tingled. A mental itch rather than a warning, leaving him with the impression Galdor wouldn't be as upset as Sunburst about his unconventional origins. He didn't know why he should feel like this, or how it worked. It was one of the larger mysteries of being a dragon.

Sunburst never tired of telling him he must learn to embrace his *perception* fully and trust his inner dragon. The Alduce part of his shared consciousness knew the yellow dragon's advice was good. Nightstar would just have to prove it by going with his instincts.

"We call our world, Sull, "Galdor continued. "A name given by our distant cousins, many generations passed. As far as I am aware," he paused waiting for Nightstar to speak, then filled the silence, "it is only a name."

"Thank you for sharing this with us Galdor," Sunburst said. "We are honoured by the trust you show in us."

"You are my guests, thus far. I would be a poor host, as Ryvind tactfully reminded me, should I fail to observe common pleasantries. Especially with visitors who have travelled as far as you have." He observed the dragons watching them from across the dividing river, aware of their silent stares.

"I will take you to the cavern of the cataract. There are many among us who are troubled to see a black dragon deep within our last sanctuary. Every one of our number has suffered loss. Blaze the Black has corrupted our brothers and sisters, brought disharmony to our lands, and invited unwanted war between dragons and humans. You will understand their caution and perhaps it will help you bear their stares of distrust. Come, follow me."

Galdor launched himself from the rocky ledge they perched upon, huge green wings lifting him up and into the grotto. Nightstar was touched by a moment of intense happiness, witnessing the once imprisoned dragon flying freely. Galdor the Green was truly an impressive sight and even more so in the air.

Sunburst scrambled after Galdor, taking flight and following him across the river, eager to keep up. Nightstar, on impulse, bowed to the assembled dragons watching from the other side of the river. He hoped his gesture would be seen as friendly and respectful. He wanted these dragons to accept him and understand he wasn't a threat, even though his scales were black. He sprang into the air and beat his wings, powering after Galdor and Sunburst.

The size of the grotto was larger than it first appeared and Nightstar craned his neck to see everything as he flew, taking in the wonders of this safe haven, aware his internal passenger was doing the same.

Galdor led Sunburst towards the waterfall, weaving left and right along the path of the river below. He gained height and then abruptly dipped downward, setting huge green wings into a fixed gliding position, aiming directly at the curtain of water at the foot of the roaring falls.

He flew directly into the misty vapour, cutting through the flickering rainbows, a myriad of sparkling colours painting his glistening hide. Water bounced from his wings as he passed beneath the cascading waterfall. The rushing torrent of water swallowed him whole and he disappeared into the shimmering curtain, vanishing from sight.

Sunburst didn't hesitate in following Galdor into the waterfall, his yellow hide showing off the rainbow colours to more effect than Galdor's green. Nightstar wanted to know what lay beyond the downpour of the waterfall. He wasn't as confident as Sunburst to blindly rush headlong into the unknown, yet he realised the time for hesitancy wasn't today. He acted on the yellow dragon's constant encouragement of *listening to his dragon side* and took the plunge.

He closed his eyes as ice cold water engulfed his entire body, flying into the waterfall, copying Galdor, his tough armour of scales protecting him from the frozen chill of liquid winter. The force of the waterfall pushed down on him and he automatically increased tension to his wing membranes, adjusting the muscles and tendons to keep himself aloft. Drumming water bounced harmlessly off his body, forcing him downward, then the pressure disappeared and he lifted slightly, emerging from the downpour. He opened his eyes and barely had enough time to brace for landing, rivulets of water splashing from his back and wings.

Spreading his wings wide and twisting them upwards, he deployed two huge black sails and slowed his forward momentum, talons searching for ground. His claws scrabbled at wet rock—coated in weedy green slime—as he fought for purchase. His weight carried him forward and he slid sideways, tail whipping out behind him and lashing from side to side in an effort to steady his onrush. He bumped down onto his tail end, bounced twice, wings and tail flailing wildly to keep balance, finally sliding to an ungainly stop between Sunburst and Galdor, legs splayed wide in an attempt to keep him from falling onto his snout.

Galdor managed to maintain his composure until he looked at Sunburst. Both green and yellow no longer able to hold their laughter. Deep rumbling escaped from Galdor's throat as he tried to stifle his amusement, unable to hold it back, which set Sunburst into fits of high pitched snorting.

"I'm sorry... " the yellow dragon huffed between snorts, small wisps of smoke curling up from his nostrils. He tried to speak again and failed, laughter roaring from his belly. Galdor joined him and added his deep growling bass to the yellow's hysteria, miserably failing to hold his own laughter at bay any longer. The sound of two highly amused dragons echoed around the cavern.

"Please forgive me, Nightstar," Galdor apologised, regaining a little of his usual composure. "That isn't how I usually treat my guests." He struggled to stay serious and was barely containing his mirth.

Nightstar pushed his sprawled legs up from the cave floor in an attempt to right himself, wishing a huge hole would appear and swallow him down into the depths of the rock. The slimy coating that covered the damp surface did not provide any purchase at all and he slumped forward into a crumpled heap, setting Galdor and Sunburst into a second round of uncontrollable laughter. The laughter rang around the cavern of the cataract, loud enough to drown out the sound of the waterfall, which was considerably quieter from the inside.

Nightstar took care to stand, slowly this time, tentatively probing the slippery rocks with sharp talons, digging his long claws though the annoying greenery like gently probing fingers. He managed a scrabbling crab walk to safety, avoiding another embarrassing fall. When he cleared the slippery surface, he snapped his wings a few times to dispel the water, then folded them to his sides, no longer needing them to keep his balance. He managed a dignified, if somewhat late arrival, to the waiting green and yellow.

"It is long since I laughed as heartily," Galdor said.

"Stick with Nightstar long enough and he'll have you snorting fire!" Sunburst said. "He certainly keeps me entertained. I could tell you stories that would curl your claws."

"Please Sunburst, no more!" Galdor snorted. "I am ashamed to find humour at Nightstar's expense."

"Do not be," Nightstar said, a touch of amusement creeping into his own voice. "It is good to hear you laugh. I think you need it after all we have heard. I was not expecting to crash land. I didn't actually know what to expect flying through a waterfall."

"One thing I have discovered when visiting Alvanor," Sunburst said, "is to expect the unexpected!" The yellow dragon sounded decidedly like Caltus, the master who had apprenticed Alduce. It was time to steer this conversation in another direction before the yellow dragon unintentionally mentioned something he shouldn't. Deep inside, the Alduce part of Nightstar stored away this observation; he would have fun reminding Sunburst of his words later and comparing the yellow dragon to his former *human* master.

"You are right, Nightstar," Galdor said. "It is good to laugh. I thank you for your gift and extend my apologies for laughing at... "

"... his rump busting!" Sunburst said. "I know. I'm cruel, but it was very funny."

"His mishap," Galdor said, attempting some diplomacy. "I suggest we put his unfortunate incident behind... "

"*Behind?*" Sunburst asked.

"...us," Galdor finished, trying to ignore Sunburst and suppressing a wicked—tooth filled—grin that was all dragon. "We have more serious matters to discuss. Now we are alone and have some privacy. My *perception* tells me there are things that are best kept between us."

Nightstar risked a quick glance at Sunburst who gave a barely noticeable shrug of his wings.

"I have a number of questions I wish to ask you both, and something I need to tell you," Galdor said. There was no trace of amusement now, his grin dropped and his expression was one of total seriousness. "My questions will help me with my decision on what we must do with you and what I can do with my own situation."

"I'm sure Nightstar has many of his own questions," Sunburst said, "It appears to be the way with you both. Questions, questions, questions."

"Then let us begin," Galdor said, "we have much ground to cover."

Chapter 24

Questions

"As you are already aware," Galdor said, "black dragons are not looked upon favourably here. Blaze has shown himself to be the enemy of all free dragons. In fact he has proved to me he is an enemy to humans as well. While I was imprisoned, he reigned down a terrible war on them, attacking their towns and cities, provoking men to fight back. He managed to destroy the peace between our races and was fixated on destroying them completely. I returned to discover his reign of destruction has almost wiped out all human life on our continent. I should have seen the signs and been more attentive when he spoke out against them."

"Topaz spoke a little of this when we first met and it was obvious she was not happy to see me," Nightstar said. "How were you to know of the darkness festering inside him? Blaze tricked you, abused your trust, it is he who is to blame, not you."

"Thank you Nightstar. It is difficult for me to not accept some responsibility. Being gone so long, Blaze was free to spend all those years unchecked. I fear now, he is too powerful. Retrospectively we are always wiser after the event. Topaz informed me of her conversation with you, but there is more. Blaze has an ancient magic and has found a way to turn free minded dragons to his cause, forcing the unwilling to do his bidding. I believe some of the dragons that still remain at the Lifting Plataea are still in control of their own actions, but are afraid if they don't comply with his demands, they will be turned. Topaz told you of the mindless blacks he controls."

"She called it the black plague," Sunburst said, "and thought Nightstar was one of his drones."

"She was right to be cautious. Our survival hinges on staying one step ahead of Blaze and his followers. However, I can clearly see you aren't like the others, Nightstar. I have encountered some of the black dragons Blaze controls and I can tell you are not like them at all." He paused then continued almost to himself. "Or like any other dragon I have encountered. You aren't like any other dragon from this land. At first I thought it was because you travelled here from somewhere far away. *Somewhere* we haven't yet established. But that isn't it or I would sense the same of Sunburst. There is something different about you. Something that nags at my *perception*, but it isn't a warning of danger. It is most unusual. Most puzzling."

Nightstar didn't know how to answer so he kept silent. Galdor needed to talk and he would let the green dragon do so. There was a time for speaking and a time for listening; he recognised this was a time for the latter.

"We will return to that subject later as I still need answers." He paused, as if contemplating just what to tell them, gathering his thoughts. "The black plague is what I wish to tell you about. It is no sickness. It is a magical corruption that changes free will into subservience. I have a unique ability to sniff out magic. Not just our own dragon magic, other types of magic too." He cast a quick glance at Nightstar before continuing. "This corruption is a malevolent magic, neither dragon nor human, and is new to me. It changes normal dragons into black drones, mindlessly carrying out Blaze's orders. He is connected to it, but I suspect not in full control. I don't believe there is a cure, once they are transformed they are lost. I sensed that their very essence is taken from them and used up. Depleted and unredeemable."

"Their dragon spirit?" Nightstar asked.

"Exactly! That's a perfect way to describe it Nightstar, *dragon spirit,*" he emphasised the phrase. "I think you have a grasp, an understanding, of what this magic takes from them. That might help. We will come back to that," he said, nodding unconsciously. "It leaves only a husk, not a real dragon. A shell of the original individual, filled with the dark corruption. There is absolutely no reasoning with someone who has been affected. I could not talk with the changed dragons I encountered—the ones that still had the ability to speak, as some could only growl—they were loyal only to Blaze, extensions of his own black heart. Their essence, their *dragon spirit* gone, nothing remained. I tried to convince them what they do is wrong. And I have failed. I encountered dragons I suspect were once friends. Free thinking dragons that would listen to reason. I must have known these individuals and I am certain they would never have turned against me or against other dragons. They are unrecognisable after they are transformed. Violent and bent on destruction. Death, I believe, is their only release. The remaining free dragons know our situation is bad but they don't know just how terrible it really is. I cannot bring myself to tell them the severity of our predicament and shatter what little hope remains. I fear we will never return to how things were before."

He looked at them both, sadness written in his eyes. "We are lost."

"That is disturbing news, Galdor. Is this why you have brought us to the cavern of the cataract? So you can share with us, strangers to you, what you are unwilling to tell your own dragons?" Sunburst asked.

"In part, yes. It is easier to unburden my concerns to you. I know you are not the enemy. I have known it all along. Forgive my pretence, I wanted... no *needed* to talk freely, to have someone who could listen objectively to my findings. The remaining dragons are too closely involved to look at this rationally. I fear they will give up what little hope they have left if they knew the truth. I need to appear strong for their sake. I'm changed from the leader I once was before my incarceration. A century of darkness and starvation can have a lasting effect on you. The never ending loneliness, the lack of stimuli and the constant absence of daylight are too much, I think, for any creature, not just a dragon. I only ever saw two other living creatures while I was trapped there. A rat and a goat. To my shame, I ate them both. I have never shared that with anyone else.

"The helplessness and despair were too much to bear. I was ready to lie down and surrender to the long sleep. When Alduce rescued me, it was as if I had been reborn, free from the blackness of that desolate cave. When I saw the sky, it filled me with a joy so great, I never thought I could feel that happy again. When I came home, I arrived to a darkness worse than any my dank cave could ever cause."

"You were lost before, Galdor," Sunburst said, "and with the help of a human sorcerer, you were rescued. You were close to giving up hope and you received aid from an unexpected source. Your benefactor was a man, a small human whose help provided you with a means to escape. One small man changed your situation for the better. His accidental involvement, tiny though it was, resulted in a massive change for you. You cannot see what the future holds, none of us can. Do not give up now. That one small change may be waiting for you. The one single event that could change your circumstances again. Believe me when I tell you I have also faced a great crisis. I too have experienced a doubt so deep I could see no return. Your colony still needs Galdor the Green. Alduce wrote about you, called you a mighty dragon, a force to be reckoned with, a dragon of unstoppable wrath, and a protector of justice. He said you were wise and steadfast, you would stop at nothing and never give up, no matter how bleak the future looked. I don't think he was wrong."

Sunburst used the words Alduce had written in the *Atlas of Dragons* and as he was apt to do, added a few embellishments of his own. He believed in Galdor and his speech was sincere. Nightstar was moved to hear the heartfelt words of Alduce, quoted back to the green dragon by his friend. He should have learned by now never to be surprised by Sunburst's eloquent words. He was too familiar with Sunburst's usual ways, quick with a joke or a clever reply, competitive and often annoying. When he spoke from the heart it always caught him off guard.

Galdor had been through much, suffered alone in the dark. To eventually escape and return home to find his world corrupted and his colony in ruins was a blow he struggled to recover from. Stirred by Sunburst's optimistic view, Nightstar couldn't stand by and do nothing. He knew Alduce felt the same.

"Sunburst is right," Nightstar said, "there must be something we can do to help."

"Maybe," Galdor mused, "maybe there is."

"It seems to me that maybe, "Sunburst said, "is usually a way of avoiding saying no. I can see we are going to have to change that."

"I think it time you answered my questions," Galdor said, "and *perhaps* there is something you can offer. A fresh perspective. Two new pairs of eyes to look upon the problem. I won't know until I learn more about you both."

"Ask away mighty Galdor," Sunburst said, "I'm sure we can find a solution to your predicament. Nightstar, as I have already mentioned, is a dragon you can count on in times of need."

"Firstly, I would know how you came to be here, on my world."

"We travelled through a portal, a passageway much like the one Alduce opened for you when you returned home," Nightstar said.

"This I already know, even if you hadn't said as much. You are strangers here. You asked the names of this land, of my world. You told Topaz you travelled far to be here. What I do not know is how you came to use this passageway between worlds. I had the help of Alduce, a human sorcerer using human magic. He employed the aid of a magical device. While I am not an expert in the ways of moving between worlds, I do know it is definitely not something that is attained by dragon magic. My *perception* is clear on this. I know it can be done, but not how. If you travelled by this same method, how were you able to conjure a passageway? Who opened it for you and why? And what magic did they use?"

"You are correct in your reasoning," Nightstar said. "It was Alduce who fashioned the passageway for us."

Galdor took a step back, his face a picture of amazement. Even Sunburst, who knew the truth, appeared a little surprised at Nightstar's revelation.

"When you made your claim to have known Alduce, I believed you had met him many years ago." Galdor said. "I know you speak the truth, but there is something you are not telling me. You say it was he who helped you come here. How can this be? When I encountered Alduce it was many years ago. Human lives are short and fade in the blink of a dragon's eye. He is still alive?

"Indeed he is," Sunburst said, "very much alive. He speaks highly of you Galdor. He shared your story with me and wanted to know what had become of the green dragon he rescued."

"Why would he open a passageway to this world and not come himself? I told him before we departed he was welcome here. If he ever had the chance to visit my world, I asked him to seek me out. I own him a great debt I can never repay. He should have travelled with you. I granted him a boon and he never asked anything of me. He was... is a humble man."

"His only boon was not to end up inside your belly. He is here in spirit, Galdor," Nightstar said. "I'm sure if he could have come—"

"Wait... " Galdor thrust his snout at the silver scales on the black dragon's chest. "Your *night star* smells familiar. It stinks of human magic!" Nightstar backed up and Galdor lunged forward inhaling deeply, huge nostrils sucking in air. "I can taste it, human magic mixed with something else. The last time I smelled that magic was when I was trapped underground. I knew there was something different about you, Nightstar. It has been on the tip of my tongue since we met." He extended his forked tongue, tasting the air like a red viper. It flicked and flitted in front of Nightstar's chest almost touching the silver scales.

"Magic. Human magic, but missing something," Galdor said softly. "I can't quite recall what... Mushrooms! Without the scent of mushrooms. The foul black fungi that Alduce came in search of. *You smell of magic and mushrooms*, I told him. Now I smell the same magic. Human magic blended with dragon magic. It isn't possible! I told you I can sniff out magic, that I'm sensitive to all kinds. Other dragons wouldn't be able to detect it, but I most certainly can. This cannot be. Yet it is. How can this be, Nightstar? Explain it to me. Now!" His tone became threatening. "If you have harmed Alduce—"

"He could never hurt Alduce," Sunburst shouted. "It isn't possible, without the sorcerer there would be no..." he stopped.

"Alduce is fine," Nightstar said. "Look into my eyes, see if I lie! I am a dragon of my word. Use your magic, you will know I speak the truth."

Galdor thrust his face close to Nightstar's, yellow eyes whirring hypnotically as he stared deeply inside. "I have memories of doing this with another. You do not lie, Nightstar, but you do not tell the whole truth either. You are extremely familiar for a stranger."

He withdrew and shook his head from side to side in denial, as if unsure of what he had seen. "You are an enigma, black dragon. I sense nothing wicked in you, but there is something else, something not of dragons. There is an unusual magic within you Nightstar the Black, and I would know more about it. Shall we reveal your secret?"

The cavern of the cataract filled with Galdor's magic, the air alive with energy. Nightstar could feel invisible tendrils probing around the edges of his silver scales. Small sparks licked gently over their surface, their touch painless, yet strange. It was no invasive assault, rather a tentative exploration, more a magical reconnaissance with the sole purpose of gathering information. Nightstar could feel Galdor's presence as he skirted around the peripheral of his own magical boundaries. He was aware he could push back and resist if he wanted, but this wasn't an attack and he didn't feel threatened.

The manner in which the green dragon's magic flowed was similar to the wispy tendrils inside the pearl of knowledge when he had touched it. Instead of the sharing experience Nightstar received from the pearl, it was his own information and secrets that were available.

Galdor followed the threads of his magic, tracing a path to his core, seeking knowledge and sampling the strange mix of human and dragon magic. He could sense Galdor's amazement as he carefully explored this new unknown magic, trying to understand the weird blend that should not exist, but somehow did. He was confused and intrigued, his mind eager to understand and Nightstar felt it all.

Galdor reached deeper, gently probing his mind and weaving his way through the complex web until he found the centre. A bright ball of blinding white energy rotated and swirled, spinning like a small sun at the centre of its universe. Thin dark threads mixed through the cloudy substance like black veins in white marble, expanding until the energy became black and the threads where white, black and white reversed. The darkness of the black was as intense as the blinding white, the blackest black with thin white lines swirling through its midst.

The energy constantly changed, slow and gradual then instant, pulsing black then white, white then black, no discernible pattern, always moving. Through Galdor's touch, Nightstar knew he was now aware of what it was he was witnessing. Galdor had discovered what made up the unnatural blend of magic. He understood his discovery.

He felt the green dragon retreat, slowly withdrawing until his touch was no longer detectable.

The cavern came back into view and Nightstar blinked until his eyes came into focus. Galdor was still in front of him, snout close to his own. His own eyes vacant for a moment as he too returned to himself, taking a little longer than Nightstar. He stared in wonder, intense yellow eyes alive with questions he already knew the answers to.

"Show me," he whispered.

Chapter 25

Answers

Nightstar backed away putting some distance between himself and the other two dragons. His own magic crackled and popped as small sparks of energy leapt from his scales and swarmed over his wings. The air was charged with anticipation and the familiar tingle of transformation gripped his body.

Nightstar let go the spell holding his dragon form and released the magic. When he had first changed into a dragon, Alduce needed to hold the spell, always aware of the sorcery he manipulated to keep his dragon shape intact. He was fearful if he wasn't careful in maintaining the spell, he would unintentionally change back.

Although there were many various ledgers, scrolls and books filled with sorcery and magic, being a sorcerer didn't come with instructions.

As Nightstar grew, a new persona emerged and his own individual dragon spirit strengthened, taking over the chore of keeping in form. No longer did the sorcerer need to hold the spell in place, fearful if he let go, his dragon's body would change back into a human. The form of the dragon remained unconsciously in place and now, no effort was required.

To change back was now the opposite of what it had once been. Rather than just releasing the spell, Nightstar was required to will the change. The dragon released his magic, relinquishing his prominence and allowed the human passenger inside to come forward. There was no conflict or struggle for control, the two halves of the one whole worked in tandem. Alduce adapted, learning from Nightstar's spirit, when in dragon form it was best the dragon persona should have control. He was still very much aware of Nightstar's experiences and emotions, present throughout. It was difficult to explain just how it felt and he would never be able to put it into words. If he wanted to explain it to someone, he would have to say it was something one must experience for themselves to understand. He didn't fully understand himself and had learned, against all his scholarly instincts, to try and accept it for what it was.

Nightstar's hold on the dragon released completely and his black scales glowed from beneath, white light shone from between the gaps, highlighting their borders and brightening the cavern. The magical sparks fused with the light emanating from within, wrapping the black dragon in an ethereal corona. The wavering shape of the dragon inside grew smaller and began to change, distorting like a shimmering heat haze.

Galdor stood transfixed, his yellow eyes reflecting in the light of transformation, like the eyes of a cat in the dark.

Slowly a new shape formed as the corona shrank, tiny in comparison to the size of Nightstar. Hard black scales faded, to be replaced by human skin tones, wings and talons changing into arms and hands, legs and feet. The magical metamorphosis finished and the air settled, leaving behind the tangy smell of ozone. Where Nightstar stood a moment before, a naked human crouched, back arched, on the cavern floor.

Alduce pulled himself up from the cold rocks, fighting to keep his balance. The disorientation of transformation passed quickly, it still remained severe and unsettling, but it passed much faster than it originally had. The duration of the pain he faced—each time he transformed—had thankfully lessened. The extreme stress his body undertook, regardless of which form he was changing into, was unavoidable. It was still agonising, but it was a small price to pay. Continued practice helped and Alduce credited the living blood Sunburst had *donated*, a key factor.

Standing straight, the giddiness subsided to something close to bearable and he stretched his arms, his joints cracking. He rotated his neck and flexed stiff muscles, working the tension from his human body, feeling a phantom loss of missing limbs from his dragon counterpart.

He took a tentative step towards Galdor, naked except for the small dragon amulet he wore on a chain around his neck. He ran human hands over his skin as if checking the soft flesh beneath his fingers, coming to rest on the now familiar yellow patch in the shape of a scale.

Changing from dragon to human did not include clothing. Dragons knew no modesty, it was a human affliction, and with Nightstar's help, Alduce had come to ignore it.

"Greetings magnificent Galdor," Alduce said, performing a flourishing bow, "I am honoured to stand before you once again. I apologise for the deception, I meant no offence. I hope you understand the necessity as to why I keep my identity hidden."

Galdor was silent, eyes flicking from the human to the yellow dragon who had moved to take a protective stance next to the sorcerer.

Sunburst's body was tense, his muscles bunched, his body at the ready, like a snake preparing to strike. Alduce wasn't sure how Galdor would react and, and from Sunburst's readiness to jump to his defence, it was obvious the yellow dragon was apprehensive too. Sunburst was a smaller dragon and any well intentioned confrontation with Galdor would result in his demise. He was outsized and severely disadvantaged. The fact his yellow friend was prepared to stand by him, no matter the outcome, spoke volumes.

A deep growling rumble grew from Galdor's chest like building thunder. Sunburst drew his neck back, claws spread wide for purchase, waiting. The growling rumble increased, but it wasn't the snarling displeasure of anger.

Galdor's growling manifested into joyful laughter, echoing around the cavern. Small trails of smoke escaped his nostrils and huge tears ran down his face.

"By flame and by fang! Once again you have impressed me, *little human*," he teased.

A great relief washed over Alduce and the tension of revealing himself to Galdor drained away. Sunburst also visibly relaxed. The green dragon had discovered who Nightstar was when he explored his magic and Alduce didn't know how he would react. Perhaps Galdor believed he owed him a debt of gratitude or perhaps he was more accepting of humans. It didn't matter, he wasn't angry and that's what counted.

"Did I not tell you, all those years ago, you would become the most powerful human to ever practice magic?"

"I believe you may have said words to that effect," Alduce said, recalling how thankful Galdor had been when he opened the portal to his freedom. "I thought it was in gratitude for my help."

"No. Not in gratitude. Green dragons have no need of flattery. I told you, I have a unique ability to sense all kinds of magic. Even though you were an apprentice when we first met, I could sense a great power in you." He cocked his head and proclaimed, "I was correct."

Alduce couldn't argue with Galdor's words. He wasn't being boastful. Like Sunburst, when he knew something was true and he was right, he stated it as a fact. He liked that dragons could be direct and to the point in this way and recorded this trait in his writings, giving it a name: *dragon logic*.

Galdor brought his snout close and sniffed at the small silver dragon Alduce wore around his neck. "You still bear the magical artefact we found on the dead mage. That's what I could smell on you, faint but present. It was a long time ago and I couldn't quite place it, possibly because it was in the guise of your silver scales. It appears you have learned to use its magic to your advantage."

"I have only scratched the surface of its potential. Though I hate to admit it, there is a lot I don't know about it. I haven't been able to find out much about its origins or abilities, although I am still searching for the answers. It holds great power and I am careful when I explore its uses."

"Cautious and clever," Galdor said. "You have matured, Alduce, but you haven't lost your humility. If only Blaze could have met you, perhaps his view of humans would be different."

"From what we have learned of Blaze," Sunburst said, "I think it unlikely. I have come to know Alduce and have grown to like him, but it was not always so."

"I can see you share more than the bond of friendship, Sunburst. The way you stood with Alduce, ready to fight in his defence tells me much. If a dragon is prepared to champion a human it is for good reason. I haven't known you long, but I can tell you are of strong moral character and a dragon of spirit. There is a tale for telling there, I am sure."

"I thank you for your kind words Galdor. When I first met the *little human*," Sunburst said, "I was prepared to flame him. However, my strong moral character has—more than once—saved his soft human skin."

Alduce groaned. No doubt he would hear the mighty Galdor's description of a certain yellow dragon, of strong moral character, time and time again.

Sunburst turned serious, "It was difficult for me to accept what he was when I first found out. It took us time and much hardship before we were able to put aside our differences. How is it you can so readily accept him?"

"I have seen inside his spirit and have touched both man and dragon," Galdor replied. "It is more than enough for me to know that there is no evil intent within either. I have lived a long life Sunburst and have seen many strange things. Perhaps I make my decisions based on my experiences.

"You are powerful, Alduce. When I searched inside your magic, your strength overwhelmed me, you are stronger than anyone, be it man or dragon, I have ever met. I am glad there is no malevolence in your soul. You could have easily pushed me away, locked me out, but you chose to make yourself free to my searching, hiding nothing. I find your openness refreshing."

"I have learned not to keep secrets from those I trust," Alduce said, "and

I'm still learning." He shared a look with Sunburst. "Ever the scholar, as my old master was fond of saying."

"You have a lot of explaining to do, Alduce. Tell me all, please. I would like you to teach me about the sorcerer, the dragon he becomes and your friendship with Sunburst. We will not be disturbed here and you can take as long as you need."

Alduce told Galdor the Green everything. He told of his fascination with dragons, even before their chance encounter, and how it inspired him to create the *Atlas of Dragons*. His desire to compile the ultimate collection of all the dragon lore he could discover. This had led to the discovery of shape shifting, the regrettable theft of the unhatched egg and his transformation spell. He told of his journeys to other worlds, what he had learned of the rare Flaire metal and the artefact they found on the body of the dead mage.

When he spoke about his time on Salverta, Sunburst's home world, the yellow dragon helped with the story. Galdor listened intently when they explained the blood sharing and their strange experiences, both taking it in turns to describe their own part in the process and how they perceived what had happened.

Sunburst took over when they told of the Extractor and his own captivity and Nightstar's role in his salvation.

Galdor was the perfect listener saying nothing while they spoke. He never interrupted and absorbed every detail.

Alduce concluded their tale with their journey through the passageway, to the world they now knew as Sull and their meeting with Topaz.

"You bound your atlas with my hide!" he laughed. "A fitting use of my gift. I imagine it looks rather spectacular."

"The magic imbued in it will protect and preserve the book much better than ordinary leather ever could." Alduce said.

"And your green dragon hide looks fantastic," Sunburst added.

"I have a few more questions, then we must return to the grotto and let the others know I have concluded you are no threat. Alduce, it would be best for all concerned if you leave the cavern of the cataract as you entered; a black dragon. We will keep your secret between us. And," Galdor performed his best imitation of a wolfish grin," I would very much like to see you transform back into Nightstar."

Even though Alduce knew he was safe, standing next to all those teeth in his tiny human body, he found the presence of Galdor's deadly grin terrifying

"I am curious as to how well you mimic a dragon and mask the human inside. I would smell human or dragon magic, so I know you don't use either. How is it you manage it so convincingly?"

"You can't smell it or sense it because it isn't magic. I used science and human sorcery, magic if you will, to initially bring about the transformation. When I change now, the spell is just a catalyst. I still need the magic to start the change, but once I transform into Nightstar, the dragon takes over." Alduce explained. "Nightstar is a real dragon. I am convinced that is why he is as undetectable as anything else. With the exception of Sunburst, you are the only other dragon who knows my secret. When I first changed, I learned to imitate Sunburst and the dragons of his colony. After I started to behave like a dragon, it became more natural, like I was acting on an instinctual level. The more time I spent as a dragon, the stronger Nightstar's presence became."

"And he managed to go undetected from our moot and our leader, Winterfang," Sunburst said. "Not an easy task, believe me, that frosty old dragon sees almost everything under his snout."

"Do not let him hear you calling him *old*," Alduce said. "I happen to know it is a touchy subject with him and it is disrespectful." Winterfang was many things, but Alduce, through Nightstar, knew he was a great leader. And fair in his judgements.

Sunburst dipped his head, "Sage advice. I'll remember that."

"When I change into Nightstar, I'm no longer human and I transform completely into a living, breathing dragon. I am convinced the spirit from the unborn dragon is Nightstar. My own consciousness is still there, buried deep within the dragon. We have learned, Nightstar and I, to let the dragon part of our unusual partnership, take control. We share thoughts and feelings and I trust him completely. He is with me now, observing everything I do, feeling everything I feel. He is me and I am him. I wish I could explain it, but I can't. It is what it is. I have accepted it, as Nightstar has. We have learned from each other and it works for us both.

"When Sunburst gifted me three drops of his living blood, the conflict between my human side and the dragon spirit lessened. This is when his persona truly emerged and started to develop. The blood was the missing ingredient that makes our strange dichotomy work. If it wasn't for the unique chain of events that led to this, I expect I would have struggled to come to terms with the sheer magnitude of being part dragon."

"You are the scholar, Alduce," Galdor said, "and even though your own understanding is limited to your experiences, I trust you are the only one qualified to make that conclusion. I am of a mind to agree with your summary; it is what it is!"

"One last thing before Nightstar returns," Alduce said. "The transformation has a rather annoying side effect. The metabolic rate of the transformation, coupled with the size and bulk of a dragon, leaves me utterly and completely ravenous."

Galdor snorted. "Ha! I have a good remedy for hungry dragons. Bring forth the black dragon, Alduce. Galdor the Green will lead him and Sunburst on the hunt."

"At last!" Sunburst said. "I love that remedy. Yellow dragons think best on a full stomach. Quick sorcerer, summon Nightstar so we can hunt. Do you have curly bucks here in Alvanor?" he asked Galdor.

"We have many species of deer, I'm sure we'll find something to your taste."

"I'm sure we will," Alduce said. "Deer, fish, cattle, anything with legs... "

Sunburst snorted, "Alduce, I would remind you of my strong moral character."

"And stronger appetite," the sorcerer said, stepping back putting enough distance between them to transform himself back into the black dragon.

Small sparks gathered on the rocky ceiling above his head and the amulet warmed his skin. The air was alive with the expectation of magic. Alduce didn't need to be outside for the transformation to take place and didn't need the open sky. The Flairo artefact could use natural lightning if it was available, but it could also pull the energy it needed from its surroundings. He swayed as blue-white light arced down from the rocky ceiling above, thin tendrils finding their target. A spidery web of lightning ran over his body, covering him in a bright light, illuminating the cavern.

The man inside the bright cloud of light fell forward and began to grow, his limbs stretched, forming into talons, flesh turning to scales. Small wings sprouted from his back, unfurling into huge black ones.

Intense pain washed through him as he changed, blood flowed through his veins like fire as the sorcerous metamorphosis reconstructed his body, expanding and stretching, transforming human flesh and bone to dragon skin and scales.

His mouth distorted, morphing into a long angular snout and filling with sharp teeth. It opened wide and issued a muted growl somewhere between agony and satisfaction.

Nightstar was back.

The black dragon reared up as much as the cavern ceiling would allow and flexed his wings, stretching and snapping them, then folded them into his sides. His tail flicked from side to side and he rolled his long neck.

He was aware it was the same kind of exercise Alduce performed when he returned to being human.

"Amazing," Galdor said, "it was the exact reverse of when you changed into Alduce." He stuck his snout in close to the silver scales on Nightstar's chest, sniffing. "Yessss, I can sense the magic, now that I know what it is. It's faint, almost undetectable, a mix of human, dragon and the Flaire metal." He inhaled again, nostrils flaring, "But it quickly fades to nothing. All I smell now is a dragon, as real as any other."

"Good," Nightstar said. "As long as it is only you that can sniff it out. I'm pleased to know that after I change, any trace of the magic dissipates quickly. I suspect this is why other dragons, who don't have your sensitive snout for magic, are unable to detect any trace of humanity."

"Don't worry, Ald... Nightstar, no other dragons have my unique snout. Your secret is safe with me."

Nightstar's belly growled, expressing a deep hunger.

"If you're finished all the sniffing and snorting," Sunburst said, "I think it's definitely time to eat."

Chapter 26

Time to Plan

"We have no way of knowing how many natural dragons are still at the Lifting Plateau," Galdor said, "and of those who remain, whether they are held captive or stay of their own free will."

"From what you've told us," Sunburst said, "I think it would be unlikely they stay because they want to. What dragon would choose to live under constant threat of being consumed by the black plague? I suspect any survivors are held as prisoners. From what you've learned from those who escaped, the last place any dragon would want to be is with Blaze and his drones."

"I would like to learn more about the dragons he has changed, the means in which it was accomplished, and how he keeps them loyal," Nightstar said. "Perhaps there is something we... or my friend, can do to help them. Reverse the spell or maybe the bond between master and slave can be broken."

"The ones who now wear the black scales are beyond any help, Nightstar." The sadness in Galdor's voice plain. "Believe me, there is nothing left inside, they are empty and their spirits are gone. Some don't even have the ability to speak. They are so far beyond any help we—or our friend can offer. While I share Sunburst's view that no dragons would stay with Blaze through choice, he is a master of deception. I do not know what lies they were fed. The dragons that escaped told me what they knew, but much remains a mystery. It is possible they are oblivious to my return. He convinced them the humans deserve to be eradicated and manipulated them into starting a war. What they believe and how he convinced them, be it his talent for twisting the facts or his magic, I cannot say. The remains of my old colony is stagnant, polluted by Blaze's corruption. I returned over four decades ago to learn of Blaze's fight against humanity. He waged a war on the southlands and razed the towns and cities there. Some of the dragons with me now were involved at first, when they thought their only choice was to defend themselves. Blaze convinced them the humans were to blame for my disappearance and the other dragons that vanished after I was gone. He enthralled them with a glamour. After the first attack, once the adrenalin of battle wore off, some dragons came to realise how they were manipulated. They knew the slaughter was wrong.

"They fled the colony before Blaze could stop them. They hid, staying clear of the dragons from Blaze's new order. After Alduce opened the way home for me, I was lucky enough to encounter a few of these free dragons and avoided blundering headlong into trouble. I have found myself to be much more cautious since my liberation."

"What magic does he wield that is strong enough to beguile a host of dragons?" Nightstar asked. "Dragons possess a natural magic and any conjuration would have to be powerful indeed if it could enthral so many."

"That is a mystery that I have long pondered, Nightstar. It is of great concern to me. There are rumours of an object of power, a secret Blaze closely guards."

"Do you have any idea what it might be?" Nightstar asked. The presence of Alduce became more prominent in his mind. This was something the sorcerer might have knowledge of. "Magical artefacts can be dangerous." He thought of the Extractor, the enemy who had once captured Sunburst. "I have seen how they can corrupt even the most powerful of magic wielders." The staff of the Extractor had once been such an artefact. Nightstar was glad it now rested at the bottom of a deep, distant ocean, safe from human hands... and perhaps dragon claws.

"Whatever it may be, it is shrouded in secrecy." Galdor expelled a long sigh. "My moot was disbanded and Blaze now uses the cavern as his own chamber. No dragon is allowed entry into his private chamber and it is guarded by his black scaled converts. We have little information and what we have learned only leads to more questions. With so many unknowns, it is difficult for me to decide on the best action to take. Do we stay hidden and do nothing, remaining comparatively safe? Or do we take action and risk the lives and freedom of every dragon not under Blaze's control?"

"We need more information," Sunburst said. "We must find out if this magical talisman exists and what it is. Once we know more, we will be better equipped to deal with Blaze and stop him. We can save the dragons he holds captive. Nightstar and I have some experience in this area."

"I admire your enthusiasm, Sunburst, but I fear for your safety. If any natural dragons still remain at the Lifting Plateau, I would see them freed. Being held in captivity is no way for a dragon to live. This is an area I have my own experience in. Though I wish I did not. I can't help thinking, why wouldn't he inflict the black plague on them all? Are we too late to do anything useful? Have they all been changed? Is it an unnecessary risk that outweighs any reward? Through time, dragons eventually fade from existence. It saddens me to know the natural dragons of Sull are no longer free to fly through the skies. Blaze believes he is changing our fate. The irony of it is that he is only speeding it up. I truly believe he has spiralled into madness. Ultimately he must be stopped but I don't want to see any more dragons suffer."

"I may have an answer to one of your questions," Nightstar replied. "It is highly probable Blaze keeps some natural dragons for breeding."

Sunburst and Galdor looked horrified.

"Let me explain. It is known that when some creatures are changed by magic their whole physiology becomes different. Infertility is a possible side effect of the black plague. His converts were once natural dragons. While they are many, your world isn't overrun with new black dragons, is it? His numbers must be made up from the original colony. Your skies are not crowded with dragons. Sunburst and I remarked upon this when we first arrived."

"What of you Nightstar? Do you think you might suffer the same affliction?" Concern crept into Galdor's voice.

"I do not believe it is the same for me. I am a real dragon, regardless of my origins, I'm *perception* sure."

"Of that, I have no doubt," Sunburst quipped. "Remind me to check with Amethyst, just to be sure!"

Nightstar tilted his head at the yellow but chose not to be drawn in by his teasing. It was Sunburst who constantly reassured him his transition was more than just a change of skin and scales. Nightstar the Black was a fully functioning dragon.

"It makes sense," Galdor said, pulling Nightstar's thoughts back on topic. "About the others Blaze has inflicted the plague upon, I mean. Even though it is abhorrent to think of it. It is something I never even considered. I fear my position as leader is woefully misplaced. Yet I can't sit back and do nothing, but I can't risk it either. If even one female is left at the plateau I must act, but I don't know what I can do. I cannot stand to see what remains of my colony slowly, year after year, decade after decade, fall to the black monster who calls himself a dragon."

"Do not doubt yourself, Galdor," Nightstar said, "you were gone for a long time and were powerless to act. It is because of you there are still free dragons living here. You are the one keeping them safe, giving them hope."

"A hope I don't truly believe myself," Galdor admitted. "I am too close to our plight and find it difficult to look at objectively. I think of Blaze and I see red. It clouds my judgement. I do not know which way to turn."

"We offered our help before," Sunburst said, "let us try." The yellow dragon looked at Nightstar and this time he nodded his black head. More often than not he would scold the yellow for his impetuous behaviour. His friend was all too prone to rashly jumping in to situations without considering the consequences. Sunburst usually acted without fully thinking things through, a victim of his own impulsiveness. Today was different. Nightstar agreed. Sunburst had the right of it. They must help Galdor.

"Sunburst is correct. We need to investigate, gather information. Once we attain a clearer picture of who remains at the Lifting Plateau and what this unknown magical talisman is, then we'll be in a better position." He eyed the yellow dragon. "My yellow friend has a charitable spirit and an inquisitive nature. He is a champion of all dragons, confident and without fear. He will rush headlong into danger never stopping to question his actions. They are traits I admire in him." It was Sunburst's turn to stare at Nightstar. "And sometimes they make me want to roar. His sense of adventure can often get him into trouble, a lot of trouble. But I'm with him on this."

"You forgot my superior intellect and clever humour." Sunburst blew a small curl of smoke from one nostril.

"I haven't forgotten. I was just thinking how I'm going to explain this extended absence to Blood Rose."

"I do not wish to endanger you both. You are guests to my world," Galdor said.

"Relax, mighty Galdor," Sunburst said, "Nightstar and I know the risk. It is just his way of looking out for me. We are both aware of the seriousness of our task. We are brothers of blood and there's no dragon I would rather have at my side."

"Thank you, Sunburst," Nightstar said. "As would I."

The yellow dragon winked one eye at Galdor, "And every good adventure needs a hero. So who better to accompany him?"

Galdor nodded his head slowly, unconsciously mimicking Nightstar. "One wing beat at a time, Sunburst. First, as you have both so rightly stated, we need to find out what's going on at the plateau. Once we know that, then we can devise a plan to defeat Blaze."

"When you put it like that you make it sound simple," Sunburst said.

"Nothing," Nightstar groaned, "is ever simple when you are involved."

"What I do know about Blaze is you must not underestimate him. He is clever and ruthless. He plotted and schemed until he was rid of me. Not only has he exploited his own species to further his plans, he has systematically attacked and destroyed the human inhabitants of this continent in an attempt at eradicating them to the point of extinction. Over the last forty years his black host have ranged farther and farther south, attacking and burning every human building, every village and town, every city.

"We have remained hidden and observed him from afar. His host is at least three times the size of our new colony and we have no way of stopping him, but we watch. Witnessing his airborne attack would have been a frightening enough sight for a dragon. I can only image how terrifying it must have been to the humans, especially when they swooped down upon their homes and families. I also know he sends his patrols to search for the free dragons that escaped. We see them pass overhead from time to time, but we are well hidden. Every once in a while he captures one of us and converts them to the black. You have observed our ways and know why we are ever cautious. We must preserve those who remain free. I shudder to imagine what would become of this world should we all become slaves to his tyranny. All life as we know it would come to an end. There would be no more humans—if any survived—and no more free thinking dragons. Blaze would rule an empire of death and destruction and no living creature, be it man or dragon, could hope to stand before him."

"Then he must be stopped," Sunburst said.

"We must find the magical artefact," Nightstar added, "and if possible, destroy it. If it is something that corrupts minds, then it has no place in this, or any world."

"It seems every course of action is fraught with danger," Galdor said. "We don't know what horrors the Lifting Plateau has in store for us. How dangerous the artefact is. We risk capture, death, or worse, the black plague, if we are discovered."

"I will travel to the Lifting Plateau," Nightstar announced. "By myself," he avoided eye contact with Sunburst. "I will find out what we need to know."

Sunburst looked to Nightstar, "No! You can't go on your own."

"I am black, you are not," Nightstar said, dragon logic the yellow couldn't argue with, "even if we disguised the colour of your scales, you would still shine with a magic that Blaze might sniff out. We have no way of knowing what he is able to do or what powers this artefact holds."

"But who will watch your back? Who will be your guide? I can't stand by and do nothing while you risk everything."

"Sunburst," Galdor spoke, "your loyalty to your friend is admirable. I know only too well how you must feel. Nightstar has the right of it. I don't like it either, but I see it is the only way."

"But—" Sunburst protested.

"Look at the dragon before you," Galdor cut in. "He is Nightstar the Black. In your own words you told me you trusted him with your life and not to doubt his abilities. I have seen into your friend's heart, looked deep down into the very core of his being. You are right... and yet he is so much more. If any dragon can do this, it is Nightstar. I trust him to return to us with the information we need. I must, I have no other choice but to put my faith in him once again. He is different from the human who helped me escape, yet the same at his core. His black scales are an advantage Blaze is ignorant of. It is as he says," he looked at Nightstar and bowed his head. "Not all black dragons are the enemy and I would count you as a friend, Nightstar the Black."

"He is a friend to all dragons," Sunburst said, "who better come back, or Blaze will know a wrath no dragon from this world has ever witnessed!"

"I do not doubt it," Nightstar grinned. "I have seen your wrath and barely survived. We will call that our back up plan, should we need it."

"Pah!" Sunburst snorted. "You've think you've seen it. I was easy on you! You don't even have a primary plan yet. Back up indeed!"

"Then let's come up with one," Galdor said. "I think we need to involve a few more dragons, Nightstar. Not to infiltrate the plateau, but you will need a guide, a dragon who knows the lie of the land."

"And I will accompany them. Just try and stop me!" Sunburst stated. His tone brooked no argument.

"Very well," Galdor said. "Are all dragons of the White Mountains as feisty as this one, Nightstar? One day I would very much like to visit there."

"There are none there like Sunburst, he is one of a kind. They are strong, it is true, but they are welcoming too. The dragons of the White Mountains have a saying. *You are only a stranger the first time you visit.* They are a colony I am proud to be part of."

"As it should be," said Galdor. "The Lifting Plateau was once like that. I hope we can take back what has been stolen and return to friendlier times."

"Then let's meet this guide and get flying," Sunburst flapped his wings. "This feisty yellow is ready to rush in headlong. Whatever the plan."

Chapter 27

The Sleeping Dragon

Topaz dropped low into the approaching valley and Sunburst followed; he was still a little too close for Nightstar's liking. The Blue female followed Galdor's request to lead them to the plateau, but she didn't like it.

Galdor may doubt his abilities as leader, but the free dragons of Alvanor had no such reservations. He was still a strong leader and his colony never doubted he would liberate them from Blaze and his black army.

Azyrian made up the fourth member of their group, a bronze shadow following Nightstar silently through the air. He suspected the quiet bronze didn't just accompany them due to his expert knowledge of the landscape surrounding the Lifting Plateau. His muscles flowed like molten metal beneath armoured scales, power rippling through his body.

Nightstar didn't have much experience with metals and was impressed by Azyrian's physical presence. While all dragons, regardless of size or colour were awe-inspiring, the big bronze reminded him of a sculptor's work of art, a masterpiece forged in metal.

There was no doubt in Nightstar's mind, Azyrian was with them in case they encountered any trouble.

Topaz landed close to a small copse of dense trees, taking shelter at their edge. Nightstar understood why Galdor had chosen the short tempered blue to guide them. She was extremely cautious and knew exactly what would happen if they were discovered. She took her task seriously and made sure they all followed her instructions implicitly. Sunburst was trying hard to keep on her good side and Nightstar silently thanked his yellow companion for not upsetting her. While Sunburst didn't challenge her flying abilities on the way here, he didn't miss a wingbeat as she weaved her way through the demanding terrain.

Topaz was aware of her bright blue scales and shrunk into the treeline to disguise her from any airborne patrols. Sunburst followed her lead, pushing his bright yellow body into the gaps between the tree trunks.

Nightstar landed in the open and made his way to where the blue and yellow dragons waited, Azyrian dropping from the sky and quickly joining them.

"This is as far as we go," Topaz said, eyeing Nightstar. "To get any closer would not be wise. Are you sure you want to do this?" Her words were less harsh than they had been when they had initially met.

"If we are to learn anything useful at all," Nightstar replied, "then it must be so. I am best suited to the task."

"I wish you luck, black dragon," she said. "It says much for your character that you are willing to help us." Looking into the sky above, she continued, "Perhaps I was wrong about you. Fly high and fly free."

"Thank you, Topaz. I will."

"I am leaving," Topaz added, "Sunburst, if you wish to return, you can fly back with me. Azyrian will wait in the shelter of these trees for Nightstar's return."

"Then I shall keep him company," Sunburst replied. "I understand why it wouldn't be prudent for me to accompany him, even though I want to. I will stay with Azyrian and await his safe return. If I am unable to go with Nightstar, I should at least be here should he need my help."

"Your loyalty is without question, Sunburst. Your friendship with Nightstar says much for his character." She faced Nightstar once more. "Understand I want only to preserve our safety. If I was blunt with you when we first met, it was not without good reason. I was not always this way." She spoke as if it was the last time she would see him.

"I will be back. I would like to get to know Topaz the *Peaceful*," Nightstar stressed the word, "in less difficult times. If she will allow me the chance."

The blue dipped her head in a curt bow, "I hope to see you all return safely." Pushing off into the air she turned her head towards Sunburst and added, "And when we don't have Blaze to worry about, I'll show you how to ride the currents of the plateau!" She sped off back down the valley, flying low to the undulating ground, using her practiced skill to utilise all available cover.

"She has flown stormy skies, "Azyrian said, "and lost many friends. We all have. We are not what we once were. These dark times are hard on us all. Especially Galdor."

"I see the way you stay close to him," Nightstar said. "He is fortunate to have you with him. Blaze has much to answer for and we are here to help. Galdor's burdens are many. His loss of years, loss of home and of his colony. The mental anguish he suffered in the caves. The dragons lost to the black plague. Blaze tricked him and betrayed his trust. It should have been enough to break his spirit. But is has not. My *perception* tells me he will not give up. It is who he is."

"And every free dragon of Alvanor will stand with him," Azyrian said.

"And he knows it," Nightstar said, "and that is also a burden he carries. He cannot bear to see his colony slowly destroyed. He needs to fight back, but struggles with putting dragons in danger."

"Shells must be broken if you want eggs to hatch," Azyrian said. "What are your thoughts, Nightstar?"

"Nightstar," Sunburst said, "is going to boldly fly his big black hide into the Lifting Plateau, sniff around with that over inquisitive snout of his, find any free dragons and locate the magical artefact. *Then*," he drew the word out, "he's going to leave with everything he needs and come straight back here, avoiding any unnecessary conflict. Simple as that!"

Azyrian cocked his head towards the yellow and Nightstar detected a twinkle of humour in the Azyrian's liquid green eyes."

"He has as a way with words," the big bronze said to Nightstar. "It is a good plan. I particularly like the part when you come back after avoiding any conflict." His clipped tone was reassuring rather than abrupt. "Be extra careful, Nightstar. Do not underestimate Blaze. You enter into the unknown. The Earth Mother knows what twisted horrors lie in wait."

"In and out," Sunburst said. "A dark shadow in a dark place. Quick and stealthy. You will need to disguise your silver scales. Impressive as they are, now is not the time to draw attention to yourself."

"I have an idea about how to do that," Nightstar said, "and want to test the results before I infiltrate the plateau."

He extended a talon and traced the edges of his silver scales with the sharp tip, stopping at the topmost point of his star. Gently at first he probed the razor sharp talon into the place where the scales overlapped, pushing harder and forcing it beneath his armour. Piercing the unprotected skin he carefully drew the sharp talon down, opening a small cut, and slid it free. A warm sensation oozed from the incision as a blend of dragon and human blood, an amalgam unique only to him, trickled down over the silver scales.

The blood spread and Nightstar used his magic to smooth it out over the scales. It crept across them like a tide covering sand, slow and with purpose, until the silver was painted with blood. The star glowed red, light emanating from within, pulsing as the magic tingled his senses, and radiated brightly before fading. The pulsing slowed and each time the brightness faded, the star grew darker. When it cycled through the phase for the final time, the silver was gone and all that remained were black scales perfectly, blended with the rest.

"Strong magic," Azyrian remarked. "Quickly dissipated. You are indeed adept in the magical arts."

"Can you sense any residual magic, now it is done?" Nightstar asked, changing the subject. A human lifetime and an apprenticeship of many years helped in his proficiency with the dragon magic. "I need to ensure it can't be sniffed out by others. The caves of the Lifting Plateau are the last place I want my deception to be noticed."

Sunburst pushed his pointed snout up to Nightstar's chest and inhaled deeply. "You look strange without it. I know where it is, yet there is no trace. Nothing magical either. It's as if it never was. What do you think, Azyrian?"

Azyrian stepped closer and mimicked Sunburst's actions. "Nothing," he declared in his economic way with words. "I smell no magic at all. A nice trick, I wonder how long it will remain and if it will it rub off accidentally?"

"The silver should stay dark for a while," Nightstar said. "I've deliberately used a small amount of magic to ensure it can't be outwardly detected, so it won't last long." He knew when Flaire was involved, the normal rules of any kind of magic or sorcery, didn't always apply. The Flaire artefact he wore as a human became the silver scales on Nightstar's chest, therefore he wasn't entirely sure how it would react. "It will serve its purpose and as Sunburst says, in and out, nice and quick, no heroics."

"Leave any heroics to me. Good plan," Sunburst said. "After all, it's what I'm good at!" He butted his angular head into Nightstar's flank. "Better make a move then. The sooner you're away, the sooner you'll be back. I'll stay here and look after Azyrian and we can get to know each other."

"I hope your ears aren't too exhausted by the time I return," Nightstar told Azyrian. "Our yellow friend has a tendency towards the loquacious."

"It means I have a charitable spirit, an inquisitive nature, and a clever humour," Sunburst told Azyrian.

"And not long-winded and chatty?" Azyrian asked Sunburst. "*I will watch over your yellow companion*," he said to Nightstar.

"I was afraid to leave our bronze friend alone with you, but I see he will be fine."

"Do not worry for us Nightstar," Azyrian said, "we will indeed be fine. There is ample shelter for us to remain hidden. It is you I worry about."

"I will be hiding too. Hiding in plain sight... hopefully. Just another black dragon amongst many, strange as it sounds. I am used to being the only dragon of my colour back home." It was true, he was the only black dragon at the White Mountain. *His* dragon home.

"Fly south from here," Azyrian said, "the plateau is about an hour's flight. Fly high and fly free, friend Nightstar. Return to us safely."

"Be careful, brother," Sunburst added.

"I will." Nightstar rose from the valley floor and circled the copse of trees where the yellow and bronze dragons hid. He dipped his wings once in farewell then veered south for the Lifting Plateau... and the unknown.

* * *

The natural feature of the plateau loomed ahead. Nightstar scanned the surrounding skies for company, but there was none. He had only seen a few other dragons in the distance, flying in other directions. He continued towards his goal unchallenged.

It wasn't the getting in that bothered him, it was getting back out. His plan, much to Sunburst's disapproval, would be to walk right into the caves of the plateau like he belonged there. It made sense. Who would stop him? A black dragon in a colony of black dragons. He would be a part of their elite and he needed to believe it. As long as he set off no alarms, in theory, it should be just as easy to stroll back out. *Should.*

Galdor said Blaze used their old moot chamber as his home. If there was anything to find it would be there. They discussed the layout of the caves that ran underneath the plateau and Galdor revealed there was a maze of old passages, not as commonly used as some, that may help him approach undetected. If he stuck to the less frequently used passageways he reduced his chances of being discovered.

He also warned that drones guarded the chamber and were under instruction not to let any dragons inside, without their leader's express permission. He would tackle that particular problem once he was inside. One wing beat at a time.

The thermal updrafts from below the plateau surprised him. Their warm air currents filling his wings and pushing him skyward. It was a sensation unlike anything experienced before. Air pressure buffeted his lower body, catching outstretched wings and propelling him high above the plateau's edge. The effortless act of soaring with the rising thermals filled him with a guilty joy. He understood why the free dragons missed the Lifting Plateau. It was a natural place for dragons to make their home. No matter how many times Nightstar took to the air, there was always something there to remind him of that first flight. The scholar deep down inside the dragon mind still marvelled at the inherent instinct possessed by the dragon spirit.

Nightstar dropped back down through the turbulent air and flattened out his approach. There were many entrances to the underground labyrinth and, with Galdor's detailed instructions, he would find one less frequented... or hopefully not used at all.

The ground rushed up to meet him and he tilted his wings, slowing his air speed enough to hover for a split second, before gracefully touching ground. A perfect landing atop the aptly named plateau and more crucially, all performed with the minimum of noise.

The plateau was quiet and nothing disturbed the earie silence except the wind through the long grass. The soft whispering exaggerated in the absence of any other sound. The colony of the White Mountain was a place filled with the noise of dragons, the sounds of life. The Lifting Plateau, for all its serene beauty, felt like mute despair. Dragon ears were extremely good, but not even the humming drone of insects or the distant cry of bird song reached him.

Nightstar's muscles were tense and he held his body in a state of readiness. His stance reflected his feelings, crouched low and ready to spring into action. Skulking through the long grass he looked for a formation of craggy rocks near the eastern edge of the plateau. A landmark from Galdor's directions, he called *the sleeping dragon*. All the rocks looked the same as he searched for a rocky outcrop that resembled anything close to a dragon shape. Maybe it looked like a sleeping dragon from the air. Galdor hadn't thought to elaborate on... wait. There it was! As he moved stealthily towards the eastern edge, changing his angle, the formation took shape before his eyes. Three large rocks, a head, a back, and tail, aligned themselves like a syzygy of celestial bodies, revealing the rather accurate silhouette of a slumbering dragon. The rock representing the head was shaped in such a way that it even appeared to have horns.

Impressive as the sight was, Nightstar couldn't help being reminded of another stone dragon. Galdor had told them of his encounter upon his returning home. At first he believed the dragon was a statue carved by some long forgotten artist. The green dragon sadly explained the stone dragon turned out to be an old friend, a blue dragon called Baelross who was once a member of his moot. He suspected, given that Baelross was in the same caves where Blaze had tricked him, the black dragon was responsible.

There was no explanation Galdor could give as to how a living dragon could be turned to stone. If Blaze was responsible for this cruelty, where would he stop? Dragons didn't usually harm their own. They had seen the aftermath of Blaze's magic enough times to know, that black dragon, followed his own path, his magic growing along with his ambitions.

The sleeping dragon perched on the rim of the plateau. Nightstar climbed onto the largest of the three rocks, atop the stony back of the beast. He pushed his neck out beyond their craggy edges and into the updraft. Wind blasted his face, rushing past his ears like waves crashing onto a storm swept beach. Eyes half closed against the blustering updraft, he fought back watery tears, squinting to locate what Galdor assured him was his best way in.

A dark cave mouth was situated on the sweeping cliff face making up the steep east side of the plateau. It wasn't as obvious an entry to the caves running through the plateau and was positioned beyond casual observation. Galdor was right. You would have to know where it was to see it. Dragons leaving the plateau rode the currents of the updraft upwards and away from the secluded cave mouth. Dragons arriving usually, according to Galdor, dropped in from above. This limited the secluded cave's exposure. If you coupled that with the out-of-the-way location, it was easy to see why Galdor favoured it. While it wasn't exactly a secret, it was reasonable enough to assume dragons who were aware of it would use a more convenient entrance. The western side of the plateau was dotted with an abundance of wide, accessible caves that led down into the underground and was the most commonly used point of entry.

The eastern cave was only just wide enough for a dragon of his size to fit through and it would be a tight squeeze, which would be difficult. Add a turbulent updraft, forcing you in the opposite direction to where you needed to be, and difficult became challenging.

Topaz insisted his experience with the Leviathan's Gullet would stand him in good stead. It was true, she had led them blindly into dangerous air. This time he could see his landing point and knew what to expect.

Leaning into the updraft and partially opening his wings, he angled himself forward. The strong currents of air prevented him from plummeting downward. He leaned deeper into the updraft grasping the rock with the tips of his talons, his weight supported by nothing but rushing air. He knew exactly where the cave mouth was and gave one last scrabbling push from the rocky back of the sleeping dragon into nothingness.

For a second he hung suspended, the air catching in the pockets created by his half open wings. The sensation was so different from the easy flight he was used to. Violent eddies swirled out from under his wing membranes, whipping and lashing with raw power as the slipstreams they created fought to twist and turn him. By fractionally opening and closing his wing he was able to control his position, neither rising nor dropping too much. This wasn't challenging at all, this was terrifying. The jagged cliff face deflected the rushing air in all directions and at any second a slight misjudgement of angle or wing position could result in collision.

His wings ached from the strain but lending magic to strengthen them was not a good idea. If Blaze was as strong as Galdor thought, using magic this close to his lair was not the wisest choice. He didn't want to take the risk, so any use of any magic, no matter how much he wanted to use it, wasn't an option. This was all down to his flying skills.

Slowly, stealing inch after inch, Nightstar crept through the air towards the cave mouth. He approached from the top, lining himself up above the apex, then closed his wings slightly and sped directly for the cave entrance. As soon as his head and neck entered into the aperture, he recognised his mistake, his front end dropping as the airflow abated, as the first half of his body passed across the rocky threshold. His tail end performed the opposite manoeuvre, lurching upward as the currents still pushed from below. Momentum carried him forward, a result of luck rather than good judgement, spinning his rear end over his head.

Summersaulting tail over snout he crashed into the cave floor, disorientated and tasting dirt. He shook his head and blew gouts of dusty snot from his nostrils. It was a difficult landing and even a seasoned flier would have found it challenging. Small consolation. If Sunburst were with him he would be reminded this was the second time in as many days his aerial expertise had resulted in a crash landing. Well, Sunburst didn't need to know. Nightstar considered himself an excellent flier. He possessed strength and speed and was nearly unbeatable when it came to altitude and stamina.

A niggling voice deep down in Alduce's subconscious surfaced to remind him of something the sorcerer's old mentor liked to say. Master Caltus was known for his pithy aphorisms and witty observations. *You are never too smart to learn a little more* or *pride comes before a fall* were a couple that sprang to mind. Nightstar felt the shared memory. He heard the voice of Caltus speak the words and saw the old man's kindly face. His aching rump reminded him that he didn't know as much as he thought he did when it came to flying.

His old master would surely have something profound to say if he met the black dragon his former apprentice now shared his life with.

Nightstar righted himself and took in his surroundings. His dramatic entry into the cave was less than quiet, but the rushing of the air as it whooshed passed the cave entrance, drowned out any sounds of his awkward landing. He hoped.

There was no sound other than the rushing air outside. The cave was dry and dusty and bore no evidence of being used recently. That was promising. He peered into the dark, eyes adjusting to the gloom. The way ahead was clear, but a feeling of foreboding filled the passageway. Something definitely wasn't quite right at the Lifting Plateau.

He set off down the dusty passage, the wisdom of master Caltus still fresh in his mind.

Don't go looking for trouble, for it will find you soon enough.

Chapter 28

In and Out

The deeper Nightstar descended into the underground labyrinth, the darker his mood became. A creeping feeling of oppression seeped under his scales filling him with anxiety and despair. The narrow cave walls emitted a stifling claustrophobia that was difficult to ignore.

He didn't feel any magic he recognised or sense a warding spell designed to dissuade. This was something entirely new to him. And he didn't like it one bit.

He couldn't begin to imagine living with these emotions every day. Any dragons exposed to these feelings continuously, must be a sorry bunch.

The free dragons spoke of the Lifting Plateau with fond memories and he was sure it wasn't always this way. If this was Blaze's vision of how a colony should be, he could see why Galdor and his followers wanted him stopped.

He followed the dusty tunnels remembering Galdor's directions and tried to remain positive. Focus on the task.

In and out; gather the information they needed, then leave.

It was a fairly straight route and so far the path presented no obstacles. Galdor worried Blaze may have sealed off the less frequently travelled passageways or they may have been rendered inaccessible due to rock falls. It didn't look like anyone knew they even existed, which was a good thing. Unless there was a rock fall and his path came to an abrupt halt. If the dragons here didn't know of these old ways, they wouldn't know they were blocked and they wouldn't be cleared.

Nightstar silently thanked his luck and desperately hoped it held out. He was overthinking things and his normal pragmatic self knew it was the feelings of gloom making him think this way, almost convincing him it was pointless to even try.

What would Sunburst say? He wondered. Thinking of his yellow friend helped him battle through the suffocating tunnels and lifted his spirits. He was always ready with a quick witted observation or a clever retort and came with his own unique view of life. Most of the time he was cheerful enough to lift the lowest of moods. Sometimes he was infuriatingly annoying. And on occasion, a force to be reckoned with. Sunburst had wanted to accompany him and now he wished the yellow was here. He knew it was risky enough on his own but right now he would have welcomed the company. The last time they had faced their dangers, it was together. It felt odd not to have him at his wing.

He could feel the presence of Alduce too, urging him forward. The thoughts in his head were clear and pleasantly calming. The sorcerer was convinced something other than the tyrannical black dragon was causing these unnatural feelings. Alduce was an authority on a number of subjects and was seldom wrong. He was like a dragon's own *human* sense and Nightstar valued his judgement.

The tunnels came to their first real intersection. Up until now it was a simple choice of left or right, or choose the widest tunnel. Galdor had told him to take the narrowest tunnel to the left at this junction. On a whim, he moved a little farther down the middle tunnel, which disappeared round a sharp bend, a strange curiosity enticing him onwards. He still marvelled at his exceptional vison in the dark, his dragon's eye an advantage he didn't take for granted.

Craning his neck around the bend, he froze. The passageway widened and offered a view that stretched out for at least half a mile. Two silent forms sat at the far end of the tunnel where it widened out to a large circular cave. They sat unmoving, like faithful hounds set to guard their master's door. Two black dragons.

Nightstar knew he still had a way to go before the moot chamber and wondered what Blaze's drones were guarding down here, away from everything. He wanted to retreat back around the corner, pull his head into the safety of the tunnel where he wouldn't be seen. But he didn't. If they happened to look his way they would surely see him. There was a faint familiar scent, almost something he recognised, yet he couldn't quite place it.

What were they guarding? It didn't make sense. They weren't keeping watch on these old tunnels, not that far away. If they were it would be much more logical to position themselves at the intersection and dragons, if anything, were creatures of logic.

What would be worth keeping down here in the depths of the plateau's cave system? Why would you have dragons this far down?

Of course! It must be where the natural dragons were held. His snout finally identified the scent.

Females. Everything falling into place.

The two black dragons sat motionless, staring off into the distance as if in a trance, and Nightstar was glad it wasn't in his direction. Their silence and lack of animation puzzled him. Was this how drones acted?

Galdor was sure all traces of their past identity were wiped out when they were taken by the black plague. They were just as much prisoners as he had once been, but at least they were no longer aware of their stolen lives. Galdor had eventually escaped, there was no escape for these poor beasts other than death. Nightstar's intense curiosity—which he believed was inherited from his human counterpart—got the better of him. Only ever having viewed a changed black dragon from afar, he wanted a closer look.

Creeping from the shelter of the bend, he slowly advanced, taking the utmost care to move as silently as possible. Every step painstakingly exaggerated as he carefully placed his talons, one after the other, in a slow motion. He knew that if the two black dragons turned around or heard the slightest sound, he would be caught. He just wanted to observe them a little closer. When would he get a better opportunity than now?

He heard Sunburst's voice in his head, reminding him not to take any risks and to be careful. He was sure these two stationary dragons were in a dormant state, appearing awake, but actually more like sleeping with their eyes open. It wasn't really that much of a risk. And he was being careful. Best not to get too close though and stick to the plan.

He studied the dragons, examining their scales. He was as close as he dared, near enough to see every detail, his excellent vision making it easy. Their scales were a duller black than his own and they lacked the pearlescent finish, devoid of the lustre of life. A painted imitation of the real thing, fashioned from dark magic. The dragons they had once been, gone forever. He could see it as well as sense it, as Galdor must have, *perception* true, no doubt in his mind there was no sign of their former lives.

He was never surer that Blaze must be defeated. These poor dragons were shells of what they had once been, their spirits gone. There was no free will, no life, nothing. They were less than drones. Empty vessels filled with the poison of corruption. Nothing remained of their former selves, no chance of salvation, their only hope of redemption would be with Blaze's defeat.

He questioned his own origin, searching the memories of the man he shared a mind with. He was nothing like these creatures. He was a real dragon. His birth was not from the egg, well not directly. His was from magic and all dragons possessed magic. He had a spirit, a dragon soul. The life that allowed him to grow into the dragon he was, given a second chance. Alduce still felt some guilt in using the unhatched egg. It was part of what he needed to do in order to become Nightstar. It was never malevolent, never evil, he wanted to become what he loved. He had waited a long time to find an unhatched, abandoned egg, when it would have been just as easy to take a healthy egg from the nests he had observed.

His desire was to live and learn, his science and sorcery a means to an end. His transformation a creation of life, a truly magnificent discovery, that grew and thrived.

The transformations Blaze created were the opposite of everything Alduce stood for. He tore the life from living dragons, stealing their spirits, taking everything from them. They were nothing but mindless marionettes, their strings pulled by an unfeeling, uncaring puppet master.

The feeling of despair that filled the Lifting Plateau was strengthened by the mindless black converts Blaze had transformed. It oozed from their scales as if they had bathed in it, but it was more than that, they were part of it, although they weren't its source. Something else was at the heart of this, something evil.

Nightstar had seen enough. There was nothing here that would help him, he had learned all he needed to know from this unfortunate pair. He twisted his neck back towards the bend in the passageway, desperate to be away from these lifeless drones, only to discover it was gone!

The entranceway to the tunnel had completely vanished. It wasn't possible. If it was magic he would have detected it. He now felt far too close to the two black dragons, even though he'd only travelled a hundred feet at most from the shelter of the bend. Inch by inch he withdrew, not knowing where he would go, but never taking his eyes from the unmoving enemy.

He didn't like to think of dragons as the enemy, but these drones were not dragons anymore. They were weapons fashioned by a cruel master, commodities to be used up in advancement of his cause. They were the enemy of all natural dragons and would not stop to consider their actions, only obey without conscience. They would kill without hesitating and were a danger to all natural dragons. They must be stopped.

He needed to put some distance between himself and these foul creatures. He backed up until he hit solid rock, unaware of what was halting his retreat. He'd come far enough that he was back at the bend, his tail end pushed against the cave wall, now able to see the vanished intersection! What was happening?

The dragons remained in position, oblivious to his presence. Safely sheltered in the passageway once more, he took a second to check his surroundings. He was definitely back where he started. The intersection behind him where it should be, and the twist in the passage in front.

Creeping back towards the black dragons just enough for his body to pass the corner in the passageway, he turned and looked behind himself. The cave wall in front of his eyes looked as if it went no farther. The rocky surfaces of the passage walls all blended together to form the illusion of a dead end. Even though his snout was inches from the corner, he struggled to see passageway beyond. If he didn't know it was there, he wouldn't have believed it.

The optical illusion must have prevented any dragons approaching. Anyone observing from the other side of the passage would be totally oblivious of anything beyond.

That was why there were no guards posted this far along the tunnel. Nobody knew the passageway existed past what they could see. His head spun as he stared at the rock face that wasn't real. He knew it was false, yet he couldn't see through it. His head swam a little as he focused his eyes trying to see passed the rocky mirage.

He doubted his own magic could have created a better illusion. Everything neatly blended together, from floor to ceiling, from the left to the right cave walls, conjuring the very real illusion of solid rock. The end of the passage. There was no reason to come into this tunnel and inspect it, everything you needed to see was right there in front of your eyes. The appearance of a dead end falsely setting the expectation this was as far as the tunnel went.

Nightstar made his way back to the intersection and stood in front of the narrow tunnel he was supposed to follow. It would be easy to get lost down here in the depths if he hadn't had Galdor to tell him which way to go. The tunnels of the Lifting Plateau were full of surprises, Galdor said, and it was best not to stray too far off track.

In and out, that was all he needed to do. Stick to the plan. He would have liked to explore these underground tunnels a little more thoroughly, but for now he would have to make do with using them to locate the moot chamber.

Taking one last look behind him at the corner of the optical illusion, he wondered what other secrets lay hidden in the depths of the Lifting Plateau.

He set off once more, entering into the narrow tunnel he hoped would take him safely to his intended destination.

Chapter 29

Discovery

The chamber of the moot was situated directly below where Nightstar lay. After hours of creeping through abandoned tunnels and passageways he was finally where he wanted to be.

Galdor had sworn him to secrecy regarding his lofty vantage point. No other dragon was aware of its existence and Galdor wanted to keep it that way.

Nightstar was pleased. If Galdor wanted this passageway to remain unknown, he must be thinking to a future where he would once more be hosting his moot from inside this chamber. Subconsciously, the green dragon was not as unsure as he thought he was.

Nightstar respected Galdor's reasoning. A moot was a private affair where leaders assembled to make decisions that would impact the colony. If dragons could observe these meetings, it would no doubt lead to rumours and gossip mongering and when it came to gossip, dragons were experts. Being a leader was never an easy job. Galdor, more than most, was aware of how his actions could be interpreted by gossips and eavesdroppers.

However, it was now Nightstar's turn to spy on the chamber below. His secret observations were crucial if they were to learn what Blaze was hiding. He pressed his belly to the floor and took his time to creep along the narrow tunnel. The floor in front of his snout was riddled with a honeycomb of holes. Holes that were perfect for a sneaking dragon to peer through.

Angling his long snout to one side and pressing his eye to one of the larger holes, he peered into the cavern below. The last time he gave way to this kind of curiosity his actions had landed him in trouble with the leader of the White Mountain moot. His own compulsion to learn secrets he wasn't ready for, had backfired. He paid the penalty for his misdeeds and came to understand his betrayal of trust. Now, irony twisted his situation and his subterfuge was for the good of others; Galdor and his colony. It filled him with the feeling of being part of something bigger. He was included by these dragons, they wanted his help.

Before he was all about himself, be it Alduce or Nightstar. He wanted to learn, to find a reason, to explain, to quantify. His journey as a dragon offered him, like the unhatched dragon, a second chance. A way to open his eyes and see life from another viewpoint. It wasn't just the transformation, the physical change. It was so much more.

Alduce the human didn't realise life was passing him by until Nightstar the dragon—unintentionally—exposed him to a completely different perspective. His scholarly ways were still important, but they were no longer just his life. Life was for living, for friendship hard earned, for sacrifice and for love. The human inside could study the mysteries of science, but he needed the dragon to teach him how to embrace life.

He would help Galdor's dragons because it was the right thing to do. He was a dragon. It was what he *must* do.

He blinked and his inner eyelid flitted across his eyeball clearing away the dust from the cave floor. He bent his neck and turned his head, finding the perfect position to view what lay beneath him.

Framed through the rough hole in the rock, the bulk of a huge black dragon was partly visible.

It could only be Blaze.

He lay curled on the floor, his front legs drawn underneath his body, tail wrapped around himself and coming to rest at his snout. He lay like a cat on a hearth, the white flash on his chest rose and fell, vivid against the dark scales. Air whistled through his nostrils as he slept, exaggerated in the silent confines of the moot chamber.

Nightstar shifted his body, turning his head around and swapped his other eye to the aperture in the rock. The change in position revealed a different part of the sleeping dragon through the limited vision of the spyhole. He starred, wide-eyed in amazement and forgetting to blink, at the sight exposed from this angle.

Sitting on the floor, partially obscured between the inner curve of Blaze's neck and his thick serpentine tail, nestled a huge glowing object.

It was perfectly round and appeared to be made of glass. It reminded Nightstar of the pearl of wisdom, the artefact Winterfang sometimes communed with. It was an ancient source of knowledge, forbidden to all but the oldest and most responsible dragons. A pearl of wisdom—or moonstone—according to Winterfang was a source of mystery and wonder. It homed many strong spells, was the keeper of great wisdom, and a source of guidance for dragons who searched its depths. It was not evil, but one must take care when consulting with it. It was an unknown magic and it was always best to be cautious when dealing with the unknown.

It was clear this giant orb wasn't a pearl. Nightstar was positive it was responsible for the feelings of misery and despair permeating the caves of the Lifting Plateau. The more he stared, the more he was mesmerized by it. It glowed with an ethereal illumination, pale light radiating out from its insides. A swirling vortex of dancing, weaving clouds raced beneath its surface. Greys and whites mixed, fading brighter then darker. As the inner light pulsed and darkened, two red pinpoints shone out, barely visible then intensely bright. Baleful eyes, hypnotically terrifying, searching for a victim.

He couldn't pull his eye from the spyhole, staring at the orb, transfixed by its swirling interior. He was drawn to its power, seduced by its hidden secrets. Alduce surfaced in Nightstar's consciousness, urging him to look away, a sense of fearful urgency prominent in the sorcerer's mind.

He wanted to break the link forming between his mind and the glowing entity below, but couldn't. He knew he must, he sensed the urgency from Alduce, could feel the pull of attraction, yet he was helpless to act.

Alduce rose up from within Nightstar's mind, pushing the dragon spirit aside. He didn't need *perception* to warn him this was bad. The sorcerer was usually content to let Nightstar guide his dragon self and be the silent observer. A passenger on-board the dragon vessel, savouring the experiences of the ride, like a sailor welcomes the deck beneath his feet. Along for the journey rather than the helmsman.

He couldn't sit back now. He must grasp at the ship's wheel and steer Nightstar from danger.

His attempt was in vain. He couldn't stop himself, couldn't pull Nightstar's attention away from the malevolent magnetism of the glowing globe.

Dizzying vertigo crashed into his brain, the cave floor spun and bucked beneath his feet... his talons. He focused his mind and tried to push Nightstar away from the threat. The divide between dragon and man grew blurry as the Alduce-Nightstar amalgam slipped from consciousness.

The dragon closed his eyes and surrendered to the blackout, breaking the bond between his physical self and the huge orb below. A feeling of falling tugged at the last vestiges of his waking mind and he descended deeper into the waiting blackness.

Alduce fell too. His fall steeper and faster. His mind spanned the distance between the now unconscious Nightstar and the orb, sucked down in a maelstrom of impossible darkness.

* * *

Alduce opened his eyes and struggled to remember. Where am I? And how did I get here? His head pounded and he tried to lift it from the floor. The floor? The grey swirling substance he lay on was not a floor of any construction he was familiar with. It supported his weight, he presumed, but did he really have any weight?

He rubbed his eyes, the action a parody of the real thing. The floor that wasn't a floor moved under him. It was like looking down from above the clouds, except these clouds were a solid surface.

The clouds reminded him of flying, of soaring, of...

Nightstar!

He wasn't a dragon anymore, he was Alduce. Yet he wasn't. This wasn't real. He sat up and the pain in his head begged to differ.

He could feel the presence of Nightstar, distant and unresponsive. He was able to brush the dragon mind but unable to wake him. The floor swirled and he looked away, nausea and disorientation fighting for dominance.

"Welcome," a voice rang out from behind.

Alduce spun around, searching for the voice's owner, the sudden movement causing a wave of dizziness. The area behind him was as empty. The distance obscured by clouds in all directions. He was in some kind of dream world or spirit dimension, separated from the physical realm.

"I do not often receive visitors," the voice spoke with a hint of cruel humour.

"Show yourself," Alduce said, forcing as much confidence into his words as he could. "Or return me back to where I belong."

A wisp of misty red vapour, transparent and thin, rose from the swirling floor. It tapered upward and formed a narrow column, expanding as it gained height, like a miniature whirlwind. It surpassed Alduce's height growing half as much again, corporeal yet without substance.

The spinning vapour thickened, darkening from red to black as it became more solid. As the whirling slowed, the vapour took shape, small tendrils and wisps filling out and moving with purpose. The rough outline of a figure coalesced from within the mist, materialising into being.

Huge feet splayed out on the cloudy floor, inhuman and grotesque. Black scaly claws with talons the colour of ancient bone. The smoky vapour rushed around the feet, growing into thick muscular legs plated with small scales, each one half the length a finger. Alduce thought of the unhatched dragon and the coat of scales he had used for his metamorphosis. The scales of the creature appearing before him were of a similar size, but possessed none of the beauty.

The figure grew, torso and arms solidifying from the venomous vapour, coated in the same black scaled armour. A thick tail lashed the air as it materialised, whipping back and forth like an angry cat, disturbing the vapour, its end tapering to a pointed blade, sharp and deadly.

Wings rose up from behind the creature, spiked, stunted tips protruding over its heavy shoulders, similar to the wings of a bat, too small for flight.

The creature's head appeared, a swirling mass of hazy steam, hissing as it completed the last part of the ensemble. Long horns swept back from the creatures skull, yellow and stained. Spikes ran from between the horns along the top of a flat head and down the creature's back.

It was the vision of nightmares, smouldering red eyes glared out from above a pointed snout. Sharp angled cheekbones tapered back to small flat ears and it was covered from head to foot in black scales of varying size. It was a human shape, all be it three feet taller than any normal sized human, with the characteristics and features of a dragon.

"Here I am," the creature said, its words as sharp as its teeth. "Cower before me, human!" Its wings snapped out, unfurling like ancient leather and it spread its arms wide. "Am I not a sight to behold?" Its arms opened to expose a jagged flash of white lightning that looked as if it had been painted across its chest with a sword blade.

The creature turned in a circle, arms outstretched, as if admiring itself before a mirror.

Alduce stood his ground. He suspected the creature couldn't harm him, not here in this realm, or it would already have tried. It was all bluster, but it didn't make its manifestation any less terrifying.

This was where the malevolent force originated from. It reeked of ancient arrogance, a felled god cast from favour, bloated with self-importance, used to being obeyed.

"Lost your tongue?" it spat out the words, flicking its own blood red tongue between pointed teeth, the gesture crude and threatening.

Before Alduce could answer, its mind slammed into his head, tearing through his thoughts. He staggered, grabbing his head with both hands, struggling to remain upright. Severe pain ploughed through his already fragile mind as the creature probed deeper.

"Get out!" Alduce screamed, forcing the creature from his thoughts and throwing up a mental barrier. He could feel it scrabble at his defences, like rats clawing inside his skull.

"A wielder of magic? Your kind are a scourge. Your defences are weak, human."

Alduce felt the scrabbling increase, tearing at his defences. He pushed his mind forward, a mental wave crashing through the creature's attack and washing it from his mind entirely.

It was the creature's turn to stagger as it felt the full force of Alduce's counter attack. The sorcerer quickly focused, seeking calm and throwing up a defensive shield. His mind was protected behind a wall within his head, strengthened by his will, closing off his thoughts and keeping any further unwanted incursions at bay.

The creature shook its head and folded its wings, "You have a strong will, Alduce the sorcerer."

Alduce stared in puzzlement, wondering how it knew him.

"Yes I know your name. I saw what and who you are. You are not the only one who possesses a strong mind. My foray inside your thoughts may have been brief, but I have learned much about your life. About the black dragon you become. I am quick when it comes to searching another's mind. You revealed much of yourself before rudely kicking me out."

"Why have you brought me here?" Alduce asked, changing the subject. "And where is here?" It concerned him that the creature had learned about Nightstar. It was loose inside his thoughts for only a few seconds. What else did it know?

"Here? This is my prison, my cell, my punishment from your kind! I have not brought you here, you fool. You have been lurking here for years and now I have finally caught you."

"I have no idea what you're talking about," Alduce said. "I've been... elsewhere. Years? Not me."

"If not you then who?" it demanded.

"I don't know! Perhaps if you tell me who you are and what this place is, I will be able to answer your questions." Alduce hoped he could get some information from the creature.

"You do not recognise me?" It sounded surprised. "You do not cower before me or feel guilt at what your kind have done to me?

"You are Blaze the Black?" Alduce asked.

"Blaze is no longer in control. He is a means to an end. I am a prisoner inside this globe and Blaze is my hand in the outside world. He will be my salvation, my freedom. Humanity have known me by many names. I am Djinn. I am Demon. Devil. Jinni. Pazuzu and Shaytan. Your kind have many names for me. I am a God. A destroyer of worlds. Civilizations weep at my deeds and tremble before my power."

Alduce recognised some of the names this mad creature called itself. He was sure it was mad. There was mention of demons and djinn in some of the books he had studied. They were powerful creatures, often corrupt and malevolent. They were known for their evil. They would tempt the unwitting into doing their bidding, controlling them like puppets. Blaze was this creature's puppet. He must get this information to Galdor. They weren't fighting a dragon, they were fighting a being with the power to destroy everything they knew. If this djinn was loosed upon the land, not only Alvanor would be laid to waste, Sull would become a wasteland. Every living man, dragon, animal, and plant would be consumed.

This creature was pure evil. A character of nightmares come to life. The orb was its prison and so far, it was contained. The djinn said Blaze would be his salvation, said he would be his freedom. He must be stopped before he could escape his captivity. It was planning to use the unfortunate black dragon to help him escape. Alduce had to find out how.

Summoning his bravery he asked, "If you are as powerful as you boast, how are you still held prisoner? Surely a djinn that can destroy worlds would have little trouble with a globe of glass."

The djinn roared. "Impudent maggot! The wizard glass is strong, but I am stronger. It will break when I have collected enough life force. Blaze was strong willed. Yet like all dragons he was mundane and complacent. His hatred of mankind was his inner demon," he laughed. "I planted the dark seed of corruption, nourished it and exploited his weakness. He was not an evil dragon, just a stupid, ambitious fool who thought he could use my power to further his cause. Little did he know it was his addiction to the power that would be his downfall."

"Dragons are stronger than that," Alduce said. Even if Blaze's hatred for humans was strong, it shouldn't have allowed the djinn to take control of him, especially if it was confined in a prison of wizard glass. Wizard glass was virtually unbreakable. If this djinn had been trapped inside a globe fashioned from the magical glass, it was for good reason.

"The wizard glass should have prevented you breaching its confines." There was no connection to exploit, no way to seize control of Blaze's spirit.

"Ordinarily, yes," the djinn grinned, "but I am no amateur." The implication that Alduce was, wasn't lost on him. "Sometimes I even impress myself." The djinn waved his hand in a gesture akin to a conjurer, pointing into the air and drawing a circle with his finger. Wisps of light moved from his hand to form a circle.

Alduce stared through the circle, like a sailor looking through a porthole, to see a scene shimmering into focus.

"I am not without some power, even trapped in here," the djinn said, indicating towards the unfolding vision. "And it's not only Alduce the sorcerer who takes what he needs from the nest of a dragon."

The vision became clearer. Alduce looked out on a land of greens and browns, the colours vividly shining through into the dull dream realm. Mountains filled the horizon, grey monoliths tipped with white. In the foreground a female dragon sat in the hollow of what could only be her nest. She rose and stretched, then leapt into the air, probably to search for food.

The unguarded nest was home to four eggs patterned with a blue-green marbling, every one unique. The ground shimmered a short distance from the nest and the grass, green and verdant a moment before, withered and turned black. A dark twisted form rose from the dead patch on the grass, shadowy and faint.

The dark shade reached out to the dragon's nest and extended a grasping claw furnished with long talons. It rested its claw on each egg, rubbing the shell lightly, as if testing each one. It moved back to the second egg, choosing this one against the others. It wasn't apparent why it favoured this egg, externally it was no different from the others as far as Alduce could see.

It placed its other claw on the egg and started to sweep both over the shell's surface, slowly at first then faster. The shell changed colour, darkening to a deep blue, then to black. The shade stopped, lifted its misshapen claws from the egg's surface and extended a finger. Resting the sharp talon on the surface of the shell, it looked directly through the hole at the djinn.

The djinn turned to Alduce and drew his hand across his chest in a diagonal motion, tracing the line of the jagged white flash. Its palm glowed as it brushed the scaly chest and he clenched it in a fist then threw a fork of lightning through the portal. It struck the dark shade's finger and its hand jerked, dragging the claw over the shell.

Alduce looked at the djinn's chest and then through the portal at the egg. The white mark carved on the shell of the egg was an exact replica of the flash on the djinn's chest.

It drew back his arm, opened his palm and pushed it forward towards its shady accomplice. The shade mimicked the action towards the egg and the jagged flash pushed through the shell, and Alduce thought, on to the chest of the unborn dragon inside.

The djinn sighed and exhaled, his breath blew through the portal, swaying the grass as it reached the egg. The surface of the shell faded from black returning to the original marbled blue-green of its siblings. The shade wavered and dissipated as the djinn's breath washed over it.

He turned away from the portal and waved a hand, dismissing it from existence.

"Easy when you know how," it said. "Not exactly what happened, but you get the idea. I gifted him my mark and my hatred for humanity. I may be stuck in here, but there are always others willing to do my bidding, scrabbling at my feet for favours. The weaker the mind, the easier the control. They know I will reward them upon my escape."

"The egg was Blaze before he hatched. He was marked by your touch from birth." Alduce understood now how the djinn was able to connect with the black dragon and manipulate him.

"I waited a long time for the opportunity," the djinn said, "and I've had a lot of time to plan."

It jerked its head around, staring out into the cloudy landscape. "The entity that lurks in the shadows is watching. I thought it was you, even though you denied it. You stand before me and it is out there still, just beyond my vision, yet I can sense it."

Alduce peered out to where the djinn stared and could see nothing. The cloudy dream realm was dull and featureless as far as... a darker streak sped out from the wispy background, barely visible. He could feel a new presence as it raced towards them. If he turned his head and looked at it from the corner of his eye, he could almost make it out. Almost.

The djinn whipped round as the dark spirit rushed passed them, lashing the air where it had been. Before vanishing from sight, it spoke to Alduce. Its voice was for him alone and sounded inside his head.

Its power is its weakness. The glass is the key.

Alduce looked to the djinn, its ugly face an angry mask. "I will find you!" it shouted after the strange force, "and when I do... " the unfinished threat hung in the air.

"What was that?" Alduce asked.

"An annoyance, nothing more. I am more interested in how you have come to be here."

Alduce didn't doubt it. The djinn must realise if he could get inside its prison, it might be able to get out the same way.

"Curiosity, I expect," Alduce said, unsure himself. He suspected Winterfang's pearl of wisdom was created from wizard glass. Nightstar had managed to see inside the pearl, even though he was trespassing. It was filled with wisdom and knowledge. His journey through its secrets afforded him the ability to travel inside its realm. A place not unlike this dream realm. He couldn't rely on Nightstar's *perception* as Alduce, yet he was positive it was the same inside the globe.

It was larger and filled with the djinn's spirit, its essence, its life force. Constructed from magic, this was a cage made to hold the djinn prisoner. It was similar to the pearl of wisdom, yet different. The manufacture of the globe was something he understood. His interaction with the pearl had given his mind the ability to come here.

"I am no amateur myself," Alduce said. It sounded like something Sunburst might say. Thinking of the yellow dragon pulled him back to his task. He was being manipulated and felt a little too relaxed. This creature was using its magic on him. It was almost undetectable. Neither human nor dragon. He was aware he was slipping under its influence.

In and out. That was the plan.

Talking to the djinn was dangerous. The more time spent inside the globe's realm, the more risk to their plan—and to himself. The djinn may be mad, but it wasn't stupid. It wanted to know how he was able to enter into its prison and would exploit any information it could glean to escape. The more they conversed, the greater the chance of letting something vital slip. It was a clever creature and Alduce needed to focus on getting away from it. The longer he remained in its proximity, the more he felt compelled to listen to its words, get lost in its voice.

He now knew what he needed to do. Blaze was controlled by the djinn. It wanted out and it was gathering power. If the free dragons could destroy the globe and its contents, they would free Alvanor of Blaze, the black plague, and the corruption of the djinn. But the globe was made from wizard glass. The djinn couldn't break the glass to escape... not yet, and it was powerful. Maybe they needed to find another way to defeat it.

"You must be wondering how I came to be here?" the djinn soothed. "You said you were curious. I see the mystery of my plight intrigues you." Alduce could feel his head swim as the djinn spoke. "I was bested by mages not of this world. They were many and they joined together to trap me. Sorcerers, magicians, mages and alchemists. Small on their own, strong together. Their prison of wizard glass was created to hold me. And hold me it has, for millennia."

Alduce couldn't imagine the time this creature had spent trapped in its glass prison. It was small wonder it was insane and bent on a path of destruction.

"I travelled to new worlds and fed on their misery. Consumed their life force and left them barren. What right did they have to stop me? Seal me up for an eternity and dump me on this backward rock."

He waved a clawed hand in the air and opened another tear in the cloudy fabric surrounding them.

Through the hole in reality, Alduce watched, mesmerized by what he saw. A robed figure stepped through a portal, a portal so familiar to him it could only have been created by the power of a Flaire artefact.

The figure stepped into a cavern lit by a purple glowing light, holding the same globe that now rested beside the sleeping Blaze. Alduce rubbed his eyes and tried to look away. He knew he must, but couldn't stop himself being drawn into the vision.

The robed figure picked its way to the rear of the cavern, carefully stepping around a water filled pool. Alduce could see into the pool, its crystal clear waters disappearing into unknown depths. The figure carried the globe like a nest of wasps, fearful of the burden and ready to be rid of it. Alduce watched as he laid the globe to rest at the rear of the cavern, out of sight and hidden.

The figure returned to the portal and took a last look over its shoulder before stepping through. The portal winked from existence, not the usual shimmering he was used to seeing where it gradually faded from view. It felt as if this portal was shut down in haste, almost as if whoever closed it couldn't do it fast enough, couldn't wait to be done with it.

Time accelerated and the images of the vision moved forward, faster and faster as decades, then centuries, sped past. So many years speeding past in seconds.

The dripping water formed into stalagmites and stalactites, calcite formations bathed in the beautiful purple glow. The sensation of passing time stretched out and the djinn's words whispered in his ear, closer than he liked, making his mind swim and his head dizzy.

"Millennia," the djinn said, "a thousand of your lifetimes I was forced to endure. Hidden away where no eyes might see. Locked inside a glass prison with little influence on the outside world."

Alduce couldn't move. His feet were like the stalagmites growing from the cave floor. His head pounded and his heart raced. The djinn's tactics changed. Its unsuccessful attack on his mind had failed, now it was attempting to burrow under the barrier while it distracted him with illusions. No longer trying an obvious frontal assault, it reverted to a slow creeping stealth

Alduce couldn't shore up his magical shield as the djinn infiltrated his defences. Blackness threatened to swallow his mind as probing tendrils of malevolence pushed harder to take control. He should have listened to Sunburst's advice. In and out. He was falling under the djinn's spell, isolated and alone, his mind adrift in an ocean of despair.

The djinn screamed. Alduce lifted leaden arms to his head, pain lancing through his skull. Fingers of agony tore at his brain and the djinn's wrath slammed into his mind. He could taste its raw anger as the dark spirit returned and disturbed its attempts to beguile him. He fell onto his knees as the djinn launched itself after the disappearing entity. Blackness rose up to engulf him and he struggled to hold on to his consciousness. The elusive spirit had distracted the djinn's attempts to trap his mind and succeeded in breaking its concentration. It was not happy at the interruption.

He could sense the hatred and the frustration of the djinn lingering in his mind. The elusive dark force was a constant source of annoyance to the djinn. It didn't know what it was or where it came from. It had assumed it was Alduce when it first confronted him. Alduce sensed it was even more annoyed now, believing it had finally caught the dark spirit, only to realise it couldn't be him.

Alduce? A familiar voice, faint and distant, called out to him. Nightstar! The connection with the dragon's mind pushed away the foggy residue of the djinn's touch.

"NO!" the djinn screamed as its hold on Alduce severed.

Come back to me, Alduce, quickly! The mind of Nightstar merged with his own and the black dragon's strength filled him. The pain in his head subsided, the fog lifted and clarity returned.

It had taken him a long time to grow comfortable with Nightstar's consciousness, two entities sharing a single space. The djinn's influence and its beguiling words distracted his mind, making him forget about the black dragon.

Now the dragon spirit was back with him, a sensation of completeness filed the void he hadn't realised was empty until Nightstar returned.

Alduce threw up his mind's defences, fortifying the barrier with his unique blend of dragon and human magic. He engulfed his ethereal spirit body in the safety of his defensive shield, spreading the protective cocoon around his form and pushing it outward.

The djinn slammed into the shield forcing its mind and body against the rekindled defences. It bounced off the barrier like a wind-blown leaf.

"What are you?" it shrieked, anger written across its cruel features.

"Leaving," Alduce replied and he stretched out his hand and rotated his arm in a circle in a parody of the djinn's earlier actions.

The cloudy fabric of the dream realm swirled in front of his hand to form a whirlwind vortex. The swirling mist grew and a portal manifested from its turbulent centre.

From the opposite end of the hole in the cloudy fabric the familiar black face of Nightstar peered through. "Hurry!" the dragon urged.

Alduce didn't need a second invitation. He stepped through the gap towards Nightstar, falling into the tunnel between realities. In his last moments of consciousness he was aware of the djinn's curses fading as the portal closed behind him.

Alduce dropped the defensive spell he so desperately clung to and surrendered, letting the blackness engulf him.

* * *

Nightstar's eyes flickered open. His snout lay on the floor of the cave, nostrils snorting up dust as he exhaled. The membrane on his eye closest to the floor worked to clear the gritty particles as he opened it wide.

He peered down through the hole into the moot chamber below.

The black dragon beneath him stirred, a low growl rising from a chest heaving from exertion. His eyes snapped open. Even from the limited vision of his hidden location, Nightstar could see they burned an unnatural red and were filled with hatred.

He reached into his own mind and felt the familiar passenger was back where he belonged.

The loss of not being able to feel the sorcerer's mind was a void he did not wish to experience again. The place where the mind of man and spirit of a dragon coexisted, should never be empty of either. He knew it made no sense, could not explain it, just knew he was right. *Perception.* It is what it is. Accepted by both entities.

The angry black dragon below, filled with the djinn's malevolent consciousness, opened its jaws and roared. The inside of the globe was a violent storm of turbulent thunderheads. Dark grey clouds roiled beneath the wizard glass, a hurricane of swirling, writhing mists pierced by two fiery points of red.

The djinn's eyes.

Nightstar drew back. It was time to move. After stealing one final look through the spyhole to see Blaze pacing the floor, snorting and roaring; it was definitely time to leave.

He didn't think the moot chamber's occupant knew he was here, inside the Lifting Plateau. The confrontation between Alduce and that foul creature wasn't in a physical place. From what Alduce recalled, now Nightstar could touch his mind again, the djinn wasn't aware of how the sorcerer came to be inside. The globe was a vessel to hold the djinn creature and it wasn't able to escape. Yet.

Over the years it had spent in captivity it managed to reach out, beyond its glass borders, to other corruptible minds, twisting them to its will and slowly, piece by piece, setting events in motion. It was forced to be patient, cultivating its resources, gathering its strength until it could make its move. It was powerful and exploited the ill-fated Blaze to capitalise on that power. The dragon's growing magic was the key to its escape. It was only a matter of time before it gathered enough to break free.

Nightstar took care, slowly and stealthily retreating from his vantage point, hopeful the noise Blaze was making masked his movements. He didn't want to be anywhere near the thing that had once been a black dragon. It may look like the dragon it once was, but was far from it.

The corruption of the djinn had swallowed Blaze whole. He was just as much a victim of the black plague as the other dragons. And, Nightstar strongly believed, was beyond redemption.

Galdor and the others needed to know the truth. The djinn must be stopped. If it broke free of the wizard glass, it wasn't just this world that was in danger. Alduce would think of something. His journey to the dream realm might have given him an idea of how they could beat it.

The globe was made by human sorcerers. They had managed to trap and contain the djinn before. Alduce was a sorcerer and his power and his use of magic were without question. Yes, he was only one man, but the blood of dragons flowed through his veins.

Nightstar backtracked through the tunnels, his mind pre-occupied with what he'd learned. Now all he wanted to do was get back to Sunburst and Azyrian, return to Galdor and inform him of what he knew. And find a way to defeat the djinn.

He could feel the urgency of his human passenger as he picked his way through the labyrinth of passageways, willing him to hurry. Alduce was concerned and when the human inside him felt like this, it was for good reason.

Adrenalin fuelled his limbs as he hurried back towards the hidden exit below the sleeping dragon. He knew the stone shapes would sleep for an eternity and wished the black dragon with the white flash on his chest would do the same.

In and out, that was the plan and it was now time to employ the *out* part. He wanted out of these tunnels and away from the feeling of foreboding. He would feel better when the Lifting Plateau was at his tail and he could feel air beneath his wings.

Chapter 30

A Council of Colours

Nightstar leapt from the secluded cave mouth on the eastern cliff face. He opened his great black wings and rode the air currents up into the dusky evening sky.

He let the updraft propel him into the night air, thankful to be out of the tunnels. Away from the influence of Blaze and the djinn. He needed to fly, put some distance between himself and the caves. Alduce was shaken at his discovery and Nightstar couldn't help feeling uneasy at the sorcerer's nervousness.

He glanced out over the flat of the plateau as he rose above its edge. The dark bulk of the sleeping dragon a blurry shape on the ground below. It looked larger than before and as he passed overhead the formation shifted. A shadowy dragon shape detached itself from the rocky arrangement and rose from the grassy flatlands. An enemy lying in wait.

Even in the darkening twilight he could see it was a black dragon. A drone controlled by Blaze, who in turn was controlled by the djinn. Red eyes locked with his own and Nightstar knew, without any doubt, any chance at a stealthy retreat was gone.

Keeping one eye on his pursuer he pounded the air, wings beating as fast as his heart. Higher and higher he rose, pushed ever upward by the updraft that gave the Lifting Plateau its name. He climbed straight up, each wingbeat lifting him higher into the twilight sky. Faster and faster he sped, rising on the rushing thermals, effortless and exhilarating.

The drone followed him, the fading pinks and reds of the setting sun, painting its black scales in pastel hues, bright red eyes glowing in the darkness and spoiling any illusions of natural beauty.

Nightstar flew higher, each wingbeat lifting him closer to the stars. Each stroke of his huge black sails taking him beyond the reach of his chaser. He was Nightstar the Black, no other dragon could best him when it came to high flying. No other could climb as high as he could. He embraced the euphoria, the feeling of escaping the plateau and the sensation of pure flight.

The air thinned. His lungs screamed out for precious oxygen. He closed his eyes and drew in as much air as he could, closing his nostrils tight and savouring the stinging sensation. Cold air cleansed his body, washing away the taint of the djinn's lingering touch. His wingbeats slowed as he levelled off, the pull of gravity's fingers slipping from his scales.

He glanced below and the tiny black speck of the pursuing drone looked like a distant crow. It couldn't keep up with him. He wasn't sure if his ability to reach greater heights was due to his unusual creation, or just something he excelled at. It didn't matter, at least not to his dragon self. Nightstar accepted it without question. It is what it is, as Sunburst would say.

Tonight was as high as he had ever been. The clouds spread out beneath him, a sea of grey vapour sandwiched between the planet's surface and the darkness of space. He could drift forever. His night star shimmered and the disguising magic dissipated, the returning silver on his chest blending with a universe of celestial siblings. One more star in the night sky.

Nightstar pushed through his dreamy, oxygen starved state, leaving behind the feelings of anxiety carried from the tunnels. Being this far above the ground always filled him with a welcome serenity.

He shook his head and tipped his neck back, staring out into the unknown. Up here the unending vista of stars made him feel small and insignificant. He was loathed to leave them, yet knew he must.

The black drone was nowhere to be seen as Nightstar fell backwards from the roof of the night sky, plunging into a dive. Free falling, he plummeted straight down through the clouds, gathering speed. Air rushed over his wings as he spiralled and twisted and small trails of vapour bled from his wingtips. His elevated position in the sky and the angle of his descent put miles between himself and the Lifting Plateau.

He levelled off and fixed his wings into an effortless glide northwards, confident he was beyond pursuit, yet cautious enough to continue scanning the sky for any signs of trouble.

The black drone was long gone and Nightstar expected it had given up the chase. It hadn't seen him emerge from the hidden cave mouth below the plateau and he was only spotted when he rode the updraft. A stupid thing to do, he reflected. He should have flown downwards instead of up. He understood why the free dragons missed living at the plateau. The updraft was thrilling and it was too strong a temptation for him to resist, his actions more typical of an impulsive yellow.

He dropped a little lower in the sky, vigilantly eyeing the terrain. The drone may be gone but that was no reason to drop his defences. These were hostile skies and it would be a mistake to think otherwise.

The djinn could see through Blaze's eyes and in turn the eyes of the drones. It may be a prisoner of the wizard glass globe, but the more it learned from the outside world—Galdor's world—the more powerful it grew. The more knowledge it possessed, the closer it came to escaping.

Nightstar would be glad when he was beyond enemy territory and back with his friends. There was once a time in his life when he was content to be alone, distancing himself from potential friends and actively avoiding involvement in their lives. It was different now. He was part of something bigger and his spirit was alive. His life was complicated and dangerous, but it certainly wasn't dull.

He sped on through the night in search of the small valley, the copse of trees, and his waiting friends.

* * *

Sunburst grasped the ledge of the Leviathan's Gullet, claws scrabbling for purchase on the hard rock. He quickly shifted his weight, hopping up into the entrance chamber beside Azyrian to make space for Nightstar.

The big black twisted in the tight space, wings barely clearing the chasm walls as he landed on the ledge. He marvelled at his friend's skill in the air, making a difficult landing look easy. He remembered teasing Nightstar the first time he landed on the ledge. The black dragon only needed to try something once to be good at it. Even though the manoeuvre was familiar with them both now, it was still a tricky landing. Sunburst found it easier now than the first time Topaz tested their aerial prowess. She could be extremely irritating when it came to sharing information. He could understand that better than any dragon, being a yellow.

It was the same with Nightstar. He was keeping his snout closed about his visit to the Lifting Plateau. Sunburst sensed the anxiety in his friend and respected his silence when he enquired about his mission. He was learning incredible restraint, only asking Nightstar a dozen or so times before resigning himself to wait. Nightstar did say one thing. He was consulting his *inner self*. He couldn't say anything in front of Azyrian about Alduce, yet Sunburst was able to interpret his meaning.

Nightstar would always be a dragon to Sunburst, no matter what. He was unique not only in how he came to be, but also in the way he was able to commune with the other half of his identity. He trusted his dragon self, but would listen to his human side too. Sunburst understood why, completely. At first he learned a grudging respect for Alduce. The more time he spent with Nightstar's human counterpart, the more he came to like the human. The man grew on you. Now Alduce was his friend and he enjoyed any time spent with him. Sunburst wondered what it would be like to walk among men, as one of them, a dragon in a human disguise, the opposite of what Alduce was to Nightstar.

If Nightstar needed time to consult with Alduce's mind then it would be time well spent. Alduce was knowledgeable and was a scholar at heart. There may be some advice he could offer Nightstar that would help.

Nightstar was eager to return to Galdor and share his discoveries and hardly stopped for breath when he landed at the waiting place. Even Azyrian cocked his head at Nightstar's response to Sunburst's questions, recognising this wasn't Nightstar's typical behaviour. The black dragon set a pace the poor bronze struggled to keep up with, being more suited for stamina than speed. Nightstar may be master of the heights, but Sunburst was impressed by his uncharacteristic turn of speed over land. His discovery, whatever it might be, was important enough to lend a serious urgency to their return.

Azyrian led them through the tunnel and into the hidden grotto. They emerged into the open area and Galdor stood waiting, Topaz and Ryvind by his side.

"I am glad of your safe return," the green dragon said. "Azyrian, report."

"We were not seen or followed, Galdor," the bronze looked to Nightstar. "Nightstar survived his foray inside the plateau and we have made all haste to return with his news."

"All haste!" Sunburst said, "We flew our wings off! Nightstar has not been himself since he returned, keeping his own silent counsel."

Galdor cocked his head. "My *perception* tells me it is important."

Sunburst would have said Nightstar looked positively pale, if black scales could appear so, but it wasn't his colour that was off. The news he carried was a burden and he would see his friend lighten his load and share it.

"Then let us retire to the cavern of the cataract, where we can discuss it." Galdor said. "Ryvind, can you please find Garnet and Fern and ask them to join us? Everyone else come with me. If Nightstar has new information, perhaps we can make plans to take back what is ours. I am tired of doing nothing. It is time to act." His yellow eyes burned with determination.

Galdor leapt into the air and Nightstar, a second behind him, was first to follow. Sunburst wondered if he was eager to get through the waterfall before the others, in case he went snout over rump again. He would keep that to himself, Nightstar's mood was serious and whatever he had to say was not to be made light of.

Azyrian joined the two airborne dragons tucking his bronze bulk neatly behind Nightstar. He liked the big dragon and felt he knew him a bit better after their time spent waiting for Nightstar to return. He wasn't as surly as he pretended to be and understood Sunburst's concern for his friend when he was off on his own. He had a dry sense of humour and kept Sunburst's mind occupied, at first telling him about the dragons of Alvanor and then asking him about his own home.

"Best fall in, Sunburst the Yellow," Topaz said, "I don't think we'll want to miss this. We are in esteemed company. Look!" He followed her gaze. Both sides of the hidden grotto were lined with all the remaining free dragons. They knew Galdor was preparing for something. A silent audience stood watching, ready and waiting for their leader's words.

"I think we are going to war." Topaz lifted from the ground, her wings a flurry of blue as she rushed to fall in line. Like Sunburst, she sensed the change in Galdor's mood. The green sounded more like the dragon Alduce wrote of. More like the leader he had once been. He was ready to take the fight to Blaze.

War. It was a sad day when dragons fought against dragons. The dragons of the hidden grotto were desperate for change. Their suffering was as much as they could take. It was their time to make a stand. Fight for their freedom or die trying.

Sunburst hoped Nightstar had a plan that wasn't a backup plan. He launched himself into the air and stuck to the blue's tail. Ryvind swooped in with Fern and Garnet flanking him. Garnet dropped back behind Ryvind and Fern pivoted tightly, the small green female last to join the group.

A line of eight dragons strung out across the grotto. Green, black, bronze, blue, yellow, brown—russet he corrected himself, not brown—red, and lastly green. A winged spectrum of serpents flying in perfect formation, snout to tail.

The steady beat of dragon wings echoed from the grotto's walls as they crossed the hidden valley. Topaz was right. They were in esteemed company. Sunburst flew with giants. His yellow chest swelled with pride to be part of their number as the silent onlookers watched from below. The hidden valley was filled with the anticipation of its residents, they sensed something momentous was happening.

One by one the dragons entered the cataract, the curtain of silvery water swallowing them whole.

Icy spray bounced from his wings as Sunburst pierced the cascade, wings tensed against the downward pressure of the waterfall. He had time to blink and clear his vision before dropping to the mossy floor and sliding to a stop. He quickly skipped up onto drier rock making way for Ryvind, careful to keep his balance and catching Nightstar's eye. The black gave a slight nod and Sunburst was happy to see, this time, his friend was still upright. He was certainly a dragon that learned from his mistakes.

Garnet and Fern brought up the rear and all eight dragons made their way to drier ground, shaking water from their wings, bodies dripping.

"Gather round," Galdor called out, raising his voice above the steady flow of the cataract. "Nightstar, your commitment to our cause is great indeed. I speak for all the free dragons assembled here, and those outside, our thanks can never be enough. I can see you are shaken. Your bravery is without question. I know some may have seen you as another black, an enemy not to be trusted, yet you were the best one suited to infiltrate the Lifting Plateau. *Your* black scales have been to our advantage."

Galdor turned to face Sunburst. "You, as well as Nightstar deserve our thanks. You have both been caught up in a fight that is not your own." There was a murmur of consent from the other dragons.

Sunburst felt the eyes of his new friends upon him. "Where Nightstar flies, I follow," he said.

"And where Sunburst flies, I follow," Nightstar said, looking a bit more like his usual self.

Since their return to the grotto, Sunburst noticed Nightstar had regained a bit of his usual composure. He wondered if it was because he was back in the company of dragons, which he found strangely comforting considering his friend's origins. Or was it because he was away from the lifting Plateau. It was obvious to him Nightstar's time inside the plateau's underground tunnels wasn't pleasant. What was it in there that disturbed him so? Well, he would find out soon enough.

"We are gathered to hear what Nightstar has learned," Galdor said. "To see if we can use his findings to rid ourselves of the black threat that strives to consume us. Nightstar, please share what you know. Help us to decide what we need to do next."

Nightstar moved into the middle of the gathered dragons and stood tall. "I have learned many things about Blaze and pieced together what I believe is happening. Sunburst. Azyrian. I apologise for pushing you to return immediately. I should have explained a little more to you both rather than rushing back at a breakneck pace, saying nothing. I hope you will both understand why, once you hear what I have to say."

Nightstar's caught Sunburst's eye. "I spent most of our return journey in reflection. Contemplating what I learned and piecing together my discoveries. As Sunburst knows, sometimes I can get lost deep inside myself when I need to think. I find that particular method of inner reflection beneficial." Sunburst knew exactly what he referred to and Nightstar's eyes shared their secret. A quick glimpse at Galdor convinced him the green dragon also understood Nightstar's meaning.

"I arrived at the Lifting Plateau unchallenged. I passed a few drones on the way there, but another black dragon was of no concern to them. It was almost too easy to fly in without being stopped. The drones are probably more concerned with dragons leaving. I was able to locate the sleeping dragon and using it as a landmark, found the entrance in the cliff face. Galdor, you were right. I don't think it has been used in a long time. It wasn't guarded, and would have remained hidden to me if I didn't know where to look. I can understand why it hasn't been used much. It was difficult to navigate into the entrance as the updrafts played havoc with my flight. They are strong! Once I was inside, I was able to follow Galdor's directions. I explored the passageways until I was deep within the heart of the tunnels. The remaining dragons not tainted by the black plague are held prisoner in the depths of the plateau's labyrinth."

The Alvanor dragons began to ask questions.

"Who did you see?" Ryvind asked.

"How many survive?" said Garnet.

"Why did you not free them?" Topaz demanded.

"Be quiet." Galdor instructed them, though not too harshly. "Let Nightstar tell his story. There will be time for questions when he is done." He turned back to Nightstar. "Continue. Please."

"I wasn't able to see as I observed from a secluded place. I'm sorry. I realise you all have friends unaccounted for. What I do know, *perception* true, is where they are being held. There were only two drones guarding the entrance to their cavern. I didn't want to risk being seen. There is a foreboding presence inside the tunnels that seeps your confidence. It weakens your resolve and fills you with a despair that welcomes defeat."

The dragons hung on Nightstar's every word, even Galdor looked like a fledgling at a grand moot.

"If I could have, I would have attempted to free them. I still needed to find out what Blaze was up to. I was aware if I blundered headlong into an unprepared rescue attempt, I was likely to alert Blaze and his drones." He looked at Sunburst. "I've had previous experience with half planned rescue attempts and was lucky before. I have learned that while luck is a welcome visitor, you can't count on it staying over long. A rescue plan is only part of what we must do.

"I managed to find the moot chamber using some old tunnels. The tunnels allowed me to get close enough to observe, but stay hidden. It's what I discovered there that concerns me. Blaze now uses the cavern as his personal chambers and he is not alone. I have found the source of his power and it is not a weapon. The black dragon is not what you think, he is as much a drone as his soldiers, yet so much more."

"What do you mean?" Galdor asked, ignoring his own instruction to keep quiet.

"Blaze is controlled by another being, a creature of extraordinary power. It uses Blaze as a vessel for its own actions. Galdor, the black dragon you knew is gone. Just as you told me the drones were beyond saving, so it is with Blaze. I suspect at first, it wasn't like this. I thought Blaze still maintained control, but over time, it slowly consumed him, stripped his mind and his spirit, his very life force, from his body. All that is left of him is an empty shell filled with the manifestation of pure evil. The entity is known by many names, some of which you may have heard. Djinn. Demon. Devil. It matters not what we call it. It is a creature of malevolent spirit. It feeds off the life force of others. It destroys everything in its path. It was trapped in a globe of wizard glass and banished to your world, hidden away where nothing should have found it. Somehow it used its power to influence the outside world and manipulate whatever it could reach. It is ancient and clever. Patient and vengeful. It seeks to escape the prison of wizard glass. It cannot take full possession of Blazes' form, not yet. The magic of the globe prevents it from taking over the dragon body completely. If it gains its freedom, it will destroy Alvanor first, then all of Sull."

The dragons remained silent and Sunburst wasn't sure if they believed Nightstar's words or were in shock.

"How do you know all this?" Galdor asked. "There is a lot of information and detail in what you say to be merely supposition."

"You are right. I learned more from my encounter with the djinn. I have seen inside its prison. It tried to beguile my mind. It was aware of my presence, but didn't know where I was in the physical world. It was as if I was in another place, a world not like this one, yet just as real. I was hidden in the tunnels near the moot chamber, safely out of sight, yet close enough to be drawn inside the djinn's realm. Blaze slept with the wizard glass globe tucked between his front legs. Beneath the glass the captured spirit of the djinn moved, its life force inhabiting the prison created by human practitioners of magic. At first I thought Blaze was in possession of a pearl of wisdom, the comparisons both outside and inside are similar, but it is definitely not a pearl as I know it."

"You have communed with a moonstone?" Galdor voiced the surprise of all gathered.

"Winterfang, our leader at the White Mountain, has one," Sunburst said. He knew of Nightstar's illicit contact with the pearl. "Nightstar was privileged enough to consult it. There was a... crisis." Sunburst felt bad about covering the truth. "Nightstar's help was required. He is quite the scholar for a black. Always looking for answers." He was aware he was rambling. Winterfang wasn't pleased with Nightstar, but it was wind under their wings. Nightstar had accepted his punishment and Winterfang's wisdom.

"It is a tale for another day," Nightstar jumped in. Sunburst was grateful for the interruption. He didn't always know when to keep his jaws closed. "My past experiences did allow me to interpret information from the globe and understand the djinn's ambition. The djinn uses its power and the life force Blaze drains from his victims. Every time it gains more life force, it grows in power. The stronger its power, the closer it gets to freedom. The wizard glass is strong, virtually unbreakable from the outside. I believe the djinn is almost ready to attempt a breach. If it is successful and manages to gain full possession of Blaze, then we will not be able to stop it. It is using the stored power stolen from the consumed life force of living dragons. The djinn has been held captive for thousands of years and its sanity is far from normal. I don't know if that's a result of its incarceration or its evil nature. Perhaps it's a combination of the two.

"I think its hatred of the humans who trapped it gave it a commonality with Blaze. Blaze the Black never stood a chance, he was marked before he hatched. Touched by the hand of a demon manipulated into doing the djinn's bidding. The white flash on his chest was demon born, a conduit planted inside him that gave the djinn a means of connection. It was his weakness the djinn used as an opening to gain its hold. It planted and exploited Blaze's hatred of humans and gained more control as it fed its thoughts and lies into the dragon's mind. I am convinced the reason Blaze trapped Galdor holds a meaning for it, a twisted sense of irony. It was trapped by man, as was Galdor. Galdor was strong enough to survive with his sanity intact because he isn't malevolent. The djinn is corrupt, a creature of evil. Its mind has festered and darkened beyond what it ever was before its capture. Its years of captivity have resulted in its loss of sanity. It is bent on revenge."

"I was lucky I was rescued when I was," Galdor said quietly. "I can understand only too well what prolonged incarnation can do to a mind."

"While Blaze isn't blameless," Nightstar continued, "he was used in a way that dragged him deeper into the djinn's clutches. The more he became reliant on the power, the stronger the hold the djinn took. It fed his addiction until there was nothing left of the dragon, stripping everything away until Blaze was just another mindless drone."

"Can it be stopped?" Galdor asked.

"The wizard glass is timeless, designed to stop it escaping. Yet the djinn managed to find a way of influencing the world outside, a realm that should have been beyond its reach. It conjured visions of how it marked the egg before Blaze hatched. It let me see where the humans hid the globe. I watched as if I was witnessing it actually happening, so great is its power. It was always a creature of great cunning, with powers of magic its human captors were unable to comprehend. It managed to reach the outside world and manipulate it in an attempt to break free. Time was always on its side. Blaze must have discovered where the globe was hidden. Perhaps he was unable to avoid the attraction, the seeds of his fate already growing inside him. Once the djinn lured him to its resting place, Blaze would have been unable to resist. Slowly, over thousands of years it planned its escape, waiting for an opportunity like this. Once it gained a hold on Blaze it gathered more and more life force, drawing it inside the globe in an attempt to break the wizard glass. The pressure inside the globe is at a point now where it is close to breaking. It was only ever created to hold the djinn's spirit, its own life force. The more it consumes, the greater the pressure inside. It is only a matter of time before the globe's integrity gives way. It could be another hundred years, or it could be tomorrow. I'm afraid I don't know."

"And once it escapes?" Garnet asked.

"If it escapes," Nightstar said, "Alvanor will be consumed. If it gets out, your land will be destroyed. Every living creature will be consumed."

Silence filled the cavern, the only sound was the rushing of the waterfall. The circle of dragons stood around Nightstar, each one contemplating the black dragon's horrifying words.

Sunburst felt like he was going to explode. Blaze, or the djinn who controlled the black dragon's body, must be stopped. Why wasn't anyone speaking? They could return through the Flaire gateway, escape the fate of these dragons, leave Sull behind and never return. He knew Nightstar wouldn't abandon these dragons and neither would he. This was Galdor's home. "Then we must fight it," Sunburst said. "Stop it before it gets out."

The dragons all turned to face him. Try as he might he was a yellow and sometimes he couldn't hold his tongue.

"Sunburst is right," Galdor said, "It is time to fight or fall."

"Fight or fall." The words echoed around the cavern as Galdor's dragons repeated his words.

"Fight," said Nightstar.

Sunburst looked at him. "Do you have a plan?"

"I do," Nightstar answered, "but you're not going to like it."

"Sounds about right," Sunburst replied.

Chapter 31

The Belly of the Beast

The dragons of the hidden grotto approached the Lifting Plateau, no longer content with sheltering in the secret valley. Galdor led the host, soaring upon the once familiar air currents surrounding the plateau. The landscape below, previously their home, now enemy territory.

He roared a challenge and the host answered, filling the air with angry voices. It was difficult killing the black drones they encountered on their way here, but necessary. They were the eyes and ears of Blaze—not Blaze, Galdor corrected himself, the djinn. It was essential they were silenced before they could raise the alarm. It wasn't easy taking the life of another dragon and Galdor cursed Blaze, the djinn, and the humans who had brought the globe to his world.

Blaze was once his friend and while he hated what he had become, he couldn't bring himself to hate the black dragon. Hatred was like a poison, infectious and all-consuming. If you gave in to the hatred it would destroy what you were, killing your spirit. He should know. He almost let it take root when he was imprisoned.

The small human had freed more than his body when he opened the gateway home. And now he was helping him again—in the form of a dragon! Galdor was still amazed at Nightstar's revelation, exposing himself as Alduce. He knew when he met the apprentice sorcerer he was different. He thanked his *perception* for his restraint in not eating him.

There was no physical difference Galdor could see between Nightstar and any other dragon. Sunburst's acceptance was testament enough at calling Nightstar one of his own. The yellow dragon treated him like a brother and the bond between them was strong.

To change from human to dragon was a feat of great magic and it was reassuring to have Nightstar on his side. Alduce was a scholar as well as a sorcerer and the man possessed a knowledge of the arcane, from a human sorcerer's perspective. Galdor hoped he knew what he was doing. Their plan depended on it. If a yellow of Sunburst's calibre could put his trust in Nightstar, then he would too.

Black dragons swarmed from the tunnels and rose from the plateau floor. Mindless drones, Galdor reminded himself. The dragons they once were are gone, already dead. They are tools of the djinn and not our brothers and sisters, regardless of their shape. We must fight for what is rightfully ours. This battle would decide who prevailed. It was all or nothing.

The heat of dragon flame burned like an anger, the fiery gorge rising in his chest. He roared again, signalling the attack and closed his wings, shedding the uplifting currents and dropped into a dive. He could feel the turbulence in the air behind as the airborne host followed him down. They were outnumbered but they had the advantage of surprise and the high air.

They gathered speed, rushing to meet the oncoming foe. The first wave of attack, a battering ram of colour against the black defenders. The line of hurriedly assembled defending dragons wavered as his host punched into their midst. Black dragons flailed as the momentum of the coloured dragons smashed their ranks. Galdor's momentum carried him through the rising black drones, talons tore through scales, ripping wings and into flesh. His claws sparked with magic as they raked and gouged the enemy. To pierce their tough scales with talons alone was difficult, but not impossible. A little magic helped break through their defences.

Galdor gripped the black drone he collided with, his talons thrust forward as the drone dropped towards the plateau, pushed backwards by the weight of his descent. Its flame roared over his head and he twisted his neck in an effort to avoid it, heat blasting over his scales. The drone hit the ground and Galdor's weight pushed down through his talons, crushing his foe. The feel of snapping bones reverberated through the crushed body as the life slipped from the limp dragon.

The noise of battle filled the grassy meadow atop the plateau. Flame spewed from the jaws of attackers and defenders alike, dragons roared and talon scraped scale. Blacks and coloureds tangled in the air above and on the ground.

A dark female swung her tail and Galdor dropped his head as the bladed appendage clove through the air where his head had been. She spun to face him, red eyes ablaze with hate, black fire spitting from her jaws; Darkflame. Tales of her foul deeds came to the hidden grotto with the lucky ones who escaped the Lifting Plateau. Her reputation for enjoying death and destruction was known to them all.

Galdor swayed, dodging the unnatural fire and pulled his talons free of the dead dragon beneath him. Darkflame didn't hesitate, lunging for his throat like a striking viper, black hissing spittle flew from her jaws. The corrosive acid sizzled as it splattered onto Galdor, his scales protecting him from the burning liquid, but not the pain.

Galdor turned as Darkflame's fangs missed their mark and twisted his own tail in spinning arc, whipping it into her side with an almighty thud. Numbing shock travelled up his tail as it bounced off the tough black scales, pushing Darkflame off balance. As she hurried to right herself, Galdor stepped away from the corpse of the dragon he had landed on and spread his talons, feeling solid ground beneath them. Darkflame crouched low, muscles bunched ready to strike, eyes locked to his own. He adopted a crouched stance facing, her head on, ready to fight.

Darkflame growled as she feigned an attack, drawing back and circling, her tail flattening the grass as it thrashed from side to side. It was too far behind her to be an immediate danger, but she was fast and Galdor would be stupid to discount it.

To his left, Topaz the Blue tore the throat from a drone, red blood clashed violently against the blue of her snout. The dying dragon's neck lolled back as blood gushed from a fatal wound. The drone tried to send one last blast of flame at Topaz, but failed, the light fading from its eyes. Topaz, finished with one combatant, leapt to Galdor's aid, lashing out and sinking her teeth into Darkflame's tail, tearing with her jaws as she pinned it with her talons. Darkflame spun to defend herself and Galdor seized the moment, leaping forward and swiping at her head with an open claw. Talon struck snout, tearing into the flesh of her lower jaw, her head whipped back and collided with Galdor's tail, this time swinging in and attacking from the opposite side. Darkflame's head bounced from the collision, her red eyes rolling, dazed and confused.

Galdor prepared to finish her with the remainder of his flame, but before he could blast the flailing black, Topaz pounced, closing her jaws on the already weakened snout. She gripped Darkflame's neck with her talons and tore, wings spread wide and beating the air, pulling back.

Darkflame's jaw snapped as Topaz ripped open her snout, blood spraying from the gaping wound and splatted the blue. As the defeated black enforcer of Blaze's inner circle fell, Galdor let loose his fire, engulfing Darkflame's head.

Galdor had reservations when it came to taking the life of another dragon, but with Darkflame he was willing to make an exception. She was instrumental in the destruction of the human cities and responsible for the deaths of many dragons. Her reputation preceded her and she was known amongst the free dragons for her cruel nature.

Topaz quickly dipped her head in a bow to Galdor then leapt to help a small green who was rolling on the ground, tangled with another black drone. He remembered when Topaz the Peaceful had been a different dragon, the peaceful female her name suggested. They were all changed. Any dragon who survived today, survived the reign of terror Blaze had brought, would be different.

More black drones were emerging from the tunnels beneath the plateau. The initial wave of defenders had taken a beating, unprepared and caught by surprise. The free dragons struck first and struck hard, pushing their advantage. Reinforcements joined the battle, swelling the black ranks, levelling the field.

Galdor hoped Nightstar and his party were close to their objective. Everything hinged on the back dragon's part in their plan. If they hoped to win against greater numbers, it was imperative they distract Blaze's forces long enough for Nightstar to succeed.

Silently he wished they would hurry, as he feared they wouldn't be able to hold Blaze's drones for long.

* * *

Nightstar led the way, Sunburst, Azyrian and Garnet followed closely behind. Galdor had insisted his two self-appointed guards accompany them and Nightstar was glad to have them. It would do no harm to have two dragons of their size with them and they knew the coloured dragons being held against their will. Friendly faces would eradicate the need for explaining who they were. He also didn't want to leave Sunburst on his own to rescue the captives held deep within the tunnels. He didn't doubt his friend was capable enough but having Azyrian and Garnet along would speed up their escape.

It was easier the second time he entered into the hidden cave entrance below the watchful stones of the sleeping dragon. His three companions were aware of the awkward approach and the strong currents after he explained what to look out for. Even Sunburst had followed his lead without question, aware of the trust Galdor placed in them all and their part in the plan. The yellow dragon recognised the seriousness of their mission and his usual light hearted banter was on temporary hold.

The out-of-the-way entrance was still unguarded and Nightstar was confident his original excursion had gone undetected. He was counting on Galdor's unexpected attack above ground, diverting the djinn's attention elsewhere, until he made his move.

The djinn knew who and what he was after he visited the realm within the globe's confinement. What it didn't know was where his physical body was located. If it suspected he was close by, it gave no indication, more interested in how he had come to be there and ultimately, his departure. It wanted out and no doubt wondered how the spirit form of Alduce was able to appear then disappear from its prison.

Wizard glass was a complex substance and the sorcerer's conscience understood its intricacies. It was designed to hold the essence of the djinn. The spells woven by the practitioners who created it—be they mages, witches, sorcerers, or magicians—would have tailored it to their needs. It was created specifically to hold the djinn. The more focussed the creation spell, the stronger it was against the individual it was aimed at. The Sorcerer's mind had managed to penetrate the globe's confines subconsciously, and he hoped he could use this to his advantage.

Nightstar's *perception* knew his part in the plan counted on this, trusting Alduce and his knowledge. He was a scholar, after all, and he'd lived side by side with the man's mind long enough to know when to let him decide for them both. Being separated from Alduce was strange. The sorcerer was confident he could visit the dream realm again, it was integral to their plan. Nightstar didn't have to like it and wondered, if anything happened to Alduce, how it would impact the dragon left behind. Man and dragon shared a unique bond and he would be happy if he never found the answer to that particular question.

He crept through the tunnels and followed his previous route, remembering Galdor's directions. The tunnels didn't feel as large this time around, three extra dragons making them cramped. They arrived at the first real fork. One half of the intersection led to the guarded chamber where the free dragons were held prisoner, the other—eventually—to the chamber where the wizard glass globe waited.

He stopped and raised his tail, signalling a halt. Cautiously he extended his neck and angled his head to peer around the corner hiding them from sight. Only one black dragon stood where previously two had been stationed. He extended his neck a little farther, making sure he was able to take in the whole corridor. The second guard was nowhere to be seen. Perhaps it had been called away to join the defenders above ground. It didn't matter. There was only one guard now. He would take whatever luck came their way. Facing one guard would be much easier than facing two, especially in the confines of the tunnels. The quicker Sunburst, Azyrian and Garnet freed the captives, the quicker they could escape. He would feel much better confronting the djinn if his friends were safely out of reach.

Nightstar backed up and slowly turned himself around to face his three accomplices, taking care to make as little sound as possible. His wings brushed the cave ceiling, the sound of falling dust like an avalanche to his ears in the silent tunnel.

"We are here," he whispered to Sunburst, who was next in line behind him. "There is only one guard."

"Good news," Sunburst whispered back.

"This is where we part ways."

"For now, Nightstar," Sunburst said, his voice almost too quiet to hear. The yellow dragon turned to the bronze and red behind him and passed on the information.

Nightstar stepped passed all three, moving into the opposite tunnel of the intersection and allowing the others to take up their positions behind the curve of the tunnel. Sunburst made the same signal with his tail to Garnet and Azyrian, biding then to hold fast as he squeezed into the tunnel with Nightstar. He extended his neck, bringing his mouth as close to Nightstar's ear as possible.

"Make sure you both come back, brother," he said, quiet enough for the other two dragons not to hear his words.

Nightstar understood his meaning. Sunburst didn't like his plan and was against it, even when he explained it was the only way. The yellow dragon had grown fond of Alduce, even if he was hesitant to admit it to Nightstar. He didn't want to lose him either and understood he was a vital part of the black dragon he had befriended.

"Don't worry," Nightstar replied, "trust in the plan. You need to hurry. Help the captives, Sunburst, they need you to lead them to freedom. I remember a dragon that wouldn't leave anyone behind." Nightstar recalled the yellow dragon when he had been held captive by the Extractor. Tortured and near death he still put the other dragons held prisoner before himself.

"Be that dragon again, Sunburst."

"I'm leaving you behind," he said. "Don't make me come back in and save your hide... again." He head-butted Nightstar affectionately on the side, turned and took up his position with Azyrian and Garnet, casting one last look at Nightstar and dipping his head in a silent nod.

Nightstar returned the gesture, leaving the three dragons to carry out their rescue.

His part in the plan was less straight forward.

He set off in search of the moot chamber, and the djinn, with less confidence than he liked.

Chapter 32

Confrontation

Sunburst emerged from the shelter of the bend, crouching low as he crept towards the black guard. The drone sat unmoving, staring at the cave wall in front of its face, as if in a trance. The djinn would be concentrating on Galdor's attack and he hoped it wouldn't be worrying about controlling a drone that wasn't defending the plateau.

As far as he understood from Nightstar's explanation, these drones were no longer alive. Their life force, their dragon spirit, was taken. All that remained was a body the djinn, through Blaze, was able to control. If it sat vacantly in pretence of guarding the captives, they would never know.

Galdor spoke of this to the remaining free dragons before they left the plateau. He was conflicted about attacking and killing other dragons but understood it was the only way to defeat the djinn. They had spent time grieving for their lost and fallen companions, he said, now it was time to avenge them. Their kin were already dead and the black abominations Blaze created must be destroyed. It was the only way forward if they were to survive.

Sunburst was close enough to the drone now to see there was no sign of life, no movement, not even the swell of its chest as it breathed. It didn't breathe, he reminded himself, because it wasn't really alive. He was providing a mercy in destroying a vessel of the djinn.

The drone's eyes burned red as it whipped round to confront Sunburst, looking far from deceased. Malice shone from its stare as it swiped its talons at his head. Sunburst dropped low and charged, ramming his short stubby horns onto the drone's throat, knocking it off balance. He spun his tail and the heavy triple bladed fins at its tip moved in a blur of yellow. The drone buckled as the heavy blades clove into its unprotected flank, cleaving scales and penetrating flesh. Its eyes dulled as the poisoned tail blade, unique to yellows, released its paralysing toxins.

Azyrian pounced from behind Sunburst and landed on the stunned drone, talons opening the wound left by Sunburst's tail. Garnet attacked from the other side of the narrow passageway and Sunburst was pushed back. She sank fangs into the drone's throat and tore, ripping into the soft flesh beneath the scales and spraying blood across the cave walls.

The drone didn't stand a chance as the red and bronze found a target for their rage. The frustration of not being able to fight back for so long, finally able to find a release, was devastating. Talons clawed and jaws tore, the two avenging dragons reaping a whirlwind of retribution.

A rustling of dragon wings alerted Sunburst to movement from behind. The now unguarded cave entrance was filled with spectators, eying the grizzly scene. Coloured dragons, mostly females by their scent. A big blue hissed a warning as their eyes met, her neck spikes rising in anger, her body tense and ready to attack.

"I am known as Sunburst the Yellow." Sunburst told her, hoping to sound reassuring. He omitted his usual introduction in favour of a calming approach. "I am friend to Galdor the Green, we've come to free you."

"We?" the blue asked, her tone suspicious. "Galdor? What do you know of Galdor?"

"I am with Azyrian and Garnet—"

"Sapphire? Is that you?" Garnet turned at the sound of the blue's voice. Sunburst was glad her scales were red and disguised some of the drone's blood. The same couldn't be said for Azyrian, his bronze scales splattered violently with red.

"Garnet! Yes, it's me," Sapphire answered, "Chestnut's here too. How does this yellow know Galdor?"

"Come on," Sunburst interrupted, "time for explanations and reunions once we're out of here."

"Sunburst's right," Azyrian said, wiping his muzzle on the dead black's flank then flicked his tongue, licking the smeared mess from his jaws. He turned his head and spat blood from his mouth. "We must hurry. How many of you are there?" he asked Sapphire.

"Seventeen of us," she said.

"Follow Sunburst," Azyrian said. "He will lead you to freedom." Sapphire and Chestnut looked from Azyrian to Sunburst, then at the dead drone. They didn't move.

"Now!" Garnet urged them on, "Quickly." She used her head to nudge the dazed females into moving. "Go! Follow the yellow, he knows the way out."

One by one, seventeen dragons emerged from the unguarded cave where they were held captive. Sunburst led the way to freedom as the line grew longer, each dragon urged out of the cave and into the tunnel, helped along by Azyrian and Garnet. He could hear them telling the dragons, *Follow the yellow, he's one of us. Sunburst knows the way.* He was a yellow, not a black, but they were suspicious of a stranger. The dragons didn't know him and he was glad Azyrian and Garnet were here to vouch for him. It was understandable they would be hesitant with an unknown dragon and he chose not to take it personally. He, more than most, could appreciate how they were feeling and knew all about what it was like to lose your freedom.

"Galdor lives," Sunburst told Sapphire over his shoulder. These dragons needed good news and some hope. That was something he could give them. "He fights for your freedom. He sent us here to rescue you."

He could hear the wonder in the voices of the freed dragons as they repeated his words. *Galdor lives.*

"He has asked me to take you to safety. We have a plan to defeat Blaze." Better to keep things simple rather than explaining about the djinn. "Galdor wants us to take you to some caves south of here. He was very explicit in his instructions. He said he will meet us there when he can."

Azyrian knew exactly where the caves were located. Once they were free of the tunnels, the bronze would show them the way. Nightstar wanted everyone as far away from the Lifting Plateau as possible. Sunburst thought that was a great idea, the tunnels beneath the plateau were not a place he wished to linger.

"Then lead us out of here, Sunburst the Yellow," Sapphire said. "We will follow where you lead."

Sunburst picked up his pace and the following dragons scrabbled to keep up. He longed to feel the air beneath his wings and the sooner he was out of these tunnels, the better.

* * *

Alduce slipped into the globe with ease, his mind focussed on the weave of the wizard glass. The barrier was designed to hold the djinn and he was able to pass through its magical defences, knowing its construction. Being a lifelong scholar of the arcane did have its advantages. It was easier than before, passing into the dream realm without Nightstar losing consciousness.

He missed the dragon's presence and felt as if something wasn't quite right without it. The black dragon was part of him and he was part of it.

It was a strange feeling being alone. He missed the dragon's presence, exaggerated by its absence. A quiet gap in his mind where the voice of the dragon lived. It was all so much easier for him to accept, thanks to Nightstar's logic, he was used to the now comfortable feeling of Nightstar's mind, his dragon spirit.

Nightstar's body waited for his return in the physical world outside the globe. He wasn't far from the moot chamber and Alduce didn't think he was in any danger. The tunnels were deserted, all the drones would be busy above ground defending against Galdor's attacking force.

The surreal misty surroundings of the globe manifested from the darkness, grey and black swirling masses at the edge of his vision. His human eyes no longer possessed the ability to see in the dark, but even if they had, he didn't think he would have seen anything more.

The air felt different from his last visit, charged and angry, a thunderstorm ready to break. A shiver passed through his being and he turned, sensing something behind him. Light flared and the djinn manifested, his entrance less theatrical than before. Red smoke twisted into a whirlwind, rising from the floor as it turned to black, the djinn solidifying from the swirling vapours.

Angry red eyes burned into Alduce as it spoke. "Why do you interrupt me human? I am busy."

"I've come to offer you a deal," Alduce said.

"I don't need your deal, I am almost free. The cowering dragons have emerged from hiding and returned to their former home. Their pitiful attempt at besting my army will fail. Once I've feasted on their life force I'll have enough power to break the wizard glass."

"It isn't my deal. I come on behalf of Galdor the Green, rightful ruler of the Lifting Plateau."

"Lies!" the djinn spat. "Galdor is dead. He could not have escaped his dungeon."

"Can you not see who leads the attack?" Alduce taunted. "The majestic green dragon has returned to confront you and extract his vengeance."

The djinn froze, his glowing eyes faded to dim pinpoints of light. It remained unmoving, head tipped to one side as if listening for a distant sound. Its eyes dimmed until the light disappeared completely, remaining dark for a few seconds, then they flared brightly again, signalling its return. Alduce suspected the djinn had taken full control of a drone, looking through the host's eyes at the world above ground. The dawning realisation Alduce spoke the truth was written on its face.

"How can this be? He was sealed away for eternity. He did not possess the ability to open a passageway back to this world."

"He had a little help from an unexpected friend," Alduce said.

The djinn glowered. "You? You are nothing. A petty conjuror who does not know his place. Ignorant of your insignificance. Leave before I consume you. I have a battle to win."

"It will be Galdor's victory, your defeat." Let the djinn underestimate him. "That is why you lured him away, plotted to be rid of him. He is powerful enough to resist you. Strong enough to stand against Blaze, even with the power you wield through him. If Blaze dies, you lose your foothold in this world. You weren't the only one to reveal hidden secrets when you tried to probe my mind."

"I will be free!" the djinn screamed, "and any who stand against me will fall. I have spent millennia inside this accursed prison. You will not stop me, Galdor will never win. I would see this world destroyed rather than accept defeat from him."

"Galdor has something you don't," Alduce said. "The free minds of all the dragons you were unable to catch. They fight for their home. You are just an interloper. You are not welcome wherever you go. No wonder you were banished to the globe."

"I tire of your words, Alduce. Remain here and when I have killed Galdor I will return and take your life force and that of Nightstar."

"I think not. If you were able to defeat me, you would have already done so. You can't fight both myself and Galdor at the same time. You are desperate to get back to the battle. The longer you remain here, the less control you have over the drones. I suspect they can only function without you for a short time. You might be powerful outside the constraints of the wizard glass, but you aren't free of it yet. If you are so eager to hurry back, perhaps you are afraid of a petty conjuror." He needed to distract the djinn and if insulting it would keep it from returning to its drones, he appeared to have hit his mark.

The djinn spun, spreading its wings like a giant bat and loomed forward to confront Alduce, whipping its tail and knocking him from his feet. "Perhaps I will stay and teach you a lesson." It stomped forward, clawed feet crashing down in an effort to squash him.

Alduce rolled away, narrowly avoiding the crushing blow as razor sharp talons tore across his back. Pain lanced along the scratches and Alduce was grateful they weren't deep. The pain wasn't as bad as the agony of transformation and he was acclimatised to that. If he could bear the stretching, ripping pain of the metamorphosis, he could bear the pain of the djinn's talons.

Ignoring the burning claw marks he scrambled to his feet. The djinn was silent and its eyes were dimmed. Checking on the battle above ground, Alduce surmised. He didn't know how his sorcery would work in the djinn's prison, but it was the only weapon he had. Drawing from the reserves of the Flaire pendant, he reached for its latent power.

Instinct took over as the magic stored within the small metal dragon coursed through him. As Nightstar, the mind of Alduce was used to the familiar natural magic that was an integral part of the black dragon. As a man, the sorcery he wielded as a human was different, raw and untamed, sharp edged, as opposed to the dull omnipresence of Nightstar's natural magic. It flowed through his being, strong and clear, healing the torn skin and filling him with power. He let the power flow from his core, pushing it into his arms and out through his hands.

Bright steaks of blue-white energy flew from his fingers slamming into the djinn as its eyes brightened, fully returning its presence back into its body. The energy engulfed the nightmare creature in an aura of light and it was slammed from its feet. The djinn roared as it landed on its back in a crumpled heap, its wings twisted underneath its body. It tipped its head back and roared again, lips curling back to expose yellowed fangs, saliva spraying from its mouth. The spit crackled as it punched through the writhing energy, breaking the spell, forcing the aura to dissipate.

It stared at him, eyes burning with hate as it rose, straightening out its wings as it gained its feet. Alduce let fly again, sending more bright energy at the djinn's head, but this time it shook off the blast as if it were nothing more than an annoying insect.

"I know your sorcery," it spat, "and how to resist it." The djinn leapt forward, wings outstretched as it attacked. Alduce threw himself aside and the djinn's arm missed its target, claws slicing the air where his head had been. It missed Alduce with its open handed swing, but it followed through with the strike, slamming its wing into him, using it like a fist.

Alduce gasped for breath as the wind was knocked from his lungs and wondered how, in this spirit realm, it mimicked the physical world. He knew everything he witnessed was a manifestation, an illusion of reality. He didn't really breathe inside the prison of the wizard glass, yet the laws of the outside world appeared to be the same. Realisation slammed into him just as hard as the djinn's wing. If he could breathe and feel pain in this place, then he could die!

The djinn spun and whipped its body, pivoting its wing sharply and launching Alduce like a stone from a sling. He landed on the strange cloudy floor, tumbling head over heels, disorientated and stunned as he slid to a halt. He climbed to his knees, visions of Nightstar's tumbling fall in the cavern of the cataract, swam through the dizziness. Of course! If he could act and feel in here, as he did in the physical world, he should be able to...

A rush of air whistled passed his woozy head and a faint voice reached his ears and echoed inside his skull; *its power is its weakness. The glass is the key.* Alduce tried to focus on the dark entity as it sped away from where he was crouched on hands and knees, his eyes only seeing a blur. It was like catching movement from the corner of your eye and when you turned to look it was already gone. A near invisible spirit too fast for his vision to catch. The djinn, however, was more than aware of its return, expressing its rage and roaring into the darkness as the dark spirit flashed by. It spun, too late to catch the fast moving entity, swiping at empty air. It was the distraction Alduce needed.

Memories of a lonely mountain top, a dark clear night, a sky full of bright stars, and a lightning strike, flooded into his mind.

His single mind.

Alduce felt the heat from the Flaire pendant radiate across his skin even though it dangled from around his neck and wasn't touching his body. Raw energy and expectation filled the air. Lightning forked out of the darkness, grounding itself on the small metal dragon hanging from the chain.

Alduce began to change.

Hands and knees spread out as black scales covered skin. Heat coursed through his blood like molten lava. Talons ripped from fingers and toes, gouging furrows in the ground as the limbs lengthened. Tendons and muscles stretched, the agony of a torturer's rack screamed from his mouth as they pulled and tore. Black leather wings sprouted from his arched back, unfurling and snapping like the sails of a galleon catching a storm. A balancing tail snaked out from behind, tapering to a sharp pointed end, scything the air as it lashed from side to side. Quills and spikes jutted out from a serpentine neck, horns grew from a head that stretched out to form an elongated snout. The pain of transformation subsided to a sharp memory, the metamorphosis complete.

A black dragon stood ready.

The djinn stared at the newly transformed dragon towering above it. The dark spirit vanished into the black once more and Alduce was grateful for the distraction.

Alduce. By himself. One mind alone.

He wore the body of Nightstar but his mind was all his own. It was only his mind that ventured inside the wizard glass, the dragon spirit along with its physical body, waited beyond, in the tunnels of the Lifting Plateau.

It was just like the first time Alduce transformed. The elation of the change, the shock of the pain... and the absence of the dragon spirit. He wore the body of the dragon like a cloak of black scales, only this time he was familiar with the shape. Confident in the change.

The first time he transformed, the sensation was new and extremely terrifying. He didn't know what to expect or how to apply any control. Now Alduce was comfortable with the dragon's form, a second skin as familiar as his own.

The form of Nightstar the Black tipped his head back and roared his challenge at the djinn. The longer he kept the creature occupied, the better Galdor's chance would be against its drones. The djinn responded, opening its arms as if welcoming the dragon into its embrace. The air shimmered around its body like the rippling heat haze from a hot summer sun. The distorted figure of the djinn began to grow, its ugly humanoid figure becoming larger until it equalled the size of the dragon.

"I will make this quick," it said, and rushed forward towards the waiting dragon.

Alduce instinctually reached for the dragon fire and sent a wave of roiling flames at the attacking djinn. The djinn protected its eyes with its forearm as the flames curled around its head. Flames that would have ordinarily incinerated their foe, did little to slow the charging djinn. It rammed into the dragon, swinging a closed fist into its side and curling its other arm around the dragon's neck as it rained blow after blow into the dragon's flank.

Alduce bucked and twisted, snapping at the djinn's free arm as it pummelled into his scales, its hand a hammer on the anvil of his body. It was fast and powerful, each punch a weakening blow. He still though of the dragon as Nightstar and relied heavily on the dragon's instincts, expecting him to take control, but this fight was his alone. The dragon spirit wasn't present and he would need to take full charge of the dragon form he wore if he were to survive.

His jaws connected with the djinn's arm, ivory teeth clamping the black scaly skin but failing to penetrate its tough armour. He twisted his head turning the blows and rolling sideways, teeth screeching as they scraped over the djinn's scales, pulling it off balance.

Djinn and dragon fell in a tangle of limbs and wings. The silver star and the white lightning flash bright against their black scales as they thrashed and wrestled for an advantage.

Alduce lashed his dragon's tail left and right, using the whipping momentum to separate himself from the djinn and pull back, freeing himself from its iron grip. He swung the heavy tail, ignoring the pain in his side, using it as a battering ram. It connected with the djinn and put a little more distance between them as it jumped back avoiding the full force of the swing.

Alduce felt his tail was like a third arm, understanding why Sunburst boasted about his own tail and how deadly a weapon it was. This time *he* charged at the djinn, leaping with rear legs thrusting forward, talons outstretched. The djinn sidestepped the lunge, deflecting the attack from his upper body as talons raked across its thick bat wings, tearing the tough membrane.

Alduce dipped one huge dragon wing and pivoted, thrusting his tail point into the torn wing with all the force he could muster. Membrane split as the djinn's stubby wing ripped apart, tatters of fleshy skin hanging from twisted bone. The djinn howled, more in anger than pain and retreated, tugging the shattered wing free of the dragon's tail. The barbs on the pointed tip caught the ragged wound widening the hole as it pulled free. The djinn growled as it freed itself, awkwardly folding what was left of the broken appendage behind its back. The white lightning flash across its chest began to glow and Alduce tasted the sharp tang of magic on his tongue. The djinn had thought to best the dragon with strength and failed. Now it counted on using its magic.

The djinn summoned its power, a corrupt magic unlike dragon or human magic. A power stolen from the life force of living, breathing creatures, purloined and exploited by a creature of ancient evil.

Alduce was ready for the attack as the djinn's powerful spell pulled at the dragon's life force. It was easy for the sorcerer to defend, Nightstar's dragon spirit safely beyond the confines of the wizard glass. The magic the djinn relied on to draw the life force from the dragon could find nothing to latch on to. As it floundered to leach the life force from its opponent Alduce retaliated with his own power, this time calling on the unique blend of magic that was neither human nor dragon, into the expectant grasp of the djinn.

The djinn recoiled as the sorcerer's forceful attack slammed into the void waiting to feast on the dragon's life force. The unfamiliar magic surged into the djinn, foreign and totally unexpected. It relied on feeding off the dragon spirit and was hit with the full force of something it had never encountered before.

Alduce felt his power sweep through the djinn's defences, straight to the core of its being. The djinn knew human sorcery and it understood dragon magic. It knew how to syphon the life force from a living being and use it to add to its strength. It had never experienced the magic Alduce now wielded and could not defend against it.

The amalgam of human sorcery and dragon magic was much greater than the sum of its parts. As far as Alduce was aware he was the only living sorcerer in possession of this highly unusual magic. It was something that should never have worked. The two distinctly different types of power were opposite forces of nature. They were so different from each other, so far apart in how they worked and how they were used. Yet the extraordinary chain of events involved in his metamorphosis and the addition of Sunburst's living blood—the key ingredient—resulted in a powerful force the djinn was unprepared for.

Alduce probed deeper, pushing to the core of the djinn's essence, its very own life force. The dark presence of absolute evil repulsed him and he fought to maintain his identity inside the corrupt spirit of the beast he sought to best. It was an arduous journey as he travelled through the malevolent mind of the djinn, clinging to his awareness and holding on to his own self. It was a battle he had already trained for.

When he first became the black dragon, the spirit of Nightstar grew inside his mind. He had expected to be a man who could change into a new shape, yet still remain a man at his source. As his old master often said, *someone who never made a mistake never made anything*. Master Caltus had many such sayings and loved to quote them to his young apprentice. Alduce had certainly made a mistake when he transformed into Nightstar and expected to be a human in dragon form. He had never been so wrong. He warred with the dragon spirit, a spirit he believed originated from the unhatched dragon egg he stole to aid his transformation. His battle against Nightstar's mind had ended when Sunburst added his blood to the equation.

Alduce would never know exactly how or why it worked. Live dragon blood held a secret magic all of its own and dragons by nature, were magical creatures. One thing he was sure of was, because of the yellow dragon's unintended donation, he survived what would have eventually destroyed him.

The experience of the dragon spirit sharing his mind, his presence, his very being, prepared him against the djinn's attack. His acceptance of Nightstar's spirit gave him the knowledge he needed to keep the djinn's at bay.

He descended into the centre of the djinn's being, shielding himself from the poison of its mind. He could see how it used the stolen life force to strengthen its power and how it constantly attacked the warding spell of the wizard glass. The djinn was using the energy from the stolen life force and compelling it into the weave, slowly eroding the barrier, piece by piece. It wasn't able to use its own magic against the complex pattern of magic the creators of the ward had set in place. The wizard glass was constructed specifically to protect against the djinn's magic. Its attack was purely brute force. If it continued to use the power and channelled it into the warding spell, it would eventually destroy what had held it safely contained for millennia.

Alduce could sense the desperation in the djinn's efforts, the desire to escape and exact its vengeance on any living beings that happened to be available. For century after century its mental state eroded, just as the barrier it was attempting to destroy was being eroded. The more life force it stole, the stronger its weakening power became. The more power it gathered, the stronger it attacked the wizard glass. If it kept drawing power from outside its prison and feeding it into the barrier that held it, it would break. It forced the stolen life energy into the weave of containment, cramming it in and creating a pressure that would eventually cause it to crack open, like an egg left to boil unattended. Eventually the shell would give.

This shell was ready to crack. The djinn was close to breaking free!

Alduce could see it clearly now, the build up of energy was almost at a point where it would tear a hole right through the barrier and destroy the integrity of the wizard glass completely. If the djinn's plan came to fruition, it would be free. If it escaped, Alduce didn't doubt he would not be able to stand against it.

The original creators of the wizard glass had weaved a complex spell, a shell of magical wards to house the evil being trapped within. Alduce didn't know if it was all they were capable of doing or if it was created in haste. He could understand the necessity of trapping and holding the djinn but it was only a temporary measure, even if it lasted millennia. It was time to employ a more permanent solution.

There was only one problem. He knew what he wanted to do but had no idea how to do it.

* * *

Sunburst crested the rim of the plateau and the updraft carried him high over the battlefield.

Dragon fought against dragon and it shouldn't be so. Conflict raged within him as he watched the fighting below. He knew he was supposed to lead the following dragons to safety, yet how could he leave his new friends when they were outnumbered and talon deep in black drones?

Azyrian caught up with him as he surveyed the carnage below. "They want to fight," he shouted through the wind of the updraft, indicating the rescued dragons. "They've been held against their will too long."

Sunburst could relate to their anger and frustration. He knew what it was like to be held against your will. The feeling of helplessness eroding your spirit and fuelling the need to lash out at your captors. He glanced back along the line and every dragon he led to freedom glared down at the swarming black drones. Every face eager to join the fight yet mindful of Galdor's instructions to flee to safety.

Sunburst looked to where the fighting was most intense. Galdor stood his ground in the midst of a sea of black. Blaze's drones flocked to the where the green made his stand. He was hopelessly outnumbered with only a few coloured dragons to aid him, a green rock floundering against the tide of a black sea.

Sunburst could not—would not—fly away and leave Galdor to be overrun.

"Flame it!" he cursed.

Azyrian met his gaze, eyes flicking to Galdor and back to Sunburst. "We must follow his orders." His words conflicted with his emotions.

Sunburst knew the big bronze was loyal to a fault and would do exactly as his leader commanded, but now was not the time for misplaced loyalty. Now was the time to act.

"There will be no Galdor the Green to follow if we leave him to the blacks. He needs our help!" His *perception* warned him if they didn't intervene, Galdor would be overrun. The green was big and Sunburst had no doubt at all he could fight, but against so many? He felt the *perception* with every scale on his body and knew it. "By claw and by fang," he called to Azyrian, "we are twenty strong. We *must* help."

Azyrian nodded his head once. "Flame it, Sunburst!" he cursed, "Nightstar was right, you are a bad influence." He grinned like a mad wolf, teeth splitting his snout, his chest rumbled as his inner flame boiled.

"Yeah, blame me if you need to, bronze." He turned his head back and roared to the others. "Galdor needs your help! Are you strong enough to fight?" The air reverberated and the answering roar rang in Sunburst's ears.

Azyrian winked at Sunburst. "If there's blame to be taken, we will share it, brother yellow."

The big bronze twisted in the air and dropped from the sky like a shining metal spear, leading the way. Nineteen dragons fell into a dive behind him as they rushed to join the battle.

Azyrian smashed into the ranks of the blacks assaulting Galdor. Intense flame leapt from his open jaws, spewing orange flames into the dark mass. The black dragons were not expecting reinforcements from above.

Sunburst matched the bronze's example and emptied his flame into the unsuspecting enemy. He flipped forward, talons raking the air and grabbed onto the first black neck they encountered. He twisted his body, pivoting his weight while holding tight to the stunned black, whipping his tail. The momentum of the manoeuvre sent the heavily spiked tail through the air with an incredible force, colliding with its target like an avalanche.

Dragons were tough creatures and were notoriously well armoured; when a dragon fought against another, that advantage was lost.

Sunburst's tail crushed into the head of a black next to the one his talons were latched into. Bone and scales sprayed friend and foe alike, the enemy dragon died instantly from the impact, its broken body toppling to the ground. Sunburst twisted and wrenched his talons through the neck they gripped, flapping his wings and adding to the force of his attack, tearing chunks of flesh from his victim. Blood fountained from the wound, spraying his talons, but there was no dragon magic or life in it. The wounded black flailed like a fish out of water from the shock of a near fatal wound, its lifeless eyes devoid of any emotion. Intense heat caused Sunburst to turn his head as Garnet released a gout of fire, flaming what remained of the black's neck. Blood hissed and sizzled as it burned, the stink of charred flesh strong as it joined the mounting dead on the plateau floor.

The free dragons pushed into the line of blacks, desperate to rally on Galdor, flame and claw clashing with talon and tail. Colours met the wall of black, a writhing mass of limbs, necks twisting, wings beating and jaws snapping, each side clawing to gain the advantage.

Sunburst stood wing to wing with the liberated dragons as they fought to gain ground, trying to push their way towards Galdor. Dragons roared in anger and screamed in pain. In the confusion of the battlefield it was difficult to tell which was which. The stench of sulphur and the sting of smoke adding to the chaos.

The weight of the enemy was too much to push through and they held their ground, unmoveable. If they didn't reach Galdor soon, Sunburst feared the green dragon would be overrun.

A black head thrust towards his neck, jaws snapping shut as he jumped backwards to dodge clear of the lethal attack. Surprisingly the attacking black dragon never moved forward to claim the forfeited ground. Sunburst feigned to the left, watching the eyes of his opponent before countering right. His teeth found their objective and clamped tightly around the black throat, open and exposed. Sunburst fully expecting his enemy to resist, waiting for the counter attack. His *perception* howled like a storm, as strong and clear as it ever had.

He knew without a doubt, Alduce battled the djinn and the creature's grip on the black drones faltered. He was sure this was why the black missed his opportunity.

Muscle and jaw worked in unison, twisting and tearing as his teeth slid between scales and punctured the skin beneath. He tore at his foe's vulnerable throat, rending and tearing until his jaws pulled free and blood gushed from the deadly wound inflicted on the black.

Spitting gore from his mouth he roared to his allies, "NOW! Forward to Galdor!" He wasn't sure if the free dragons heard him above the roar of the battle or they sensed the change in the black dragons too. It didn't matter what the reason was as long as they took advantage as the enemy hesitated.

A dark blue female crashed into a dazed black as it floundered to hold its ground. A ball of twisting black and blue limbs catapulted into the black ranks and coloured dragons poured into the break in their line.

All over the battlefield black dragons slowed. Sunburst didn't know exactly what Alduce was doing, but whatever it was, it was working. He knew the risk his friend took and hoped his plan would work and he could win his battle.

Dragons of all colours swarmed over the flagging enemy with no mercy. The tyrant's rule was harsh and cruel, but the vengeance of the free was brutal.

Galdor exploded from his surrounding attackers, tossing black bodies left and right as the fight went out of them. He spun and whirled, wings and tail throwing enemies as easily as leaves in the wind. It was a terrifying sight to witness and Sunburst was glad he was on Galdor's side.

The drones were broken and the free dragons pressed their advantage. This was a fight to the death and they knew their enemy was beyond saving. The only way to win this war was to eradicate them all.

Sunburst grieved for the fallen. He knew the black drones were already dead but that didn't make it any easier to destroy them. Dragons shouldn't fight dragons.

He withdrew from the final purge, allowing the free dragons to finish the fight. It was their battle and they, along with Galdor, needed to see it through to the end.

    Finding a clear spot near the edge of the plateau, away from the blood and scorched grass, he slumped down and waited for the killing to end.

Chapter 33

The Glass is the Key

Alduce probed the wards, feeling his way about the magic, searching for an opening he could use. The djinn's uncouth method of weakening the spell was to constantly bombard it with energy. The warding spell that maintained the integrity of the wizard glass was strong and he wanted to make it stronger, but that wouldn't solve the problem of all the extra energy the djinn had gathered.

If he wasn't careful and made the slightest mistake, his attempts at keeping the djinn contained could help release it. He knew what he wanted to do but couldn't see a way to penetrate the spell and bypass its protective wards.

Its power is its weakness. The glass is the key. The words from the dark spirit came back to him. It took him a moment to understand the message the mysterious words it contained; and then a sudden realisation hit him.

Of course!

He knew it was a huge risk. In his heart he understood it was a risk he must take to save not only the dragon population, but the entire world of Sull.

If sweat existed in the ethereal prison of the wizard glass it would have been running down his face. He waged a war on two fronts. The first against the djinn's mind, holding it at bay, the second as he weaved his own spell into the ward. While Alduce was able to penetrate its magical weavings, it wasn't easy, the ward was designed to withstand any tampering. Now he understood what he must do, his approach would be different.

The key *was* the glass. The excess power would be the weakness *he* could use.

He constructed a new weave, focussing on the wizard glass, a weave that added more than just the containment it was originally designed for. He used his own knowledge of sorcery, the unique blend of human and dragon magic, and the djinn's stolen life force. He twisted each different thread of magic around the others lacing them together, crossing them back over themselves, and tucking them into a complicated structure. The strands fought to repel each other, like opposing magnets, pushing apart when Alduce wanted them together.

The weave was dangerous and an error would result in the magic backfiring and that would be disastrous. If he made a mistake it could mean the destruction of them all. The opposing magic, coupled with the power the djinn had gathered, all reacting against each other, contained enough magical energy to potentially destroy a world.

Alduce used the energy the djinn had reaped from its victims and pushed it into the new weave, winding it into the structure of the wizard glass. This time the weave would no longer be just a shell to hold the djinn's essence. He added his own design to the construction, pulling it tight through the braided weave, binding it into the spell holding the barrier in place.

The djinn pushed at his defences and Alduce sensed its anger. He kept it from accessing what it desired for so long, while he was able not only to see how it worked, but alter it.

Tighter and tighter he bound his design to the existing spell, each weave, each strand, each fibre dancing to his touch, a musician of magic conducting his finest symphony. The effort of reconstructing the magic and shutting out the djinn took its toll. He only needed a few more minutes to finish but he was tiring fast.

And then the presence of the djinn disappeared.

Alduce renewed his concentration. Without the distraction of the djinn trying to force its way through his defences, he doubled his efforts. The sorcerer in him took over, finishing the work as if it were second nature. Weaving and spinning, bending and shaping. He used the power to strengthen the crumbling defences, adding his own blend of magic to the mix. Just like Sunburst's blood to his own transformation, the unique magic he wielded, allowed him to take liberties with the laws of magic, changing the wizard glass to his own design. He knew his alterations would hold and do what he intended them to. A warm feeling of satisfaction, coupled with exhaustion, washed through him as he wound the final strand of magic into place and tied it off. He gently tested the spell, lightly probing the wizard glass, feeling the subtle adjustments he made. Content with his work, he opened his eyes.

The djinn was no longer facing him.

Where the man shaped demon had been, a majestic black dragon now stood. A huge black dragon with a white flash of lightning adorning his chest.

"Blaze the Black?" Alduce asked, still in Nightstar's form.

"I am Blaze. Yes," the dragon's melancholy voice answered. "Or what's left of him. I wish we were able to meet under better circumstances, Nightstar the Black. We would have had a lot to discuss."

"Where is the djinn?" Nightstar looked around, anticipating some deception or trick.

"I believe you have tired it out, but only for a short time. I feel it writhing inside me. Its corruption makes me sick. What it has done, what I have become because of its influence."

"Can you not escape and return to your own body? Leave it behind. I have a plan to..." Alduce stopped. Blaze was possessed by the djinn and even if he was in control just now, as he appeared to be, there was no telling when it would be able to assert its dominance over the dragon again. If he were to reveal what he had done and the djinn was privy to Blaze's memories, it would know.

"Best not tell me anything about any plan, Nightstar, I don't know how long I'll be able to keep this up." A weariness oozed from the black dragon's voice. Weariness and so much regret. "I will hold on to my form for as long as I can. Hopefully it will give you enough time to do what it is you are planning. I would see an end to this. The suffering and the pain are bad enough, but knowing it was me who unleashed this evil into our world is unbearable."

"Is there no way—"

"NO!" The black dragon's eyes were like hot coals, red embers burning from the inside as the djinn tried take control. Blaze tossed his head. "Not yet," he murmured. When he made eye contact, Alduce could see his eyes returning to normal.

"I am too far gone," Blaze said. "My punishment for my part in this. I have seen this creature's memories and know the horrors it has inflicted. It is an evil I do not wish my world to face. If it escapes, what you have seen up until now is nothing. It will destroy everything and revel in the misery, take pleasure in the destruction. It will suck the life from my world and leave it a barren wasteland. Once it has taken everything, it will move on to another world and start again. The human mages who trapped it were powerful. They were lucky to catch it inside the wizard glass. Other worlds have not been as fortunate."

The scholar inside Alduce wanted to know more, yet any time spent learning of the djinn's past would use up valuable time. Time they didn't have. He wanted to explain this to Blaze but couldn't risk the djinn finding out what his plan was. He could see the black dragon was beaten, struggling to maintain his grip and resist the power of the djinn's will.

"I must leave this place," he told his black counterpart. "I promise you I will do everything in my power to defeat the djinn. You have my word, dragon to dragon." It was the most solemn oath a dragon could swear and he believed it to be true. If the djinn was able to read Blaze's thoughts he would know Alduce truly believed he was able to stop him. It might help sow the seeds of doubt.

"Another time then, brother black," Blaze said. "Go do what you must. Tell the dragons of Alvanor, Blaze the Black is truly sorry for his mistakes. I cannot put into words the remorse and the regret I feel. And how stupid and selfish my actions have been. I have one final battle to fight, hopefully it will give you the time you need."

Blaze lay down and closed his eyes and muttered, "Earth Mother guide you." The black dragon slipped into a restless slumber, twitching and snorting like a dreaming dog. Small wisps of smoke drifted up from fluttering nostrils and Alduce could only imagine the inner turmoil Blaze faced holding the djinn at bay.

The dark spirit appeared, no longer flitting beyond his vision. It buzzed around the sleeping form of Blaze. It was still difficult to distinguish what it was. It moved this way and that and was still fast, yet with the presence of the djinn gone for now, it seemed less agitated.

Alduce suspected he knew what the dark spirit was now, and perhaps it still had a part to play. He concentrated his will on the silver scales that formed the night star on the black dragon's chest. A small blue wisp of magical energy formed around the silver scales, then rose like smoke from a snuffed out candle. The dark spirit flitted like a hummingbird, dancing around the glowing magic, moving in and out as if testing it. It slowed, floating alongside the thread of magic and turned, winding the wispy thread around its misty body. The magic glowed brightly and then the dark spirit absorbed the energy, drawing it inside until the blue light was gone. With renewed vigour it shot off into the darkness looking a little bluer and brighter than before. Alduce sensed it was time for him to leave too.

Just like the first time he attempted to transform back, he reached for his human body. There was no panic this time, only the feeling of change. He was only a man without the spirit of Nightstar, slipping back into his own vessel. The black dragon's metamorphosis to a man almost instant. There was no feeling of discomfort or pain.

Alduce opened his mind and reached out for what he was missing. Nightstar.

A swirling vortex of energy took shape and a portal broke the void, opening a passageway from the realm of the wizard glass prison. The irony of ease in which he was able to reach out to his counterpart and step from this realm back into the physical world, wasn't lost on him. The djinn, even with the power it possessed, would never be able to cross the boundaries put in place to contain it.

The black vortex pulled him in and carried him home. Home to the waiting body of Nightstar.

* * *

Nightstar opened his eyes. He was no longer alone. The mind of Alduce was back where it belonged. He could feel the sorcerer's presence below the surface of his consciousness. He knew what the man had encountered inside the realm beyond the physical world. He knew what he had done. There was no need to commune with the mind of Alduce for an explanation, their shared presence conveyed everything.

Time was of the essence. He needed to get back to Galdor and the dragons above ground and lead them to safety. If Alduce's plan worked, they needed to be as far from the Lifting Plateau as possible.

He scurried back along the tunnels, his memory guiding him back the way they had come. Even if he hadn't been able to count on his memory, the path of clawprints left by the escaping dragons would have been easy enough to follow. He arrived back at the eastern cave entrance without encountering any resistance.

Perching on the outer rim of the cave entrance, he tipped forward and spread his wings, jumping out and catching the updraft, allowing the thermals to catch his outstretched wings and propel him up over the plateau's edge.

Galdor perched on the stone back of the sleeping dragon, the only living dragon remaining atop the plateau. A grim reaper of green for the lost spirits of all who were turned to black. It was as if he stood vigil for the dead, a green sentinel standing on the black stone. The symbolism of the imagery was not lost on Nightstar. He tilted his wings and angled his glide towards the waiting green.

Bodies of black drones and coloured dragons were scattered over the scorched grass. The black bodies outnumbered the coloured ones. As he drew close he could see Galdor's yellow eyes were filled with a deep sadness. The green moot leader knew they would have to fight and kill. The colour of the dead didn't matter to him, he grieved for them all. Every spirit gone was a loss to all dragonkind.

"I am sorry it came to this," Nightstar said as he came to land beside Galdor. "It saddens me to see the death of so many dragons."

"It is indeed a terrible day when we must sacrifice so many. They were all dragons once, regardless of their colour."

Nightstar could feel Alduce deep inside mourning their loss too. The man understood what the loss of so many dragon spirits meant to their population. Many of the fallen would not have the chance of rebirth, their life force torn from their bodies, no longer part of the Earth Mother's cycle. There were many worlds where dragons no longer flew in their skies, only remembered as myth.

"Where is Blaze?" Galdor asked, "Did you kill him? Is the djinn dead?"

"No, not quite. We don't have the time to discuss it here. Are the others..."

"On their way to the caves as you suggested. I sent them on ahead when the fighting here was done. The resistance of the drones faltered, as if the life went out of them."

"I think I was able to occupy the djinn long enough for it to lose some of his influence, or maybe control, over them."

"Whatever you did, it turned the tide of battle. We were almost lost and then the drones just... gave up. The slaughter that followed was horrible, Nightstar. I never wanted this."

"None of us wanted this but it was the only way. Let's join the others," Nightstar said. "The sooner we're far from here and are safely underground, the happier I'll be." His nerves were at breaking point, he needed to be flying. The time spent without Alduce, the knowledge of the djinn, and the plan the sorcerer had set in motion, were beginning to take their toll.

"C'mon," he called to Galdor, "I'll tell you all about what happened with Blaze and the djinn as we fly. Don't spare your wings. Fly like you've never flown before!"

As if to emphasise his words, a distant rumble of thunder rolled down over the plateau. Black thunder clouds gathered in the distance and Nightstar was thankful they weren't in the direction they were headed.

He sprang back into the air, throwing his weight over the edge of the Lifting Plateau and launched himself skyward. Turning his head, he was happy to see Galdor less than a tail length behind.

"Fly high, Nightstar the Black. Fly high and fly for freedom!" Galdor trumpeted into the darkening sky. "Show me how a dragon of the White Mountain flies."

"Make haste Galdor. Don't fall behind."

"That sounds like a challenge, black dragon," Galdor bellowed above another peal of thunder and his pounding wing beats. "You sound like you have a little of Sunburst the Yellow in you," he added, lightening the ominous mood.

"More than you can know," Nightstar returned, grinning. He did have a piece of yellow in him and Galdor knew it.

Chapter 34
The Dark Spirit

Nightstar followed Galdor into the caves as they made their way deeper inside. The corridors were filled with dragons of all colours. None of them black. The survivors from the battle of the Lifting Plateau and the dragons Sunburst had helped free were all gathered here. Nightstar believed this was the best place for them to shelter and Galdor agreed.

Their losses were minimal and could have been much worse. Many of the dragons bore scars of battle. Claw, fang and flame were not kind adversaries. Nightstar believed when Alduce engaged the djinn inside the wizard glass, his power over the drones was lessened. Its focus of dealing with the sorcerer had distracted it enough for Galdor and his dragons to deal with the defending drones, despatching them quickly when they were at their weakest.

And Blaze had helped. Nightstar needed to make sure the dragons of Alvanor were aware of how the black dragon resisted the djinn's hold, allowing all the dragons the time to retreat here.

A giant black storm had taken up residence above the plateau and could be seen for many miles. The turbulent air currents clashing with the wild winds and heavy clouds was an unnatural reflection of another battle being waged far below the ground.

In the former moot chamber an inner turmoil raged. Blaze fought against the djinn and knew he could never win. Mind against mind, the dragon battled with the demon that had corrupted his spirit. There would be no reincarnation back to the egg for Blaze. This was his last stand and he was destined to lose. The storm was about to break and Blaze would break with it.

"Quickly," Nightstar said to Galdor, "we still have one last thing we must do." Blaze couldn't hold the djinn back forever.

Galdor led them on until they arrived at the cavern where the stone dragon stood. The cavern was packed with dragons and they picked their way to the statue that had once been Baelross the Blue.

Sunburst waited with Azyrian, the smaller yellow and the big bronze now the best of friends. Beside them, a large blue and a deep brown, both females, stood. Galdor had told Nightstar of Sapphire and Chestnut's rescue on the flight here.

Garnet stood guard over the entrance to the cavern with Ryvind and Topaz and they stepped aside as Galdor hurried through.

"Nightstar has need of our help," Galdor addressed the dragons. "Heed his instructions as you would my own," he panted, the exertion from their flight still fresh. Nightstar's heart pounded and it wasn't just from catching his own breath.

He bowed formally to the assembled dragons, dipping his head in respect.

"You have lost many friends to an evil that plots to destroy everything you know and love. It has corrupted your kin and stolen their lives. We have one chance to stop it and it is now. Lend me your voices, dragons of Alvanor and lend me your strength. Together we can defeat it for good."

Galdor stepped forward and dipped his head towards Nightstar, "Show us the way, Nightstar the Black. By fang and flame we are ready!"

"Galdor, Sapphire and Garnet, to the left of the stone dragon's flank. Sunburst, Chestnut and Azyrian, to the right." Nightstar stood at the head.

"What about Topaz and myself?" Ryvind asked.

"Seven is a magical number," Nightstar answered. "Stand guard at the entrance and let no others wander in and disturb us. We will need to use all our magic," he told the other six, "to complete what I've started." He leaned his head and rested it upon the stone head of Baelross.

"Each of you touch the stone." His voice echoed around the now silent cavern. The dragons followed Nightstar's lead, resting their heads upon the stone flanks of Baelross. "Now do as I do," Nightstar said, wrapping his tail around the base of Galdor's, black curling round green. Galdor linked his tail with Sapphire, green on red. Each dragon in turn twisting their tail to the dragon next to them until finally Sunburst closed the circle linking back with Nightstar.

"Now push your magic into the stone, slow and steady." Six dragons released their magic as Nightstar instructed. The silver scales on the black dragon's chest began to glow, filling the Flaire wrought star with dragon magic. Brighter and brighter the silver shone as threads of magic rose like wisps of steam, drifting up along Nightstar's neck. Little ribbons of magic crept onto the surface of the stone dragon, flowing like rivers of light along the depressions between its stone scales. The light infused all seven dragons, flowing from each one to the next, tails shimmering in a bright circle surrounding them all.

The cavern grew brighter as Nightstar weaved his magic with the other six dragons, channelling their combined power. He searched for the dark spirit trapped within the djinn's prison, recalling its words, *its power is its weakness. The glass is the key.* The dark spirit was the final part of the spell. Alduce had paved the way and it was up to Nightstar to finish what the sorcerer started.

He closed his eyes and rode along the conduit opened by the combined dragon magic, searching for the weave Alduce had planted within the globe. He could see inside the wizard glass prison as if looking from the outside in. The fury of the djinn's spirit seethed as it lashed out against the dwindling life force of Blaze. The dying black dragon's spirit struggled to hold back the djinn, slipping a little more each time the djinn battered against its defences. For a second, Nightstar touched the mind of the corrupted black dragon. Blaze sensed Nightstar's presence and knew his job was done and dropped his defences.

The djinn roared as it smashed into the remaining mind and spirit of Blaze, shattering his defences into oblivion and sweeping him from existence. No longer held in check it attacked the new wards Alduce had weaved, pent up rage fuelling its power. It relentlessly smashed into the magical barrier again and again, each strike weakening the spell and bringing freedom closer.

Nightstar called out into the void, "Baelross! Come home. Call him back," he told the dragons. "Call your lost brother back to the stone!"

"Baelross," six dragons chanted, "Baelross. Baelross. Baelross!" Filling the cavern with their voices, rising higher each time they spoke the blue dragon's name.

The dark spirit appeared above the djinn's head, buzzing around it like an angry wasp. The ethereal essence it once was, gained substance and colour. A bright blue corona pulsing with life.

"Baelross. Baelross. Baelross!" With each chant the spirit of the blue dragon brightened.

"Come back to us!" Nightstar called and opened the way. A small tear in the barrier pierced the ward and the light radiating from the cavern where the blue dragon's stone body stood, beamed out into the dream realm, lighting the way for Baelross.

The glowing blue spirit flew from the djinn, directly towards the rent in the barrier, passing through the gap in the globe's defences. The djinn screamed and launched itself after the disappearing blue spirit as Nightstar began to close the gap, weaving threads of golden light like a sewing needle. The fabric of the dream realm began to knit together closing the djinn's escape. It seized the tear with huge clawed hands, pulling the golden stitches apart and rending the gap wide open.

Nightstar tried to pull the tear closed, feeding his magic into the growing wound in the barrier. The djinn countered it with ease, using every last piece of the power it had gathered, pouring it into the gap. The giant influx of power split the tear wide open with a sound like shattering glass and the golden strands of magic vaporised.

And Nightstar dropped his magic.

The djinn sensing victory threw itself into the growing tear, forcing itself into the gap the spirit of Baelross had passed through. And the trap Alduce set sprung closed.

The hidden spell Alduce wove into the wizard glass, activated when the djinn threw its power into the gap. There was no passage for the djinn as there had been for Baelross. Nightstar could feel the sorcerer's consciousness and sense his relief. He also detected something else, a self-satisfied feeling, and a single thought: *amateur.*

The power of the life force was too much for the wizard glass to hold. The more power the djinn gathered, the stronger the pressure had been on the ancient ward. It counted on that strength to break free, which was what Alduce hoped.

The wards Alduce reworked were fashioned to absorb the power the djinn released, turning it back on itself in an endless loop. The new construction of the wizard glass no longer weakened, the rearranged wards of the barrier increased the power and poured it back into the changing spell.

Nightstar fed the dragon magic of six dragons, adding his own magic to the mix and amplifying the power, forcing his powerful magic into an already volatile concoction. The expanding energy grew and grew, transferring his spell into the ward.

The original properties of the barrier started to change and it began to shrink. The smaller the area inside the djinn's prison realm became, the faster the tsunami of magic moved. Wave after wave coursed through the weave, each one growing in power and feeding more magic, more energy, and more pressure, into the mix.

The djinn writhed and thrashed as it tried to break free from the trap. The ever decreasing wards slowly crushed, strangling and constricting the djinn. The more it struggled and tried to use its power, the more it fed into the spell, a magical noose pulling tighter and tighter.

The djinn was unable to escape the wards holding it in place, the pressure increasing like a constrictor crushing its prey. As the energy rose to dangerous levels, Nightstar knew it was time to withdraw. With the ever increasing power cramming into the shrinking vessel, he knew it would only remain stable for a short time.

The inside of the wizard glass was like a pot of oil. The supercharged magic like the raging flames of an inferno. The hotter the flames grew, the greater the heat of the oil. The magic Nightstar poured into the warding spell was the flames. The wizard glass prison was the pot of oil. It would only hold so long before the growing pressure broke free.

Nightstar lifted his head from the stone head of Baelross. "Stand away!" he commanded.

Six dragons staggered back, exhausted and drained of magic.

The stone statue of Baelross the Blue shimmered like a mirage, rippling blue waves washing over the dull grey stone.

"Move back," Nightstar panted, his breath hot and his voice wheezy. The six dragons dragged themselves to the edges of the cavern as Baelross began to change.

Stone cracked and splintered and huge chunks of debris flew from the stone dragon, turning to vapour and hissing like steam as they blasted out into the cavern. Vaporised stone filled the air and when the dust settled a blue dragon stood where the statue had been.

"Welcome back, Baelross," Galdor said, his voice thick with emotion.

Baelross slumped to the cavern floor. "My legs are like lumps of rock," he rumbled, "think I'll lie down for a while." He turned his weary head to Nightstar and nodded. "Thank you," he said, before laying his head on the floor and closing his eyes.

"Will he be alright?" Sunburst asked, tentatively sniffing at the prone blue dragon.

"I think he will," Nightstar replied. "He needs rest and time to recover."

"Legs like stone! He has a sense of humour," Sunburst snorted.

The ground trembled and a deep rumbling filled the cavern. The roar of a thousand hurricanes filled the air, building to an ear splitting crescendo. The dragons fought to stay upright and Nightstar was glad Baelross wasn't standing. Dust and small rocks rained down from above and the cavern walls shook.

"I need to see," Nightstar said, above the roaring, and staggered from the cavern on wobbly legs.

"Come on," Sunburst shouted to Galdor, head-butting the green's flanks. "If I've learned one thing about being friends with Nightstar, it's that it's never dull when he's around. We don't want to miss anything." He stumbled after Nightstar, fighting to keep upright as the tremors continued.

Nightstar fought his way along the crowded passageway, each step unsteady as the floor moved beneath him, bumping off the cave walls as he made his way outside.

He emerged from the tunnel, the skies above crowded with ominous dark clouds. Sunburst came next, standing beside him, joined by Galdor and then Azyrian.

To the north, above the Lifting Plateau, a storm of epic proportions raged. Even from this far away it was obvious something was happening. Clouds gathered above the plateau, dark foreboding shapes holding back the light. Lightning flashed through the dense storm, jagged silver streaks bright against the dark canvas of the sky. Nightstar was glad of the distance between himself and the plateau. Despite the safe distance the lightning gave him cause for concern.

The howling wind abated and the quaking ground returned to normal. A quiet stillness followed as if the wind had blown itself out. The air was heavy with anticipation, charged with expectation and electricity, tingling like the moments between the rumble of thunder and the strike of lightning.

A spooky tranquillity after the raging of the wind, the absence of sound a noiseless calm.

The calm before the storm.

Nightstar held his breath, staring north, his eyes fixed to the stormy sky. Waiting.

"What are we—" Sunburst began to ask. Before the inquisitive yellow had time to finish his question, the sky exploded. A huge ball of white light swallowed the dark storm clouds, blasting up into the sky and lighting up the dull afternoon. It swelled like a miniature sun, painful to look at as the light intensified and then, with an almighty explosion, it blew apart. An eruption of light spread out from the centre in a huge circle as it tore across the sky.

The dragons turned their heads, averting eyes from the blinding flash. Orange flames chased the white light and Nightstar blinked away the dancing afterimage. A mountain of flame burned the sky, wave upon wave of roiling fire curling into the troposphere. The orange faded to yellow as it travelled up into the stratosphere in rippling waves.

The earie silence was shattered with the almighty crash of the explosion that followed, tearing through the air, a tornado filled with detonating magic.

The force of the explosion reached the barren lands where the dragons stood, heat blasting over them. Nightstar closed his eyes from the dust storm as a wave of pressure deafened his ears, exhaling through his snout to keep from inhaling the swirling dust. He bowed his head, sheltering from the oncoming windstorm, waiting for it to abate.

"Look!" Sunburst called out above the howling winds.

Nightstar open his eyes, squinting through the dust. A huge mushroom cloud of black smoke rose up from the Lifting Plateau, swirling as it expanded, flashes of flickering flames crackling though the dense cloud. It moved and swayed, changing shape and coalesced into the smoky shape of the djinn.

A horned black head emerged from the rising mushroom cloud, piercing eyes of red fire blazed hatred from a face of pure evil. A shiver ran through Nightstar's body, malevolent and cold after the heat of the explosion. The mesmerising gaze from the smoke-formed djinn was broken as another shape appeared out of the swirling vortex. The head of a dragon rose up, jaws growing as it twisted and swirled into substance. The dragon head turned and faced the djinn, gargantuan jaws opening wide as it lunged. A black cloudy maw swallowed the djinn whole, snapping silently shut.

The cloud reformed, reverting back to a rising mushroom, slowly softening around the edges as it began to dissipate.

Bright flashes of colour were visible through the smoke, weaving and swirling as they ascended. Reds and yellows, blues and greens amongst the more vibrant. Nightstar stared in awe as the stolen life force of the dragons Blaze had consumed—believed to be gone forever—were finally freed. The colourful spirits burned brighter until each one became a blazing white star, shooting into the atmosphere. Liberated dragon spirits, returning to the cycle, as the Earth Mother intended.

Nightstar turned to see Sunburst shaking his head, as if he doubted witnessing the final throws of Blaze and the djinn. The silence grew as the four dragons stood an unplanned vigil, watching the smoke as it curled and faded, each one lost in their own thoughts.

It may have been minutes or hours, Nightstar didn't know how long they stood staring, until at last the silence was broken by the sounds of dragons emerging from the caves.

"Is it over?" Galdor asked. "It feels over. Feels... better, somehow. Clearer and cleaner, like the air after a summer storm."

"The djinn is gone," Nightstar said, "of that I am certain. Nothing could have survived that much magical energy exploding."

"What's next?" Sunburst said, raising one bony eyebrow at Nightstar in an all too human gesture.

"What indeed," Galdor replied.

"Well, I could do with something to eat," Sunburst said. "All this excitement has made me *very* hungry."

"Eat?" Baelross the blue appeared at Sunburst side. "Yellow dragon, I believe that is an excellent idea. And a bath afterwards? I need to wash the stench of dust and rock from my scales."

"I like him," Sunburst said to no one in particular. "I am known as Sunburst the Yellow," introducing himself to Baelross, "my—"

"Scales are the colour of the sun. When I take flight I burn across the sky like a celestial fire," Galdor and Nightstar finished.

"Pah!" Sunburst snorted.

Galdor rumbled with laughter. Nightstar joined the green dragon. It felt good to laugh. Sunburst grumbled a little chuckle adding to the happy sound.

Baelross looked at the three of them, a puzzled expression on his face.

"It's not that funny really," Sunburst attempted to explain to the blue dragon.

Nightstar and Galdor looked at each other and renewed their laughter, proving the yellow dragon wrong.

Excerpt for the private journals of Alduce.

The Djinn.

Djinn come in many forms and are known by many names and are commonly referred to as demon or devil. The longer they live the more powerful they become. They are adept in magic of their own, more akin to human magic rather than that of the dragon, yet different from both these more familiar types.

While some djinn are content playing the role of trickster and enjoy granting wishes that usually come at a price, not all are so. Djinn have the capacity to tempt the unwittingly with promises for their own advancement and in certain cases can become extremely malevolent and corrupt. They are extremely good liars and are sparing with the truth.

Djinn have the ability to influence feelings, create addictive states of wellbeing or euphoria, or terror and foreboding. They prefer to remain unseen and hide in the shadows, using their power to manipulate and corrupt. Djinn can take on many forms and use this ability to blend into their surroundings. Their victims, once under the djinn's beguiling spell, will unwillingly protect their identity without realising their actions are not of their own volition.

Many cultures have their own version of the djinn and my research, while limited, has allowed me to study and learn from the records I have found, building a clearer picture of how these creatures act.

I believe the djinn encountered on Galdor's world, Alvanor, saw itself as a god. It was an ancient being of incredible power and intelligence. While it most probably was always corrupt, as in their nature, this djinn appeared to have been driven mad by its need to punish its captors. Its continued incarceration, added to its inability to lash out and extract vengeance, would most likely have contributed to an already unstable mind.

Note: it is unclear whether the djinn was male or female and there was no evidence to determine one way or the other what gender it was.

The djinn appeared to have been imprisoned and contained, then deposited on Alvanor, hidden out of harm's way by captors from another world, not of its origin. The power of the magic wielders who trapped it was limited, even though they were able to travel to another world. I am unsure whether dumping a creature of this power, even contained, was an irresponsible or desperate act.

The djinn was able to influence Blaze the Black, drawing him to its resting place, and used him in an attempt to free itself. It possessed enough magic, even when imprisoned, to reach out and corrupt the black dragon before he hatched.

The explosion that destroyed the Lifting Plateau and ultimately killed the djinn, was fuelled by the stored magic contained within the wizard glass globe. Simply put (although sorcery of this intensity is never simple) the magic I was able to weave into the containment spell in order to continually increase the power inside the globe, grew to such a level as to create an explosion powerful enough to end the creature.

I am confident most djinn never reach anywhere near the level of power, or live as long as the specimen encountered on Alvanor. They are generally content to lurk in the background of the societies they inhabit and this one was the exception to the rule.

Epilogue

Nightstar, Sunburst and Galdor made a final circle around what was left of the Lifting Plateau. Most of the plateau was gone, replaced by a huge crater. It looked as if a volcanic eruption had laid waste to the once scenic home of the dragons of Alvanor. The intensity of the exploding magic had changed the landscape forever, destroying the Lifting Plateau and the air currents that it had taken its name from.

The dragons of this land would remain at the hidden grotto and would not be returning home to the plateau. Nightstar imagined it would no longer be called the hidden grotto. There was no need to hide now Blaze and the djinn were gone.

Leaving the ugly crater behind, Nightstar peeled away from the scarred land. It was time to go home.

The three dragons flew in silence for a while until Galdor pulled alongside Nightstar. The mighty green dragon took the lead, Nightstar and Sunburst following. When a regal dragon like Galdor leads, thought Nightstar, it is easy to sit back and follow.

Galdor spiralled purposefully down to a clifftop where a waterfall dropped into the valley beyond. They landed on the rocky shores where the water cascaded over the edge, a misty spectrum of colours filling the spray. It reminded Nightstar of the liberated spirits. All the colours of the rainbow, he thought, but no black.

"I will leave you here," Galdor said, "to carry on your own homeward journey yourselves. I have much to do. A new moot to choose. Leaders to appoint. Dragons to feed. We must build a new home, start again."

"And with no evil black dragon, or a life sucking djinn, I am sure Galdor the Green can handle it," Sunburst quipped. "His deeds are legendary."

"Thank you for your confidence in me, Sunburst," Galdor returned. "Yet, it is Nightstar the Black whose deeds won the day."

Nightstar bowed his head to the green dragon. "We all played our part."

"We did," Sunburst said. "Daring rescues, battles, and magical explosions. Did I not say it is never dull when Nightstar's around?"

"Blaze also wiped out most of the humans on your continent," Nightstar said, his voice low. "While I don't agree with what he did under the influence of the djinn, I don't think you will need to worry about mankind for a very long time." The three dragons sat in silence for a minute, the sound of the waterfall soothing and peaceful after all the violence.

"I think I have another debt," Galdor said, "to our friend. Once more he has helped me. He, and you both, are welcome to return to Sull anytime you wish. I am still in awe of you both and glad to call you my friends."

"Our pleasure," Sunburst said, missing Galdor's meaning.

"It is what it is," Nightstar said. "We do what we must."

"I have no boon to offer you this time," Galdor said. "However, you are still welcome to stay and take a place of honour on our moot."

"I am flattered, Galdor, but we must return. The White Mountain is my home." He looked at Sunburst. "And who would keep this yellow out of trouble if I stayed?"

"Pah!" Sunburst snorted.

"Very well," Galdor rumbled, humorously. "Fly high and fly free." He sprang into the air, huge green wings beating down through the spray as he dropped over the waterfall's edge and out of sight.

"While it is nice to travel and see new worlds," Sunburst said, "it is good to be going home."

"With tales of more bravery and daring rescues?" Nightstar asked.

"It is what it is," Sunburst replied. "We do what we must."

"Sometimes," Nightstar sighed, "I regret giving you one of my scales."

"No you don't," Sunburst said.

"Let's fly," Nightstar grinned as he dropped from the ledge, spreading his wings and following Galdor's path down through the waterfall's spray.

Acknowledgements

Writing and self-publishing a novel isn't as lonely an adventure as can often appear to be. While sometimes it does feel that it can be a lonesome road, there are some people who remind me their support and encouragement is there when I need it.

I can't discuss my story like I can a favourite TV show, where everyone knows what's going on. For me, it helps to speak with someone about what I am writing. No one can see inside my head (thankfully) so having a like-minded writer to chew the fat with, discuss the plot, brainstorm an idea, or even just tell them you finished that chapter... eventually, is a pretty cool resource to have.

If that person is willing to read your novel multiple times, assist with the editing and throw you a bone on how to improve something, then that support goes above and beyond.

It doesn't hurt to get totally honest feedback or criticism either, be reminded how many times I used the wrong word! (Lifting/Landing, Stripe/Spike) or if a sentence doesn't make any sense, is poorly written, or just downright terrible.

So wouldn't it be great to have someone like that?

Wait I do! Thank you Chris Coleman for all the support, foresight and the late night discussions until stupid o'clock! I missed the acknowledgements page in Bound in Scales, and it should have been said earlier. Your insight and keen eye keep me honest. I wouldn't be writing now if not for your encouragement and support. I look forward to reciprocating soon. I would also like to thank my Alpha and Beta readers (special thanks to Jim for being both) for their feedback and investing their time and faith in my story.

Steve.

March 2020

Printed in Great Britain
by Amazon